"YOU DON'T WANT ME."

"I said I couldn't want you. Not that I didn't want you." Noah's gentle voice reached out to her, offering a soothing balm for all the words he could not speak. "I know it makes little sense to you. But believe this, Emily," he said, reaching out to grasp her hands in his. "I have *wanted* you since the first day I laid eyes on you, and I've never stopped wanting you. I have been fighting with myself ever since you walked into the salon today, holding myself back, trying not to touch you"—he took a step closer, unaware he'd moved—"trying not to want you." Noah reached up to touch her hair, silky and soft, shining like spun gold laced with pearls.

"But why?" she asked, her eyes wide and confused.

He frowned. "Because I would only hurt you and I'd do anything to spare you that," he said fiercely. A surge of protectiveness shot through him, startling him with its intensity. He would protect his wife. Even from himself.

"Oh, Noah," she murmured, reaching a hand up to stroke his cheek. "I love you." She smiled a small smile, like a child giving a homemade gift uncertain if the receiver would accept it. "I have loved you for so very long."

Noah grabbed her shoulders, his insides raw and aching. He felt as if he'd taken another beating, but this one left deeper wounds, more scars. "No, Emily. You can't love me. You can't."

"But I do, Noah," she said, smiling again, tears glistening in her large gray eyes. "Love me. Love me, Noah," she whispered, rising on tiptoe to brush a kiss across his lips.

BOOK YOUR PLACE ON OUR WEBSITE AND MAKE THE READING CONNECTION!

We've created a customized website just for our very special readers, where you can get the inside scoop on everything that's going on with Zebra, Pinnacle and Kensington books.

When you come online, you'll have the exciting opportunity to:

- View covers of upcoming books

- Read sample chapters

- Learn about our future publishing schedule (listed by publication month *and author*)

- Find out when your favorite authors will be visiting a city near you

- Search for and order backlist books from our online catalog

- Check out author bios and background information

- Send e-mail to your favorite authors

- Meet the Kensington staff online

- Join us in weekly chats with authors, readers and other guests

- Get writing guidelines

- AND MUCH MORE!

**Visit our website at
http://www.zebrabooks.com**

INNOCENT
BETRAYAL

Mary Campisi

Zebra Books
Kensington Publishing Corp.
http://www.zebrabooks.com

ZEBRA BOOKS are published by

Kensington Publishing Corp.
850 Third Avenue
New York, NY 10022

First Printing: May, 2000
10 9 8 7 6 5 4 3 2 1

Printed in the United States of America

Chapter 1

England—1818

"Be damned! He's done it again," Noah Sandleton muttered under his breath. He'd been watching the boy for a full ten minutes. If his count was correct, the little ruffian had just pickpocketed his third victim. Not that lifting coin from this group would be a difficult task. Many of them, especially his own men, were plunging into various stages of drunkenness with the same gritty determination they employed while manning his ship. They deserved this night of reckless abandon after weeks at sea and Noah planned to let them have it. But he was not about to sit by and watch some scrawny urchin steal from them.

He peered through the gray haze, trying to concentrate on the boy's actions. The Fox's Tail was crowded and smoky, making it difficult to see clearly, but Noah thought he had figured out the boy's game. Each time the little tough edged up to an unsuspecting victim, he would lean in close, whisper in his ear and then depart, shaking hands as he faded away,

taking his booty with him. Noah leaned back in his chair and
took a long draft of ale. He was a patient man. Odds were that
soon enough the boy would approach one of his men and then
Noah would teach him a lesson. He smiled at the thought.

His dark eyes scanned the pub, taking in the scene around
him. The Fox's Tail attracted all breeds of men, from sailor to
nobleman, oddly bound together by the port and ale that flowed
freely through the establishment, loosening their tongues and
their purses. Its walls housed the latest whispers of scandal,
whether they were social or political. And it was no secret that
the rooms upstairs were frequented by customers wanting a
quick tumble with one of the pub's well-endowed barmaids.

It was all available for the right price. Rumors abounded
regarding the illegal trade pushing up and down the coast. Silks,
lace, spices. A half smile played about Noah's lips as he thought
of the crafty merchants who bought their wares straight off the
boats only to sell them to unsuspecting noblemen for nearly
three times their worth.

The boy hadn't moved from his spot. He seemed to be waiting
for something or someone. Was he a Bow Street Runner?

"Will ye 'ave another?" A blond barmaid leaned over, her
huge breasts spilling out of the peasant's top she wore. Noah
saw the hint of a pale pink nipple. She smiled at him, and he
recognized the invitation in her warm brown eyes.

"Is there anything else ye be wantin'?" Her voice was low
and husky.

Noah's dark eyes swept the length of her full figure, then
settled again on her breasts. "Later."

"Me name's Hazel," she murmured, running her tongue
slowly over parted lips.

He smiled at her.

"Later," she repeated before picking up her tray and disappearing amid a group of raucous seamen.

"Ah, Noah, I see the women are flocking to you, as always,"
a voice boomed from behind him.

Noah turned to see his first mate, John Judson, settling his bulky frame into a nearby chair. He grinned at the old man, then leaned back in exaggerated resignation and closed his eyes. "I know, John, but what's a man to do?"

"Hah!" the older man bellowed in laughter. "You've a way with the women—that's for sure." He paused only long enough to take a healthy swallow of ale before he continued. "They all love you, from England to the Orient, princess to barmaid, and not a one of 'em has ever been able to catch you."

Noah smiled, his eyes still closed. "Oh, they catch me when I want them to, John, but keeping me—now that's a different story."

John chuckled, slapping Noah on the back. "One day, boy, one of them will. You'll see, or my name isn't John Judson."

Noah's eyes snapped open as he remembered the pickpocket. The boy had edged closer to a group of scruffy seamen, two of whom were Noah's deckhands.

"John, look at that boy standing over by Amos and Jeremy." He pointed a long tanned finger toward the group.

John squinted his faded blue eyes. "The scrawny thing in the black cap?"

"That's the one. He's been fleecing unsuspecting victims all night, and I'm about to teach him a lesson."

"Are you sure he's stealing?" John's bushy white eyebrows drew together as he studied the boy. "He looks like the same one that's been asking around for Gerald Thackery."

"The *Matilda*'s captain?" Noah asked.

John nodded, rubbing his white beard thoughtfully. "The lad's been quizzing everybody in the place, looking for the captain. Said he wanted to sign on as a cabin boy." John's blue eyes twinkled. "We pretended we didn't know where Thackery was." He leaned his big bulk toward his friend and whispered, "We didn't have the heart to tell him the good captain was taking his pleasure upstairs."

Noah frowned. "I don't believe it. It's just a ruse to cover what he's really been doing, and that's stealing."

"Why would a boy bent on stealing strike up a conversation

with the person he's about to rob? Especially an urchin like
that one. From what I heard and from what I can see, he's no
more than fifteen or so and he is so scared he can't even give
a straight look in the eye to ask a question.''

Noah said nothing as he watched the boy sneak up to one
of his men.

''I know you find it hard to believe a person would want to
go to America,'' John continued, oblivious to his friend's lack
of response, ''but there's many a man who believes it's the
land of opportunity.''

Noah ignored the comment. ''Did you see that? Did you see
him brush up against Amos?'' He stood up, towering over John.
''That's the last coin he'll steal tonight,'' he muttered, pushing
away from the table and moving with steady purpose through
the crowd.

A glass broke behind him, crashing to the floor, followed
by yelling and the sound of fists connecting. Noah turned just
in time to avoid the blunt edge of a bottle hurled in the air by
some drunken sod. It landed squarely on the head of the man
next to Noah, toppling him to the ground. Within seconds, an
all-out brawl exploded. Noah pushed his way toward the boy,
grabbing him and hauling him up and over his shoulder toward
the stairs that were a few feet away. Ignoring the kicking legs
and squirming body on his shoulder, he took the stairs two at
a time. Flinging the first door open, he thrust the boy inside
and almost laughed as he watched him scurry to the farthest
corner of the room, trying to put as much distance between
them as possible.

''Unless you're planning on jumping out that window, you
have no other means of escape.'' Noah settled his large frame
against the door, blocking the only other exit in the room.

The would-be thief scanned the whole room quickly, then
scanned it once more. ''What ye be wantin' from me?'' His
voice sounded gruff and forced.

''Now there's a question.'' Noah laughed shortly, pulling
away from the door. ''What I 'be wantin' from ye,' '' he

drawled, "is to see how much coin you stole downstairs." He advanced on the boy, capturing and pinning him against the wall with one large hand. "We'll see how much booty you collected tonight," he said, working his free hand inside the boy's oversize pockets. They were empty. He opened the front of the jacket and looked for hidden pockets. "Did you steal this jacket too?" he asked, fingering the fine silk lining. He received no answer—not that he really expected one. But he had expected to find pockets filled with money and so far he hadn't found that either.

"Where's the money?" he demanded. "I know it's here somewhere." Ignoring the look of panic in the boy's eyes, Noah reached out and ran his hands slowly along the oversize shirtfront. He felt two soft mounds. "What the devil . . . !" he growled, grabbing the shirt and jerking the buttons open to reveal full breasts straining against the confines of their heavy cotton binding. *A woman!* She tried to cover herself, but Noah caught her small hands in his large ones and forced them to her side. The shirt fell open to reveal the creamy swell of her bosom, and he found himself wishing he could have a peek beneath the layers of cotton binding.

Forcing himself to look away, he gazed up into a pair of smoky gray eyes. They were soft and shimmering, surrounded by a thick fringe of lash. How had he missed those eyes?

"So," his soft voice mused, "the *he* is a *she.*"

She tried to bolt from him, but Noah was too quick, clamping down on her arm with lightning speed. He closed in until they were no more than a hairbreadth apart. Locking his eyes with hers, he reached out and jerked the stocking cap off. A tumbling mass of golden locks spilled about her shoulders, cascading down her back in a riot of curls.

She was beautiful—of that he was certain. Her full pink mouth trembled with what seemed like fear. He wondered absently what she would taste like. Sweet and fresh would be his guess. Of course, there was always one way to find out, but that wasn't why he had brought her up here, he reminded himself. Until a moment ago, he had thought her to be a thieving *he,* and whether female or male, beautiful or not, she remained a thief.

"I saw you stealing," he said bluntly.

"I did no such thing!" she protested, all trace of the cockney accent she'd used a moment before gone.

He frowned. "Who are you?"

She didn't answer him for the longest time, and when she did, her words weren't really an answer at all. "I'm looking for Captain Gerald Thackery. He's sailing his ship to America."

"I've heard of him. What do you want with that scoundrel?" Noah held little respect for a man who cheated his men out of honest wages and spent the better part of his life in drunken excess.

"I"—she hesitated a moment—"am trying to secure passage to America and thought I might travel as a cabin boy."

"Oh," Noah scoffed. "More deceit. Exactly how did you plan to carry it off?" His eyes lingered on her breasts, and he took perverse pleasure in the crimson color spreading on her cheeks.

She yanked her jacket closed and shifted about uncomfortably. "I had planned on disguising myself as a cabin boy."

Noah laughed outright. "With Thackery as captain? You wouldn't stand a chance. He'd sniff you out a mile away." He leaned in close to her, the scent of lilac filling his nostrils. "Listen," he whispered. Loud grunting moans and soft sighs traveled through the walls. A man's voice, deep and commanding, rasped out words of pleasure that made her flush ten shades deeper than a moment before. "Sail with him and that's how you'll be passing your time."

He paused a moment, his expression grim. "I think you're lying. If you wanted to get to America, there are legitimate ways to go about it. You wouldn't need to come to a dockside pub dressed as a boy looking for a man you know nothing about."

"I had no choice," she spat out.

"There's always a choice," Noah said gruffly, turning away from the woman and running an agitated hand through his hair. Out of the corner of his eye, he saw her reach two fingers inside the heavy binding that covered her breasts. She seemed to be trying to get at something. Or hide something. *What the devil was she up to?* He swung around, moving quickly for a man his size, and hauled her to the narrow bed in the corner.

Her booted foot kicked out, just missing his groin.

"Damn you!" Noah stilled her squirming body with one arm. He thrust his free hand inside the binding, ignoring her protests, and pulled out a bunched-up scrap of paper.

He stared at it a long time, barely noticing Gerald Thackery's name scrawled on the fine linen stationery. His eyes studied the name on the letterhead.

Ian St. Simon.

How in the devil did she get hold of my best friend's stationery? Before he could question her, he felt a sharp, searing blow to his temple. "Aghh," he moaned, clutching his head as the pain roared through his brain. Noah doubled over, crouching on the wooden floor among shards of glass. A fine stream of blood oozed from his right temple, but he ignored it. He heard her cry and lifted his aching head just in time to see her flee, her long golden hair trailing behind.

Moments later, Noah hurdled the steps two at a time, racing out the door in pursuit of his quarry. He was oblivious to the dull throbbing in his head as his trained eyes scanned the darkness, searching for her. He knew she was out there somewhere, probably hiding in one of the warehouses. The docks of London could hide a person for days.

There were no signs of life, save an elegant black carriage traveling several yards ahead of him. She was gone. *Damn her.* Turning back toward the pub, he swiped at the wetness on his cheek. Staring down at the bright red blood on his fingers, he cursed all women, but one in particular, to everlasting hell.

* * *

The carriage rolled away from the Fox's Tail and toward the comfortable familiarity of the Gregorys' drawing room.

Emily St. Simon lay back against the burgundy velvet squabs with her eyes closed. She dared not open them yet for fear of falling apart, one tear at a time. If she kept her eyes firmly shut, perhaps the last hour would fade away into the vagueness of a bad dream.

"Emily, what happened?" Isabel Fleming's concern for her good friend was evident in the slight trembling of her voice. "Something's happened, hasn't it? It's finally gone too far."

"Just let me rest a moment, Belle." Emily spoke in a low voice. "Just a moment and then I'll be fine."

"Then we'll talk," Belle added, settling back against the cushions as the carriage whirled through the noisy streets of London. Training her golden eyes on her friend, she watched and waited.

Emily tried to make the vision go away but the events of the evening were too powerful, too heavily embroiled in her mind to be whisked away with the brush of a hand or the blink of an eye. He kept coming for her, a bronzed warrior, towering over her, blocking all thoughts of escape. The breath caught in her throat. What would he do when he caught her? He turned then and she saw his face, dark and foreboding. A stray lock of dark brown hair fell over his forehead while the rest trailed to his shoulders in wavy disarray. His nose was slightly crooked, his jaw too square. Eyes, deeply set, were a rich brown, like fine French chocolate, smooth and decadent. They bored into her as he closed the distance between them. She stood frozen in place, unable to move.

The man backed her up against a wall. She inhaled the spicy male scent of him, felt his warm breath on her hair, watched his strong, firm mouth moving closer. Her fingers pressed into the wall, bracing for the onslaught of his kiss. There was no escape. His mouth descended, stopping mere inches from hers.

His full lips opened, revealing even white teeth. Fear warred with anticipation as she waited, wondering if he could hear the wild beating of her heart. He spoke to her then in a whisper. "Liar." His next words were louder. "Thief."

Emily's eyes flew open. She blinked twice, hard, and rubbed her temples with the tips of her fingers. What if he knew Ian? She had seen the way he stared at the paper. Could he have recognized the St. Simon name? Emily forced the thought aside. It would be highly unlikely, she assured herself. The monster at the inn wasn't even an Englishman—she had known that as soon as he spoke.

"I had some trouble tonight, Belle." She leaned over, avoiding Belle's watchful gaze, and grabbed one of the boxes that held a carefully wrapped rose gown and various layers of undergarments.

"What happened?" Belle's golden eyes widened with concern and fear.

"I wasn't careful enough. I couldn't think of anything but meeting Captain Thackery and I let my guard down." Emily shook her head and reached for her camisole. "There was a man . . ."

"And?"

"He accused me of stealing. And he found the piece of paper with Captain Thackery's name on it." Shimmying out of the gray breeches, she pointed her toe into a rose-colored stocking.

"Well, that would tell him nothing."

Emily closed her eyes, fastening her garter. "It was on Ian's letterhead."

Belle frowned, worry showing in her lower lip. "Let's remain calm. Ian doesn't frequent such places. Besides, our families only travel to London a few times a year, so how could this man possibly know your brother?" She shook out a frilly petticoat.

"I'm sure you're right." Emily sighed. "If Ian ever knew we were masquerading as boys in taverns, he would have our heads."

Belle smiled, a twinkle of mischief in her eyes. "We did it all last season and he never found out."

"But this is the first time at the Fox's Tail. And it's nothing like the quaint little taverns we're used to frequenting." A vision of a fierce warrior's face intruded on her thoughts. "It's seedy and wild, with all sorts of untamed characters milling about. You wouldn't have liked it at all, Belle."

"I'd choose that any day over attending another boring, predictable soirée," Belle said, fingering her pale pink satin gown. "Dance cards and demure smiles with silly introductions and the latest *on dit.*" She sighed, leaning back against the burgundy squabs. "Why can't our families accept the fact that we don't want to marry? Period."

"Duty." Emily gathered the rose gown and worked it over her head. "We've been born and bred to it, Belle. My brother's an earl; your father's a duke. It's expected."

Belle helped Emily pull the gown down, smoothing out wrinkles with her small hands. "Expected perhaps, but accepted never. I'll not conform to it."

"Nor will I." Emily shook her head. "That's one of the reasons I'm so determined to go to America. I'll have the freedom to make my own choices without societal constraints." She paused. "And I'll be with Christopher."

Belle laughed. "You mean, you can talk Christopher into anything, even ignoring 'societal constraints.' "

Emily wrinkled her nose. "You needn't be so blunt about it, Belle. Chris and I have a very close relationship. Need I remind you that he was the only member of my family who didn't desert me?" It had always been just she and Christopher from the time she could remember. The only image she had of her dead mother was a small locket with her picture in it. As for her father, Jonathan St. Simon had found little time for his family, instead spending most of his hours in other women's company. Or their beds, as Emily had heard.

And then there was her oldest brother, Ian, the current Earl of Kenilworth. Seventeen years at sea had made him a legend, a hero, a god. A stranger.

"I know you love your brother, Emily, and Christopher loves you. But you must admit it was much easier to get Christopher to do your bidding than it is Ian."

Emily rolled her eyes. "There is no comparison, Belle. Ian wants to control me, see me settled in a manner befitting a woman of my station, as he says. And to him that means marriage."

"I think he's trying to make up for all the years he was gone." Belle reached for the silver brush in Emily's hand. She pulled the brush through her friend's golden tresses. "He might never tell you, but Ian does love you, Emily."

"Of course, he loves me." Emily sighed, pushing a few stray tendrils of golden hair aside.

"You must admit he is quite noble," Belle grinned.

"To a fault. He had his reasons for leaving and I respect them, but Christopher is my brother too. And *he's* in America. He understands me, Belle."

"He also lets you get away with your outrageous antics."

Emily raised her hands in frustration. "Chris used to tease me about being too outspoken and independent, but he also encouraged me to be that way. Now, Ian wants me to 'repress my forward behavior and adopt a more demure air,' " she mimicked. Her hand slashed the air. "I won't do it."

"There's not a lot about you that's demure," Belle chuckled.

"My point exactly. And now, because of some meddling man, I have most probably missed my opportunity to meet Captain Thackery, and he was my last hope of gaining passage to America."

"Well, you can't go back there after what happened tonight. You have no alternative but to speak with Ian again."

"And hear him lecture me for the hundredth time about how I am a young woman of proper breeding who needs to be thinking about a husband and children rather than traipsing halfway around the world?"

Belle smiled but said nothing.

"Well, no, thank you." Emily crossed her arms over her chest, angry that she had to wear this uncomfortable gown and attend this ridiculous ball. All because her brother and society deemed making a match essential in securing a comfortable position in life.

"And of course," Emily rattled on, feeling the heat rise to her face, "my dear brother would never miss an opportunity to tell me that, at twenty-one, I am not really a *young* woman anymore."

"Ah, yes, I do see a smattering of gray among all this gold," Belle said as she wound Emily's hair high atop her head, securing the golden locks with small pins. "You are an old creature." Emily could hear the laughter in her friend's voice. But all trace of humor was gone from her next words. "Try speaking with him once more. Ask him under what terms he would consider sending you to America, if any. Just one more time, Emily."

"I really think the effort will prove futile." Belle didn't know Ian the way she did.

"You have no other choice at the moment." Belle sighed. "If I thought one of my brothers would secure passage for you and not tell my father, I would have made the arrangements long ago. Unfortunately, they would tell the duke straightaway, and you know he would not be pleased."

Before they could consider their predicament further, Emily felt the wheels of the carriage grind to a halt. "Oh, no," she groaned. "We're already at the Gregorys' and I'm not finished dressing." Reaching for her rose slippers, she asked, "What's our story tonight?"

"We told Ian that we were coming with my aunt, and vice versa." Belle tapped a slim finger to her chin. "Then Auntie got sick midway to the Gregorys' and we had to return her to her residence. Thus, the extended lapse in time. We were not concerned about chaperons, because we knew that Ian and Augusta would be here." Belle's eyes narrowed. "As long as

Ian doesn't talk to my aunt, we'll be all right and our honor will be safe.''

"And Higgins?" Emily's head inclined toward the front, where the ancient driver sat. Their usual driver on such nights of adventure had taken ill and Belle had asked Higgins to fill in.

"Higgins is my friend," Belle assured her. "You have nothing to fear from him. He'll never expose us." Her voice lowered to a whisper. "I've got him wrapped around my little finger. Just like the rest of my family." She smiled smugly. "Being the youngest child with five older brothers does have its advantages."

"So you've said." Emily smiled in amusement, thinking of the truth in Belle's words. The Fleming brothers were giants, with quick tongues and ferocious snarls that disappeared the moment they saw their little sister. Belle could cajole, scold and tease them to extreme and receive no more retribution than a hearty laugh or a lift in the air. Emily couldn't even imagine having that kind of a relationship with Ian.

Belle grabbed the sapphire-encrusted combs from the tissue and placed them in Emily's hair. "Perfect. Unfortunately, we're off to a night of sheer boredom. I must admit I wish I had been the one to have your adventure in the Fox's Tail tonight. At least then I would have something exciting to think about while I danced with my latest would-be suitor."

Emily's eyes widened with fear as the image of her dark abductor crossed her mind. "No," she said in a shaky voice. "Do not wish that, Belle. Above all things, do not wish for that."

It had been a sleepless night. Emily gave up looking at the clock sometime after two in the morning. Her mind kept racing with what she would say to Ian in the morning, her one last attempt to convince him to let her follow her heart's desire. If she could only make him see reason, then she could set sail for America within a fortnight. On the other hand, if this meeting ended with her oldest brother's staunch refusal, as all the others had, then Emily would have to resort to desperate measures, though at the moment she wasn't quite certain what those would be. Christopher was in America, and from the moment he had told her he was leaving, she had planned to join him. Just thinking about him made her feel warm inside.

There was only one obstacle standing in the way of her freedom. Actually, she admitted, it was a very big obstacle, mountainous to be exact, with a will to match her own. And it had a name. Ian St. Simon, Earl of Kenilworth, was not a man to trifle with. Nor could she sweet-talk or wear him down the way she could Christopher. Punching her pillow, she settled on her stomach to plan her final attack. If this one failed, she was doomed.

Emily awoke with a start at the sound of a horse's whinny. She scurried out of bed, nearly tripping over her long batiste nightgown, and rushed to the window, throwing back the heavy velvet curtain to peer below. Ian sat astride a huge black stallion; his wife, Augusta, accompanied him on her own sleek chestnut mount. The pair made a startlingly attractive couple and Emily couldn't help but smile at the obvious love the two shared.

Augusta had been her best friend when they were children. It had seemed only natural, as their estates bordered one another and their fathers were best friends and business partners. But it had all ended with the scandal that ripped the families apart, pitting them against one another in vows of revenge. Emily didn't like to think back on those pain-filled days or the innocent part she played in pulling Ian and Augusta apart. Fortunately, love had prevailed for them, but it was a subject carefully avoided by all.

Emily watched as her brother leaned over and whispered in his wife's ear, lifting a strong tanned hand to caress her neck, trailing it down over her bosom. Emily stepped back from the window. She felt like an intruder witnessing a very intimate act. What would it feel like to be touched in such a manner? Heat pooled low in her belly as she recalled a stranger's hands roaming about her body, fitting his hands to her breasts. She thrust the image from her mind and prepared to meet her brother.

A short while later, Emily ventured out of her bedroom. She knew Ian would be poring over his ledgers. Her stomach rolled with anxiety as she fixed herself a quick cup of tea, dismissing the sideboard laden with hearty breakfast fare. There would be time enough to sample Mrs. Florence's scrumptious sausage and biscuits later.

Unless Ian rejected her request again. Then she would be too depressed to eat. Chiding herself for already anticipating defeat, she pasted a smile on her face and headed for the study.

Drawing in one last deep breath, Emily hesitated only a moment before knocking on the heavy oak door.

"Come in." She heard the annoyance in Ian's voice. He disliked interruptions and she wouldn't have disturbed him if it weren't necessary. But Emily didn't think she could wait another minute for his answer. In a very short time, she would either be elated beyond belief or on the edge of despair.

Ian looked up as she entered the room, and the irritation faded from his handsome features at the sight of his sister. "Good morning, Emily. Did you enjoy the ball last night?"

"As much as I do any of those sorts of things," she answered vaguely, avoiding his eyes and plopping herself onto the gold and burgundy sofa.

"Ah, I see." Ian leaned back in his chair, clasping his large tanned hands behind his head. She felt his eyes on her. "Too many suitors vying for your affections, all of them dandies living off of their father's money."

Emily smiled at Ian's very accurate assessment of her stead-fast opinion of the ton. "Something like that," she said.

"No wonder you've got them all falling over your skirts," Ian commented. "You're beautiful, witty and intelligent. A rare commodity in women." He laughed at her sour expression.

"That Barton fellow has asked me for the third time if he may call on you. I can't put him off much longer."

Emily rolled her eyes, letting Ian know what she thought of Andrew J. Barton, Viscount Arondale.

Ian laughed again. "My thoughts exactly. You'd be miserable with that sniveling creature." He leaned forward and jotted a note to himself.

Emily watched her brother, admiring the aura of strength and power that emanated from him. He had returned to England three years ago and she had lived with him for two. But she didn't really know him. No one did except his wife. Ian and Emily had shared many meals, attended balls and soirées, conversed at length and ridden horseback with each other. And yet he always managed to remain a little aloof, a little restrained.

How she longed for sweet, affectionate Christopher.

The two brothers didn't even look alike. Ian was a big man, standing well over six feet with a body of bronze and muscle honed from years at sea. He possessed none of the conventional looks deemed handsome by England's standards, but that didn't stop women from seeking him out. He had high cheekbones, a straight nose, a square jaw and the most arresting pair of indigo eyes. His jet black hair traveled several inches past his shoulders, definitely longer than the current fashion. And the small golden hoop he still wore in his left ear served as a reminder of his years at sea. Whether he had sailed as merchant or pirate, no one really knew and he never said. But the very fact of not knowing the truth only added to the alluring enigma of the man.

She looked at those watchful blue eyes and willed herself to be strong. Swallowing twice, Emily gathered her courage and smoothed her lemon yellow day dress. Forcing herself to meet her brother's gaze, she smiled, but her quivering lower lip gave away her nervousness.

"Emily?" Ian prodded. "Is something wrong?" She must be strong, she told herself even as the tears brimmed on her lower lashes. "Emily? For heaven's sake, what is it?" Ian rounded the desk in a matter of seconds, his deft movements belying his size. Grasping her small pale hands in his strong tanned ones, he sat down next to her, pulling her into his embrace.

He spoke gentle, soothing words as he caressed her back. Those acts of kindness from her usually stoic brother broke her resolve and a single tear trickled down her cheek, followed by another and yet another. Hot, sorrowful, burning tears fell and only touched the edge of her grief. She loved Ian and appreciated his caring, but Christopher understood her and supported her need for independence.

But he had headed for America, leaving her with a head full of ideas and dreams that didn't fit in with English society.

Fresh tears rolled down her cheeks as the events of last evening came rushing at her again. Desperation had led her to the Fox's Tail and left its indelible mark on her.

"Emily, please don't cry."

She knew he hated tears, but she couldn't seem to stop them. Lifting her head from his damp shirtfront, she met his gaze. "I don't fit in here, Ian," she stammered. "And I can't be something I'm not. I've tried," she murmured, shaking her head, freeing wisps of gold from her braid.

Ian frowned. "Christopher did you no favor by letting you have free rein of Marbrook. He encouraged your outrageous behavior and led you to believe that it would be equally acceptable to walk into a room of crowded people wearing breeches instead of a gown."

"He only wanted to make up for our lack of family." As soon as the words were out, Emily wished she could take them back. She felt Ian tense but his expression remained unreadable. "Oh, Ian, I'm sorry. I didn't mean you. I know you had a very good reason for leaving."

A full minute passed in silence, save the ticking of the old oak clock resting on the mantel. Emily cursed herself for her thoughtlessness. Hadn't Belle just told her last evening that Ian was overprotective because he'd been away for so long?

His deep blue eyes darkened, then gentled. "Expectations are different for a woman, Emily," he said, holding her hands in his. "Women aren't given the freedom a man enjoys. Unfair as it may seem to you, that's just the way it is. It would be best if you tried to understand and accept that fact."

"But why?" she insisted. "We come to London every year so you can display me on the marriage market." Her hands flew up in frustration. "I don't want to get married. Now or ever. Marriage just makes me some man's chattel and no matter what you say, I know that's what happens."

Ian raised a black brow.

"Except in your case," Emily continued in a rush. "You and Augusta love each other and you treat her like a queen. She's the one person you can't intimidate with your deep voice and stern looks. Don't deny it," she said when she saw the muscles in his jaw twitch. "You share something rare and beautiful, and I'm very happy for you. But I'm not willing to risk loving someone who doesn't love me. The pain would be too deep to watch him cast me aside for his mistresses."

"And what do you know of such things?"

Emily shrugged her shoulders. "Gossipmongers abound, whether in London or the country. I've heard enough whispered tales about our father and his women to make me vow never to marry." She smoothed an imaginary wrinkle from her gown, concentrating on the soft muslin fabric. "So you see, there's really no reason to refuse my trip to America."

"Not all men are like Jonathan," Ian countered.

"But many are. And besides, it's more than just the idea of marriage. I'm a St. Simon. Adventure is in our blood. Once, long ago, you left this life and found another. Now Christopher has done the same thing." Her voice gathered strength. She would try one more time. "Can't I please have the same freedom to make my own choice?"

Ian's blue gaze bored into her. She could almost see his mind thinking, studying and assessing. He ran an agitated hand through his long black hair and frowned. "I know I have fought

your traveling to America every step of the way," he admitted.
"But there are several reasons I don't want you to go. Some
of them are selfish. Chris left and if you go too, there is little
chance we will see each other more than once every five to
ten years, and I don't want that, for Augusta or myself. And I
want Lucas to know his Aunt Emily as a person, not just as a
bedtime story." He paused a moment, his words settling over
Emily like a warm embrace.

"But aside from my own selfish reasons for wanting you to
stay here, I am concerned for you. I've traveled the world and
it isn't always a kind place." He sighed, tightening his hold
on her. "You have led a very sheltered existence at Marbrook,
with only occasional trips to London. Granted"—he laughed—
"it has been said that if one survives London, one can survive
anything. But I'm talking about foreign lands with different
and sometimes unfriendly and dangerous people preying on
unsuspecting victims. Not to mention the basic backward ele-
ments of living in an undeveloped land."

"But that's part of the excitement, is it not?" Emily's words
held a faint glimmer of hope.

"And danger," Ian said tightly.

She sat up, pulling out of his embrace, and turned toward
him. "First of all," she began, "Christopher will protect me
from any undesirables. Second, I am quite capable of adjusting
to a different lifestyle. Why, I could even perform housekeeping
duties if necessary."

"Hah," Ian laughed. "I doubt you would be able to find
your way to the kitchen."

"But I could," she persisted.

"Emily," Ian began in that placating manner that annoyed
her to no end. "To my knowledge you have never been in a
kitchen other than to steal a tart. And if the rumor is true,
you'd be buried alive under your clothing if it weren't for your
personal maid. I dread to consider what would happen if you
tried to mop a floor."

"Just because I haven't done any of those things doesn't mean I can't," she said, folding her arms across her chest.

Ian's dark brow shot up. "It would be a disaster."

A wonderful thought struck her. "If I could do all of those things you mentioned"—she paused, pinning him with her gaze—"then would you permit me to go?"

"Cooking and cleaning?" He sounded incredulous.

"Why not?"

"That's ridiculous," he said, slashing his big hand in the air. "You are a woman of quality. Even in America, you would not be expected to perform such manual labor. You would lead a privileged lifestyle, and be waited on by servants, much as you do here."

"I know all that," she said, clinging to the hope that he might change his mind. At least this discussion had gotten further than all the previous ones. "Christopher has written all about the black slaves and the tobacco fields. What I'm asking you is, if I can prove you wrong by doing something you're certain I can't, such as learning housekeeping, then will you admit that you could be wrong about America?"

"And let you go?"

"And let me go." She held her breath, waiting for his response. Perhaps. Just perhaps he might agree.

Ian said nothing for what seemed like ages and Emily knew better than to interrupt him. He would make his decision when he was ready and no amount of prompting or impatient urgings would hurry him. She leaned back against the soft cushions of the sofa, preparing to settle in for a long wait. Closing her eyes, she thought of the books she'd been reading about America. New lands, new people.

Endless possibilities.

"I'll agree on one condition." Ian's words sliced through her thoughts. "For the period of three weeks, you will become a servant here at Greyling Manor. You will dress the part, work with the servants and not socialize with any of your friends."

"That's all?" she squeaked, unable to believe what she'd just heard.

Ian's blue eyes narrowed. "You will cook, polish and scrub as directed."

"Fine. Is that all?" He was really going to let her go!

He hesitated, obviously surprised by her rapid consent. "You will wear serviceable gowns. No more silks or satins."

Emily smiled at him.

"And no soirées or balls either," he spat out.

"That should not pose a problem." She lowered her head to hide another smile. This servant business had her brother in a major huff. He certainly didn't seem to like the idea, which made her all the more determined to succeed.

"Are you positive you wish to go through with this charade?" he asked, rubbing the back of his neck as though he couldn't wait to be done with this conversation.

"If it is the only way I can obtain passage to America, then it is what I want," she replied.

"Before you give me your final answer, there is one more small condition we must agree upon."

"Yes." Emily didn't need to hear any more. She would agree to any condition as long as it got her on a ship bound for America.

Ian pinned her with his gaze. "If you fail to carry off this little ruse, fail in any way to meet the terms, then all talk of America will cease." He placed his strong tanned hands over hers. "Then you will accept your fate and remain in England."

Emily bit her lip, trying to control the wave of emotion that ran through her. If she failed, Ian would prohibit her from traveling to America. Ever. She would be forced to stay in England, and whether or not he spoke the words, she knew he would eventually try to coerce her into a marriage.

"Emily?"

"I agree," she blurted out. "If I fail, then I won't mention America again. You have my word."

Ian smiled then and gathered her into his warm embrace.

She knew he thought he would beat her at this game of wills.
In truth, he probably didn't think she would make it past a day
or two. But she would show him. She would succeed, she
told herself, and then quickly amended that thought: She must
succeed.

Chapter 2

Emily could hear the companionable chatter of dinner conversation as she approached the dining room, laden with a tureen of creamed asparagus soup. Ian's hearty laughter echoed to her, making her smile. She approved of their dinner guest, Noah Sandleton, though she had yet to meet him. Anyone who could lighten Ian's somber countenance and make him laugh in earnest was someone she would hold in great esteem.

Not to mention the fact that he was the man responsible for getting Christopher to America. Oh, yes, one mustn't forget that little bit of information, Emily reminded herself as she turned her thoughts to the scant tidbits she knew about their guest. He was an American, though a displaced one, having had a falling out with his father several years ago. Noah Sandleton had met Ian at sea, though the conditions of their first encounter remained unknown. They had been adversaries, two men of equal strength and power who later became best friends, sailing the sea together, exploring distant, exotic lands. Emily was more than a little curious to meet this man, and she secretly hoped to hear more news about Christopher's new home.

"Are you all set to bring in the soup, Emily?" Mrs. Florence grinned, barely able to control her mirth. Emily smiled back at the plump cook, who had been preparing delectable dishes for the St. Simon household for almost twenty years.

"I think I am, Mrs. Florence." Her gray eyes sparkled. "I only regret that I won't be feasting on your roast pork or spiced apples."

"The earl said this was to be a special dinner for his good friend, Mr. Sandleton, so I fixed one of the family's favorites." She bent her gray head toward Emily and whispered, "I'll save you some in the kitchen, Lady Emily."

"You're a dear. It will be scrumptious, as usual," Emily said, lifting the tureen of asparagus soup. It was much heavier than she expected. "How on earth do you manage these things?"

Mrs. Florence let out a booming laugh. Behind her, Emily heard the soft tittering of two young maids as they watched her wrestling with the huge bowl. She grinned at them, knowing her transition from noblewoman to servant had created quite a stir at Greyling Manor. There were even whispered rumors that bets had been taken as to whether she'd succeed in her mission.

"Good luck to you," Mrs. Florence whispered, her kind blue eyes twinkling as she opened the door for Emily. Concentrating on the creamy green liquid in front of her, Emily took slow, careful steps toward the dining room, where her family entertained their honored guest. As she entered the ornately decorated elegance, her eyes shot to an empty spot on the linen tablecloth. Just large enough, with a little room to spare, she thought, as she edged closer to the table.

"Christopher will have his work cut out for him, but he'll do well in Virginia." A very deep, very familiar voice spoke to the right of her.

The tureen clattered loudly onto the table, sloshing asparagus soup onto the pristine tablecloth. Emily withdrew quickly, her startled gaze riveted on the man who'd just spoken. *It was him!* Dark brown eyes sliced over her, widening briefly in recognition. Just as quickly, his face became an unreadable mask and he looked away, leaving her gawking at him.

"Emily!" Ian fairly roared. "What is the meaning of this? You are staring at our guest. And look what you've done to his shirt." Ian motioned toward Noah's white shirt. Pale green spots had splattered the front in a random pattern. "If you can't conduct proper decorum in the dining room, then I will have you permanently installed cleaning chamber pots!" he warned, his commanding voice filling the room.

Emily felt the heat creep into her cheeks. How she wished she were anywhere but in this room, standing alone, feeling utterly humiliated.

"Emily, why don't you see if you can find something to clean up this little accident? I'm sure Mr. Sandleton bears you no ill will." Augusta's soft voice cut the tension in the room. "As we all know, accidents do happen." She shot her husband a murderous look, her emerald eyes flashing. Ian ignored the warning, piercing Emily with his blue stare and preparing to continue his diatribe.

"Augusta is quite right." Noah's rich, deep voice interrupted Ian's attempt. "It's nothing, Ian. Really. Best to let it just be forgotten," he drawled.

Best to let it just be forgotten. Those had been Noah's own words, but he'd spent the rest of the supper hour anticipating the return of the maid named Emily. But she didn't return for the rest of the evening. And somehow, he'd known she wouldn't. Still, he waited, more than a little curious about this maid who dressed in boy's clothes and frequented taverns.

What had she been after? And more to the point, did it have anything to do with Ian? He had to find out, had to be certain Ian was safe from his past, for God knew Noah wasn't.

Noah recalled the conversation he and Ian had had in the library after supper. They had been enjoying a fine brandy and reminiscing about the old days at sea.

"How much have you told Augusta?" Noah asked, eager to allay his concerns.

Ian's dark brow shot up. "She only knows I was a merchant tradesman." His jaw tensed.

Noah nodded, wondering how to broach the subject they had both vowed never to speak of again. "Nothing else?" he asked, his voice low and cautious.

"Of course not."

"Good." Noah crossed one booted leg over the other and stared into his snifter. "He saw me you know." There. Finally, after seven years, he'd said it.

"Impossible," Ian spat out.

"No," Noah corrected, "most definitely possible." He threw back his head and downed the rest of his brandy in one swallow.

Silence followed, filling the room with memories—dark, ugly images of men lying in pools of blood, gasping for one last breath as the life oozed out of them.

Noah was the first to speak. His voice sounded distant, cold, emotionless. "I didn't leave right away. I had to be certain the files were destroyed." He paused a moment, his fists clenched. "I pulled off my mask, the damn thing was so hot, and watched the building go up in flames. And then I saw him at the window, staring straight at me. A few seconds later, the fire took over and he was gone."

"Jesus," Ian said, looking at his best friend. "We checked the building. It was empty."

"Who knows?" Noah shrugged. "He could've been hiding or even entered once the fire started."

"Peter Crowlton stood to become a very wealthy man. But only if he had the files," Ian said, sipping his brandy.

"The bastard was willing to sacrifice all of us," Noah bit out, thinking of the brutal murders of twelve fellow espionage agents. Crowlton had sold their files and exposed his own kind for money and power.

"But we stopped him," Ian said. "The files were destroyed. We completed our mission. The Crown was satisfied."

"But they never found a body," Noah said, trying to keep his voice casual. "Not even in all the charred ashes of the building. Don't you find that odd?"

"He's dead, Noah." Ian placed his forearms on the oak desk and leaned forward. "It's been seven years. The man's dead."

"Logic says you're right," Noah agreed. "But every once in a while, something out of the ordinary happens—say for instance, a stranger taking an unusual interest in me, asking a lot of personal questions about my past. Or a person who just seems out of place in a particular situation. It makes me think about Crowlton and the fact that his body was never found."

Ian laughed. "Nonsense. That life is behind us now. I'm a respectable businessman, titled no less, with a wife and child. And you"—he paused a moment—"you are a wealthy, philandering merchant wanderer who roams the world in search of excitement."

Noah smiled. "You forgot to include British-born American. That makes me sound more interesting. Like an unsolvable puzzle." He swirled the brandy in his snifter and took another drink.

"That's because you *are* an unsolvable puzzle, my man," Ian said. "And you like it that way. It makes you irresistible to all those women who trail after you and your American accent with that Virginia drawl. If they only knew you were as British as I am, they'd be very disappointed."

"But they'll never know, will they?" Noah asked, his voice full of humor.

"Not from me they won't."

"I knew I could count on my best friend." He paused a moment, his brow furrowed, his smile gone. "And you're probably right about Crowlton. Most likely he's dead. But if he were alive, we both know he'd be hunting me." Noah looked up from his snifter to see Ian give a slight nod of agreement. Noah's fists clenched and unclenched. "And part of me wants nothing more than to meet him, face to face, so I can repay him for killing his own,'' he said, his voice little more than a low rumble.

"Nothing's worse than a traitor," Ian agreed.

"If by some crazy stretch, the bastard were still alive, he'd only be after me." Noah hesitated a moment, measuring his next words. "Or those I care about. I don't have to tell you what to look for. We were both trained together."

"Is there some particular reason that you're telling me this now? Has something happened?" Ian asked bluntly.

Well, here it was. Time to confess. "I don't trust your new maid."

"Which one?"

"The woman who spilled the asparagus soup on me. Emily, I believe."

" Emily?'' Ian's voice sounded incredulous. His lips curved up a little. Was he hiding a smile?

"There's something about her. She's not what she appears." *Even when she isn't dressed in boy's clothes,* Noah thought, but he saw no need to bring that point up at the moment.

"Really?"

"She dresses in maid's clothing, but carries herself with the grace and elegance of a well-bred lady. And her speech tells of education, unless she's an awfully good imitator." Noah frowned. "And she was quite flippant, with little regard for social class, which is unseemly in a maid, but actually quite refreshing in a woman."

"Emily is a maid," Ian said, the harsh note in his voice filling the room.

"And her skin is too soft," Noah said, thinking of the velvety swell of her bosom, the soft satin skin of her hips. . . .

"Her skin?" Ian boomed. "What in the hell do you know of Emily's skin?"

Startled from his thoughts, Noah quickly recovered. "Why nothing other than what my observant eye relays to me."

"You think Emily is hiding something?" Ian's expression

was blank, his voice cautious, as though he were trying very hard to show no emotion.

"Perhaps. How long has she been in your employ?" The question was straightforward, innocent enough.

Ian's eyes narrowed a moment, almost imperceptibly, but Noah didn't miss the action. Nor did the slight twitch in Ian's jaw escape him.

"She's been here less than a week," Ian said, looking down and shifting a few papers on his desk, moving them from one pile to another.

"Where was she previously employed?" References would be easy enough to check.

"She said she'd been taking care of an ailing grandmother in the country for the past two years." Ian shoved the papers aside and leaned back in his chair, strumming his fingers on the massive oak desk in front of him.

"So there are no other employers to vouch for her work?"

"None."

Not the kind that would admit it anyway, Noah thought, a blurred image of Peter Crowlton swimming before his eyes. Was it his imagination, or was Ian avoiding the subject of his new maid?

"Judging from the skills she's displayed, it's hard to believe she's really a maid. There was more asparagus soup splattered all over the place after she cleaned up than when she actually spilled the stuff." Noah twirled the brandy snifter between his fingers and waited for Ian's reply.

"Out with it, man. What are you saying?" Ian demanded.

"Maybe," Noah began, looking up to meet Ian's steady gaze, "she's here on a mission."

"To do what? Steal Mrs. Florence's lemon tart recipe?" Ian's laughter sliced the tension in the room.

"Maybe she's spying on you. Maybe Crowlton is still alive. Admit it. It is a possibility," Noah persisted.

Ian laughed again and reached for the brandy decanter. "It

is most definitely not a possibility. Emily. A spy." He chuckled, shaking his head.

The whole idea was beginning to sound ridiculous, even to Noah. But what if Ian knew about her escapades as a boy? Would he feel any different? Should Noah tell him? Something inside told him to wait, not to divulge Emily's secret just yet. If there were proof to be found, he would find it. Then he would go to Ian and expose her.

Noah took a drink, savoring the burning sensation traveling down his throat. It tasted good. Damn good. Maybe tonight he'd just get drunk and forget all the nagging, unanswered questions swimming in his head.

"Noah?"

Noah looked up from his drink.

Ian held his glass out and saluted him. "Thanks for telling me."

Noah nodded.

"And you know," Ian continued, "if Crowlton weren't dead, which I'm certain he is, planting a spy in my house would be his style. He'd use a go-between to gather information for him, someone nonthreatening." He paused a moment before adding, "Like a beautiful woman."

Ian's words stayed with Noah, nagging him with uncertainty. Was Emily a spy, sent by a half-crazed maniac bent on revenge? Did she have a rendezvous with him at the Fox's Tail the other night?

The evening ended a short while later with Emily's image shrouded in mystery, a tantalizing enigma wrapped in a dangerous cloak of lies and deceit. Noah paced his room for the better part of an hour, his thoughts on the beautiful servant who spoke with more refinement than many of his titled acquaintances.

There were so many unanswered questions. But Noah would have answers. He planned to seek Emily out himself and question her. And she would talk. He would give her no choice. Noah had to know if Peter Crowlton had sent her. Was the Serpent still alive, slithering back into his life for one final attack? He clenched his fists, his thoughts on the golden-haired beauty who might well prove to be the link between past and present, good and evil, life and death.

Emily rushed about the guest room, plumping pillows and folding fresh linens. She'd secured the heavy emerald draperies with thick, golden tassels and thrown open the window to admit light and fresh air. A soft, gentle breeze swirled throughout the room. The late-afternoon sunshine peeked through, casting its sunny warmth on the objects within, illuminating them with its gentle radiance. The fragrant beauty of freshly cut honeysuckle overflowing from a large glass vase wafted through the air.

Emily stood in the center of the room, drinking it all in, eyes closed, senses alive as the touch, feel and smell of summer blanketed her.

Times like these brought her such peace that she could almost pretend Noah Sandleton didn't exist. Unfortunately, they were short-lived because the man seemed to be everywhere she turned, watching her with his slow, steady gaze. And now, thanks to her hardheaded brother, she would have to face him daily because Ian had invited him to spend the remainder of his visit at Greyling Manor. Another three weeks. It was too much.

How would she possibly tolerate the man for that length of time? Of course, she had considered seeking out Augusta and beseeching her to change Ian's mind and make that dreadful man go away. But what reason could she possibly give? None, without revealing the incident at the Fox's Tail, and she'd die before she admitted to that. It also seemed that Noah Sandleton possessed a few scruples and had decided to remain quiet on the matter as well.

Emily sighed. It was bad enough that he haunted her dreams at night, but now she was going to have to tolerate him during her waking hours as well. And a living, breathing Noah Sandleton was just plain dangerous. What was she going to do?

Somewhere in the far recesses of her mind, she heard a door open. Pulling herself from her disturbing thoughts, she whirled around to stand face to face with her tormentor.

Noah's dark eyes pinned her, stripping away her defenses with their intensity, leaving her exposed. His lips thinned into a tight line, the brackets at the side deep. Emily watched the small muscle twitching in his jaw and knew he was angry.

He reached her in four long strides, towering over her, poised and waiting. "Looking for something?" he inquired, a smirk playing across his full lips.

Emily took a step back, trying to distance herself from him. "I-I," she stammered. "I came to prepare your room." The admission sounded weak even to her, and she knew it was true.

His eyes scanned the room quickly before settling back on her face. "I keep my purse with me," he said, patting his vest pocket.

"I had no intention of taking your belongings," she fumed, eyes blazing.

Noah lifted a dark brow. "Oh really?"

"Yes, really. I had duties to attend in this room now that you are staying at Greyling Manor." She didn't try to hide the faint tinge of bitterness that crept into her words. Why couldn't he just go away? He watched her every move and she feared he might go to Ian and tell him about her. It had been bad enough seeing him in the dining room last evening, but now the thought of having him underfoot as a resident turned her stomach. But it also did strange things to her insides, leaving her a little breathless.

She didn't relish either feeling.

She had to get away. Her eyes darted around the room, searching for an escape. Without a moment's hesitation, Emily leapt for the bed, planning to roll over it and head for the door behind. But a large forearm reached out, catching her in midair and slamming her slender body onto the emerald counterpane. Noah threw one of his long legs over both of hers, blocking any thoughts of escape.

Emily struggled to free herself, pushing and squirming against his harsh grip. Her hands struck out at him, nails turning into talons as she clawed at his jaw and neck, drawing blood.

"Stop it, damn you," Noah ground out, catching her wrists with one hand and forcing them above her head. Emily met his angry look as he pushed her farther into the bed, shifting his weight to rest more fully on her. He was going to crush her right into the emerald stitches of the counterpane, she was certain.

"Let me up, you beast," she gasped as she lay breathless and panting beneath him, her chest heaving from exertion and anger.

His eyes were on her, watching her, burning with quiet intensity. They moved from her face, slowly traveling down her neck to settle on her breasts. Emily felt the heat of his gaze warming every fiber of her body. Her heart beat a rapid staccato against her rib cage, the sound deafening in her ears. Surely Noah Sandleton heard it. How could he not when it pounded in such loud cadence?

Her gaze settled on his face, strong and formidable one moment, yet warm and gentle the next. His rich brown eyes remained fixed on her chest as though lulled into a seductive trance by the rise and fall of her breasts. Emily's nipples hardened into small peaks, and she prayed Noah wouldn't notice. But when he lifted his head to meet her eyes, the small smile playing about his full lips told her the thin muslin had shielded nothing from his view.

Keeping his eyes on hers, Noah trailed his free hand up her rib cage, his long fingers nearly brushing her breast. Emily wanted to cry out, wanted him to put his hand on the swollen peak of her breast and soothe the ache he had created with that one heated look. With great effort, she forced her body to be still, giving herself up to the unknown pleasure of his feather-soft touch stroking its way toward her neck. The pads of his fingers circled the hollow of her neck in a slow, gentle rhythm.

Her body felt light and heavy at the same time as she turned toward his touch.

Noah smiled again, this time a slow smile, revealing white teeth and wrinkle lines at the corner of his eyes. He was devastating when he smiled. He still held her hands above her head, but his hold gentled as he rubbed one of her wrists with the pad of his thumb. Small shivers ran through her body. Was that from his touch or had it happened with just a smile? It didn't matter. Nothing mattered at the moment other than the sensations this man was creating in her.

Noah's free hand reached up to stroke her hair. He pulled a pin out and tossed it on the counterpane. Then he reached for another and another until her unbound hair spilled into his hand. He closed his fingers about the golden mass, lowering his head to breathe in her scent.

"Lilac," he whispered, his voice low and gruff.

Emily nodded, then realized her foolishness. Noah had his face partially buried in her hair, his eyes closed, the hint of a smile playing about his mouth.

"I prefer lilac over rose," she blurted out, wondering about his fascination with her hair. She'd always thought it to be something of a nuisance, a big unruly mass that refused to stay in place. But Christopher had always told her it reminded him of their mother's hair and so she had battled with it to please him.

"I definitely prefer lilac," he murmured, "especially on you."

Her heart skipped a beat as his words washed over her, soft, smooth and seductive, like fine sherry on a winter night. His grip on her hands lessened and she reached up to stroke his cheek.

He groaned low in his throat as he lifted his head, moving closer to her, so close that she could see golden flecks in his brown eyes. She hadn't noticed them before. Or the small scar above his right eyebrow. Her gaze roamed his face, settling on his mouth.

The sound of voices in the hallway startled them both. Noah reacted first, raising a finger to his lips.

"I'll just check with Noah and see if he'd care to take an afternoon ride with us," Ian said.

"That's a splendid idea." Augusta lowered her voice. "I just wish your sister could go along with us."

"Absolutely not," Ian said. Emily wondered at the sudden coldness in Ian's voice.

"But I think they would get along quite well," Augusta countered, seemingly nonplussed by her husband's behavior.

"No," Ian said. "You don't understand, Augusta. Noah's not husband material." His tone gentled. "Despite what she says, Emily will settle down one day."

"But perhaps it could be with Noah. She might just tame him," Augusta whispered. "Look what happened to you." There was a very long pause, followed by Augusta's giggle. "Stop it, Ian. Stop it now. Not in the middle of the hall," she whispered, giggling again.

"That's not what you said last night," he whispered back, laughter in his voice. There was another long pause, followed by a loud rap on Noah's door.

"Noah?" Ian's deep voice filled the room.

"Yes, Ian?" Emily met Noah's gaze and their eyes locked. Would he expose her? She held her breath.

"Augusta and I are going for a ride on the grounds this afternoon and thought you might like to accompany us."

There was a brief pause. Emily could feel her heart pounding against her ribs. "Certainly. Just give me a few moments to change and I'll meet you at the stables."

Emily kept her eyes trained on the door long after the voices faded away. Noah eased himself off her and leaned back against the mahogany bedpost.

"Who are you, Emily?" he demanded, his voice low and quiet.

She refused to meet his eyes, certain that if she looked at him he would see the vulnerability there and take full advantage of her weakness. He mustn't learn her identity or America would be nothing but a broken dream, forever lost. Gathering her courage, she pushed herself up from the wrinkled counterpane and began collecting the pins that lay scattered before her.

"My name is Emily Barry. I am a servant at Greyling Manor." She must not reveal too much.

"And before you were employed at Greyling Manor?" His tone was stiff and impersonal now, all trace of gentleness gone.

"Why, I was employed elsewhere." Why must he be so persistent and so cold? How could he pretend nothing had passed between them? Emily could feel his gaze on her, dark and forbidding. She had to find a way to escape his scrutiny.

"As what?" He was losing his patience—she could hear it in his voice.

"What does that mean?" If she feigned ignorance, he might ease up on his questions. Then again, he seemed to be the persistent type.

"It means," he bit out, "I intend to find out who the hell you are and what you're really doing here."

Emily's eyes widened but she said nothing.

"I find you at a seedy tavern dressed as a boy one day and in the home of my best friend wearing maid's clothes the next. How is it," he asked, his voice accusing, "that a simple servant has the speech and grace of a well-bred lady?" Noah leaned over, his face mere inches from hers. "I don't expect an answer from you because whatever comes from your lips will most likely be lies."

He reached out and grabbed a mass of hair, forcing her to meet his gaze. "I'll be watching every move you make, Emily Barry." He spat out her name as though he'd tasted sour milk. As though he thought it wasn't her real name at all. "When you think you're alone, turn around and I'll be there. Watching you." His words were dark and threatening. "I intend to expose you. And if I find that you are in any way involved in a scheme to harm Ian St. Simon, as I suspect you may well be, then I will personally cart you off to Newgate."

"I would never hurt Ian!" she cried out, clenching her fists.

"Ian? My, how familiar you are. Even a wayward American like me knows that a servant doesn't address nobility in such a manner." Releasing his hold on her hair, Noah rose from the bed and headed for the door. He stopped, rested his hand on the knob and turned to face her. His smile didn't quite reach his eyes. "Just remember, Emily. I'll be watching you." Then he was gone, closing the door quietly behind him.

"Now Emily, I'll tell you my secret to making a meat pie." Mrs. Florence leaned over, her round body crowding out the work area, and whispered, "It's all in the crust."

Emily smiled and nodded. "The crust," she repeated, knowing there was much more to making a meat pie than those simple words. In the last few days, she had gained a whole new perspective on food that had nothing to do with eating it. She hadn't known it could be chopped, shredded, sauteed, broiled, fried and steamed. Never again would she look at a plate of food as a simple means to fill an empty stomach.

"Now you add the water to the flour like this," Mrs. Florence said, pouring a healthy amount into a big bowl. "Then you add butter and start to mix, using two forks. Don't be afraid to get the dough on your hands. It washes right off." She smiled at Emily and worked the two forks into the big lump, cutting and slashing with her pudgy fingers until the pastry resembled hundreds of small peas.

"And that's our crust?" Emily knew Mrs. Florence was an excellent cook, knew she had eaten her meat pies for years, but she had to admit she had serious doubts about the mass of tiny, shredded lumps in front of her. It didn't resemble anything she'd eaten before, nor did it look like it had any chance of turning into a flaky, mouthwatering crust.

"Of course it's our crust, child. But it won't be unless it's properly cut up," Mrs. Florence said, turning the pastry over with her forks.

"Cut up," Emily repeated, adding that word to her list of food activities. One could also cut up something.

"Now you give it a try. Go ahead." Mrs. Florence pushed the bowl toward Emily, handing over the long forks. "That's a girl." She chuckled as Emily struggled with the utensils. After several more attempts and a few kind words from her mentor, Emily got the knack of using the forks and cutting the pastry. "You've cut it up but good." She chuckled again, slicing a hunk of pastry and placing it on the floured counter. "I like to make pastries when I'm troubled about something." She winked. "I can cut to my heart's desire and nobody gets hurt."

"Like Mr. Florence?" Emily teased, thinking of the wizened stableman, who was several inches shorter and many pounds lighter than his wife.

Mrs. Florence let out a hoot of laughter, shaking her rolling pin at Emily. "When I'm mad at Mr. Florence, child, I make bread."

Emily balled her fists and struck at the big lump. She left an imprint where her knuckles collided with the dough. Laughing, she punched again. Soon her fists were moving in earnest, attacking the dough with vengeance.

Punching the dough one last time, she poked a finger in the middle to test for softness. It bounced back slowly, not unlike Mrs. Florence's upper arms had done a little while before when Emily had accidentally bumped into her.

Mrs. Florence had pointed to the huge sack of flour that morning and announced that today was bread-making day, which meant she must have had a tiff with her husband. Emily's suspicions were confirmed when the cook growled at the flour mixture and pummeled it with such force that a fine spattering of white landed everywhere: the counter, floor, her apron, Emily's nose. When she'd exhausted her frustrations, she pushed the bowl to Emily and encouraged her to have a go at it.

Emily spent several minutes punching the dough. She understood why Mrs. Florence did this when she was angry. The technique proved quite effective to relieve stress and required only minor instruction before a person was ready to attempt the process alone. Emily didn't even need an imaginary villain to pound on. A face appeared each time she punched. It was dark and brooding with deep brown eyes flecked in gold. *Bam!* She struck his already crooked nose. *Pow!* Her knuckles connected with his square jaw. *Whack!* Wiped that crooked grin off his mouth. *Bam! Pow! Whack!*

A fleshy hand stilled her arm. "That's enough, child." Mrs. Florence's soft voice reached her, dragging her away from the taunting image of Noah Sandleton.

Pulling back, Emily grasped the edges of the large bowl, stilling her shaking hands. She had actually imagined she was doing all of those nasty things to Noah Sandleton's face. The worst part of it all was, she had been thoroughly enjoying herself. Disgusted with her lack of control, she wondered when she had fallen so low.

The kitchen door swung wide, banging against the wall, interrupting Emily's self-chastisement. Her gaze focused on two rosy-cheeked young girls who stood facing each other, giggling behind their hands.

"All right, you two," Mrs. Florence said, a hint of laughter in her voice. "Out with it. What are you both up to this early in the morning? Hmm?" Her bright blue eyes ran over the girls.

"Oh, mum, 'e certainly is a beauty." Bridgett, the shorter of the two maids, twirled about and ended on a sigh. "With 'is deep accent an' 'is slow smile, I was all tied up in knots."

"And those eyes," Heather, the other maid, piped in. "I thought 'e could see right through me. They was the same color as the shavings we put on Lady Emily's hot chocolate."

Emily looked down at her dough-crusted hands and began rubbing at the sticky stuff. She would not get into a discussion about *him*. She would not do it.

"Strange though," Bridgett said, her full, pink lips turning down. " 'E complimented us on the meal and the like, but then 'e asked where you was this morning, Lady—I mean, Emily."

Looking up into three pairs of curious eyes, Emily could feel her face growing warm. Why would he say something like that? She shrugged and tried to make light of the inquiry. "Wouldn't you want to know where the she-devil was that spilled asparagus soup on your shirt, cream in your lap and tea on your shoulder?" she asked, a sardonic expression on her face.

The two girls clamped their hands to their mouths, trying to suppress another round of giggles. Mrs. Florence hid a smile. "Out with the two of you now. There's plenty to be done. Shoo."

Bridgett and Heather scurried out of the kitchen, whispering as they went. Emily bent to the task of removing the rest of the drying dough from her fingers. It was starting to itch and would soon be unbearable if she didn't get it all off.

"Come, child. There's an easier way to get your hands clean," Mrs. Florence's gentle voice offered. "If you keep up with what you're doing, your hands will be raw." She took Emily's elbow and guided her to a large basin of warm water, where she handed her a bar of soap and a towel.

Emily could feel the other woman's watchful gaze on her as she lathered her hands.

"Mr. Sandleton is quite a looker, don't you think?"

"I hadn't noticed." She rubbed more vigorously.

"Really? That's odd. I thought you'd be particularly interested in him, seeing as he's an American and all. And we all know how much you want to join up with Lord Christopher."

Mrs. Florence was no fool. "I don't need him. I've got my own plan." She pulled at the globs of dough, watching them float in the water a moment and then sink. Too bad she couldn't get rid of Noah Sandleton that easily.

She heard the cook cluck her tongue and knew a lecture was about to follow. The old woman was never disrespectful, but she had little regard for titles and such when there was a lesson to be learned. And from the way she was watching her, Emily knew there would be no escape from her this morning.

"Everybody needs somebody at one time or another." Mrs. Florence crossed her arms over her ample middle. "And we usually need a body most when we fight it the hardest." Her blue eyes misted. Emily hazarded a glance at her and knew she was thinking of Mr. Florence.

"Well I certainly don't need Noah Sandleton for business or otherwise," Emily said, inspecting her clean hands. She grabbed the towel and began drying her chapped hands.

"Do you mean to tell me you haven't felt those blue eyes following you around the room?" Mrs. Florence demanded.

A vision of deep, rich chocolate swirled before her. Without thinking, Emily burst out, "His eyes aren't blue. They're a rich chocolate color with tiny golden flecks."

No sooner were the words out of her mouth than Emily realized her error. She hazarded a glance in Mrs. Florence's direction and saw the huge grin on the other woman's face. She had set out to trick her and the ruse had worked.

"You haven't noticed him, eh?" The older woman threw back her head and laughed, jiggling the extra flesh on her ample chin.

Emily could feel the heat in her cheeks. She rubbed her hands on the towel in swift, jerky movements, trying to gather her thoughts.

"Well, I guess I have noticed those eagle eyes on me," she admitted. "But only because I know he's just waiting for me to mess up again. He unsettles me and the harder I try to concentrate on the task, the more I seem to make an absolute muddle of things."

"I must admit, he was a tad upset when you spilled that cream on him."

"But I tried to wipe it up right away."

Mrs. Florence chuckled. "Lesson number one child: never wipe up anything that's fallen on a man's lap. Period."

Emily agreed, remembering Noah's stunned face and the sudden viselike grip of his hand stilling her actions. He hadn't spoken for several moments, and when he finally did, his voice was low and gruff, commanding her to get out. Immediately. Thank heavens, there were no other witnesses to the disastrous event save Mrs. Florence, who had stood by in shocked horror. Ian would have killed her.

"Your wager will be over soon enough and then you could present yourself to Mr. Sandleton as Lady Emily St. Simon."

"Never!" He could never know her real identity. If he found out she was Ian's sister, Noah would waste little time exposing her escapades and all chance of traveling to America would sink as quickly as the dough had a few moments before. Ian was not that understanding or forgiving. He would see her little jaunt to the Fox's Tail as a major betrayal and would marry her off posthaste. She must protect her identity at all costs until Noah Sandleton was safely away from them, sailing off to his next adventure.

Chapter 3

The next six days passed with relative ease. Of course, there were a few minor mishaps where Noah Sandleton was concerned, but nothing so severe that a careful laundering wouldn't remove. Emily wondered, though, if the cranberry juice stain on his shirt cuff would be permanent. Well, she wasn't going to feel guilty about that or the claret spill on his trousers either. He shouldn't have tried to grab the silver pitcher or glass carafe from her as though she were an incapable goose. She knew how to serve refreshments. She had even acted as Christopher's hostess on occasion.

It wasn't her fault that Noah Sandleton unnerved her to the point that she lost her wits around him. His steady stare, following her every movement, was enough to make her spill, drop, bobble or overturn most everything she got her hands on. Things would progress quite smoothly if he would just leave her alone and not watch her every move like a cat about to pounce.

Well, it would all be over soon enough, she reminded herself. One more week and she would be through as Emily Barry, wearer of scratchy dyed muslin and cotton hose. One more

week and she would win her wager with Ian and begin making
plans to sail for America. It might even be possible to begin
her journey the next week if she were fortunate enough. Belle
had told her about a ship setting sail in three weeks' time.
Certainly, she needn't wait any longer than that.

After all, Ian was in the shipping business and knew many
of the vessels coming in and out of port. He would arrange
passage for her. He had given his word.

Emily hummed a light tune as she placed the warm biscuits
in a serving dish.

One more week. That was all. Seven more days of falling
under Noah Sandleton's dark gaze following her around the
room, taunting her. Her hand closed around a biscuit, squashing
it with her fingers. He would be leaving soon for his ship. Was
it seven or eight days? Not that she cared. The sooner he
was gone, the better. Good riddance. Another biscuit crumbled
between her fingers.

How dare he accuse her of wanting to harm Ian? The man
was a beast. Very soon, she'd never have to see him again.
Never again. A third biscuit suffered the fate of the others, bits
and pieces of it falling through her fingers onto the floor. Then
another and another.

"Good heavens, child." Mrs. Florence rushed up to Emily,
grabbing her arm. "What are you doing?"

Emily looked down at the half-crumbled biscuit in her hand.
Tiny crumbs clung to her fingers. Larger ones were strewn
everywhere: on her apron, the table, the floor.

"Oh my goodness!" There were only four biscuits remaining
in the serving dish. She had destroyed twelve without even
knowing it! Emily started scooping up crumbs and large chunks
of biscuit into her apron, then went to the rubbish pail and
shook out its contents. A small mountain of white heaped from
the pail, threatening to spill over onto the floor. Emily stood
staring at the rubbish, a small tear forming in the corner of one
eye.

"It's all right, child." Mrs. Florence's voice was soft and

soothing. She placed a plump hand on Emily's arm. "I'll serve for you tonight."

"No!" The word flew out of Emily's mouth with more force than she intended. "No, Mrs. Florence," she repeated on a quieter note. "I'm fine. Really." Patting the cook's fleshy forearm, Emily offered a weak smile. "I don't know what came over me."

"Well I do, and I say it's about enough of the two of you going at each other." Mrs. Florence nodded her gray head. "Why a body's got to be blind to not see it. Plain and simple blind, if you ask me." She crossed her arms over her ample breasts and snorted.

"See what?"

The look Mrs. Florence gave Emily said she was no fool even if Emily thought she was. "Hmpph." The old woman leaned against the kitchen table. "Why do you think you've been so clumsy lately? Have you thought about it?" Mrs. Florence smiled. "And you've only blundered about around one certain person. Don't you find that odd?"

"He makes me nervous." Emily could feel a slow heat creeping from her neck to her cheeks.

Mrs. Florence remained silent.

"And he's always watching me," Emily complained. "Everywhere I turn, he's looking at me with those dark eyes. It's like he sees something I don't and it unsettles me." She paced around the kitchen table. "*He* unsettles me. When I'm near him I can't think straight." She stopped to push back a stray lock of hair. "And I get all fluttery inside."

"It makes you a mite angry," Mrs. Florence said knowingly.

"Furious," Emily admitted.

"Well, that about sums it up, I guess," the older woman said, clucking her tongue.

"What do you mean?" Sometimes Mrs. Florence could be very confusing.

"You've taken a liking to him and he to you."

"Never!" Emily blurted out.

The older woman shrugged her shoulders, smiling at Emily's outburst.

"I don't even like him." *How could she think such a thing?*

The cook's smile turned into a wide grin.

"He's a mean, selfish bully." *Even if his touch is as gentle as a summer rain.*

This time, Mrs. Florence actually threw back her head and laughed.

"And he detests me." *But I have noticed the heat in those rich, brown eyes when he thinks I'm not looking.*

Pushing her large frame from the table, Mrs. Florence took a few steps to stand in front of Emily. Her kind blue eyes misted with tears as she reached out to take Emily's hand. "Oh, child, you've so much to learn." She sighed, a deep sigh that puffed out the apron covering her ample bosom. "The man may glare at you, bully or ignore you, but one thing is for certain." She leaned in closer and whispered, "He wants you like a man wants a woman or my name isn't Gertrude Florence."

Emily swallowed hard. She felt her cheeks burning.

"Now don't go getting all embarrassed on me. I don't imagine with your mother gone so many years that anyone has ever talked about such things with you. You could do worse than a gent like Noah Sandleton."

"Ian would never permit such a match," Emily said. But would *she?* Of course not, she told herself. She'd have to be crazy to consider a match with a man like him. Or any man for that matter.

"No, I don't suppose he would. More's the pity, if you ask me. You'd make a fine match. Fine children too, with your golden hair and his brown eyes." Mrs. Florence sighed again. "Aye, more's the pity."

A vision of a golden-haired little boy floated before her. He was no more than four or five, with a smattering of freckles across the bridge of his nose. He was laughing—a musical, joyous sound that filled the air. But it was his eyes that made her breath catch in her throat. They were a deep, rich brown, like fine French chocolate.

Noah's eyes.

Emily felt heat pooling deep in her belly and clutched her middle to stop the sensation.

"Ah, well," Mrs. Florence continued, "supper needs to be served. Why don't you plead a headache and go to your room? I'll explain it all to the earl."

"I can't," Emily said, smoothing her apron and wiping off a few stray crumbs. "I won't give Ian any reason to go back on our wager." She forced a smile, pretending a confidence she didn't quite feel. "It's only one more week. What else could possibly go wrong?"

Twenty minutes later, Emily carried a tray laden with roast duck and potatoes into the dining room. She kept her eyes trained on the platter in front of her, determined to ignore Noah Sandleton. The low murmur of voices drifted to her as she edged closer, Augusta's soft tone mixing with Ian's deep one.

"We are going to miss you, Noah," Augusta said.

Not all of us, Emily thought, eyeing a large space of white tablecloth. Perfect. She leaned over with the large platter balanced in her small hands.

"I'm sorry I won't be meeting your sister," Noah said.

The platter landed on the table with a loud thud. A few small potatoes went rolling off the side, followed by several slices of duck and a healthy measure of juice that slopped on the pristine tablecloth. Emily closed her eyes, dreading Noah Sandleton's smug expression more than Ian's reprimand, which would be forthcoming any moment. If only she could will herself away.

Dead silence filled the room. Emily hazarded a look in Ian's direction.

"It's all right, Emily." Augusta's sweet voice sliced through the tension blanketing the room. "Let me call Mrs. Florence to help clean up this little accident." She put her napkin aside and rose from her chair, squeezing Ian's hand. He sat there, staring at Emily, his jaw working back and forth, a small muscle twitching on the left side.

Emily swallowed twice, hard. He was furious.

Noah's soft laughter broke the silence. "Well, at least the duck and potatoes landed on the table and not on me." His eyes filled with mirth as he sought Emily's gaze. "As you must know, Miss Barry, I can ill afford to lose any more shirts or cravats."

"They were honest accidents, all of them." How dare he be so indelicate as to bring up her past mistakes. Couldn't he tell Ian was fuming?

Noah lifted a dark brow. "I should hope so. I would hate to think that you were intentionally dumping food and drink on me." He grinned at her, seeming to take pleasure in her obvious discomfort. "Though I must admit, the thought had crossed my mind."

Emily shot him a dark look. She wanted to tell him what he could do with his thoughts, but Ian would never forgive her and the closest she'd get to America would be in her dreams. She bit the inside of her cheek to keep quiet.

"I apologize for Miss Barry's clumsiness." Ian's deep voice filled the room as he trained his eyes on Emily. "I am thinking that perhaps she might be better suited as a scullery maid. Permanently." He leaned back in his chair and took a sip of wine, his blue gaze never leaving hers. Emily stared back, the silent threat hanging between them, thick and heavy, permeating the room with heated anger and unspoken accusations.

He was waiting for her to apologize to his guest.

Emily looked away first. *Might as well be done with it,* she thought, turning toward Noah. Soon enough, he would be out of her life forever. Her hands clenched and unclenched at her side. Forever. Her nails dug into the soft flesh of her palms.

Focusing her gaze on Noah's cravat, she forced the words out. "I apologize for my accident." *I only wish the potatoes had landed in your lap.* "I did not intend to disrupt your meal." *That's a lie. I'm delighted I disrupted your meal.*

"Apology accepted." She could feel his gaze on her, moving over her like a warm summer breeze. Emily tried to concentrate on the perfect folds of his cravat. He was doing it to her again. He was making her forget her anger, making her all hot and cold at the same time. And jittery, like a hundred butterflies fluttering about in her stomach. It was his eyes that did it, dark and rich and full of heat.

She would not meet his gaze. She would not. Under no circumstances, she told herself, straining to find the most minute fold in Noah's pristine cravat.

Mrs. Florence chose that precise moment to enter the dining room in a flurry of starch and white muslin, cleaning towels draped over one arm and a fresh platter of potatoes and roast duck in her hands.

"Oh dear me, I do apologize, my lord," she gushed, bustling forth, her plump cheeks puffed out and rosy. "The countess told me about the little ... er ... accident." She shot a sympathetic glance in Emily's direction before setting the new platter down and scurrying to clean up the soggy mess that sat congealing in the middle of the table.

"Accidents do happen," Augusta inserted, laying a hand on her husband's shoulder as she brushed past him to take her seat beside him. Ian grunted in response, but his blue eyes warmed at her touch.

Thank heavens for Augusta, Emily thought. *If not for her, Ian might just spill the beans, wager or not.*

"There you go, good as new," Mrs. Florence said, inspecting the white linen she had placed over the gravy-soaked spot. The errant potatoes and slices of duck had been disposed of and the new platter wafted delectable aromas about the room.

"Thank you, Mrs. Florence," Ian said. He stared pointedly at Emily. "I would like you to have Miss Barry report to Mrs. Bloomfield in the morning. Let's hope she shows a greater aptitude for polishing than she did for serving." With that comment, he stabbed a hunk of roast duck, and without looking up said, "That will be all for this evening, Miss Barry. You may be dismissed."

Outraged and humiliated, Emily turned on her heel and left the room, head held high, eyes staring straight ahead.

Oh, how she wanted to tell Ian just exactly what she thought of his high-handed manner. How dare he treat her this way! She wanted to turn around and run back to him, screaming and yelling. And kicking. She bit down hard on the inside of her cheek and kept moving toward her small room in the servants' quarters.

He wanted her to lose her temper, wanted her to fly at him in a fit of rage. Then the wager would be completely settled and she would be the loser. No more talk of America or Christopher. Her life would be over.

She wouldn't allow it to happen. She *couldn't* allow it, not when she was one week away from winning her freedom. And if it meant pasting a sweet smile on her face and gritting her teeth for the next seven days, she would do it.

No one would draw her off course. No one, she told herself, not even that arrogant American who crept into her dreams at night. As she fell into bed, she vowed to push Noah Sandleton so far from her mind that by morning he would be no more than a vague memory.

Eunice Bloomfield took her duties as head housekeeper very seriously. Emily had never met a person with so many rules and restrictions about the proper way to do things. Not even Miss Fielding's *Proper Comportment for a Lady* contained as many "thou shalt nots."

Mrs. Bloomfield had a particular method for accomplishing every task down to the most minute detail. And she seemed intent on making certain Emily followed in her footsteps.

"Now, this very useful apparatus is called a feather duster." She held up a wooden handled contraption with thousands of black feathers protruding from it. "It is a wonderful tool for reaching high places, brushing off ornately carved objects and ridding a room of a fine film of dust.''

Emily watched in amazement as Mrs. Bloomfield glided about the room, flitting from candlestick to mantel to windowsill, whirling the feather duster before her. She reminded Emily of a ballet dancer, albeit a gray-haired one, bending and swaying her tall frame like a sapling in the wind.

"The key to proper feather dusting is movement," she said, flicking the duster over a crystal vase in several short, quick motions.

Rumor had it that she had worked in the queen's court years ago as head housekeeper. Emily didn't doubt it. She'd never met a servant with a vocabulary or diction like Mrs. Bloomfield.

"And then one must twist and bend," Mrs. Bloomfield continued, aiming the duster at the clawed legs of a green velvet sofa. "Now flick, twirl, flick, twirl. Like this."

Emily hid a smile. She liked Mrs. Bloomfield despite her bending, twisting, twirling idiosyncrasies, of which there were many.

"Now, dear," Mrs. Bloomfield said, handing over the feather duster, "let's see you work your way towards the sidetable, beginning at this chair. And don't forget to twist."

Noah stifled another laugh. He'd been watching Emily whirl about the green salon, bending and twisting as she swatted the oak furniture with her huge feather duster. First a dip and a swipe at a chair leg, then a turn and a bow toward a sidetable. On and on it went, the dips and curtsies, twists and turns, until Noah felt dizzy from watching her.

And to top it all off, she was singing. Singing! The melody couldn't reach him from his vantage point on the other side of the wide French doors, but he could see her lips moving in rapid animation.

Noah shook his head in resignation. The woman was mad. Absolutely mad. And she looked ridiculous dancing around the room, slicing the feather duster through the air as though it were a mighty sword and she a great warrior heading to battle.

He continued watching her for several more minutes, concluding that Ian had been right. Emily was no spy. How he ever could have entertained the idea, even for a scant moment, that she could possibly be involved in espionage, he didn't know. The whole idea seemed absurd to him now as she scooped up the duster and batted it over her head, flicking a brass sconce so hard it almost fell off the wall.

Emily Barry was too clumsy, pure and simple. A man as precise as Peter Crowlton would never risk getting involved with someone as unpredictable, undisciplined and uncoordinated as Emily, no matter how beautiful she may be.

Noah breathed a small sigh of relief. She wasn't a spy. He was certain of it. Thank God. He'd hated thinking she might be involved with the likes of the Serpent.

He frowned. If she weren't a spy, then that left only one other option: thief. Noah frowned again, not pleased with that possibility.

Peering through the small white pane, he saw Emily turn abruptly and run toward him. He thought for a brief moment that he'd been discovered, but she stopped several feet from the glass doors and dug her heels into the Aubusson rug. Bending down, she untied the laces of her heavy black shoes and kicked them off, one at a time, smiling as they sailed in opposite directions.

What was the woman up to now? He watched in amazement as Emily lifted the feather duster high above her head then brought it down in a grand arc and sweep, hurling it back and forth between her hands, faster and faster. Then, in one final motion, she flung the duster in the air and caught it behind her back.

Noah smiled again. Never, never could this woman be a spy. Not even in his wildest imagination. He must have been mad to have even considered the notion.

Now she was a candidate for Bedlam. That was something he could visualize for one Miss Emily Barry.

His thoughts were cemented to certainty when he saw her leap in the air, land squarely on both feet and then start spinning, head thrust back, arms outstretched, duster in hand. Round and round she went, faster and faster, until finally she fell over, collapsing on the thick, wheat-colored rug.

Quietly, Noah slipped through the French doors and edged his way toward Emily. She was lying flat on her back, arms and legs outstretched, chest heaving from her latest acrobatics. And the damn duster was still in her hand!

"Would you care to dance?" He stood over her, trying his damnedest not to smile.

Emily's eyes popped open. "You!" she nearly screamed. "Where did you come from?" She tried to straighten herself up into a sitting position, but her last ten spins must have been too much for her and she fell back down on the rug.

"I'm dizzy." She lifted her hand up to massage her forehead. Her eyes drifted closed.

"I'm not surprised," Noah said. "I was just trying to figure out if you belong in the ballet . . . or the circus."

"You're despicable," she muttered, not bothering to open her eyes.

"And you are," he paused, tapping his forefinger to his chin, "outrageous and crazy. Put the two together, and there you have it. Outrageously crazy." He frowned, then smiled. "Or is it crazily outrageous?"

Emily giggled and opened her eyes. "Which one is it, Mr. Sandleton?" she asked, a faint smile playing about her lips. "Am I crazy or just outrageous?"

She had moved into a semi-sitting position, with her elbows supporting her upper body. Her plain gray dress was gathered and bunched around her legs, revealing their firm shape. He could see a good deal of ankle clad in a heavy stocking material. Wisps of golden hair swirled about her neck and trailed down her back. Her full pink lips were slightly open.

Noah felt his groin tighten. Emily was too beautiful to be wrapped up in such common trappings, tucked away in servant's garb with nothing better to look forward to than marrying some commoner and having a brood of whiny brats.

She belonged in silks and satins, not broadcloth and muslin. Her horizon should span the Orient and the West Indies, Egypt and Africa, not just a city and country home in England. She should be waited on, attended to and looked after.

Emily Barry should be his mistress.

The shock of what he was thinking hit him like a lead ball in the gut. He gasped for breath, blinking his eyes to refocus on anything but the vision of Emily, golden and beautiful, lying beneath him.

"Noah?" Her voice, low and throaty, reached him, moving over him intimately without her lifting a finger. His manhood hardened, ready to burst.

He stood mesmerized as Emily's small tongue darted out to run over her full pink lips. He could explode just thinking of the numerous possibilities for that delectable mouth.

"Noah? Are you all right?" Emily scrambled up to stand beside him, but not before he saw an ample amount of leg and thigh. God, he felt like a miscreant. What was wrong with him, practically peeping under a woman's skirt? And getting hard, very hard, in the process?

She reached out to touch his arm, but Noah flung it away.

"Have you no sense of decency, sprawling before me like a dog in heat?" he spat out. His gaze narrowed. "If you've got an itch that needs to be satisfied, then just say so and dispense with the coquetry."

Her hand moved too fast. Actually, he hadn't thought she'd have the nerve to slap him. But she did, hard and square on the cheek. The resounding crack filled the air, followed by deafening silence.

"Touché, Emily Barry." Noah bowed, low and deep, his voice as hard as steel.

Emily backed away from him, one slow step at a time. She

was as white as a ghost, her lower lip trembling. But he didn't see fear in those huge gray eyes that never left his face. Determination, wariness, perhaps even a bit of remorse. But fear? Definitely not.

Noah wanted to laugh. She should fear him. Men twice her size feared him. Always had. But that was during wartime when his reputation as the Chameleon spanned the continent.

It was a lifetime ago. Noah found it extremely ironic that this slip of a girl should meet him face to face and not be afraid.

He hid a smile as he watched her slowly edge toward the great oak doors. Emily was no fool. She knew when to cut her losses and make her exit.

He waited until her hand touched the doorknob. She was inches from escaping. Noah couldn't resist.

"Emily," he called out to her, his voice low and steady. "Just remember, if you're ... uh ... feeling ... uh ... restless ... you know where to find me."

"Beast," she hissed, throwing open the door and running into the hall.

Good, Noah thought. Let her think he was a real swine. That way she might just stay out of his way. If he didn't see her, maybe he would stop wanting her.

Or maybe it was already too late.

Emily Barry was working her way under his carefully constructed façade and he didn't like it. Not one bit. He found himself actually caring that he might have hurt her feelings. No one got that close to him. No one. Ever.

Noah looked down at the Aubusson rug for a moment, remembering how Emily looked lying there, a vision of innocence and seduction. Innocent? Emily? Now that was a real laugh, though suddenly, he could find nothing remotely amusing about the situation.

He turned on his heel and strode toward the French doors, uttering a string of curse words under his breath.

* * *

"I never thought you'd pull it off." Ian's lips curved into a half-smile as he gazed down at his little sister. They stood in the green salon, surrounded by afternoon sunlight and heavy brocades. Emily felt ready to burst, as bright and full as the pansies outside.

She had won! Unable to contain her excitement, she twirled around in her simple muslin gown and heavy black shoes, laughter tinkling from her.

"I can't believe it," she gasped, twirling around again and ending in a plié. "I'm actually going to America. Oh, Ian, isn't this just grand?" Her words spilled over one another in her excitement.

Whatever melancholy had possessed her spirits the last several evenings was gone now. She felt alive and excited with new possibilities and now Ian was about to help make her dream a reality.

He stood with his broad back to her, staring out the window. Perhaps he hadn't heard her or was engrossed with something outside. She moved next to him to peer out the window. Nothing but bustling carriages and cobblestone.

"What's got you in such a dither, Ian?" she laughed. "Are you upset because I beat you at your own game? Admit it, you never thought I would make it. You expected me to muddle it up and quit somewhere around the second day."

"You're right. I did." His quick, somber response startled her. She chose to ignore the possibility that his dissatisfaction had anything to do with her.

"Well, I surprised you," she said saucily. "But I knew I could do it. Of course, my hands will never be the same." She surveyed her red, chapped knuckles with a frown. "And my feet ache from wearing these heavy shoes." Emily shook her head in amazement. "I think we should redesign the servants' garb. It's actually quite uncomfortable, what with the scratchy underthings that rub against your leg. And the stockings," she sighed, "are just dreadful." Pulling up her gown to her ankle, she surveyed the heavy cotton stockings and made a face.

"But," she continued, a huge grin on her flushed face, "all in all it turned out to be a great coup for me. In three weeks' time, I learned how to roast a duck, make bread and earn my passport to America. I'd say that's a rather huge accomplishment." Ian still hadn't spoken. "So," she rounded on him, "when can I leave?"

He turned to face her, looking much like a sleek panther considering his prey. She didn't like to think of herself as prey, especially if her mighty brother was the predator.

"Emily."

She knew that tone. It didn't bode well coming from Ian. It usually meant he was about to tell her something disappointing. Something she didn't want to hear. But what? Last night he had agreed she'd won their wager, so what could possibly have happened between last evening and this morning to dampen his mood?

"I have to talk to you." There it was again, that same tone with just a hint of sympathy thrown in.

"Ian, forgive me for being so bold, but what could possibly be more important at this moment than making plans for my trip to America?" Sometimes her brother frustrated her beyond belief.

He cleared his throat, took a deep breath and cleared his throat again. Tiny prickles of dread inched up her spine.

"Actually, it's about your trip." He paused for what seemed like an eternity. She watched his jaw twitch and his black brows knit into a straight line. That definitely meant trouble. Had he somehow heard about the creamer incident with Noah? Dear God, she didn't want a silly thing like that to ruin her chance to get to America.

"The first available ship that meets my standards is not leaving for another six months." His indigo eyes searched her face.

Emily spun around so he wouldn't see her tears. She stuffed

her fist in her mouth to keep from shouting about the injustice of it all. He *knew* she hadn't meant to wait six months to sail to America. And yet, he had never promised it would be any shorter. Truth be known, deep down he probably never even planned on her winning the wager. "How can that be?" she asked, her voice a mere whisper. "There must be some way."

"I'm sorry, Emily." She felt his large, strong hands on her shoulders. "I wish there were."

"What about Noah Sandleton?" she choked out. "Isn't he sailing in a few days?" As much as she disliked the man, she was desperate now.

"No." The harshness of his response sliced through Emily's misery and surprised her. His voice leveled. "Noah can't take you."

Emily turned to look at his face. "Not even if his best friend asks him?" she pressed on.

"No." He shook his head. "No."

"I see," she said, though she didn't see at all. Emily bowed her head and swiped at a stray tear. She couldn't even book passage with that miserable miscreant.

Ian's strong hands settled on her shoulders, drawing her into his embrace. It felt cold and empty. There was no longer any security there. No comfort at all.

In that moment, Emily realized she could not wait six months, six weeks or even six days. Somehow she had to make her own plans. She had to choose her own destiny, here and now, because Christopher and America were getting farther away every day. She would get to them, she vowed. No matter what it took, she would get to them.

"I had hoped you might consider extending your visit," Ian said as he handed Noah a snifter of brandy.

"Sorry old man, but you know I don't like to settle in one place for too long. Besides, it's time I sailed home for a little while and checked on my lands." Noah sipped at his brandy.

It would be their last night together for quite some time. The *Falcon* was setting sail on the morrow for a six-month excursion.

Ian smiled. "Are you certain that's the only reason you're going back? There wouldn't happen to be a special *someone* waiting for you? Maybe one of those beauties from the Far East?"

Noah shook his head, grinning. "Ian, there are always many 'someones' as you well know, but never that *special* someone." He shrugged. "I prefer it that way. Less complicated."

Ian's laughter rang out beyond the closed study door and into the hallway where Emily had her ear bent to the door. She ignored the slight twinge she felt when Noah referred to his limitless supply of female companionship. After all, why should she care when she detested the man?

And she did detest him, didn't she?

She had spent the better part of another long night driving the beast from her thoughts and had finally convinced herself of her success when she had heard his name announced. No longer under the guise of servant garb, Emily had raced up the stairs and hidden in little Lucas's nursery for the remainder of the evening.

Unfortunately, her stomach got the better of her a few hours later and she decided to sneak into the kitchen for a glass of warm milk and a raspberry scone. As she tiptoed past the library door, Noah's drawl reached her, stopping her in her tracks.

Though she didn't believe in spying, she had to admit there were times when it did prove quite useful. Noah Sandleton was going home to America! Her mind raced as she listened to their conversation. Would Ian tell her? Would he reconsider and give her an opportunity to leave in a few days' time? Somehow she didn't think so. Well, it didn't really matter because she had just figured out the perfect plan. All she needed now was a little assistance to pull it off. Belle would help her. She was certain of it.

A small smile played about her lips as she congratulated

herself on her spying efforts. They had paid off well, and very soon her little plan would be set in motion. Easing away from the great oak door, Emily hurried down the hall to the kitchen, her thoughts on Christopher and their impending reunion.

"I just don't understand why you can't wait and go to America with Ian's blessing!" Isabel Fleming whispered from the darkened interior of the carriage. As arranged, at precisely midnight the Fleming carriage had quietly rolled past Greyling Manor, stopping only long enough to pick up a darkly clad youth dressed in breeches and a stocking cap.

"Don't you see, Belle, this is the perfect opportunity." Emily pulled off the black cap and shook out her hair. It fell past her shoulders and halfway down her back. "Noah Sandleton is going to America. I heard him say so with my own two ears." She leaned toward her friend, speaking in hushed, earnest tones. "Who knows when and if Ian will truly permit me to go there in six months or six years? It's not that he would ever be deliberately deceitful, but Ian has a way of making things work to his advantage. You know that yourself, Belle."

"But he told you if you won the wager that you could go, did he not?"

Emily waved her hand in agitation. "Of course that's what he said because he never thought I would win. Now that I have, I find there's a caveat and more time is involved. He's hoping I'll get married and forget about it."

Belle smiled. "We both know you won't let that happen."

"Absolutely not. That's why I must leave now when I have the perfect opportunity to do so."

"But what do you know of Noah Sandleton?" Belle queried, gnawing her lower lip.

"He's Ian's best friend." Emily could feel her cheeks growing warm and was thankful for the darkened carriage.

Belle shook her head. "Ian will be furious when he finds out. But what of this Mr. Sandleton? How do you think he'll react when he finds out his best friend's sister has stowed away on his ship?''

"He'll be more than furious.'' Emily smiled at the thought. "He'll want to shoot me at the very least, but by the time I'm discovered, we'll be well on our way to America.'' She hesitated a moment, placing her hand over Belle's. "I have a small confession to make,'' Emily said sheepishly.

"What have you done now, Emily?'' Belle asked, sounding like a mother hen about to scold her chick for a misdeed.

"Well, you know that man I told you about at the Fox's Tail?''

"The one who caught you and accused you of stealing?'' Belle's voice rose an octave.

Emily nodded. "It was Noah Sandleton.'' She winced at the colorful expletive that flew out of Belle's mouth. "I know what you're thinking, Belle.'' The words rushed out of her mouth. "But he's my last chance. If Noah knew I was Ian's sister, he'd march me to him, posthaste. Can you imagine what Ian would do to me?''

Belle sighed. "Probably nothing you don't deserve at the moment. If I thought it would do any good, I'd try to dissuade you from this scheme of yours. But I know you'll do it with or without my help and I'd rather know what you were up to.''

Clasping her friend's hands in her own, Emily's voice was low and serious. "Thank you, Belle. You're a true friend.''

"A foolish friend is more like it.'' Belle shook her head and sighed again. "All right, Emily, tell me what you want me to do.''

Chapter 4

Noah Sandleton watched the black conveyance ride away from Greyling Manor. He knew it was the same carriage that had been at the Fox's Tail the night he'd met Emily. And he'd lay odds that the figure hurrying into it clad in boy's clothes was Emily as well. Interesting. Although the carriage remained a fair distance away, it was obvious that it belonged to someone of wealth.

Was Emily Barry a thief? Or could she be a rich man's whore? He hadn't considered that possibility. The question nagged at him, pounding in his head as loud as a star percussionist. He had to know if she was bartering her delectable body or stolen goods to the slimy bastard in the black carriage.

Noah frowned, growing impatient. He stood in the shadows of Ian's brick townhouse, hidden from the occasional passerby. Damn it, where had she gone? What was she doing? And who the hell was she doing it with?

Emily was a beautiful woman, that fact was more than obvious. His jaded thoughts turned to the obvious: She was being used as a plaything by some wealthy nobleman. But dressed as a boy? Noah had seen more bizarre behavior over the years and had long since stopped thinking about the sexual appetites or preferences that abounded in society. Still, the thought of Emily engaging in some sordid, perverse sexual escapade sickened him.

Perhaps she *was* a thief. He almost wished she were. For some reason, thievery seemed more palatable than the other possibility he was entertaining.

Half an hour later, the same black carriage stopped a few hundred feet away and a lone figure emerged. Noah stamped out his cheroot and trained his eyes on the carriage. The absence of a family crest or other marking that would signify the owner disturbed him. The conveyance was new and sleek, its fancy design speaking of wealth and privilege. As it rolled by him, Noah thought he saw one of the curtains move. Then it disappeared into the night and his thoughts flashed back to Emily.

He recognized her soft swaying walk and lithe figure, despite the bulky clothes she wore. She waited for the carriage to move on before she cut down a side alley leading to the back entry of the townhouse. Noah raced down the other alley and crouched behind a row of rubbish bins to wait for her. In a matter of minutes, Emily emerged, whistling softly as she moved toward the old iron door of Greyling Manor.

She took no more than a few steps toward the door before Noah grabbed her, hauling her back against his hard chest. His large hand clamped across her mouth, stifling any attempt to scream.

"What have we here?" His words were crisp, biting. "If it isn't the little she-boy."

Emily struggled against his grasp, but she was no match for his strength. He pinned her arms to her sides with scarce effort and backed her up against the old brick of the building, quite content to let her exhaust herself with useless struggles.

When she quieted down, he leaned over, his voice a mere whisper in her ear, and said, "If you can behave yourself, I'll remove my hand from your mouth."

Noah watched as the stocking cap bobbed up and down in silent agreement. He eased his hand away, releasing his hold on her, but did not step back. They stood mere inches apart, staring at one another, locked in silent battle.

"Don't even try it," he warned, guessing at her next move. "I can read that devious little mind of yours, but you're not going anywhere without my consent."

"What do you want?" she spat out.

"For starters, I'd like to know where in the hell you went in that black carriage dressed like a boy."

He watched her closely. The moon cast a faint light on her face, making it easy to detect the slight flaring of her nostrils and the momentary widening of her gray eyes. She was scheming. In his short acquaintance with Emily Barry, he knew that much of what came out of her mouth was untrue. He also knew that she was a terrible liar and one look at her face usually proved enough to distinguish truth from untruth.

"I do not see where my affairs are any of your concern, Mr. Sandleton." Her voice held all the haughty grandeur of a lady. Noah wanted to laugh, but her manner struck him as odd. Not for the first time, he wondered at how easily she slipped into the role of the upper crust. As though it were second nature.

"I see you're employing the speech of a lady this evening. Where might you have acquired that fine skill?" he taunted, studying her with keen interest.

She looked away and settled her eyes on an old tomcat that sat perched on one of the rubbish bins. "Augusta . . . I mean Lady Kenilworth has set a wonderful example and encourages proper speech and etiquette, even among the servants." Her eyes remained averted.

"But that's not where you learned those things, is it?" he persisted, his voice as soft as the night's breeze.

"Of course it is," she shot back, glaring at him. "Where else would I have learned them?"

"Where else indeed," he said, letting the unspoken accusation that she was lying hang between them.

"What is it you want from me?" Emily demanded.

Noah laughed a short, humorless laugh. "In case you have forgotten our last chat, I have every intention of getting to the bottom of whatever little scheme you are involved in." He grabbed her small chin, forcing her to look directly at him. "Were you thieving or whoring?"

Emily's hand flew up to slap his face, but Noah caught her wrist. "You might have gotten away with that once, but don't ever try it again," he said through clenched teeth.

"You're hurting me," she hissed.

Loosening his grip on her wrist, Noah tried a different tactic. "Did you steal something from Lord Kenilworth?"

"No!" she shook her stocking-capped head in firm denial.

"Or anyone in that household?" There was just a hint of sarcasm.

"Absolutely not."

"Hmm." She had looked very uncomfortable with that last question. What could she have taken? Jewels? He had to find out for himself. "Then you won't mind if I check for myself? Just to make certain you aren't harboring any stolen goods or money? We've done this before, remember? So you know the routine." Ignoring the shocked look on her face, he forced Emily up against the rough brick and parted her large jacket. His hands traveled down the front of the oversize shirt, moving over her soft curves in a brisk, businesslike manner. Noah tried not to think about the soft swell of her breast or the smooth, taut skin beneath the shirt. His hands slowed. He wanted to remain apart from the touch and feel of this woman, apart from the rapid little breaths and the swollen peaks he'd brushed a second before.

"Nothing yet," he said, his voice ragged. God, but she felt good. He knew he should stop this game now before it got out of hand. But he feared it was already too late and, in some ways, it had been since the first time he'd laid eyes on her.

His hands shook as he reached up to stroke the firm, ripe flesh of her breasts through the thin cotton of her shirt, lingering

on the soft, full mounds. Her small breasts fit perfectly in his
hands. She whimpered as he molded them, grazing the taut
peaks with his knuckles. His own body tightened in response.

Noah cursed under his breath and forgot all about searching
for stolen property. Emily was in his blood. There was no use
denying it any longer. He had to get closer to her. His hands
worked their way to her ribs in slow circular motions, then
trailed back to her breasts, brushing the swollen nipples with
the pads of his fingers. She moaned low in her throat. He cursed
again and pulled her to him, needing to feel her body pressed
against his, hot and wanting.

His dark head bent over hers, seeking her full, pink lips. Her
face was turned away toward the wall. Noah leaned forward
and placed a soft kiss on her jawbone. He could hear Emily's
sharp intake of breath. He followed the silky path of skin,
planting light kisses, until he was but a hairbreadth away from
her mouth.

"Turn to me, Emily. Give me your mouth." His voice
sounded raspy and unnatural, even to himself.

Slowly, her head turned and she met his gaze. They stared
at one another in silence, speaking only with their eyes. Noah
raised a hand and stroked her cheek. His hand shook slightly.
Emily's head fell back against the wall and her eyes fluttered
closed.

Lowering his head, he sought her mouth. He wanted her,
wanted all of her, with a depth and passion he had never known.
When their lips met, the kiss was not gentle, but demanding
and possessive. He ran his tongue along her full lower lip,
urging her mouth open. Her lips parted and he dove into the
sweetness of her mouth, touching, tasting, wanting. His hands
roamed her body, pressing her against his own hard length.

The black night enveloped the two lovers, closing around
them in a warm embrace as the breeze carried the quiet sounds
of night through the air. Noah was oblivious to everything but
the soft, pliant woman in his arms who fired his blood. He
could feel his swollen manhood pressing against Emily's belly.

Just the thought of sinking into her warm flesh, with her legs wrapped high around him, had him hot and throbbing. God, how he wanted her.

"Tell me where you went tonight," he whispered into her mouth. He had to know; he had to hear her admit her treachery and lies. Then he could forgive her and lose himself in her sweet, hot body.

His mouth trailed light kisses over her face and along her jaw, continuing down the slender column of her neck. Her choppy little breaths told him she wanted him as much as he wanted her. Well, she would have him soon enough, but first he'd have his answers.

"Tell me, Emily," he coaxed, sliding his fingers down the length of her body, pressing his palm between her legs. She felt hot and wet through her clothes, her nubbin hard and swollen. Noah moved his fingers, flicking his fingertips over her heat in slow circles.

"I can't," she moaned.

His fingers stilled.

"Can't? Or won't?" he demanded in a whisper-soft voice, pressing his fingers over her woman's heat.

She jerked involuntarily toward his hand. "C-c-can't," she murmured in a ragged voice.

Noah's fingers stilled again. *She'll lie even in the heat of passion.* He released her, disgusted with himself for his lack of control. Taking a step back, he reached in his pocket and pulled out a cheroot. His hand shook as he struggled with the light.

Damn her! She wasn't going to tell him. He wanted to shake her until her teeth rattled. *Damn witch!*

"It's not what it looked like," she finally spoke.

"Oh? And what exactly did it *look* like?" He would not make this easy for her.

Emily winced. "Well," she stammered, "perhaps it looked like I was somewhere I shouldn't have been."

"Perhaps?" He threw down his cheroot, smashing it out

with his booted heel. Why in the hell was he so upset over this girl when it looked like she was up to no more ill than meeting her lover for a midnight tryst? The thought of someone else's hands on her was driving him insane. He had to know. "Do you want to know what I think you were doing?" Without waiting for her reply, he continued, "I don't think you are a thief because I found no evidence of such and God knows I looked." To hell with her tender sensibilities.

"So," he continued, raking a hand through his hair, "that only leaves one unexplored possibility."

He waited for her to respond. Time stretched before them, the voice of the night engulfing them in a mysterious cacophony of sound. When at last she spoke, her voice was little more than a whisper. "What do you think I am, Noah?"

"A rich man's whore." His words were dry and flat.

That seemed to shake her up a bit. She gasped and balled her hands into fists, but remained silent, neither admitting nor refuting the accusation. *Damn but she's not only a good liar, but a fair actress as well,* Noah thought. He could almost believe she was outraged. Almost.

"What else could you be?" he flung back. "You leave in the middle of the night dressed as a boy, which is strange even by my standards. Who knows," he scoffed, "maybe your nobleman lover likes to pretend you're a street urchin until he deflowers you to discover the beautiful woman underneath." Noah paused a moment as the image of Emily, trapped and naked beneath some fat old nobleman settled in his brain and tore at his guts.

"That's it, isn't it?" he bit out. "That's what excites him."

She wouldn't answer him. Instead, she huddled against the brick, turning her body away from him as though to shield herself against his hurtful words. Well, sometimes, the truth was an ugly bedfellow and Emily might as well accept that fact.

"I do have one question." He knew he should just turn

around and walk away. His ship was setting sail in a few days. He'd never have to see her again.

She turned farther into the wall. Why did it bother him so much to find out she was a whore? He'd been with whores in his day. Plenty. But she had seemed different. As annoying, mouthy and frustratingly impossible as Emily Barry had been, she had touched him somewhere deep inside where his real feelings lay lost and hidden.

"I just want to know," he asked, trying to keep his voice calm and unaffected, "why you were so hot for me when you had obviously just been with your lover?" *Why, damn it? Why couldn't you be different?* "Or are you like that with any man?"

She whirled on him like a she-cat. Was she angry or hurt by his words? "Yes," Emily bit out, "I lie with every man who appeals to me." He winced, surprised at the viciousness of her words.

"Whenever, wherever, however, from nobleman to stable boy. It doesn't matter and neither do you. You were just one more face," she paused, her breath coming in harsh, heavy rasps, "or I should say one more body among a string of countless others."

Pushing herself away from the wall, she took a step toward him, planting her feet squarely and pointing a finger at him. "But you're not worth the trouble." Noah watched as she turned and walked away, her head held high, her steps graceful, almost regal.

And for the hundredth time since he'd first set eyes on her, he asked himself the same question. *Who is Emily Barry?*

Slightly before dawn three days later, two small figures darted toward the nearly deserted docks. The morning was cool, with little activity save for a lone sailor or two. Conditions were perfect.

They had spotted their prey, the *Falcon,* a huge, well-made vessel. As they edged closer, Emily felt as though her heart was in her throat. Finally! Today she was sailing to America!

"Are you certain you won't reconsider and do this whole thing in a more civilized manner?" Belle whispered from her crouched position behind an old wooden barrel.

Emily shook her stocking-capped head, her eyes still glued on the deck of the *Falcon*. She'd seen movement a moment before, a darkly clad, round figure ambling about. Where had he gone? "You know I can't, Belle."

"But a stowaway aboard a ship full of men? That's extremely dangerous."

Emily let out a low snort and turned to face her friend. "So are a roomful of marriage hunting 'gentlemen' in London." She leaned in close, her voice barely above a whisper. "And most show no mercy or discretion when vying for the largest purse."

"I know," Belle sighed. "I just wish you were on better terms with Mr. Sandleton." She gnawed her lower lip. "It would make things a lot easier."

"Nothing would ever be easy with that man," Emily said, her head starting to pound at the mention of Noah Sandleton's name. She'd battled a ferocious headache for the past three days.

Ever since she decided to stow away the *Falcon*.

She was not afraid of him, she told herself. She was not afraid. The words ran through her brain, a silent chant that imbedded itself in her thoughts and would not be driven away.

A tall, dark figure came into view aboard the ship. From the distance, Emily watched the proprietary stance of his well-muscled frame. Noah. It had to be him. Emily's nails dug into the flesh of her palms.

"Is that him?" Belle whispered.

"That's him," Emily said, trying to control the jumpiness she felt at the sight of him.

What could he do to her if he found her hiding on his ship? Kill her? Certainly not. Have her thrown in Newgate? Possibly.

Take her back to Ian? Most definitely. Well, it wouldn't be an issue, because Emily didn't plan on getting caught. She hadn't figured out how to manage it, but she would come up with a plan. She had no choice.

"We'd better get you on board while the crew is still light," Belle said, watching a few straggling crewmen walk down the wooden planking toward the massive ship.

Emily turned to Belle and squeezed her hands. "Remember our plan. Ian thinks we're shopping for the day. He'll find the note I left him in his study." A small smile played about her mouth. "He'll be so thrilled, thinking we're decorating ourselves for the duke's ball, that he won't question a thing."

Belle nodded. "And I am to wait until exactly seven o'clock and present him with this note." She patted her pocket.

"Then he'll know I've taken off to America with my unwilling host and it will be too late for him to stop me." She tried to keep the triumphant note from her voice, but it was difficult.

"I'll miss you, Emily," Belle said, her soft brown eyes shining with unshed tears.

"And I you," Emily choked out. She swallowed hard. "I'll never be able to thank you enough, Belle." A stray tear escaped, trailing down her cheeks. Why did she suddenly feel like she was deserting everyone who cared about her and loved her? She thought of Ian, proud, unbending, fiercely loyal Ian, and the victory she'd felt a moment before dissolved into fresh tears. Perhaps one day he would find it in his heart to forgive her.

"Go, Emily. Go. Now," Belle said, giving her friend a quick, hard hug.

"I'll write to you as soon as I get settled. I promise." The tears kept coming.

"I know you will, Emily," Belle whispered.

"I'll work on a plan," Emily sniffed. "A plan to get you to America." She tried to smile. "You know me, I always have a plan."

Belle smiled. "Take care of Christopher."

"I will." Emily hugged her friend one last time before straightening up and heading toward the ship. She flung her canvas bag over one shoulder and concentrated on imitating the purposeful swagger of the sailor in front of her. Unfortunately, he was several inches taller and many pounds heavier than she, making Emily's attempts more comical than serious.

A hard slap across the shoulders almost sent her flying over the roped railing. "Wot ye got in yer trousers, mate?" came a deep, gravelly voice from behind. "Is it bugs or a slithery snake?" Emily kept her eyes down, ignoring the loud guffaws and hoots that followed.

"Aw, now, I didna' mean ta hurt yer feelins," the old sailor said, draping his burly arm about her small shoulders. "Wot's yer name, boy?" he asked, skewering his face so close that Emily was forced to stop. Stealing a quick glance in the sailor's direction was much more than she wanted to see. Or smell. His black, beady eyes scrunched almost closed as they studied her. A long scar ran from his forehead to the left side of his jaw. He had several teeth missing and when he smiled, which he was doing now, she could see great black gaps in his mouth.

Emily couldn't tell if the foul odor emanating from the man was coming from his mouth or his body. Either way, the result was a sour, garlicky-onion smell, mixed with rotten cabbage. She felt the bile rising in her throat.

"Ease up, Big Tom. Ease up." A jovial voice rang out to the right of her. Emily hazarded a glance in the direction of her savior. He was a short, robust man with a ruddy face and long white hair and beard to match. With his bright blue eyes, he reminded her of St. Nicholas.

"Ah, John, I didna' mean no harm," the giant said.

"We're traveling light as it is this trip, Tom, and we can't have you scaring off the new crew, now can we?" the man named John said.

"No, sir," Big Tom said, bowing his head low. He reminded Emily of a too-playful puppy who'd just been caught with his owner's shoe.

"No harm done, no harm done," the older man said, walking alongside Emily. They were less than twenty feet from the ship. "What's your name, boy?"

Emily hesitated, cleared her throat and squeaked out a small reply, "Simon."

"Ah, Simon," John repeated. "Fine name. My uncle's name was Simon."

Emily nodded, not knowing what else to do.

"You'll like the captain," John continued in his soothing voice. "He's fair and decent. A true gentleman." He paused, then pointed a stubby finger. "There he is. Look. Over there."

"Hmmm," Emily mumbled, darting a quick look up. It was Noah Sandleton, all right. Proud, arrogant Noah Sandleton. In command, as usual. Her head dipped low. She kept her eyes to the ground, lest he spot her and recognize her from the fear in her eyes. And it was there. She could feel it enveloping her whole body. It covered her like a blanket, smothering her, squeezing the breath from her chest, filling her nostrils with its scent.

She was so close. She could not fail. She would not fail, she told herself as she inched closer to her destiny.

"Be damned. Where's he got himself off to now?" John said in a puzzled voice. "Ah well, no matter. You'll meet the captain soon enough."

Emily's eyes shot up toward the spot where she'd last seen Noah. She let out her breath in a great gush of relief. It was empty. Noah Sandleton was gone.

She was going to die. Emily was certain of it. And right now death would be a welcome relief from the endless rocking of the ship. She'd decided that hours before when the ship first left port and encountered choppy waters, but her sentiments had increased tenfold with the rocking of the ship. Her quarters were dark and cramped and she could barely feel her legs anymore.

What could she expect when she was stowed away in Noah Sandleton's armoire? How long had she been in here? Three hours? Four? There'd been no time to seek out a safe haven, what with all the crew moving about, shouting commands, readying to set sail. Then she'd heard *his* voice and panicked, stealing into the first cabin she saw. Not until she lay crouched in the armoire did she smell Noah's spicy cologne and realize her mistake.

The ship rolled again, sending Emily's stomach somersaulting. If she could only get fresh air, a breath, perhaps, of something other than the spicy cologne and stale cigar smoke that filled her nostrils. Then maybe her insides would settle and stop their continuous flips and turns.

She struggled to her knees, burrowing her way through the pile of clothing, seeking a different, less offensive scent. Her fingers landed on a swatch of silk material. Odd that silk should be in Noah's chambers. Emily pressed the fabric to her nose and sniffed the sweet, overpowering fragrance that emanated from the material. A woman's perfume? It certainly smelled like it, but it wasn't anything like the lilac water Emily preferred. No, this was more of a compelling, exotic blend, demanding and bold, like the wearer would be.

Unable to contain her curiosity, Emily ran her fingers over the silk again. Behind it were other garments, definitely a woman's, made of soft filmy fabrics. The last one she touched was but a wisp of satin with gaping holes where they shouldn't be. Emily withdrew her hand quickly.

Damn Noah Sandleton. Damn him for accusing her of something that he himself was doing. And damn him for making her care.

The ship pitched again and Emily flew back against the side of the armoire. At least everything was bolted down so there was no fear of toppling over. Unfortunately, the same could not be said of Emily's stomach. She felt as though at any moment, she would lose the few biscuits she'd stolen from Mrs. Florence's pantry.

Taking a deep breath, she ignored the sour taste in her mouth, trying instead to think about her family.

Soon, Belle would deliver the letter, a single sheet of scented lilac paper, telling them only that she was sailing aboard Noah Sandleton's ship to meet Christopher and asking them to forgive her dishonesty.

Emily prayed they would understand. Perhaps not right away, but in time they might understand and find it in their hearts to forgive her. Her fingers reached into her coat pocket, patting a small packet of papers.

Christopher's letters. There were six of them, worn and tattered from so much handling. A few had smudges on them where Emily's tears had mingled with the ink.

Her hand closed over the letters. Soon, very soon, it would all be over thanks to the help of her friend Belle and, she grudgingly admitted, Noah Sandleton.

Just the thought of the man unsettled her. She refused to dwell on what his reaction would be if he discovered her aboard his ship. He would not find out, she told herself. He simply would not.

Her stomach did another flip-flop. Squeezing her eyes shut, she huddled into a small ball, resting her weary head on her knees, and drifted into a deep, troubled sleep.

"What the hell!"

Emily jumped, fully awake. Her eyes flew open to find a furious Noah Sandleton glaring down at her. He stood towering over her, drenched from head to toe, looking as wild and untamed as the storm outside. Tiny droplets of water fell in a steady stream from his long, wavy hair, which, when wet, looked almost black. His broad arms crossed over his chest, revealing a mass of dark hair above the half-opened shirt that clung to his well-muscled body. His breeches looked like a second skin. Emily felt the heat rush to her cheeks.

She tried to scoot farther back into the armoire, but there was nowhere to go.

"You!" Noah roared, grabbing her arm. "What in God's name are *you* doing on my ship?" He narrowed his gaze, pinning her with eyes as dark and unfathomable as the storm outside.

"I can explain," Emily began feebly.

"Get out of there," he demanded, yanking on her arm. "Get out now, before I drag you out."

She tried to move, tried to unfold her legs to stretch out and stand up, but her limbs refused to cooperate. They felt weak and lifeless after so many hours scrunched in a corner. She looked around for a stronghold, trying to find something to hang onto and pull herself up, but she was weary and disoriented.

The ship pitched and flung her back, slamming the doors to the armoire shut. Emily flailed about inside, feeling weak and dizzy.

A few seconds later, Noah tore the armoire open, almost ripping the doors from their hinges. He flung aside several garments trying to reach Emily. She hit at his face and kicked with her feet, squirming and yelling as she felt him grab her arm. She would not go down without a fight, she vowed as he half lifted, half dragged her out of the closet. Hoisting her into his arms, he carried her across the swaying room toward the bed, mindless of the wet spots he was making on her shirt and breeches. Emily turned her head into his shoulder and bit. Hard.

"Witch," Noah yelled, throwing her onto the bed.

Emily hit the firm surface with such force that her teeth rattled in her head. Her stomach jumped and flipped like a bouncing ball, threatening to explode. She eased onto her side, moving slowly, trying to settle the queasy feeling and taste of bile and biscuit.

It wouldn't do to disgrace herself. Not now, in front of this odious man. Closing her eyes, she concentrated on her breathing, trying to ignore the ominous figure standing over her.

Go away. Please go away and don't come back.

She heard a door close, and she let her body relax, sinking her head deeper into the pillow. It smelled of spices. Noah's cologne. Groaning, she shoved it away and looked toward the door. She gasped, surprised to see *him* standing there, staring at her. He pushed away from the door and walked back to stand beside the bed.

He was frowning, his deep brown eyes piercing her with their intensity, holding her, looking into and through her.

The shivers that ran through Emily's body had nothing to do with her damp clothes. Her stomach rolled. She wondered if Noah was prone to violent physical outbursts. He looked like he wanted to throttle her. Should she be afraid? She looked at him again, noting the flaring nostrils and twitching jaw. Maybe.

But he was a gentleman, wasn't he? John, the older crewman with the white beard, had even said so. And after all, Noah *was* her brother's best friend. Certainly, that counted for something, didn't it? Of course it did, she assured herself.

But he was *not* an Englishman, her mind screamed at her.

No, he was not an Englishman. He was an American. Would he revert to some primitive behavior and scalp her, like she'd read the savages did when they went on a warpath? They liked blond hair. She fingered her curls. Curly, long, blond hair. She scooted farther back toward the wall of the berth.

"Get back here," Noah boomed.

Emily crept forward a few inches, taking deep breaths to calm herself and her stomach.

"Now tell me what in the devil you're doing here." he demanded.

She opened her mouth to speak. Her stomach lurched with the ship. She wasn't going to make it.

"Talk, damn you," he said through clenched teeth. "Now."

Please don't let me disgrace myself. Her stomach rolled again. Sweat broke out on her upper lip. "I think I'm going to be sick," Emily said, her voice low and drained.

"Don't think I'll fall for another one of your tricks," Noah barked. "Now talk."

Emily didn't hear his words, didn't hear anything but the sound of her own rapid breathing as she tried to will herself not to be sick all over Noah Sandleton's bed. But it was too late. Clapping a hand over her mouth, she jumped up from the bed, frantic and wild-eyed, searching for a chamber pot.

She must have looked as dreadful as she felt, because Noah's demands ceased as he clasped her arm and guided her to the far end of the cabin. Within seconds, Emily proceeded to relieve herself of her breakfast. When she was certain there was nothing left in her stomach, she rinsed her mouth out with the glass of water Noah handed her and allowed him to help her back to bed.

Too weak to protest, Emily watched him remove her shoes and pull a warm blanket over her chilled body. He remained silent as he placed a cool cloth on her forehead and smoothed back her hair.

"We'll talk in the morning." His voice was gruff. His fingers touched her cheek, stroking gently for a moment before he drew his hand away. She closed her eyes, comforted by his touch, and let sleep take her.

Emily yawned loudly, stretching her arms over her head and luxuriating in the early morning quiet. All was silent save for a gentle swishing sound and the distant cry of a bird overhead. She moved her legs, extending them the full length of the berth and hit a hard, unmoving object.

Her eyes flew open to find Noah Sandleton's large frame settled at the end of the bed, watching her. He appeared relaxed, his broad shoulders resting against the wall with one booted leg crossed over his knee, his muscular arms folded across his chest. But there was no calmness in the dark, brooding eyes that followed her every move. They stalked her, a predator closing in on its prey, and she knew there would be no escape this time.

"Talk," he said tightly.

Emily scooted to the top of the berth, placing what little distance between them she could, and eyed him warily. What to tell him? Well, she supposed it was time to come clean and tell the truth. At least some of the truth, she amended.

"And a good morning to you too, sir," she replied, raising her eyebrows. She was stalling, deciding what and exactly how much to tell. Noah's dark look told her he knew her ruse and it wasn't going to work.

"Well," she began, toying with the blanket and carefully avoiding his eyes, "I do suppose I owe you an explanation." She tried a feeble attempt at a laugh. "After all, I'm certain I gave you a bit of a start when you found me in your armoire." Emily looked up and managed a weak smile. Noah stared back at her, saying nothing.

"Things aren't quite what they seem. You were right about that, but I do have a very good explanation." She paused a moment, hoping he would help her along just a little. But that obviously wasn't going to happen, not if the rapid twitching of his jaw or the further narrowing of his eyes were any indication. No, he wasn't going to make it easy on her.

"Your little game is up," Noah ground out. "You've got exactly one minute to talk, and it had better be a damn good explanation."

"Oh, all right." Emily frowned at him. "But you don't need to be nasty about it."

"Emily," he warned.

She fidgeted with the blanket again, glanced around the cabin twice and finally settled her gaze on his stern face. "I'm not really a maid, if you haven't guessed. My name is Emily Elizabeth Barry and my brother is an earl." Well, that was partly true. Barry was her mother's maiden name and her brother was an earl.

Noah looked at her a full moment, saying nothing. Then he threw his head back and laughed.

"What exactly do you find so amusing?" The man could be most annoying.

He laughed once more, shaking his head. "Emily, I have to hand it to you. You really should be on the stage. Have you ever considered that as a profession?" he asked with mock sincerity.

"But I *am* a woman of quality. The St. Simons are friends and the maid act was just a ruse, a silly game. Nothing more." Could he really not tell she was of noble blood?

In the next instant, Noah leapt toward her, grabbing her forearms in a death grip, his face mere inches from hers. All traces of humor vanished as he ground out, "I am tired of your games. You have insinuated yourself upon me since the day we met. Now, you will tell me who you are and what you are about."

She looked into his furious face and wondered again if he were capable of bodily harm. Upper lip curling, nostrils flaring, eyebrows pulled together in a straight, unforgiving line, shadowing eyes that had turned black with anger, he reminded Emily of a wild animal. In that moment there was nothing civilized about the man. Or human for that matter.

Yes, she feared he could cause her much harm if he chose to. "My name is Emily Elizabeth Barry." *St. Simon,* she added to herself. Emily couldn't tell him her real last name. Not with him snarling at her like that. He might just decide to snap her neck in two. She eyed his huge hands. Or squeeze the very life out of her. He'd probably do just that if she told him she was Ian's sister. Correction. His best friend's sister.

Noah let out a string of profanities, flinging her away from him as he rose to pace the small cabin. Emily watched him walk over to the desk and retrieve her satchel, then return and dump its contents onto her lap. "I suppose," he replied with a smirk, "that these are yours as well?"

Sparkling jewels winked back at her in a colorful array of

dazzling brilliance. Her hand closed over a ruby necklace and an emerald hairpin. "These were my mother's," she said softly. "Now they are mine."

"Like hell they are," Noah growled, snatching them from her and thrusting the pieces back into the burgundy satchel. "This jewelry belongs to the St. Simons and you stole it from them."

"But—"

"Enough! If I hear you say you're a member of the nobility one more time, I swear I will be forced to use extreme measures." The murderous look in his eyes kept Emily from challenging him.

"Now, you will speak and tell me why you are on board my ship."

"I'm on my way to America. To see Christopher." She paused. "Christopher St. Simon." She ignored the warning look he gave her and plunged forward. "Ian St. Simon and I had a wager. I've known the St. Simons forever and am especially good friends with Ian's wife, Augusta. They're like family to me, more so than my own. Ian agreed to help me get to America if I could prove to him that I could survive there. You see," she rushed on, relieved that Noah appeared to be listening to her, "he didn't think I would do well there, being a woman of quality such as I am. Every time I broached the subject of sailing to America, he put me off with one excuse or another. Then, he came up with the wager. If I could survive as a servant for three weeks, performing all of the duties required, he would arrange passage for me."

"So why are you on board *this* ship?"

"Ian told me there wouldn't be a ship suitable to take me for another six months." Emily sighed. "I couldn't wait. I won the wager, fair and square, but I just couldn't wait any longer. So, when you said you were going home," she shrugged, "well, you seemed like the logical choice."

"When did I say I was going *home?*" he demanded.

"In the study, when you were talking to Ian one night."

"Oh, so we can add eavesdropping to your list of crimes."
He smiled then, a cold, ruthless smile. "I must say, you do
seem to be quite resourceful. Unfortunately for you, your
duplicity has caught you in quite a predicament."

"What . . . what do you mean?" Dread washed over her.

"The last time I consulted my map," he said, pinning her
with a dark stare, "we were headed for the West Indies."

"What?" she shrieked.

"You heard me, you little minx." He scowled at her.

"But," she pleaded, "I have to get to America."

"Then you've got a problem."

"But I don't understand. You said you were going *home.*"
Fear crept into her voice, she heard it herself. She had to keep
it at bay so he wouldn't notice. She had to get to America. She
had to get to Christopher.

"I am. To the West Indies." His smile was cold, brutal.
"It's been my home for more years than I can remember."

She started to panic. Fear wrapped itself around her, choking
her ability to reason. "Take me to America," she pleaded.
"My jewelry's worth a small fortune. You can have it all."

"I can have the jewelry you stole from my best friend's
family? No thank you."

"Then Christopher will pay you when we get to America."

Noah raised one dark brow in response.

"All right, I don't blame you for not trusting me," she said,
massaging her temples in slow circles, "but I have no other
way to pay you."

Noah stared at her a long time, saying nothing. Silence hung
between them, thick and heavy. "I can think of a way," Noah
said, his expression unreadable.

"You can?" He was going to help her. But how?

His bold gaze roamed her body, slowly and seductively,
caressing her flesh with his eyes, lingering on her breasts and
stomach. Emily felt the heat creeping up her face, spreading
to her cheeks, as the meaning of Noah's words sunk in.

"You want me to barter my body?" she asked incredulously, embarrassment turning to cold, raging fury.

He shrugged his broad shoulders. "I seriously doubt it's the first time." His words dripped sarcasm.

"You bastard!" Emily screamed as she sprang from the bed and headed toward him. But Noah was too quick. He was on the other side of the door, the heavy key rustling in the lock before she'd taken more than three steps.

Emily banged on the old wooden door, screaming and cursing him to the devil. *How dare he? How dare he?!*

Chapter 5

Noah tried to ignore the blasphemous curses that came from his cabin, the ones that wished him to perdition in the form of a two-headed goat. When the banging on the door and crashing glass started, he acted like it was an everyday occurrence. His men tried to do the same, but it was difficult pretending not to hear a crazy woman likening him to a particular part of a horse's anatomy.

He'd wring her neck, by God, Noah vowed. And he'd take great pleasure in it. At least then she'd be quiet.

Noah rubbed the back of his neck, cursing the day he first laid eyes on Emily Barry.

"Noah," John Judson said as he placed his hand on the rail and stared out to sea, "it might not be any of my business, but you seem to be in somewhat of a predicament."

"You're right, John." Noah stared off into the distance, watching the gray waves lap up over one other. "It's none of your business."

Emily chose that moment to let out another wail. He should have gagged her. The sound of metal crashing against metal reached them. And tied her up. To the bed. Spread-eagle. That would have given her something to think about.

"It does seem rather odd, if I do say so myself," John commented, stuffing his pipe with tobacco.

"What does?" Noah asked, looking up at the dark clouds looming overhead. He found himself hoping for another storm, loud enough to drown out all manner of sound.

"Well," John said, puffing on his pipe, "I can't recall a time when any of your women ever raised their voice to you, let alone haul out a string of curses like that little miss in your cabin. I'd say she's downright hostile towards you." He smiled, his blue eyes twinkling.

"She just had a little upset. She'll be fine," Noah said, frowning. "And she isn't my woman."

John lifted a bushy eyebrow. Noah could feel his steady gaze on him. "Oh?"

"It's hard to explain." He kept his eyes on the water. It calmed him, even at its fiercest moments. Right now he felt restless and much in need of calming. "I found her in my armoire."

John threw back his head and laughed a rich, hearty laugh that filled the air, drowning out Emily's blasphemous tongue. "Found her? In your armoire?" Another wave of laughter rolled over him.

Noah shot him a warning look. "She was hiding there."

"Hiding?" John's round face scrunched up. "She's a stow-away?"

Noah nodded. "She thought I was going to America." He laughed, but the sound held no warmth. "Can you imagine, John," he said, turning to face the older man, *"me* going to America?"

John puffed on his pipe a moment before answering. "No, I can't say as where I can actually picture you setting foot in America again, Noah. At least not yet."

"Not until I receive word that my bastard of a father is dead and buried," Noah bit out.

John said nothing. A loud screech came from below deck, followed by another and another.

"What are you going to do with her?" John asked, inclining his white head toward the sound.

"I know what I'd like to do with her," Noah said, shooting a quick glance at the choppy gray water before them.

John grinned. "But you're too much of a gentleman to hoist a female overboard."

"But she's no lady, John. Of that, you can be sure," Noah said, thinking of how she had insisted she was nobility. And he was the king's uncle. Noah shrugged his broad shoulders. "I've been debating my situation for the better part of the night." *When I wasn't getting hard listening to the little witch's soft moans and long sighs.*

"And?" John queried.

Noah rubbed his chin. He needed a shave. "We're too far out to take her back now, so I was thinking about proceeding to the West Indies and then shipping her back once we arrived." He paused a moment.

Another scream filled the air, a loud, piercing howl that made him wince, followed by a string of curses that would make his men blush. Noah closed his eyes, trying to gather his patience.

"If she'll just shut up," he bit out, enunciating one word at a time, "I'll promise to send her to America."

John let out a long sigh, relief evident on his round face. "That's the best idea I've heard in a long time."

Two hours later, Noah turned the key in the lock and entered the cabin. Emily had been quiet for a full fifteen minutes and he hoped she was asleep. No matter, the situation between them must be dealt with and the sooner the better.

She sat in a corner, on the far end of the bunk, staring at him. There were no curse words, no blasphemies, nothing. Only a cold, steady stare. What was she up to now? Did she have a weapon hidden under her skirts? He tried to remember if the pistol he kept in his desk drawer was loaded.

Noah walked toward her, his gaze locked with hers. She remained perfectly still, her hands clasped in her lap. Good, Noah thought. If she had found the pistol, he'd be on her before she got a shot off. He reached the berth and stood towering over her. If the woman had any sense, she'd be afraid of him.

Emily lifted her head slightly, her wide, gray eyes watching him. She sat cross-legged on the bed, her skirts billowing about her. Noah could tell from the way she was sitting that she wore no petticoats. His body tightened in response. Her golden locks hung freely about her shoulders, curling just under the swell of her breast. Noah cast a quick glance in that direction. Fatal error. Was that the outline of a nipple he'd just seen? He shook his head to clear his thoughts. It couldn't be, unless she wore only a light chemise. Or nothing at all. His manhood strained against his breeches.

He ran a hand through his hair. He had to get his thoughts back on course. After all, he was in charge of the situation. Emily should be cowering in a corner, begging forgiveness for her treachery.

"I've been thinking," he said, his voice low and rough. God, but she had the most beautiful neck. Long and slender.

"I accept your proposal," Emily said, her voice flat and emotionless.

Proposal? What proposal? He looked at her blankly.

"I'll come to your bed if you take me to America."

Her words struck him more forcefully than his own pistol would have. "You would sell your own body to be with Christopher St. Simon?" The very thought made him even angrier.

"If there were no gentlemen available to honor other forms of payment."

Her words stung. *She* was acting the wounded victim, the same woman who had told him nothing but lies from the moment he'd set eyes on her. Emily Barry was nothing more than a common thief and a manipulator.

"I haven't decided what to do with you yet," Noah lied,
not wanting to give her the satisfaction of letting her think
she'd gotten her way. *Let her stew for a little while. Let her
think she has to barter that delectable body of hers.*

Emily glared at him. "Oh? So now you are withdrawing
your offer?" She raised a light brown eyebrow. "It would
appear you are untrustworthy as well as unscrupulous, and I
unfortunately am currently at your mercy."

Noah smiled thinly and replied, "So it would appear." The
woman's tongue was more deadly than any weapon he owned.

"Well," she said, tossing her hair back, "when you decide
my fate, would you be so kind as to inform me?"

Noah leaned over, moving his face mere inches from hers.
"My dear, sweet Emily, you will be the first to know." He
bestowed a dazzling smile on her. "In the meantime," he said,
his voice dropping to a low, husky drawl, "you might try to
be a little more congenial. You used words today that made
my men blush and that just won't do." He lifted a lock of hair
from her shoulders, fingering its soft, silken texture. "You see,
I've never had a problem with the ladies and your behavior
today makes it seems as though you don't hold me in very
high regard."

"That's because I don't," she said, her gray eyes shooting
daggers.

"Well now, that just won't do," Noah said, letting her hair
glide through his fingers in a shimmering golden cascade. She
tried to move away from him, backing up until she hit the wall
of the cabin. "You know," he continued, leaning closer, "my
crew might even think you don't like me."

Emily said nothing. Noah tipped her chin up with his finger.
She remained silent. He knew it was killing her not to open
that pretty little mouth and start spouting off all manner of
blasphemies at him. She was a proud woman. Proud and beautiful.

"But that can't possibly be true, can it, Emily? You do like
me, don't you?"

Noah paused to see how she was reacting. As anticipated, her face flushed crimson, her eyes narrowed and her dainty nostrils flared.

She was furious.

"It is imperative that you treat me with great affection during the remainder of the trip." His fingers tightened on her hair.

"Go to hell." Emily's chin flew up, but she could not release herself from his grip.

"And deep admiration." He started winding her hair around his hand, forcing her closer.

"Rakehell." She tried to pull back, but he gave a quick yank and she let out a yelp.

"And utmost respect." Their faces were almost touching.

"Incorrigible wastrel."

Noah turned his head slightly to hide a smile. He didn't think he'd ever enjoyed a woman so much out of bed as he did this one. Emily with her quick, saucy tongue was an exhilarating challenge for him. So different from the weak, simpering females he'd known who were content to bat their lashes and agree with everything he said, no matter how outrageous. One thing was certain, Emily would never hesitate to speak her mind or voice an opinion, solicited or not.

"Fool. Idiot. Bully," she spat out.

"Enough."

"Lecher."

"Lecher?" He was upon her in an instant, his hands roughly gripping her shoulders. His voice was deceptively soft. "If you are interested in finding out about lechers and lecherous activity, my dear Emily, I have only to open this cabin door and tell my men you are fair game." He saw the fear in her huge gray eyes.

"Just remember as long as you are under my protection, you will be safe. Push me too far and who knows what will happen?" Her face had gone pale under the weight of his words. Good. She was afraid. Fear often kept people from making foolish mistakes.

"Now," Noah continued, releasing his tight grasp on her shoulders and reaching up to stroke her golden hair again. "Do we have a deal? Will you play the role of a woman thoroughly besotted with her 'lover'?" He smiled, knowing she had no choice but to agree to his terms.

She wrapped her arms about herself and turned her head away.

"Oh, yes, I forgot one small point. It would never do for my crew to think we had not been, ah, shall we say 'intimate'?" He shook his head, brushing his fingertips across her neck. He couldn't resist torturing her. "Bad for my reputation and totally unbelievable, I might add."

Emily buried her face in her hands but said nothing.

"Well, what do you say, Emily? Do we have a deal?" He couldn't see her face with her head bent forward, golden curls cascading down. Her small body slumped forward, as though in weary defeat. Perhaps he had been too harsh with her, made too many demands. She looked so small and defenseless.

Noah reached out to stroke her hair once again, the scent of lilac drifting toward him. Her hair was beautiful, as soft and shimmering as moonlight on quiet waters. As beautiful as spun gold, he thought, bringing his hand closer.

"I'll do it." Her words were empty, devoid of emotion. Noah jerked his hand back. He would not feel sorry for her. He would not feel anything for her. She was a schemer, a master manipulator and a grand liar.

He would do well to remember that when dealing with Emily Barry, he reminded himself as he turned away and headed for the cabin door.

Morning dawned bright and clear. Emily was still abed, though she'd been awake for hours, pondering her current dilemma. She knew from his constant tossing and turning last night that Noah hadn't slept much either. She had been afraid for a moment that he would demand to share the bed, but he'd done nothing more than scowl at her and toss his bedroll in the corner.

But what would happen today? Would he demand the use of her body in exchange for safe passage to America? Just the thought of his crude proposal made her cheeks burn. He wouldn't go through with it. Would he? He was Ian's friend. He was a man of honor. Wasn't he?

Emily's head pounded with unanswered questions. What a mess she'd gotten herself into. She had to think, had to reason her way out of this horrible situation.

A raucous yell above deck caught her attention and reminded her of Noah's warnings. *Stay close, smile sweetly, act like a lover. Act like a lover?* How on earth was she supposed to do that? Well, she was not about to ask him. He would only laugh at her.

Barbarians, Emily thought, *the whole bloody lot of them.*

The cabin door opened and Noah entered carrying a tray laden with food. He glanced in Emily's direction and seemed surprised to find her awake.

"It's early. I thought you'd still be asleep," he said, setting the tray down on the bed.

"I . . . had a rather restless night, I guess." Emily propped herself up in bed, feeling suddenly awkward with the intimacy of the moment.

His strong, tanned hands spread strawberry jam on a biscuit. "I doubt you've ever slept on a ship before."

Or in the same room with a man. "No, this is a whole new experience for me." *One I'd just as soon forget.*

Pouring a steaming brew from an old metal pot, Noah said, "My crew's not English and none of them are tea drinkers. I brought you coffee, but it may not be to your liking."

Why was he being so polite to her, so considerate? What was he up to now? She inched away until her back hit the front of the bed.

"Coffee is fine, thank you." She reached for the mug in Noah's hand. Their fingers touched, a feather-light brushing, nothing more. He pulled his hand away and snatched a biscuit from the tray, tearing into it with a vengeance. They ate the rest of their meal in silence, save the occasional clatter of silverware and the muted voices of the crew.

When Emily could stand the tension no longer, she ventured to speak. "Would it be possible to get a little sunshine today?"

"Maybe," Noah replied, spearing a piece of bacon.

"Thank you," she said quietly.

His head shot up, his eyes narrowing on her face. "Stop acting like a damn scared rabbit!" He threw down his napkin and stood up, hands on hips. "I'm not going to throw you to the wolves!" Muttering an oath under his breath, he strode to the door. "I'll be back in fifteen minutes to take you on deck." Then he was gone.

Scurrying out of bed, Emily performed her morning ablutions as best she could and changed into a pale blue day gown. It only took her ten minutes to dress since she was minus most of her undergarments. What a difference it made not to have to worry about petticoats and the like. She was grateful that packing had prohibited such items. Wouldn't it be wonderful if she could dispense with them permanently?

She'd wondered what American women wore and prayed the encumbrances were less and not more.

America, she thought, closing her eyes to recreate the pictures she'd seen in her books. She must continue to plan, to believe in her dream, because one way or another, Emily was going to America. Even if it was by way of the West Indies. Her eyes flew open. Ian! The note she left him said she was sailing with Noah to America, but he knew Noah was headed for the West Indies. Would he follow her? What would he do? The numerous possibilities drenched her already sagging spirits.

A brisk rap on the door brought her out of her dark reverie.

"Come in," she called out.

The keys rattled in the lock and the heavy wooden door opened. Noah stepped inside, his presence filling the room.

His eyes raked over her body. "Where are the rest of your clothes?"

"Excuse me?"

"Your undergarments," he said impatiently. "I can see the entire shape of your legs and your"—he stopped midsentence, eyeing her bosom—"and the rest of your person. It's indecent."

"It's all I have except for a few pairs of breeches."

"Worse yet," he muttered in disgust. "I've seen you in breeches and let me assure you, they leave little to the imagination." He ignored the bright red flush that crept up her face and strode past her to the armoire. Flinging the doors open, he pulled out a pale pink sateen gown with black, frilly lace and handed it to her. "Put this on."

"I will not."

"Emily," he warned.

"I refuse to wear that gown," she said peevishly. "It will make me look like a courtesan."

"Well at least that's a step up," Noah ground out. "Because right now you look like a streetside doxy."

"I won't wear that gown. Besides, it's too big." There, she'd see what he had to say about that. Emily knew she was being petty, but the very idea of her wearing a gown that belonged to one of Noah's mistresses was just too much.

"I see what you mean," he commented after a minute, studying her intently. "You are rather small," he said, his eyes trained on her breasts.

"Why you crude—"

"Time to go," Noah said, grabbing her arm. "And remember, my sweet Emily, you love me more than the air you breathe."

"How 'bout another bowl 'o soup, Miss Em'ly?"

"Why thank you, Amos, but I couldn't eat another bite." She smiled at the grizzly old man, her gaze drawn to his half-toothless grin. He reminded her of the color gray: gray hair, gray eyes, a gray beard, gray complexion, gray shirt and breeches. Even the five teeth left in his mouth were gray.

"More ale, Miss Emily?" Jeremy asked, his face turning as red as the ruffled mop of hair on his head. He couldn't have been more than fifteen. Emily wondered how he came to be aboard the *Falcon*. Perhaps she could talk to him later. First, she had to get him past blushing every time he looked her way.

"I've had one and that's really my limit, Jeremy. But thank you for asking."

"Where'd ya say ya come from?" Big Tom bellowed, ripping off a hunk of bread and stuffing half of it into his mouth.

"That's wot I'd like ta' know," Amos chimed in. "Us men sees all a' the cap'ns visit'rs, 'specially the women." He scrunched up his faded gray eyes and scratched his head. "But we nev'r seen the likes a' you."

Emily felt the heat rushing to her face. "Well, no, you might not have seen me," she hesitated. "Or rather, *recognized* me, because, you see"—she let out a nervous laugh—"I didn't look exactly like I do now. As a matter of fact—"

"She was with me in my cabin, and hardly wearing appropriate attire to greet my men," Noah cut in. "Isn't that right, my dear?"

Emily wished at that moment she could sink through the wooden planks into the deep, dark waters of anonymity, never to be seen again. Noah had just confirmed their suspicions. She was his whore. It was one thing for them to speculate they were lovers and quite another to hear their captain admit to the liaison in such a crude manner.

"Emily?" Noah's deep drawl pushed through her thoughts, pulling her back to the present. Emily heard the silent challenge in his voice. She wanted to jump from her seat and claw the smug look off his face. Instead, she balled her hands into tight fists and raised her head to meet his intense gaze.

The table fell silent. The wooden floorboards creaked back

and forth in rhythmic cadence with the waves beating against the ship. All eyes settled on their captain.

John Judson broke the silence. "Well, now, it doesn't matter how Miss Emily got aboard or that none of you sorry men saw her." He smiled at Emily, his blue eyes twinkling with sympathy and encouragement. "I for one am just happy that we'll be sharing company with such a beautiful, charming young woman. It makes for a much shorter trip."

Amos lifted his mug. "Hear, hear. I agree. Miss Emily is a might bett'r look'n than any a' you old cusses."

"She's the most beautiful woman I've ever seen," Jeremy said, blushing.

"She sure is purty," Big Tom grinned, making the scar on his forehead crinkle.

"Enough!" Noah slammed his fist on the wooden table.

"Captain?" John Judson asked. "Is something wrong? The men were just trying to make your guest feel welcome. Like you always tell them to do when you have a *visitor* aboard."

Emily lowered her head to hide her smile. Noah was not pleased that his men had come to her rescue and saved her from further humiliation. Her heart warmed to all of them, for despite their outward appearances and obvious lack of manners, they all possessed good intentions and kind hearts.

Unlike their captain, who was nothing more than a blackguard and a boor.

Yet Noah had wanted her to fear his men. Why? He'd led her to believe they were lechers, not to be trusted where a woman was concerned. Yet she was probably safer with these men than she was with their captain.

The meal proceeded with the entire crew, minus Noah, exchanging delightful stories about life at sea and traveling the world. Emily listened with an eager ear, trying to understand and absorb everything they were telling her. She learned about Istanbul, Paris, Greece and Peking. By the end of the hour, her head was spinning.

With the meal finished and the men scurrying off to their

various duties, Emily found herself alone. Without thinking, she sought out Noah. He was standing off in the distance, gazing out to sea, his chestnut hair windblown and tousled from the steady breeze. His strong, dark features were set against the brilliant backdrop of the afternoon sun, reminding Emily of a fierce warrior returning from battle. He seemed troubled and it surprised her that she could discern that fact. Well, when two people spent vast quantities of time together, wasn't it to be expected that they would learn each other's likes and dislikes? It seemed plausible. But this *knowing* of Noah went deeper. Much deeper and it disturbed her.

She was beginning to sense his moods from a look or word. Even the quirk of an eyebrow told her there was so much more to the man than what was readily visible. And it scared her to think of it, scared her to acknowledge that she might be interested in scratching the surface of that hard exterior to find the real man beneath. And, Emily *knew* there was a very different man behind the cold façade Noah showed her. Unfortunately, only a fool would open herself up to the pain and heartache of loving Noah Sandleton and Emily St. Simon was no fool.

"Miss Emily, if ye don't go below deck or put a hat on soon, ye'll be as red as a lobster come sunset."

Dragged from her thoughts, Emily turned to the old, grizzled sailor who had just spoken. "Why thank you for reminding me, Amos. I was so enjoying this fine weather that I didn't even consider my skin." She frowned. "Unfortunately, I find myself without a hat or bonnet, which means I suppose I should return to the cabin until the sun sets."

"But the cap'n has one o' them big straw 'uns he wears in the Indies," Amos said.

"The captain's not in a mood to be disturbed right now," John Judson said, casting a look in Noah's direction. "We'd best call it a day for now. I'll escort Miss Emily to her cabin."

Emily hazarded another glance at Noah. He was staring straight at her, his face dark and foreboding. The fierceness of his expression frightened her. She turned quickly, clasped John Judson's arm and followed him belowdecks.

"Is he always like that?" she whispered as they reached the cabin door.

John shook his head, smiling. "He's never like that, Miss Emily. Leastwise, not unless the subject of his family comes up, which it rarely does." His blue eyes twinkled. "Noah's as carefree and easygoing as they come. And he's always had a way with the ladies, a real charmer that one, with his sweet words and that big smile. Women go crazy over him."

Emily snorted indelicately. "Pardon me for my rudeness, Mr. Judson, but that description does not fit that man out there on the deck. That man is crude and overbearing."

John grinned down at her. "I'm seeing that, Miss Emily, and I couldn't agree with you more." He paused a moment before adding, "If I were a betting man, I'd say he's got it bad, real bad. And it's about time."

"Got what bad, Mr. Judson?" Emily stared at him.

John's smile only deepened as he pushed open the door for her. "You'll find out soon enough, Miss Emily. Rest assured, you'll find out soon enough."

Chapter 6

No one seemed to notice that Noah was silent through supper the next evening. He and Emily were sitting among his crew, eating barley soup and hard rolls with chunks of ham. He'd had to get out of that damned cabin. She was too close, too accessible. Emily was insinuating herself upon him slowly, minute by minute, hour by hour, working her spell, making him crazy with wanting her.

Wherever he turned, he saw her fresh beauty, her tantalizing smile. The sound of her voice enveloped him, calling to him with whispered promise as he listened to the velvety notes of soft humming or, God pardon his sick mind, her little moans and sighs of sleep. Even her anger was drawing him in, the spark in her soulful gray eyes captivating him as no other woman had. And he dared not think of that luscious body, though even the thought of *not* thinking about it made him as hard as a rock.

Why her of all people? he thought angrily. Why did just the thought of her make him ache with need? She drove him crazy and he didn't even think he liked her, with her waspish tongue and shrewish ways. Oh, but he wanted her. There was no denying that any longer, he admitted grudgingly, biting fiercely into a chunk of hard bread. He told himself it was because he hadn't bedded her yet and once he did, she'd be relegated to the ranks of the scores of other women who'd come before her. But there was this gnawing feeling deep down in his gut that told him she might just be different from all the rest, and that's what angered him the most.

"Noah, tell Miss Emily about the silks we brought back from the Orient," Jeremy said, interrupting Noah's dark musings.

"I doubt Miss Emily has much to do with silks," he responded, his gaze settling on the plain muslin gown she wore.

Emily gasped. His men fell silent. Noah cursed his foolish behavior. Even loud, burly men like these knew a direct cut when they heard one. What was the matter with him? He had always had a reputation with the ladies, young and old alike. They all loved him and his carefree, debonair style and rakish grin. Within minutes, he usually had them eating out of his hand.

But not this one, he thought. She would just as soon cut his hand off if the opportunity presented itself.

He looked over at Emily. She had a smile pasted on her face, but he didn't miss the flaring nostrils or the wide-eyed stare. Noah would bet that she probably wanted to strangle him for his rude behavior. And he couldn't say he blamed her. He *had* been ill-mannered and inconsiderate toward her. He just wished to hell he knew why.

She was looking at him now, her gray gaze intent on his mouth. Noah felt his manhood stiffen as he watched her lean toward him, her full, pink lips stopping a breath away from his own. He stared in stunned silence, unable to breathe, as she placed the softest of kisses on his lips.

Though he expected the contact, even yearned for it, when her warm mouth touched his, the union startled him, sending shards of raw sensation through every fiber of his body. Noah jumped back, wiping his mouth with the back of his hand.

"Jesus, Emily, what did you go and do that for?" he demanded.

The smile she gave him was sweet and innocent, and totally unlike the Emily Barry he knew. Damn her, but she was taking great pleasure making a fool out of him in front of his men. She leaned closer, whispering in his ear, "You told me specifically that I was to show you great affection in front of your men." Her small teeth nipped his earlobe. "And that's all I'm trying to do, Noah. Honestly." Her hands reached up to touch the curls at the nape of his neck.

"Damn you!" he whispered through clenched teeth, jerking away from her and hastily rising from the table. He turned on his heel and stalked off, muttering a string of oaths under his breath.

All eyes followed their captain's retreating back. When he was out of sight, they turned back to their bowls in silence, sopping up broth with chunks of bread. Several minutes passed without a word. Jeremy snickered first, a low snorting sound, followed by Amos's high-pitched howl. It matched the piercing cry of the seagulls overhead. Within seconds, the whole lot of them broke into gales of laughter, deep, full-bellied laughs that started and ended with hoots and hollers.

Emily laughed too, though she really didn't know why. The last few days had proved more than a little trying on her person and right now she felt close to wit's end. But she refused to examine the motive behind her sudden giddiness, other than to acknowledge that Noah Sandleton was nowhere to be found and she felt relieved, almost weightless. It was a welcome feeling.

A large ruddy hand covered hers, squeezing gently. Emily turned to look into the twinkling blue eyes of John Judson. She liked this kindly man with his shock of white hair and even disposition. He smiled at her, gently reassuring her as though he'd sensed her false bravado and was proud of it nonetheless. Emily returned his smile weakly, saying nothing.

"Care to take a walk in the setting sun with an old man?"

"I'd be honored, John. Truly honored."

They made their way to the stern of the *Falcon* and stood side by side gazing out over the dark, endless water. There was not even a hint of land in sight, and Emily marveled again at the wonder of these men who could find charted lands with only a map and compass. Brave, fearless souls with passion in their veins and purpose in their hearts. Men like John Judson and Ian and, she hesitated only a moment, Noah. They sought and found their destiny with a single-mindedness that she deeply admired. Thinking about them gave her fresh courage and renewed her determination to see her destiny fulfilled. She would get to America, she vowed, one way or another, and she would reach her soul mate.

"Don't be too harsh with Noah, Miss Emily," John said, breaking into her thoughts. "He'll come around soon enough."

Emily leaned close to the older man. "No he won't, John," she said, shaking her head. "He most certainly won't." Small wisps of golden hair escaped from her long braid and whipped across her face. She reached up, brushing them aside. "He's not happy I'm here." There was a moment's hesitation before she added, "I think you should know I stowed away in his cabin."

John winked at her and grinned. "That's what I heard. Well done, young lady," he commended her, laughing. "Well done indeed."

Emily looked at him blankly. "Did you hear what I said, John? I stowed away, hidden in his armoire."

"I heard you well enough, Miss Emily, and I applaud you. Noah needs a woman who will stand up to him instead of those frilly, gushy dress-ups that swoon when he looks their way and would never dare let him know they have an opinion."

"But you have it all wrong, John. I'm not Noah's woman."

John raised a bushy white brow but said nothing.

"Truly I'm not. Noah just wants us to act like a couple for appearance' sake. He said it would ruin his image if I didn't fawn all over him," she finished, rolling her eyes and letting him know what she really thought of the whole idea.

John let out another laugh. "The truth will come out soon enough, Miss Emily. It always does, whether we like it or not."

Emily wanted to argue the point further, but held her tongue. John would believe what he wished, no matter how strongly she and Noah denied it.

"Noah did tell me that you were headed for America," John said.

Emily nodded. "John," she began, choosing her next words with great care, "why doesn't Noah consider America his home?"

"Now what do you know about that?" John asked, a small frown playing about his usually cheerful face.

"He said he considers the West Indies his home." She pressed on. "Did something happen in America?"

John sighed and leaned back against the ship's railing. He crossed his arms over his rounded middle and studied Emily. When he spoke, his voice was quiet, as soft as the gentle swaying of the ship. "I've been sailing the seas for some thirty plus years." His bushy eyebrows pulled down in thought. "Met a lot of men in my day, most of them running from something, usually their past." He paused and stroked his white beard.

"Noah's a good sort. It was his father's doing. Old Noah Senior drove him away." He shook his head sadly. "Noah comes from a long line of Sandletons, each one of them prouder than the one before. They own hundreds of acres of tobacco and cotton in Virginia. Since Noah was the oldest son, his father expected him to remain at Willow Oaks and carry on the family tradition. Of course, Noah wanted none of it. Not even the little rich girl his father had picked out for him. He couldn't ignore the wanderlust in his blood, but his father would hear none of it and threatened to disown him if he left. That didn't stop Noah. He took off anyway, barely sixteen at the time."

"And he's never returned?" A dull ache started in the middle of her chest. She knew the pain of being the one left behind.

"He went back once, seven years ago." John's blue eyes darkened. "It turned out badly. The old man started on him again. Tried to hoist the Willow Oaks legacy back on him. I was there and it wasn't a pretty sight. Noah swore he'd never return as long as the old man was alive. Frankly, I can't say I blame him."

Emily fell silent, sifting through this new knowledge of Noah Sandleton. She could easily see why he and Ian were such good friends. They had both been in similar circumstances as the eldest sons of powerful families, duty thrust upon them at a young age like a vise, twisting and imprisoning them in its harmful grip.

"Does he have any brothers or sisters?" she asked softly, suddenly needing to know if others had suffered as she had.

"He's got a younger brother and twin sisters." John cleared his throat and turned to look at Emily. "I've spoken more than I should have." He touched her arm gently, smiling into her upturned face. "When the time is right, Noah will talk to you," he said, patting her arm. "Now, we best get you back to your cabin."

Emily sat cross-legged on the bunk, combing out her hair. When she'd bid John good night and entered the cabin, it had been dark save for a pale light shimmering in the corner. Noah's obvious absence had caused her to feel equal amounts of relief and disappointment, though she couldn't say why. Actually, she'd been hoping to gently prod him into talking about his home life and family. John had told her just enough to whet her curiosity about the strange land and the enigma of Noah Sandleton.

Did he plan to return after his father's death? Would he stay? What of the brother and twin sisters? Were they old enough to remember him? And what of the pretty little rich girl he was to marry? The questions teemed in her brain, one after the other, until she began impatiently watching the door for his return. Emily was so lost in her thoughts that she hadn't heard the light rap on her door.

"Miss Emily?" Jeremy's young voice called out to her.

Emily scurried off the bed and pulled the door open. "Yes, Jeremy?"

She stood dumbfounded, as Jeremy and Amos entered the cabin carrying a huge wooden tub. "The captain thought you might enjoy a bath." Jeremy grinned at her. "We've been collecting this water"—he motioned to several steaming buckets behind him—"but it's been a devil to heat." They set the tub down in the middle of the room and proceeded to empty the buckets into it.

Emily looked on in awe. Tears threatened to spill at the tenderness of this gesture, initiated by the man who was becoming more of a mystery to her with each passing minute. He confused and angered her with his high-handed manner and sarcastic tongue, but he also beckoned her with his heated gaze and soft caress. She wondered, now for the hundredth time, who was the real Noah Sandleton?

"Enjoy your bath, Miss Emily." Amos grinned at her and she smiled back, wondering if the old sailor had ever seen bath water. Somehow, she seriously doubted it.

"I thank you fine gentlemen for thinking of me. I shall most certainly enjoy my bath."

"It weren't nothing, Miss Emily," Jeremy piped in. "It was all the captain's doing. You might want to thank him."

"Yes, well . . ." she hesitated a moment. "I most certainly will."

As soon as the two men left, Emily hurried over to the armoire and pulled out her travel bag. She ruffled through its rumpled contents until she located a small bottle of lilac water. Unscrewing the top, she poured an ample amount into the tub and closed her eyes. The scent of lilac filled her nostrils and she breathed deeply, luxuriating in the heady fragrance.

Hazarding a quick, cursory glance at the door, she decided she could trust Noah to respect her privacy, and she began unlacing her gown. Seconds later, she sank into the steamy, scented water and lost herself in her own private heaven.

More than an hour later, she sat on the bed, battling with her long hair and wondering when Noah would return. She'd donned a prim batiste nightgown that covered her from head to toe.

"Ouch," she snapped, pulling at a large knot of hair. She could see why Julia, her lady's maid, mouthed curse words and dropped subtle hints about opting for a more fashionable, shorter style whenever she had the task of combing out Emily's hair. Bending her head forward, Emily began the painstaking chore of sorting through the golden strands, trying to untangle the matted mess. Perhaps it was a tad too long. She wondered if Noah possessed any scissors.

The door opened, signaling Noah's return. She lifted her head and watched him enter without a single glance in her direction.

"Thank you for the bath," she said softly. "It was most enjoyable."

Noah shrugged. "You're welcome." He walked over to the tub and stood beside it, looking down into the water as though something inside was of great interest. Emily studied his broad back, wondering at the man who called her a whore one minute and sent her bath water the next.

Was he really as cold and heartless as he wanted her to think? She was beginning to wonder.

"I was thinking of a bath myself," Noah said, turning toward her, his expression unreadable. "Would you mind?"

The thought of Noah naked turned Emily crimson. "Why no," she stammered, trying desperately to gather her wits and not appear the ninny. If Noah could appear so nonchalant about his nakedness, then why couldn't she? Because for all her bluster, she had never in her whole life seen a man naked, and it petrified her. It also intrigued her, she secretly admitted to herself. Silence stretched in the small cabin. "I wish I had known," she mumbled, grabbing for something to say. "I wouldn't have put the lilac water in the tub."

He smiled tightly. "Consider it just one more step in our ruse."

She looked at him blankly. "I don't understand?"

"Don't you?" he drawled. "When my men smell your scent on me they'll have no doubt that we're lovers. They'll picture those lovely long legs wrapped around me as I give you pleasure. And that is our plan, isn't it?" he asked, his voice soft as silk. "Pretend to be lovers?" Without waiting for her response, Noah turned around and began unbuttoning his shirt.

Emily hesitated a moment, unable to look away as he pulled off his shirt, revealing a darkly tanned, well-muscled back. When he bent to remove his boots, his tightly clad breeches stretched to expose the finely carved muscles of his thighs and buttocks, leaving Emily a vision of what his unclothed body would look like.

She swallowed hard. He was perfect. His head bent as he worked the buttons on his breeches. Emily's breath caught in her throat, her eyes glued to his strong hands as they slowly worked the fabric down over his slim hips. Then he stopped and jerked his head around swiftly, his dark brown eyes boring into her startled gray ones.

"Unless you'd like to help, you'd better turn around now," he said gruffly.

Emily gasped, humiliated that she'd been caught in the act. She swung herself around, burying her head in the pillow. But no matter how deeply she burrowed, she could not block out the deep, rich sound of Noah's laughter.

Noah stood over the still form, watching the slow, even movements of her breathing. Every once in awhile, she would make that small mewling sound she made, followed by a sigh. He'd counted ten in the last fifteen minutes. That's how long he'd been standing over her, filled with desire, close to bursting. He tried to ignore the painful throbbing of his manhood, tried to deny the need that had been building in him for a long time now, ever since he'd laid eyes on her.

This woman had no special hold over him. None, he kept telling himself. It had just been a long time since he'd been with a woman. Disgusted with his behavior, he moved to leave her and then was reminded of the reason he'd been standing there in the first place.

He'd meant to place her under the covers, keep her warm from the chill of night. Leaning over, he tried to nudge the blanket down from under her sleeping body. She moaned softly and shifted position, exposing one long, slender, golden leg. His dark eyes ravaged her body, mentally stripping her of the thin cotton material that covered her exquisite curves. She was bewitching him, even in her sleep! He tried to pull the blanket back yet again, with no success. After three more attempts, he decided there was no way to get her under the covers without lifting her, which meant touching her body, and torturing himself with her forbidden sweetness.

Cursing under his breath, he bent low, scooping her gently into his strong arms. Her body was soft and warm with sleep as she snuggled against his bare chest. She made a low mewling sound like a contented cat and nuzzled her nose against the dark mat of hair on his chest.

"Emily," he choked out, "stop it."

"Mmmm," she murmured, reaching a slender hand out to stroke his chest.

Noah let out a strangled sound and hastily flung back the covers and laid her on the bed. Emily's arms snaked around his neck, pulling him toward her. She caught him by surprise and he lost his balance, tumbling on top of her. Her laughter was low and throaty, a siren's call, as she tightened her arms and shifted her body slightly beneath his. That was all it took.

His manhood throbbed, pushing against his breeches, poised and ready.

"Emily," he groaned, "I'm no saint."

She smiled, her eyes still closed, and moved again, rubbing herself against his engorged shaft. Sweat broke out on his forehead as he fought to regain control. "I've dreamed this a thousand times with you," she murmured, her soft, tantalizing voice washing over him.

Emily's words slowly registered. She'd dreamed this intimate act a thousand times with him, a man she clearly loathed and fought with at every turn? Hardly. A sickening feeling settled in the pit of his stomach. She was still sleeping, dreaming about Christopher, her lover. He was the one she wanted to wrap her sweet body around, not him. How could he have been such a fool?

"A thousand times and more," she moaned softly, running her fingers along his shoulders. "Oh, Noah."

His head snapped up. She'd said his name. "Emily, wake up," his harsh command startled her out of her slumber. Her eyes flew open to find Noah staring at her, his weight pressing her into the small bed. "You were dreaming."

"Was I?" Her huge gray eyes stared at his stern face, then dropped to his full mouth.

"Don't, Emily," he said, his voice low and rough. Emily ignored his words and lifted a shaky hand to trace his lips with her fingertips. God, she was killing him, one sweet touch at a time. His tongue shot out to trace a pattern over the pads of her fingers, his eyes never leaving hers.

"If you want me to leave, say so right now," he rasped, "because in another minute I won't be able to."

Emily looked at him, touching her fingertips to his lips again. "Stay," she whispered.

Noah groaned as his mouth sought hers, releasing all of the pent-up passion and longing he'd harbored for so long. Emily returned the kiss with a fire of her own, her tongue seeking and mating with his, tracing his lips, sucking his tongue, exploring the velvety recesses of his mouth. She moaned, holding him to her as he moved his hard body over her, enveloping her with his heat. Noah shifted his weight slightly, settling his throbbing manhood between her thighs.

"I can't wait any longer." His hand skimmed down her thigh, grabbing the hem of her nightgown and yanking it up to her waist. He stroked her creamy flesh, his long fingers brushing over her woman's heat with feather-light touches. Her low, pleading moans unraveled the last shreds of his control. "I've got to have you now," he ground out as he tore at the buttons of his breeches, releasing his engorged manhood in one swift movement. Noah grabbed her buttocks, lifting them off the bed, and positioned himself over her. Their gazes locked for one brief moment before he thrust deeply into Emily's small, trembling body.

He heard her scream just as he tore through the resistance of her untried body. *A virgin! Be damned! How could that be?*

"You're killing me!" Emily yelled, beating her fists against his broad chest. "Get off of me, you beast!" She wiggled and squirmed, trying to dislodge him.

"Be still!" he spat out. His manhood was near to bursting. He couldn't think when each small movement of her luscious body took him to the edge of control. One more little wiggle and he was going to forget her tender sensibilities and pump into her with all his force until he spilled his seed deep inside her soft, warm body.

Her movements stopped. She seemed afraid to breathe. Noah held himself still, his body rigid. But not without great effort. He could feel the sweat beading on his face, the muscles in his neck straining, his forearms tight in their effort to support the bulk of his weight.

And he could feel his manhood pulsing inside her woman's heat. He cursed under his breath, willing himself to regain control. He was close to going berserk. One little jerk, one little movement or sigh and he'd be pounding into her like a madman, thinking of nothing but his own release.

Sweat rolled down his neck. His muscles started to ache with the strain of holding himself so still. If he could maintain control for just one more minute, he'd be in command again. Then he could ignore Emily's exquisite tightness and withdraw himself from her. Just one more minute.

"Are you in pain?" Emily asked, her voice little more than a whisper.

Noah refused to look at her. He almost had it, his mind had almost blocked out the feel of her body. Just a few more seconds.

"Noah?"

He would not look at her. He didn't want to see those big gray eyes, because that would only make him want to look at her mouth. That luscious mouth with those full, pink lips. His manhood pulsed involuntarily.

"I'm sorry if I overreacted," she said shyly. "It—it—" she stammered and he knew her face was bright red. "You're not hurting me anymore."

Blood rushed into his groin, and his shaft throbbed against her tightness. He couldn't speak.

"I just feel this kind of fullness . . . down there," she continued. *Why wouldn't she just be quiet?* "It's actually not unpleasant."

Noah groaned. If she kept talking, he was going to fill her up to the hilt. Then she'd know what real fullness felt like.

"So if you want to proceed . . ."

His control burst and he plunged into her, deeply, wildly, wanting all of her.

"God forgive me," he groaned, burying his face in her neck, "I can't help myself." Emily responded with a heat of her own, wrapping her legs tightly around his waist, pulling him closer to her. She met each thrust with a powerful need of her own, bucking off the bed, moaning his name, pleading for release. Noah worked his fingers between their bodies and stroked her swollen nubbin with his fingertips. That was all it took as Emily's climax came in a rush, spilling over her, draining the very life from her limbs, leaving her spent and exhausted. Noah pumped into her once more, shouted her name and spilled his seed deep inside her womb.

"Emily?" Noah was the first to speak. He lay on his side, studying her as she pretended to sleep. It was evident from her uneven breathing and squinting eyes that she was not sleeping, but merely avoiding this inevitable confrontation. "Emily, give over." Noah's tone held a note of exasperation. "I know you're awake."

Emily's eyes inched open.

"And you're naked," he said, enjoying the shocked look on her face as she tried to cover herself with the rumpled sheet. She'd have to work a little harder if she wanted the damned thing, since most of it was nestled between his legs. He smiled as he watched her let go, her face turning crimson.

"Don't," he said, lifting her hands from their feeble attempt to cover her breasts. "Your body is beautiful. And I've seen it all. Every delectable inch." Her face turned even redder. Noah traced small circles on her palm, his voice a soft caress, "I've been undressing you in my mind practically from the moment we met."

"You have?" She seemed shocked.

He nodded, smiling. "But reality is so much better." Leaning over, Noah planted a small, chaste kiss on her lips. His body leapt in response.

"Why didn't you tell me you were a virgin?" he asked quietly.

"Would it have made a difference?" She tried to sound light, carefree, as though his answer wouldn't affect her either way, but Noah heard the hint of desperation beneath her indifference. It did matter to her. Very much.

"Hell yes!" he barked. The woman could be impossible. Even in bed. "I'm not in the habit of seducing young virgins."

"Well, now you've made an exception," she said.

"Because," he continued as though she hadn't spoken, "I've always been able to tell the difference." He felt like a bastard as soon as the words were out of his mouth. Emily stiffened and pulled her hand away from his. Noah saw the momentary shock on her face, but then it disappeared so quickly that he thought he might have imagined it.

She turned her face away, lips in a straight line, eyes glued to the ceiling, steady and unblinking.

"I apologize," Noah stumbled with the word. He wasn't in the habit of saying he was sorry to a woman. Especially in his bed. It had never been necessary before.

"We had a deal. I've kept my part." Her eyes looked bright and shiny.

"A deal? What deal?" he asked, rifling a hand through his hair. The woman would make a saint lose his patience.

Emily continued to stare at the ceiling, blinking several times. Trying to keep the tears at bay, Noah thought. Bold, proud Emily.

"You told me you would take me to America if I came to your bed." Her lips barely moved as she said the words.

"And you thought I'd actually do that!" Noah boomed. "What kind of a beast do you think I am?" He grabbed her chin, forcing her to look at him. "I intended to send you to America once we reached the West Indies. Bedding you was never part of that plan."

Her lower lip started to tremble. "It wasn't?"

"Of course not," he growled, angered that she should think so little of him. "I've wanted you in my bed since the first time I saw you and it had nothing to do with any bargain."

She smiled then, a small faint tilting of her lips that made him think she was pleased with what he'd just said. That made him angry. She'd just gotten him to admit a weakness for her. Damn the woman! And damn her to hell for sleeping with *him* as part of a bargain.

"You, on the other hand, believed that sharing my bed would insure your passage to America." He paused. "To Christopher

St. Simon,'' he added, his voice cold and distant. ''My scent still clings to your skin and already you're thinking of another man.''

''No!'' she said, shaking her head. ''What happened between us has nothing to do with my getting to America.''

His eyes narrowed. ''Is that the truth, Emily, or just another lie?'' He laughed, but the sound was brittle and humorless. ''It's so hard to tell, you know, there have been so many lies. I'm beginning to think the only truths we've shared lie right here in this bed.'' He reached for a lock of golden hair, fingered its silky texture and brushed it against her nipple, watching it harden in response.

Emily turned her head away.

''I won't marry you, Emily.''

That got her attention. Her head whipped back around. She stared at him, eyes round as saucers, a look of shock on her face. ''And I *won't* marry you, Noah.''

He looked at her, dumbfounded. Had she just said she *wouldn't* marry him? He must have heard her wrong. Women from all over the world wanted to marry him. Of course she *wanted* to marry him, she was just being coy because he'd said he wouldn't marry *her*. That was the way of it, he was certain.

''Oh, come on now, Emily,'' he said, wanting to force an admission. ''You know if I offered for you, you would accept.''

''No. No, I would not,'' she said, looking horrified at the prospect. That sounded like a definite no. Her words irked him. He couldn't believe it. Perhaps she was trying an angle to lure him in and get him to offer marriage.

''No?'' he asked again.

''No,'' she repeated, her voice rising.

''What if your father demanded it?''

''My father's dead.''

''A brother then. What if he forced the issue?'' This was becoming a matter of pride.

Her face turned white. ''I tire of this game, Noah. We are both in agreement. There will be no marriage.''

Noah studied her a moment. "Tell me why the mention of a brother made you look as though you'd seen a ghost," he demanded.

Emily turned to him, her gray eyes wide with concern and perhaps a little fear. "If my brother finds me, he'll drag me back to London by my hair."

"Not if I have anything to say about it," Noah vowed, a little surprised by his fierce need to protect her. "No one will harm you, Emily. I'll get you to America, if that's where you truly want to go."

"Unless my brother finds me first," she murmured, turning on her side.

"What did you say?"

"Nothing. Nothing at all." Her words trailed off, but he heard the concern in her voice. Did she think he wouldn't protect her?

Noah reached out to stroke her hair. It felt like soft, golden strands of silk. His hand trailed down her hip, his fingers splayed over her velvety skin in quiet worship. He heard her breath catch in her throat as she turned back toward him, placing a small hand on his chest. She raised her gaze to meet his and the passion flared between them, full and hot, threatening to explode.

Noah wanted her, now, with a fierceness that was foreign to him. He felt himself harden with desire. It amazed him that this woman could make him burn with anger one moment and drown in desire the next. Noah refused to dwell on their differences right now, not with Emily's sweetness so close to him. She was his tonight. And tonight was all that mattered. Tomorrow was too far away to consider.

Jeremy summoned John Judson above deck. "I think you might wanta take a look at who's approachin', sir," he said, barely able to contain his excitement.

"It had better be worthwhile, Jeremy," John said, grabbing

the spyglass and squinting through it. "You know I'm a sight older than you young bucks and I don't appreciate being roused in the middle of the night for no good reason."

"You'll see, sir," Jeremy said. " 'E's the stuff of legends."

"Oh no," John grumbled, adjusting the glass. "What did that overactive imagination of yours conjure up this time?"

Jeremy laughed. "It's the real thing. I swear."

"Well, I'll be damned," John murmured, looking through the glass and smiling to himself. "If it isn't the *Raven*."

"Should I call the captain?"

John shook his head. "No need to wake him yet. He's got nothing to fear from his best friend."

Ian St. Simon, Earl of Kenilworth, stood towering over John, quaking with barely controlled anger.

"Where is he, John? Where is that bastard hiding?" Ian spat out, clenching and unclenching his fists. He was dressed in black from head to toe, save the small golden hoop in his left ear.

"John," Ian's deep voice boomed, "I want him. Now."

"Ian." John's blue eyes shone with concern. "In God's name, what's happened?"

Ignoring the old man's question, Ian demanded, "Is there a girl on board, blond hair, gray eyes?"

Warily, John nodded. "Yes, that's Miss Emily."

"Where is she?" he growled.

"Ian, please. Let's talk," John pleaded.

"The time for talking is done. If he touched her, he'll wish he were dead." Turning on his heel, he strode toward Noah's cabin and started pounding on the door.

The loud banging startled Noah awake. Jumping out of bed, he grabbed his breeches and threw them on.

"What the hell—" he flung the door open and was met with a right cross to the chin, follow by a left. He stumbled backward, careening against the bed. His attacker stormed after him, pum-

meling him with both fists. A right and a left connected with
Noah's left eye, then his right cheek. Noah staggered to the
desk, blood oozing from his face. He tried to straighten himself,
get his bearings to deliver his own blow, but the man charged
at him, sinking his fist in Noah's belly. Doubling over, Noah
clutched his stomach. He had to get in his punch, take control,
he thought as a wave of dizziness passed over him. Damn, but
he'd been blindsided and now he couldn't seem to catch a
breath. He felt two large hands on his shoulders, dragging him
to the ground, followed by a direct blow to the nose. A sick
cracking sound filled the air. Blood spurted everywhere.

There was a scream. "No! Please don't kill him!"

The assailant looked up and Noah recognized Ian. *What the
hell?* Why had his best friend practically beaten him to a bloody
pulp? He fell back onto the wooden floor, clutching his head,
trying to still the pounding pain that throbbed within.

"Emily, for God's sake, cover yourself," Ian commanded.

With great effort, Noah turned his head toward the bed. Out
of the corner of his left eye he saw Emily crying, covered in
nothing more than a thin sheet. She looked so helpless, so
alone. He watched as she yanked a blanket from the bed, threw
it over her shoulders and scurried out of bed.

"Emily! Don't take one more step," Ian warned. She hesitated a moment before letting out a small cry and rushing to
Noah's side. Kneeling beside him, she placed her arms over
his chest. As though to protect him. Noah winced. Even her
light touch hurt. His whole body felt beaten and bruised. If he
weren't in such pain, he would laugh. This slip of a girl thought
to keep him safe. She was a little late for that now, he thought,
as blood oozed down his cheek. His right eye was almost
swollen shut and his left seemed blurry. He knew his nose was
broken. Again. Maybe he even had a cracked rib or two.

"Emily, get out of the way. Now!" Ian said, grabbing her
arm and hauling her back to the bed. "Stay there," he warned.
He turned and strode back to the still form lying on the floor.
"Fight me, you bastard. Fight me," Ian challenged.

Noah tried to focus on Ian, but he was just a blur. A huge, black blur towering over him. He opened his mouth to speak and tasted blood. "Ian . . ." he rasped, "what the hell is this about?" God, but it hurt to speak. Maybe his jaw was broken too.

"You ruined my sister, you bastard!" Ian yelled.

"Your . . ." the word stuck in his throat ". . . sister." It was more of a statement than a question. A sick feeling of dread crept through his beaten body. She couldn't be his sister. *She couldn't be. She couldn't be,* he told himself over and over, even as the dawn of knowing twisted about him, squeezing, choking, threatening to strangle the very life out of him.

"Please, Ian," Emily begged, scrambling off the bed again, the blanket trailing behind her as she ran to Noah's side. "Please don't hurt him anymore. He didn't know, I swear to God, Ian. He didn't know."

The small room filled with silence, save Emily's tearful pleading. "N-N-Noah," she stammered. "I'm so sorry for what I've done," she whispered. "I lied to you and you suffered because of it. Please forgive me." Noah closed his eyes, blocking out the golden beauty beside him. He didn't want to see her tears or the anguish on her face. She was to blame for this bloody mess. Emily could have told him who she was days ago, when he first discovered her on his ship, but then he would have returned her to her brother. Immediately. And she knew that. Her lies and deceit had placed the noose around his neck. Her silence had tightened it.

"P-please, Noah," she begged. He turned his head away.

Emily sniffed and cleared her throat. "Ian, are you taking me back to England?" Noah heard the dread in her voice, thick and heavy with loathing.

"On the morrow," he said flatly.

"And then?" she asked, though Noah knew she already suspected the answer.

"Then it will be up to your new husband to decide what becomes of you," he said. A sinking feeling settled in the pit of Noah's stomach. He opened his left eye and slowly turned his head to meet Ian's harsh stare.

"Husband?" Emily whispered. "What husband?"

"Of course, how remiss of me. You haven't been properly introduced," Ian said, his voice cold and brittle. His expression was hard and determined as he turned toward her. "My dear, meet your betrothed, Noah Sandleton. Noah, meet your betrothed, Emily Elizabeth St. Simon. *My sister.*"

Chapter 7

Emily rested her head against the rough wall of Ian's cabin and tried to still the pounding in her head. The past few hours had been a nightmare that she would just as soon forget, but the memories flooded back to her, taunting and pulling, driving her mad with remembering. Her last vision of Noah flashed through her mind. He was standing on board the *Falcon,* looking out to sea. In profile, he looked the fierce, angry warrior. Cold. Hard. Unforgiving.

There had been no wistful looks or hushed words between them. No tender good-byes. No good-byes at all. He hadn't looked at or spoken a word to her since Ian's ruthless attack. Nor had he argued when Ian announced they were to be married. Noah had remained impassive, as though the decision was of little consequence.

Emily was the one who fought the announcement, begging Ian not to force the issue. His only reply had been marriage or a duel, which left Emily no real choice at all. She abhorred the possibility of either man suffering an injury. Or worse.

How had she gotten herself into such a mess? She was to

be married posthaste to a man she had repeatedly deceived, one who would never forgive her and most certainly never love her. Or let her go to America. These were sad and depressing thoughts, but the realization that she had fallen in love with such a man was the most depressing of all.

Noah knew Ian would search him out once Emily was gone. There were matters to be settled, things that needed said. He didn't look at her as she boarded the *Raven,* not even when he felt her sorrowful eyes on him, begging for some kind of sign. Some kind of forgiveness. Noah slammed his hand against the wooden railing. Well, he'd be damned if she'd get absolution from him. Because of her lying, scheming ways, his whole life was about to be turned upside down and there wasn't a damn thing he could do about it.

"We need to talk." Ian spoke from behind him.

Noah nodded, turning away from the black, curling waves of the sea. Even the water provided no solace for him this day. He made his way below deck, to his cabin and the bottle of whiskey that was waiting for him. He needed a drink. He needed several drinks to ease the pain in his body. And several more to dull his brain into accepting the inevitable.

Pouring two whiskeys, Noah handed one to Ian and downed the other in one healthy swallow. It burned as it traveled down his throat, hot and inviting. The second felt even better. After the third, he set his glass down and waited.

"You *will* marry her," Ian said, his words cold and stiff. *A stranger's voice,* Noah thought, *not that of my best friend.*

Noah poured another whiskey, saying nothing. He felt like hell and probably looked a lot worse. The whiskey was beginning to ease the dull aching in his battered body, but his brain pounded in his skull whenever he thought of Emily St. Simon.

Dear God, what a mess! Marriage! He knew she was trouble the first time he laid eyes on her, even before he discovered she was a woman. Uncovering that luscious femininity beneath those oversized clothes had thrown him into a constant state of need and arousal that he could not deny. She had been like a fire in his blood, burning and scarring him but good.

He would have to marry her. He realized there would be no alternative with Ian. Trapped. He hated that feeling. If only she hadn't lied to him about her identity, then none of this would have happened, Noah told himself. He never would have touched her. But even as the words ran through his head, he doubted their truth. And that sickened him more than anything.

Ian's deep voice interrupted his thoughts. "Noah? Did you hear me?"

"Of course I did, Ian," he said, not trying to hide the bitterness in his voice. "You want me to marry your sister and provide her with the luxuries befitting a woman of her station." His fingers tightened around his empty glass. "A grand estate, diamonds and rubies, silks and satins. She and I will then settle into a comfortable, married existence in the country and raise a passel of children." His smile was forced and tight. "In short, my life will be over."

Ian's smile was equally forced, his voice deceptively soft. "Not exactly." His indigo eyes turned the color of the turbulent waters they sailed. "Emily needs the protection of your name because you have compromised her. Once she has that you may consider your obligation fulfilled."

Noah's eyebrow shot up. "Perhaps you would care to explain." *What in the hell was Ian talking about?*

"I'll be quite clear about your responsibilities, lest you get confused at some point and try to change them. You *will* marry Emily and give her your name. Period. That is the only requirement necessary to be her husband. You will not provide a home, clothing, jewels or any other possession for her. You will be free to sail the seas and visit your exotic lands and pursue your other . . ." he paused to press the point ". . . pleasures. But," his eyes narrowed, "it is to be understood that my sister will not be one of those pleasures."

"And if Emily disagrees with your plan?" Noah asked

testily. He refused to acknowledge the tightness in his gut. Ian was granting him as much freedom as any man in these circumstances could hope for. That's what he wanted, wasn't it? *Why in the hell didn't he feel relieved?*

"She won't. Not when I tell her you only agreed to marry her if you would be granted freedom to roam the world, free of husbandly duties and the burden of a family. If that fails," Ian said as he shrugged his broad shoulders, "I'll tell her about all the women you're bedding while she pines for you at home."

"And if she happens to be with child?" *Pregnant. With my child.* His anger lessened.

Ian's face turned to stone. "It won't be your problem," he said, his voice colder than the battering gusts of wind outside.

"Why?" Noah ground out. "Why are you set on doing this?"

Ian rounded on him, fists clenched, the cords of his neck strained and pulsing. "If you weren't my best friend, I'd dispense with all this unpleasantness and just shoot you for what you did. I have to protect Emily. You can't love her." His voice shook with emotion. "You're incapable of love. You'll use her until you tire of her and then toss her aside. I know you, Noah. I've seen you do it more times than I can remember." He ran a hand through his long black hair. "But Emily will fall in love with you, if she hasn't already. She'll wait for you to return from one trip or another until finally you won't return at all. I won't let you destroy her."

Noah stiffened at the cruelty of the words. "And if I refuse?"

"You won't. Remember Istanbul? I saved you from getting a knife in your back. You owe me and I'm calling in your marker."

"Bastard," Noah spat out. Of course, he remembered Istanbul. The Serpent and his greed had almost landed him dead. Ian had saved his life.

"Maybe," Ian agreed. "But I protect what's mine."

Noah squeezed his eyes shut a moment, willing the pounding in his head to still. *Emily needs the protection of your name*

*because you have compromised her. Once she has that you
may consider your obligation fulfilled.* The words beat in his
head like a drum, pounding the same rhythm over and over.
*Obligation fulfilled . . . obligation fulfilled. And if she's with
child? It won't be your problem . . . won't be your problem.*

"Do you agree?" Ian asked, cutting into Noah's thoughts.

The movement was so minute, nothing more than a slight
dip of his head, but Noah knew Ian had seen his response. He
turned away, grabbing the bottle of whiskey and pouring two
fingers into his glass. He needed a good drunk right now, he
decided as he brought the glass to his lips. He'd lost too much
this day: his friend, his freedom, Emily. He was not going to
lose the blissful numbness that waited for him in the depths of
the amber liquid.

It couldn't heal him, but it sure as hell could make him numb
for a while. And that's what he needed right now. To stop
feeling. The pain in his aching, bruised body would heal
eventually, though his nose might have another crook to it.
But the regret, he thought, as he took a healthy swallow of
whiskey, now that's what would eat at him long after the alcohol
wore off.

Regret that he'd ever met *her*. He'd tasted her, touched her,
made love to her and somehow, without his mind's knowledge
or his heart's consent, opened up to her. There was no use
denying it any longer. She was inside of him now, a living,
breathing part of him, and there wasn't a damn thing he could
do about it. It didn't really matter though, he thought while he
drained the rest of the whiskey, because the marriage would
be a farce, a sham. And perhaps one day he would regret that
most of all.

"He should've been here by now," Ian ground out, stabbing
a piece of roast beef with his fork.

"It's only been a week. Besides, the wedding isn't for another
four days. He'll be here," Augusta said as she cast a quick

glance in Emily's direction. Head bent forward, Emily kept her eyes on the small mountain of peas in front of her. *He isn't coming. He hates me for what's happened.* Her left hand dug into the fold of her peach gown.

"Two more days," Ian muttered. "Two more days and I'm going after him."

He couldn't even look at me when I left.

"He'll be here, darling," Augusta said. Lifting a forkful of peas to her lips, she tasted them, chewing slowly. "Mmm," she murmured, "aren't these peas delicious? So sweet and tender."

"If he doesn't show, I swear to God, I'll call the blackguard out."

"They really are quite good," Augusta went on, as though Ian hadn't spoken.

"I'll find him," Ian vowed, fists clenched.

"With just a hint of crunchiness."

"He'll do his duty."

Augusta shoved a forkful of peas into her husband's open mouth.

"Taste them, Ian," she ground out.

"Aggh," he choked, spewing several peas onto the white tablecloth. He fell into a fit of coughing, his face turning beet red. Augusta jumped up and gave him several sharp whacks between the shoulder blades.

"Augusta," he coughed out, "what the hell are you trying to do? Kill me?"

"No, of course not, dear," she said, giving him one last whack. "But you've been so busy talking, you've barely touched your dinner."

Ian cast her a dark look and grabbed his water goblet, draining it in one healthy swallow. He looked down at his plate and frowned. "Who would know where he's hiding?" he murmured, blue eyes narrowed in thought.

Augusta let out an exasperated sigh.

Emily picked up her fork and jabbed at the peas, smashing

them into a pile of green mush. *Probably gone to the West Indies to be with one of his mistresses. He hates me.* She picked up her knife and started shredding her roast beef. *I wish I could hate him.*

"He's still got four days. He'll be here, Ian," Augusta said, laying her hand on her husband's arm and nodding toward Emily.

Ignoring his wife's silent plea, Ian plowed forward. "He's got two days, Augusta. Two days to show himself." His hand shook as he grabbed a glass of claret and emptied it.

Emily said nothing. She studied the design on her plate. An array of smashed peas and shredded beef adorned the setting, creating a pattern of color and contrast. Interesting, Emily thought as her fork traced a path through the green and brown concoction, swirling it around, mixing it together. Only a small spot of white and gold pattern remained visible on the plate, where three small boiled potatoes sat. Her fork attacked the little white balls, flattening them with quick, sure strokes. *Gone. Gone. Gone. And I don't care,* she told herself, even as she felt the huge lump in her throat grow and swell.

"Emily!" Ian roared.

Her head snapped up.

"What in God's name do you think you're doing?" Ian demanded.

Emily blinked. Once. Twice. What had she been doing? *Thinking of Noah Sandleton,* she admitted. She looked at her hand and the fork she held as though they belonged to someone else, almost as if she were outside of her body, watching a stranger. Her eyes roamed over her plate and she gasped at the brown heaps of chunky mush that covered it.

Ian and Augusta were staring at her as though she'd gone mad. She stared back at them and then scooped up a forkful of the brown muck that resembled the contents of a chamber pot and took a bite, pretending it was one of Mrs. Florence's finest preparations.

Scooping up another forkful, she smiled at her brother and

sister-in-law and extended the fork. "Care to try any? It's actually quite tasty."

They both shook their heads, eyes trained on her fork. Emily waved the utensil toward them and plopped its contents into her mouth.

"Mmmm," she said as though it were a great delicacy.

She wondered if she really was going crazy. Crazy wouldn't be so bad. At least then she wouldn't *feel* anything. No disgrace over being considered "ruined." No humiliation when Noah did not show up for their wedding. No despair over her lost dream of America. No sorrow for what might have been. But most of all, no pain for loving a man who would never love her.

No, she thought, chewing thoughtfully, crazy would not be such a bad thing.

There was no way out. Three bottles and four sleepless nights later, Noah accepted his fate. He had to marry Emily St. Simon. And then he had to leave her. Forever. Strangely enough, the latter part was beginning to bother him the most.

He would have to walk away from her golden beauty, quick wit and sunny smile. Forget those clear gray eyes and full, pink lips. Pretend he'd never sampled the secret treasures of her womanly body, touched her silken curves, lost himself in her sweetness. He would have to erase her throaty laugh and gentle touch from his memory.

He would have to forget her. There was no choice. It was for the best.

Cursing under his breath, Noah berated himself for letting the little temptress break down his defenses. How had she done it? He never let anyone get close enough to hurt him, to cause him pain or grief, and yet Emily had done all of those. Quickly and thoroughly. He raked a hand through his hair. How? Curse the witch. He needed another drink.

A knock at the door stilled his hand on the bottle.

"Come in," he rasped, his voice hoarse from too much drink.

The door handle turned and Noah heard someone enter. Ah, that would be the maid, he thought, delivering another bottle. He listened as the footsteps crossed the plush golden carpet of the huge apartment he'd rented a few days before.

"Just put it on the sideboard next to the other one." Noah's words slurred and spilled over one another. He was slouched on the moss green velvet sofa, head flung back, eyes closed. The footsteps stopped directly in front of him. Damn it, why couldn't he just be left in peace?

"Noah, my boy," John Judson said, his voice laced with equal amounts of concern and disgust. "What are you doing to yourself?"

Working his left eye open, Noah recognized the portly form of his long-time friend. "Celebrating my nuptials, John." Noah's mouth turned up slightly at the corners. Damn, but it hurt to smile. He really needed another drink. "And ... and ..." his mind blanked a second while he grasped for the word. "Recuperating. That's it," he drawled, the words moving over his tongue like tiny pebbles. "Re-cu-per-a-ting."

Shaking his white head, John leaned over and wrested the bottle from Noah's grasp, setting it on the table beside them. "Give it up, Noah. No more whiskey."

"Just one more, John," Noah slurred. "Have one with me." His hand waved at the bottle, then dropped with a thump to his side. His head fell back farther into the cushions.

"No more." John's voice was firm, commanding. "You've got to pull yourself together. Why look at you, Noah. You haven't bathed or shaved since"—he hesitated—"since Miss Emily left."

Noah jerked his head off the cushions, ignoring the splintering pain that shot through his brain. His good eye narrowed to a dark slit. "This has nothing to do with her," he lied, his words clear and precise. Not that he was willing to admit to anyone anyway.

"It sure as hell does," John said, plopping himself down next to Noah. The force of his weight hitting the sofa jarred Noah's aching body, making him wince. He knew he needed another whiskey. He shouldn't feel pain. Of any kind.

"John," he said on a ragged sigh, falling back against the cushions, "my body's been beaten and bruised. My nose is most likely broken and my left eye's swollen shut. Whiskey eases the pain."

"To my way of thinking," John continued as though Noah hadn't spoken, "you could do a lot worse than Miss Emily. She's pretty, well-spoken—"

"John," Noah warned.

"Charming, witty, graceful—"

"Enough."

"Sincere, caring—"

"Stop!" Noah roared.

John smiled, his blue eyes crinkling at the corners. "But you already know all that, don't you?" His voice was soft and understanding.

Noah said nothing.

"Then why don't you just marry the girl? Marry her and settle down. Raise a bunch of little ones." His smile disappeared. "Don't make the same mistake as me, Noah. The sea is a tempting mistress when you're a young buck like yourself, but time passes too quickly. In the blink of an eye, you're an old man with nothing but a hard bunk for a bed partner and a lifetime of regrets."

Noah turned his head toward John, surprised at his words. He looked old, so much older than he had yesterday. In all the years they'd been together, this was the first time John had ever mentioned a woman. And not just any woman. This one must have been very special. Noah could tell from the tears of sadness in John's eyes, the furrowed brow and slumped shoulders. They spoke of loss. And a woman was the cause of it, Noah thought grimly.

Damn all women.

"You don't understand, John," Noah said wearily, rubbing the stubble on his chin. How long had it been since his last shave? Two days? Three?

"What's to understand?" John shot back, all traces of his earlier moroseness gone. "You bedded your best friend's sister. You marry her. Period."

Noah's lack of response seemed to irk him. "I know you never wanted to get married, boy. But, like I said, you could have done worse. Remember that sheik's daughter a few years back? The one that hid in your bed? We were lucky to get out of there alive."

"I never touched her."

"Didn't matter," John said, pulling out his pipe and tobacco. "Point is, we all know you *did* touch Miss Emily. Ian just wants you to do right by her." He lit his pipe and took a puff on it. "So marry her." He puffed again. "Have a passel of kids. Golden-haired ones with big gray eyes." Another puff. "Be happy." Puff. Puff.

"Stop it, John!" Noah said, slamming his hand on the sofa. He didn't want to hear any more about what he should or shouldn't do. "I never said I wasn't going to marry her."

John blinked, his blue eyes searching Noah's face. "So." He paused. "You are going to marry her." It was as much a statement as a question.

Noah nodded once, keeping his eyes fixed on a small gold vase in the corner of the room.

"Good," John said, his voice laced with uncertainty. "Good." He puffed on his pipe again. "And that's the problem?" he guessed.

"She'll be mine in name only," Noah said, refusing to meet John's questioning gaze. "After the wedding, I disappear from her life. Forever. Ian's got it all worked out." The words came out forced, brittle as old bones. "He saved my life. I owe him." He raked a hand through his hair. "She'll think I deserted her." His voice trailed off.

"Jesus," John whispered, his pipe resting on his knee, long

forgotten. He spied the whiskey bottle sitting on the table and grabbed it, throwing his head back and taking a long, healthy swallow. When he was finished, he wiped his mouth with the back of his hand and thrust the bottle at Noah.

Noah brought the bottle to his lips and savored the burning taste traveling down his throat. It was his cure, his medicine, his salve, albeit temporary, from the pain that festered and swelled inside. One day, it would ooze out, but not now. Not today.

"Noah?" John accepted the proffered bottle and took another swallow. "Are you saying you *want* to marry Miss Emily?" he asked, his words a jumble of surprise and confusion.

Noah looked away, saying nothing.

"Sweet Jesus, you *do* want to marry her," John whispered, tilting his head back and chugging more amber liquid down his throat.

"It doesn't matter," Noah spat out, a muscle twitching in his jaw. God, but the whiskey wasn't working fast enough. "What's done is done. I've given my word. After the wedding, Emily will never see me again."

Two days and several bottles of whiskey later, Noah sent a message to Ian, confirming their "meeting" two days hence. He couldn't bring himself to say "wedding." Probably because it wasn't really a wedding. It was more of a farce than anything else. A great big façade to protect Emily St. Simon's reputation. As though she cared what polite society might say.

Noah smiled. Emily couldn't care less, that much he knew. She'd begged her brother not to force the marriage. His smile disappeared as he recalled her mournful words, pleading Ian to reconsider. Noah's mouth curved downward. She really *didn't* want to marry him. That fact amazed him, considering the bevy of females around the world who would do anything to become Mrs. Noah Sandleton. Anything at all: lie, cheat, play the whore or the sophisticate, whatever it took to trap him.

But not Emily. What would she say when she found out she had a husband in name only? After Ian told her his twisted version of Noah's wedding terms, she would feel hurt and betrayed. Anger would set in, red, hot, searing anger, wrapping itself around her, tighter and tighter, choking out all feeling except one. Hate. Hate for him. The husband who deserted her.

An unbidden thought crept into his mind, clutching at his gut, tearing at his soul. Did Emily harbor any tender feelings toward him? Affection? Warmth? Perhaps love? Cursing under his breath, Noah called himself a thousand kinds of fool. It would do no good to torment himself with games and guessing. Only one thing was certain.

He had given his word and he meant to honor it. There were a few minor details to take care of, and then Noah would leave. Glenview Manor, the country estate Noah had inherited from his uncle ten years ago, sat in readiness, awaiting its new mistress. It was nestled in a small village about two hours' riding distance from Ian. It would afford Emily a certain amount of independence but would be close enough for Ian to visit regularly.

His man, Billington, had overseen the tidying up of the place, and his last report two days ago indicated the staff was eager and ready to meet the new Mrs. Sandleton. Noah smiled. He and the tall, lanky Englishman had been conducting business for more years than he could remember. Billington was a most discreet man, who rarely smiled or showed emotion of any kind. He hadn't even batted an eye when Noah gave him his latest assignment: spy on the future Mrs. Sandleton.

It would be easy enough. Billington would pose as the butler of Glenview Manor and track Emily's comings and goings. Once a month, he would send a report to Noah at his last known address. If there was any threat to Emily's health or welfare, Billington was to enlist a special messenger to locate Noah. Immediately. Not that Noah thought it would be necessary. The most upheaval he expected to disturb the quiet, staid existence at

Glenview Manor would be a stray animal on the grounds.
Perhaps a deer or fox.

Or a Serpent. A dark, faceless form emerged, shattering his
thoughts like a broken mirror into hundreds of fragmented,
terrifying possibilities. Peter Crowlton. If he was still alive,
Emily would be in grave danger. Noah felt his pulse quicken.
Tiny beads of sweat formed on his upper lip. He yanked at his
cravat, trying to loosen it. The folds of cloth wrapped around
him like a snake coiling and constricting, tighter and tighter.

But he's dead, he reminded himself. Dead. He'd spent the
last several days convincing himself of it.

Noah cursed loudly. He had driven himself mad with a mission that was over seven years ago. God help him, he had even
thought for a time that Emily might be a spy. That showed
how cloudy his judgment had become. She was no more capable
of spying than Ian's cook, Mrs. Florence.

Ian believed Peter Crowlton was dead. He'd been fairly
adamant about it. The Crown thought so too. So why had it
taken Noah seven years to accept his death and forget about
the Serpent?

Because there had been no body.

Noah squeezed his eyes shut, trying to still the clamoring in
his head. Crowlton had always been the reason Noah never
announced his arrival when he made his periodic visits to
Glenview Manor. He came in the night and left the same way,
shrouded in a cloud of mystery and intrigue. The servants at
the manor were loyal and dedicated carryovers from his uncle's
days, their families having served generations of Sandletons.
They never questioned their master's odd comings and goings.
Nor did they share gossip with the neighboring estates. It was
one of Noah's few demands and for all of his generosity, that
request seemed a meager exchange.

Soon, he would be entrusting Emily into the capable hands
of his staff. He would not let his mind torment him with visions
of Peter Crowlton slithering into his thoughts any longer. The
Serpent was dead. Dead. Probably nothing more than a bag of

bones lying in an unmarked grave. In seven years, there had been no sign of the Serpent other than in the dark imaginings of Noah's brain. It was time to move out of the dark shadows of his life, time to stop looking behind him at every turn, time to go on with his life. Noah would slay the Serpent in his mind's eye, swiftly and surely. And permanently.

The vision of a faceless Peter Crowlton, clad in black, glided toward him, slowly and steadily, stopping mere inches from him. Noah raised his sword, wielding the shiny blade high over his head, preparing the blow. The Serpent struck out, wrapping his hands around Noah's neck and squeezing. The sword came down with a loud thwack, splitting the back of Crowlton's skull open. Blood spurted everywhere. The Serpent fell back, his hands sliding from Noah's neck, and stumbled to the ground dead.

Noah smiled and opened his eyes. He had slain his worst nightmare. The Serpent was dead.

Emily stood before the full-length mirror and studied herself. The woman staring back at her seemed more ready for a funeral than a wedding. She was oblivious to the striking picture she made in an empire-cut satin gown, ivory in color, decorated with rows and rows of tiny seed pearls. Nor did she take notice of the elegant beauty of her upswept golden locks, interlaced with ribbons and pearls. She blinked past the long, slender neck and smooth expanse of golden skin to study her face.

The eyes that peered back were large, luminous pools of gray, deep and mournful, as though they had seen a thousand tears fall. Her golden brows pulled into a straight line, her full, pink lips turned down at the corners. There was no sparkle, no glitter to her expression.

No smile.

A slight rap at the door interrupted her thoughts.

"Come in," she called, her voice a mere whisper.

The door opened and Augusta entered in a swirl of gold and

mauve brilliance. Emily glanced at her sister-in-law through the mirror and managed a weak smile. Augusta looked beautiful as usual in her elegant gown, with her auburn hair piled high atop her head and her emerald eyes glowing. Ian was very lucky to have her for a wife. And he treated her like a queen.

But of course, *they* loved each other.

She blinked several times.

"Emily, are you all right? Is something in your eye?" Augusta asked, rushing to her.

Emily looked at Augusta's concerned face, watching her in the mirror. She blinked again and sniffed. *Yes*, she wanted to scream. *Something is in my eye! And in my heart, and in my soul, and in my very being. And it's called pain. Pure pain, so deep and real it knocks the breath from me. And it's all because I love a man who doesn't love me, who will never love me.* But instead of uttering the unbearable truth, she murmured, "I think I may have gotten something in my eye, but I'll be fine." Placing her fingertips to the corners of her eyes, Emily pressed gently. "There. All better."

"You look beautiful, Emily."

"Thank you," Emily managed.

"But I wish you would have consented to a real wedding dress, not just an elaborate ball gown."

Emily shook her head. They'd been through this before. "It wasn't necessary to go to all the trouble."

"But it's your *wedding*," Augusta said, sounding so sad that Emily wanted to comfort *her*.

"A gown doesn't make a wedding. Nor does a vow make a marriage," Emily said, her voice cold and flat.

"Emily! Give him a chance," Augusta pleaded. "Noah is a wonderful man. He'll get used to the idea of marriage. He's just in a bit of a shock right now."

"No," Emily said, meeting Augusta's gaze in the mirror. "He'll hate me because I was the reason this marriage was forced on him. I lied and deceived him, but I never meant to hurt him. Never," she whispered, her lower lip starting to quiver. "When I tried to apologize, tell him how sorry I was, he wouldn't believe me." A single tear escaped, trailing down her cheek.

Augusta put her hands on Emily's shoulders. "Listen to me, Emily. Things *will* work out," she assured her. "Why, look at Ian and me. If you recall, we did not exactly have a smooth go of it early on." Her emerald eyes darkened as though she were remembering less pleasant times.

That got Emily to smile. "You are being too kind to my brother. He was an utter fool and we both know it. I thought he'd never come to his senses."

"At least he had sense enough to get rid of that odious man I was supposed to marry," Augusta shuddered.

"And conveniently fill in as the groom," Emily added, recalling Augusta's wedding day.

"Yes, well, that was convenient for him, I must say. But I would have much preferred to have found out my future husband's identity *before* I walked down the aisle."

Both women smiled. "There's a girl," Augusta whispered, giving Emily's shoulders a gentle squeeze. "Things will work out. Truly."

"Oh, Augusta, I wish I could believe that," Emily said. She turned to face her sister-in-law. "Sometimes I think it would almost be better if I were marrying someone who had been"— she hesitated over the word—*"selected"* for me." Seeing the surprised look on Augusta's face, Emily pressed on before she lost her nerve. "That way, both parties would know the rules. There would be no expectations or disappointments. Everything would be understood. With Noah, nothing is understood."

"You love him, don't you?" Augusta's quiet words startled Emily.

"Is it that obvious?" Emily asked.

Augusta smiled. "To me it is. You once said you never wanted to marry. Yet your whole concern these past several days has been for Noah. Would he blame you for the forced marriage? Would he forgive you? Would he hate you? Would he ever love you? Not once did you say, 'I don't want to marry the man.' Not once.''

"But I really didn't want to before," Emily said, puzzled at Augusta's words. There was truth in what she said. Emily hadn't fought the marriage since she left Noah's ship. Why? The question floated through her mind, softly at first, then faster, gathering momentum and spinning like a top out of control before crashing recklessly, with a loud thud. Out of the wreckage emerged the answer, clear and true. Emily loved Noah Sandleton, loved him with a depth and strength that frightened her. Her concern had not been for herself, but rather for the proud man she loved.

"But you do now?" Augusta prompted in a soft voice, clasping Emily's cold hands.

"Yes," Emily admitted, full of equal parts awe and despair. "Yes, I do want to marry him, despite our differences." A tiny shred of hope began unraveling with her words. "Oh, Augusta, do you really think we could have a chance?"

"Absolutely," Augusta assured her, squeezing her hand. "And who knows, one day he may even take you to America."

"Damn you Noah, that was an underhanded thing to do," Ian barked.

Noah looked at him, careful to keep his expression blank. It wouldn't do to let Ian see how important this was to him. Best to pretend indifference. "Listen, Ian, I am a man of means. My wealth at least equals yours, as we both know. I want to provide for my 'wife' as befits a Sandleton and that includes setting up a household."

"But that wasn't part of the deal." Ian stood in front of Noah, fists clenched at his side.

"It wasn't part of your deal," Noah corrected. "I always intended to provide for Emily." He shoved his hands in the pockets of his black trousers. "It's the very least I can do."

"I wanted her to remain with us," Ian said, his voice rising. "She'll need time to adjust."

"Exactly," Noah cut in, his tone sharper than he'd intended. "And exactly how will she adjust when she is a married woman with an absent husband, living in her brother's home?" Shaking his head, Noah shot him a look of disgust. "It's a pathetic sight and don't think Emily won't feel it the first time the gossipmongers come around to get a glimpse of *Mr.* Sandleton. What are you going to do, Ian? Fight off each one single-handedly, until the last old lady lies in a heap at your feet with your sword through her heart?"

Ian threw him a look that would have made a lesser man cower. Nostrils flaring, eyes narrowed, jaw tensed, he moved to within inches of Noah. Noah squared his shoulders and met his dark blue gaze.

"I won't give in. She deserves some independence. Tell me you'll let her go," Noah demanded.

Ian said nothing, his expression as hard as a wall of granite.

"My God, man," Noah exploded, forgetting his vow to keep his emotions in check. "How can you be that insensitive to the woman? Can't you leave her with some measure of pride?" Noah's deep voice filled the room. "Let her go. She'll have a household to run in the country. Great expanses of land to roam and ride her horse and garden and do whatever she wants." He stopped a moment to catch his breath. "She'll be free of both of us. We've got to let her go," he finished quietly.

Ian's gaze bored into him, burning with intensity. Noah shifted his weight from one leg to the other, avoiding those watchful eyes that saw too much. He hadn't meant to become so impassioned. He hadn't meant to give Ian any reason to become suspicious of his true feelings for Emily. He hadn't meant to act as though he cared so much, he thought grimly. But the hell of it was that he did care. A lot.

And it was becoming increasingly difficult to pretend he didn't.

"Let her go, Ian," Noah repeated, his words a soft command.

Ian opened his mouth to speak, hesitated, then closed it. He tilted his head to one side, studying Noah, his eyes narrowing to little more than slits. Noah felt like a trapped rat. What was Ian thinking? Had he guessed his true feelings? Small beads of sweat popped out on his forehead. He was hot, too hot with all these formal clothes on. Wedding clothes. His wedding.

"She may go," Ian said, then turned away and walked to the oak sideboard to pour himself a whiskey.

Noah let out a long breath. He hadn't even been aware that he was holding his breath. Had Ian noticed? He hoped not. It wouldn't do to let him think he had the upper hand where Emily was concerned.

He pulled a gold watch from his pocket and glanced at the time. Four forty-five. In fifteen minutes he would meet his bride. Snapping the lid shut, he stuffed it back in his vest pocket.

Fifteen more minutes. He could feel the tiny box containing Emily's wedding ring in his right trouser pocket. The ring had been in the Sandleton family for years, a gift given him by his grandmother on his last visit to Virginia. He wondered if Emily would wear it after he was gone.

Anxious to be alone for a few minutes, Noah headed for the doors, preparing to wait in the green salon for the ceremony to begin. He also wanted to get away from Ian's watchful eyes.

His hand was on the knob when Ian's voice reached him.

"Noah?"

"Yes?" He paused, not bothering to turn around. *Here it comes.*

"Forget about Emily. You can't have her."

"I know," Noah said, trying to ignore the tightness in his chest. *But will I ever stop wanting her?*

"Tomorrow, you'll sail out of here and into the arms of Monique or Isabel or even Desireé, and Emily will be less than a memory," Ian said matter-of-factly.

"And if she isn't?" Noah asked, unable to stop himself.

"A vague memory at best," Ian continued, as though Noah hadn't spoken.

"And what do I do, Ian," Noah asked, clutching the doorknob until his knuckles turned white, "when that memory haunts me day and night, until it becomes more real than life itself? When the only peace I find will be in and through that memory? When nothing and no one will soothe me but that memory. What do I do then?"

Noah didn't wait for a reply. Instead, he flung open the oak door and strode down the hallway toward the green salon, leaving his future brother-in-law staring after him.

Chapter 8

"And do you, Emily Elizabeth St. Simon, take this man, Noah Alexander Sandleton, to be your lawful wedded husband? To have and to hold, for richer, for poorer, in sickness and in health, 'til death do you part?"

Emily felt herself tremble. She wished Noah would look at her, acknowledge her presence at least, but other than a brief nod when she'd first entered the room, he'd said nothing. And now the priest was asking her to pledge herself to this man beside her who felt more like a stranger than a husband.

"Emily?" Father Gerard's gentle voice reached her through her distress.

"I do," she said softly, hazarding a quick glance at Noah. He stood tall and proud, looking straight ahead, much like a soldier doing his duty. *Duty,* Emily thought sadly. *He's marrying me out of duty, nothing more. He can't even look at me.*

She wished she could say the same, but since she'd entered the salon, Emily hadn't been able to keep her eyes off of him. It had seemed so long since they'd last been together, a lifetime ago. She wanted to feast her eyes on Noah, take all of him in, from his blackened eye and broken nose to the sleek lines of his cutaway jacket and polished shoes.

Emily wanted to place soft kisses all over his battered and bruised face. She wanted to clasp his strong hands to her heart, press her body to his solid form, reach up to brush that ever-errant lock of cocoa-colored hair from his forehead.

She wanted to be his wife. Augusta had said to be patient. Noah would come around. Emily hoped that was true.

"Noah Alexander Sandleton," Father Gerard continued, "do you take this woman, Emily Elizabeth St. Simon, to be your lawful wedded wife? To have and to hold, for richer, for poorer, in sickness and in health, 'til death do you part?"

Emily held her breath.

"I do," Noah said, his voice strong and steady. Almost as though he meant it. *Had* he meant those two little words that possessed the power to change their lives forever?

Father Gerard smiled. "You may place the ring on her finger." Emily held out her hand as Noah pulled a small velvet box from his pocket and flipped the top open.

The priest continued, "Now place the ring on Emily's finger and repeat after me. 'With this ring, I thee wed.' "

Noah removed the sapphire and diamond band from its case and grasped Emily's hand. She felt a tingle where his warm fingers touched hers. He looked at her then, his deep brown eyes seeking hers, burning into her, through her, marking her with their heat. His grip on her hand tightened, pulling her closer to him. Their bodies were almost touching. Almost.

Ian cleared his throat loudly and the spell shattered at their feet like shards of glass. Noah tore his gaze away and placed the ring on her finger. "With this ring, I thee wed," he repeated, his voice hard and distant. His grip loosened and he stepped away, leaving a respectable distance between them. Gone was the man with the hungry eyes of a moment before, replaced once again with the polite stranger. *Why?* Emily wondered. *Why does he act so aloof when I saw the fire in his eyes a moment ago?*

"I now pronounce you man and wife." Father Gerard smiled. "You may kiss the bride."

Will he choose a peck on the cheek or a kiss on the hand? Emily wondered. She turned to Noah and waited.

He faced her, stepping forward, his dark eyes locking with hers. Raising his hands, he placed them on either side of Emily's face and leaned forward slowly. It seemed to take an eternity for his lips to touch hers, to melt together, feather-soft at first and then deeper, with more urgency. Emily opened her mouth under Noah's gentle coaxing, meshed her tongue with his, sucked him long and deep as he had taught her, and gloried in the low groan that escaped from him. He pulled her close, their bodies molded to one another, his arousal pressing hard and urgent against her belly. She moaned. *He wanted her.*

Her moan turned to a shocked gasp as she felt strong arms thrusting her away, breaking the kiss. Her eyes flew open to find Noah staring at her, his breathing deep and uneven. Noah had pushed her away. Why? It would have been less humiliating if Ian had been the one to pull them apart. Or even Father Gerard, though the stout old priest would have been hard-pressed to complete the task. But Noah? What could be more humiliating than to be tossed aside by one's husband, at one's own wedding ceremony, no less?

Emily wanted to slap Noah's face. How dare he make her want him so and then cast her aside like a bit of useless baggage? She could feel the anger seething through her veins, as hot and pulsing as the desire had been a few moments before. Well, she would show him. Two could play that game.

"Hmm," Father Gerard said after he cleared his throat. "We just have to sign the register and everything will be official."

"Fine," Noah said, motioning Emily to follow the priest.

"Fine," Emily huffed. "And when we're through, I'd like a word with you, Noah." She squared her shoulders. "In private."

If she weren't so furious, she might have laughed. The look on Noah's face was priceless. One might have thought she'd just asked him to lay a golden egg. He was avoiding her for some reason and she was determined to find out why.

"Oh Emily," Augusta crooned, coming up behind her as she turned away from the register. "You make such a beautiful bride. Doesn't she, Noah?" she asked, gracing him with a dazzling smile.

"Yes, she's beautiful," Noah said cautiously, as though the words were being dragged from him, one letter at a time. Somehow, his acknowledgement of her beauty sounded to Emily's ears more like a confession than a compliment.

"And so are you, my dear," Ian cut in, draping an arm over his wife's shoulders. Noah shoved his hands in his pockets.

"If you'll both excuse us," Emily said, clasping onto Noah's arm. "Noah and I have some very pressing, private matters to discuss."

Ian raised a brow. "Oh?"

"Yes, Ian, you heard me correctly. I haven't seen my husband in days." She tapped her foot with growing impatience. "Eleven to be exact and we have much that needs to be discussed." Emily turned to go, trying to tug Noah with her. It would have been easier to move a mountain. He didn't budge.

"I think it would be rude to desert family right now, Emily." Noah's voice touched her, chilling her in its cold, impersonal manner.

"Oh, do you really?" Emily asked, not trying to hide the anger boiling within. "Then is it not also rude to desert one's betrothed until the wedding day, showing up mere minutes before the ceremony is to begin?"

A dull flush crept up Noah's face, blending with the purple and blue bruises that already marked it. Was that a flush of embarrassment or anger? Emily wondered. Or both?

"I was detained," Noah said, flashing a look at Ian.

Oh. Detained. As with a mistress, no doubt. She felt like blackening his other eye. Well, there would be no more mistresses. Her hand clenched in the folds of her gown. Emily didn't care if mistresses were widely accepted among her class. She would not share her husband with anyone.

"Go with her, Noah," Augusta coaxed. "We'll see you at seven for supper."

Noah and Ian exchanged looks and Emily thought she saw Ian shake his head. What was going on?

Before she could think on it further, Noah turned and headed for the doorway, practically dragging her behind him.

"Now, madame wife," Noah said, closing Emily's bedroom door, "what is so pressing, so urgent, that you required my immediate attention?" He turned the lock. In less than five minutes, he'd have her running out of this room. "Or is it that you can't wait to lie beneath me again?" Make that four minutes.

"How did you guess, Noah?" Emily asked, walking up to him and running her slender fingers down his arms. What in the devil was she up to?

"What do you think you're doing?" he demanded, taking a step away from her. She followed him, reaching for his neck cloth, loosening the folds. Noah grabbed her hands. "Stop it, Emily."

Emily smiled up at her husband, a siren's smile full of sensual promise. Did she know what she was doing to him? What she was offering? His body leapt in response.

"I've missed you, Noah," she whispered, leaning into him and pressing her body close. He took a step backward, trying to get away from her softness, and ran into a large mahogany dresser. Emily raised her head and smiled, running her tongue slowly along her upper lip. "Why have you been ignoring me, Noah?" she purred.

"Stop it, Emily," he growled, grabbing her arms and placing her away from him. Didn't she understand that he *couldn't* look at her, not without wanting her in a most primitive, elemental way? Right now, he wanted nothing more than to throw her on the bed, toss up her skirts and bury himself deep in her woman's heat. One more joining with her, hot and explosive, to carry him through the long cold nights ahead. But it would not be enough. It would never be enough, he realized. Not with Emily.

The scent of lilac filled his senses. Emily. She floated through his mind, constantly teasing and taunting him with her golden beauty and soft laughter. But the living, breathing Emily was something else altogether. She made his pulse quicken and his body throb with need.

"Noah, make love to me," she whispered. He could feel her breath on his neck, warm and soft. Dear God, but he wanted her. When she placed her hand on the bulge in his pants, he thought he would explode.

"No!" he roared, pulling back and turning away. His breath came in great gulps as he tried to steady himself. *Control. Stay in control,* he told himself, even as his manhood pulsed at the thought of Emily.

"I'm sorry," he said quietly, turning around to face her.

"No," she whispered, shaking her head, her shoulders slumping forward. "I'm the one who should apologize." Her gray eyes sought his. "I tried to tempt you, to make you want me as I've wanted you every night since you left." Emily's gaze fell to the carpet. "Then I was going to reject you."

"Why?" He had to know.

"I wanted you to feel the pain of wanting and not having." She sniffed. "But it doesn't matter now. The joke was on me all along." Another sniff. "You have to care about something in order to want it." Emily swiped at her eyes. "And it's more than obvious that you don't."

"Don't what?" Noah asked, stalling. He wanted nothing more than to gather her in his arms and comfort her, but he couldn't. He thrust his hands in his pockets.

His response seemed to irritate her. She flung her head up, standing straight and proud, like an angry golden goddess. She bit out, "Don't care about or want *me.*"

"I can't want you, Emily," Noah said, willing her to understand something he himself did not.

"Hah," she said. "You were too busy with your mistresses to even think about wanting me. That's it, isn't it?" She balled her fists, placing them on her hips. "Of course," she went on, not waiting for his response, "you went straight into the arms of Desireé or Monique or whatever her name is and"—she stopped midsentence. "It's Desireé *and* Monique, isn't it?"

"There have been no other women," Noah said quietly.

"You have two mistresses!"

"No one since you."

"Or do you have more than two?" Her gray eyes narrowed. "I heard your men talking. They mentioned more than one name." Emily crossed her arms and started tapping her foot. Was she waiting for an explanation?

Noah sighed. The woman was acting the shrew already and they hadn't even been married an hour. He'd love to tell her she was spilling out of her gown with her arms crossed that way, but thought better of it. This was the woman who had toppled him with a pitcher at the Fox's Tail.

"Well? I want to know their names," she demanded.

"For what purpose?" Noah's curiosity got the better of him.

"So I may pen them each a note and tell them their services are no longer required."

Noah stifled a laugh. If she were going to pen each of his women a note, then she had better begin immediately and perhaps in three weeks' time she would complete the task. He smiled. Emily would kill him if he mentioned that fact.

"I should like a meeting with John Judson. He can provide me with details such as addresses and the like."

"I'll be sure to mention that to him." John would roar with laughter.

"And," she added peevishly, "you may discard those clothing items in your cabin. They are much too large for me and in extremely poor taste."

"Yes, m'lady." He liked Emily better naked, anyway.

"Good," she finished, cocking her head to one side. "And I think you should know, I'll not share you with other women."

"Oh?" Noah smiled. He was enjoying this game. Too bad it wasn't for real, he thought, feeling a sharp pain in his gut. He'd even tolerate the shrewish part. Anything if he could be with her.

"No. I will not," she said, her full pink lips pulling into a straight line.

"Listen to me, Emily," Noah said, his smile fading. Every minute that ticked away brought him closer to leaving her. "There have been no women since I met you. No one."

"No one?" she echoed.

"No one," he repeated.

"Why?" she demanded.

"Why?" he asked, not understanding the question.

"Yes," she said, tapping her foot again. "Why have there been no other women? It's obvious that you're a very"—she hesitated—"virile man." Her eyes darted to his groin.

"Thank you," Noah grinned.

A deep crimson flush spread slowly from her neck to the roots of her golden hair. "You have quite a reputation with women. It would not be out of character for you to have seen one of them at some point during the last eleven days."

Noah fought to keep a smile from his face. His expression remained bland as he responded, "Perhaps none of them appealed to me."

"None of them?" she asked, looking astonished.

"Perhaps none compared to you, fair wife." The words slipped out, but the truth had a way of doing that sometimes.

"Must you make fun of me, Noah?" she cried. "Can't you see I'm humiliated enough having to ask you about your mistresses?" Emily's chin flew up two notches.

Noah sobered. The game was up. "I was speaking the truth, Emily."

"But you don't want me. You said so yourself." Her voice was a mixture of confusion and irritation.

"I said I couldn't want you. Not that I didn't want you."
Noah's gentle voice reached out to her, offering a soothing
balm for all the words he could not speak. "I know it makes
little sense to you. But believe this, Emily," he said, reaching
out to grasp her hands in his. "I have *wanted* you since the
day I first laid eyes on you, and I've never stopped wanting
you. I have been fighting with myself since you walked into the
salon today, holding myself back, trying not to touch you"—he
took a step closer, unaware he'd moved—"trying not to want
you." Noah reached up to touch her hair, silky and soft, shining
like spun gold laced with pearls.

"But why?" she asked, her eyes wide and confused.

He frowned. "Because I would only hurt you and I'd do
anything to spare you that," he said fiercely. A surge of protectiveness shot through him, startling him with its intensity. He
would protect his wife. Even from himself.

"Oh, Noah," she murmured, reaching a hand up to stroke
his cheek. "I love you." She smiled a small shy smile, like a
child giving a homemade gift uncertain if the receiver will
accept it. "I have loved you for so very long."

Noah grabbed her shoulders, his insides raw and aching. He
felt as if he'd taken another beating, but this one left deeper
wounds, more scars. "No, Emily. You can't love me. You
can't."

"But I do, Noah," she said, smiling again, tears glistening
in her large gray eyes. "Love me. Love me, Noah," she whispered, rising on tiptoe to brush a kiss across his lips.

Always. I will always love you, Emily. He was losing the
battle with his conscience. All the reinforcements were turning
into casualties, along with his first line of defense that had been
good intentions and honor. Noah felt himself slipping fast into
the abyss of love and desire. He wanted Emily beyond reason,
with a depth of feeling that left him breathless and shaking.
One more attempt. Integrity emerged from the reserves to make
one final valiant effort.

"You'll hate me tomorrow," Noah said, his voice low and

ragged as he tried to fight the butterfly kisses landing on his lips, his chin, his neck.

"I could never hate you," Emily whispered. "Never." She opened her mouth and ran her tongue along his neck, sucking gently. Integrity fell to its knees, shattered by an explosion of desire.

"God, help me, Emily. I can't fight you anymore." Noah crushed his mouth to hers, plunging his tongue inside, stroking, sucking, mating with hers. His hands moved over her body like a starving man, feeding on the feel of her satin skin against his callused fingers. He lifted her gown, grazing his fingertips along her thigh, kneading and stroking her buttocks, trying to absorb all of her.

It had to last him a lifetime. He worked his way to the bed, worshiping her mouth with his tongue, her body with his hands. Noah followed Emily down onto the counterpane, pressing his hard body into her soft pliant one, his manhood nestled in the cleft of her thighs.

He was moving too fast. He should savor the sensations, he thought, rubbing himself against her. God, but she felt good. His senses were on fire, burning where she touched him, leaving a hot trail of aching need where her fingers had been. If he didn't slow down soon, he'd spill his seed before he got his clothes off.

Emily moaned low in her throat, a pure sound of pleasure as her fingers explored beneath his shirt. She stroked his back with her nails, exciting him with her touch. Her hands played over his buttocks, grabbing and kneading the muscles, pulling him closer to her woman's heat.

Emily jerked her hips up, a pure involuntary reaction, Noah was certain. But a silent plea to join their bodies. His manhood throbbed. Patience, he told himself, take it slow. Think of Emily. His manhood throbbed again. No, don't think of Emily. Think of her pleasure. He almost exploded. Correction. Think of anything but Emily.

She moved again. This time, the movement was slow and

determined. And damned exciting. Too exciting. The little witch knew what she was doing now.

"Noah," she whispered, "love me." Her low, throaty words hurled him beyond the edge of reason to a place where nothing remained but sensation. Pure sensation, wild and primitive. Noah wanted to lose himself in the touch of her satin skin beneath his fingertips, the sound of her low moans dying in his mouth. He wanted to revel in her innocent beauty as she reached her woman's pleasure, bury himself in the lilac scent that covered her body. Taste the honeyed nectar on her lips.

He wanted her and, God forgive him, he had to have her. Now. He could take no more. Noah jumped off Emily, flung her gown up to her hips and pulled down her pantaloons. Pure sensation. Emily lay before him, bare and exposed. And beautiful. Wild and primitive. Noah tore at the buttons on his trousers. His manhood sprang free, full and erect. Pure sensation.

Bending over Emily, he spread her legs wide. His hands stroked her silky thighs, easing them farther apart. She lay like a goddess, half clothed in her golden beauty. Noah could wait no longer. He climbed onto the bed and knelt between her legs, lifting them high, placing them on his shoulders. Her eyes widened in surprise and confusion. Noah stroked the back of her legs, his manhood straining. Wild and primitive. He thrust into her, burying himself to the core of her heat. Pure sensation.

Emily raised her hips to meet his driving need, clutching his forearms with her hands, moaning his name. Her face lit up with pure pleasure as he worked her body fast, then slow, then faster still.

"Oh, God, Emily," Noah rasped, unable to bear much more of the sweet agony. His manhood throbbed, pulsing with need, threatening to explode. Noah plunged into her twice more, deep and hard, reaching for the very center of her. Emily let out a cry, her eyes wide with surprise as her body convulsed in climax, gripping his shaft, hugging it tightly. Wild and primitive. He drove into her one more time, groaning her name as he poured himself into her, hot and wet. Pure sensation.

Wild and primitive, he thought as he drifted off to sleep, curling Emily's warm body close to him. That was how he felt around her, whether they were making love, arguing or just sitting together. She evoked the need in him to protect, to cherish, to love. Emily Sandleton. His wife. He smiled.

A short while later, Noah stood fully dressed, looking down at his wife's sleeping form. She lay curled on her side, cocooned in the mauve counterpane, golden hair tangled and loose, a slim ankle peeking from beneath the heavy material. A sleeping beauty in wanton disarray. If only she could stay nestled in sleep and ignorance, then she'd never discover the heartache that awaited when her slumber ended.

Noah frowned. He would not regret what had happened between them in this bed. Emily touched him as no woman had ever touched him before. He had needed to feel that closeness, if only one more time. Noah clenched his fists. Damn honor. Damn integrity. Damn Ian St. Simon.

He leaned over to touch the cascade of golden hair fanning from her head like a crown. The scent of lilac drifted to him, drawing him in, tantalizing him with memories. Noah extended his hand, hesitating, hovering mere inches above the silken mass. He withdrew his hand. He would not touch her. Not again.

"I love you," he whispered to her sleeping form. "I love you, Emily Sandleton."

Then he was gone.

Emily emerged from slumber, stretching slowly, like a cat basking in the sun on a lazy afternoon. Twilight filtered through the half-drawn ivory curtains, casting shadows on the bed.

The bed. Emily felt the heat rush to her face as she recalled what had transpired there. Noah. Her body tingled in response. Where was he? Probably downstairs with Ian and Augusta. Ian hadn't looked too pleased earlier when she'd announced she wanted a private word with Noah. No, he hadn't looked pleased at all. Come to think of it, his expression was rather fierce, almost downright hostile. Emily sighed and tossed back the counterpane. She hoped the two of them would settle their differences soon. After all, Noah was her husband now. And would be for a long while. She smiled at the thought.

Pushing herself off the bed, she started brushing at the wrinkles in her gown, suddenly very anxious to see her husband again.

Emily emerged from her bedchamber and descended the staircase. She forced herself to slow her step. It wouldn't do to let her new husband know just how much she wanted to see him. Or Ian for that matter. Her brother might have forced the marriage, but something told her he wasn't overly thrilled with his best friend marrying his sister.

"Lady Emily, may I help you?" someone squeaked out behind her.

Emily swirled around to find Pierce, the butler, staring down at her. All six foot five of his lanky self. Emily liked the new butler. And not just because he happened to be Mrs. Florence's nephew. John Pierce was young, about her age, extremely well-mannered and very serious about his position at Greyling Manor. She sent him a smile that turned his pale face ten different shades of red.

"Actually, I'm looking for Mr. Sandleton. Could you tell me where he might be?"

Pierce turned redder still. Magenta? Yes, that was the color, Emily thought as she watched the hue deepen and spread from his long neck to his ears.

"M-M-Mister Sandleton isn't here," he managed, sounding like someone was choking the words out of him.

"Oh." A wave of disappointment washed over Emily as she took in the news. Where had he gone? When would he be back? It wouldn't do very well to quiz poor Pierce. Next he'd be passing out in front of her and that wouldn't bode well for him. A mental picture of Pierce's tall, lanky form thudding to the ground came to mind. He would block a good portion of the hallway and the dining room door, depending on how he landed. Emily almost giggled. His arms and legs would be flung straight out, navy waistcoat askew. Ian would find no humor in this young man's body sprawled on the floor, of that she was certain. He could be such a stickler at times and Emily didn't want to do anything to jeopardize Pierce's new position with the family.

"B-B-But," he stammered, "the earl and Lady Augusta are in the dining room."

"Good." She patted him on the arm and smiled again, hoping the gestures wouldn't send him into a state of apoplexy.

Pierce cleared his throat once. Twice. Three times. "Will there be anything else, Lady Emily?" he asked, his blue eyes darting around the room, fixing on a sight directly behind her right ear. Why wasn't he looking at her? The color in his face had settled back down to a dusty rose. Thank goodness. Poor Pierce seemed quite undone tonight.

"No thank you, Pierce. That will be all," Emily said, turning toward the dining room door.

She breezed into the room with a smile on her face. This day had turned out far better than she could have hoped. A new husband. A new beginning. Now, all she had to do was find that husband, she thought wryly.

"Emily."

Emily shook herself out of her musings and threw her sister-in-law a bright smile. "Hello, Augusta. Hello, Ian." Her eyes lit on the roast duck sitting amidst bowls of peas and potatoes and corn pudding. And asparagus soup. Her heart did a little flip when she looked at the tureen of green soup.

"I'm famished," she announced, plopping herself in the

seat next to Ian. "Asparagus soup. My favorite," she giggled,
casting a sideways glance at Augusta.

Apparently, Augusta found no humor in her words. She sat
very still, staring at her plate, her beautiful face as stoic as a
soldier heading for battle. Perhaps Augusta had forgotten the
incident with Noah and the asparagus soup. Well, Emily would
never forget it, not the shocked look on his face or the splattered green on his white shirt. She stifled another giggle and
looked in Ian's direction. He was staring at her, his blue eyes
as hard and cool as shards of ice.

What is the matter now? Emily wondered, staring back at
him. She was tempted to stick out her tongue or cross her eyes,
anything to get a reaction from him. Ian was not going to ruin
her wedding day. She would not let him be an old spoilsport
about this marriage business. And she would bet that was the
source of his current displeasure. He always seemed to be
displeased with her about something. Well, he would just have
to get used to the idea that Noah was her husband, she decided
as she picked up the soup ladle.

"You know, I must thank you, Ian," she said casually, filling
her bowl. "If it hadn't been for your insistence, I would never
have married Noah." Emily picked up her spoon. "And I do
believe it will all work out for the best," she added, leaning
over to nibble at a tiny piece of asparagus.

"Emily," Ian's deep voice reached her, washing over her
with its intensity. "There's something I need to tell you."

Tiny alarms rang in Emily's brain, signaling a warning, but
she refused to heed them. Ian was always trying to lecture her
about something, feed her some piece of bad news and then
offer his advice, like an oldest brother, or an earl or head of
the household, of which he was all three. She scooped more
soup into her mouth. Well, not this time. Her spoon scraped
the bottom of the bowl. He would not ruin this day for her.
She vowed not to listen to his dismal, doomsayer voice again.

"It's about Noah."

There was that voice again. But she was not listening to it, she told herself. Emily grabbed a golden biscuit and took a big bite.

"He's gone."

She stuffed more biscuit into her mouth, heedless of the crumbs tumbling onto her lap. He's gone? Gone? Too bad she wasn't listening to that voice. She refused to listen to it, because that voice had just said her husband, the man she loved, was gone. Emily felt something wet on her cheek. Tears. She was crying. Why? She didn't believe those horrible words Ian was saying, did she? Another tear slipped, unchecked, down her face.

"I'm sorry, Emily. It will be better this way," Ian said, touching her shoulder. She jumped. How had he gotten there? When had he moved?

"Oh, Emily," Augusta sobbed. "I'm so sorry for you." Emily could hear her sister-in-law weeping in the background, hear the words she was saying, but they seemed displaced, removed, far away. Like a play, she thought. A play with a tragic, twisted ending, with herself as the solo audience.

"Damn him," Ian muttered under his breath. "I thought he told you. I thought you knew."

Emily felt the pressure of his fingers on her shoulders. His words kept coming, pounding against her brain like a crazed messenger demanding entry. Slowly, against her will, the meaning penetrated her body, seeping through her veins. Noah was gone? When? Where? Why? The questions spun in her head like a child's top, around and around, twirling aimlessly, heading nowhere. Squeezing her eyes shut, she willed the questions away, willed away the soft sobs of her sister-in-law and cold words of her brother to the far recesses of her mind. He was saying things she couldn't bear to hear. Noah had planned to leave? It was part of an agreement?

No. That could not be true. The man who had looked at her so tenderly, touched her so deeply, loved her so passionately, could not have done so knowing he would leave her forever when he left her bed.

Emily tasted blood in her mouth. Slowly, she lifted her hand to touch her lips. She felt something damp on her fingers. Forcing her gaze downward, she stared at the faint red splotches on the tips. Blood.

The blood was real. The tears that streamed down her face were real. Ian's words were real. Everything about this whole horrible scene was real.

Emily bent her head and gave herself up to the grief she felt. Her body shook with the pain of betrayal and love lost as understanding stamped out denial. Her cries echoed a soulful mourning over hopes and dreams, lying like burnt offerings, charred in the ashes of deceit. A huge gaping hole lay in the middle of her heart. A gift from her husband.

She felt strong arms around her, trying to protect her, pulling her from the pain of her grief. But it was too late, much too late. As welcoming darkness called her forward, Emily gave herself up to its bliss and drifted into blackness.

Chapter 9

"I've had it, Augusta. I'm calling the doctor." Ian's words floated to Emily through her bedroom door. She heard the sharpness in his voice. He was angry. What had she done now?

"Give her a little more time, Ian. It's only been a day," Augusta said.

"One day too long if she is mourning over that good-for-nothing bastard," Ian growled. Who were they talking about?

"Ian! How can you speak that way about a man who has been your best friend for years?" A heavy, sinking feeling settled in the middle of her chest.

"He's no longer my friend," Ian said. A face appeared, dark and brooding, with deep brown eyes the color of French chocolate. Emily stamped out the vision.

"People make mistakes. Have you forgotten the early days of our relationship?" Augusta asked. "You left me as well." Emily squeezed her eyes shut, fighting the vision, forcing him back into the dark corners of her memory.

"That was different," Ian pointed out. "I loved you." Emily felt a tear trickle down her cheek.

"Hah!" she scoffed. "I see your memory has failed you, dear husband."

"Augusta," Ian warned.

Emily heard soft tinkling laughter, followed by silence.

A few moments later, Augusta spoke, her voice low and faintly husky. "One day, you *will* need to settle things with Noah. If for no one else's sake, then for your own." Emily heard the name she was trying so hard to forget.

"And if he never returns? What then?" The challenge of Ian's words smothered her, blanketing her like a piece of granite, hard and cold. She turned on her side, burrowing deeper under the covers, blocking out Augusta's response, blocking out the world as she descended once again into darkness.

Emily's room was awash with light. She felt it, even though her eyes remained closed. Why was she still abed when the sun peeking through the draperies hinted it must be late morning? She should have been up by now, roaming the hills and enjoying the countryside with her chestnut mare, Allegra.

"Emily?" a voice called from the other side of the bed.

Emily moved her head with the speed of a tortoise. Her whole body felt heavy, weighted down by some inexplicable force seeping the energy from her bones. Augusta had spoken her name, coaxing her back from the hazy cloud of confusion that blanketed her. Emily opened her eyes.

"Oh, thank God," Augusta cried, clasping Emily's hands. "Thank God you're finally awake."

"Emily? Are you all right?" Ian's deep voice reached her. He had risen from his chair to stand beside her bed. Her gaze crept to him, an inch at a time. His handsome face, always so calm and unperturbed, look drained, lined with shadows of fatigue that matched the rough edges of concern she heard in his voice.

"How long have I been asleep?" she asked.

"Two days," he said, his lips forming a straight line.

"What—" she started to ask, and then stopped midsentence as memories flooded her brain. Noah. Emily closed her eyes a moment, fighting back tears. Noah had deserted her after less than a day of marriage. She would not cry again. He had made his choice and it had not been her. But she would not let that knowledge destroy her.

"What exactly did he say?" she asked, barely recognizing the cold, empty voice that spoke as her own.

"What do you mean?" Ian's words were equally devoid of emotion.

"Noah. How do you know he won't be back?"

Ian's eyes narrowed slightly. "He told me."

"What were his exact words?" She had to know. Every minute detail. It was the only hope she had of exorcising Noah Sandleton from her mind. And her heart.

Ian cleared his throat and hesitated a moment, his blue eyes moving from her face to her clenched hands. "There was an agreement between us. It was to be a marriage in name only. Noah would marry you and give you his name, and then he would leave, free to sail the seas without any"—he paused, seeming to search for the proper word—"encumbrances."

Encumbrance? That's what she had been to him? Not a wife, not a friend. Not even a lover. She had been an encumbrance. The word pierced her heart like a dagger, drawing the blood of her pain and grief.

"I see," she managed in a small voice.

"He's gone. He won't be back." The dagger twisted.

"But he has set you up with a very fine country house in Bath," Augusta rushed in, wringing her hands. "There is a full house of servants waiting to see to your needs. And I heard Noah say Allegra is to be transported as well."

Emily looked at Ian. He stood glaring at his wife, as though silently chastising her for saying too much. Augusta seemed unaware of his dark mood as she continued to smile at Emily like an angel, offering hope where none existed.

"Ian?" Emily asked. "Is this true?"

Ian shoved his hands in his pockets. "You don't have to go, Emily," he said, frowning. "Bath is at least two hours from Marbrook. You're a woman alone. You should stay with us, where you will be cared for."

A woman alone. The words sank into Emily's brain, leaving an imprint. A woman alone. In that moment, she knew she would leave, must leave. Noah might have bound her to him in marriage, but he had freed her as well. Now she could move about as a married woman without threat of disgrace or ruination. She could roam the countryside, dance barefoot in fields of sweet-smelling grass, ride bareback at sunrise, the wind rifling through her unbound hair. Freedom. At last. A vision of Noah flashed before her, his dark eyes boring into her very soul. She frowned. He had given her the gift of freedom but had stolen her dream of America as well as her heart, locking her in a prison where he held the only key. One day, perhaps, she would be able to forgive him. One day. Perhaps. But not today.

"I have much to do," Emily announced, throwing back the covers. "I'm leaving in the morning."

"Oh, Ian, why didn't you tell her about the letter?" Augusta asked, her voice soft and full of sadness. She dabbed at a stray tear with her lace handkerchief as she watched the carriages roll away.

"There was no point," he said.

"No point?"

"He'll never change. Noah has probably sent hundreds of missives to hundreds of women telling them how much he missed them and regretted having to leave them, from Istanbul to France. Emily is just one more. Even if she is his wife. I won't let him dally with her any longer."

"But what if he is sincere? What if he really does miss her? What if he's in love with her?" Augusta persisted.

Ian's arm went around his wife, pulling her to him. He

looked down into her emerald eyes end smiled. "Noah? In love? Impossible."

The sun climbed over the horizon, nudging its way past the somber tones of night. Emily raced down the hill on Allegra, the feel of the wind in her face, the sound of the horse's hooves beating the ground in rapid staccato. Freedom. Freedom. Freedom. She threw back her head and laughed, a rich glorious sound that filled the morning air.

Horse and rider reached the bottom of the hill, panting and gasping for breath. "Good girl," Emily whispered, stroking Allegra's neck. The horse nickered, throwing her head up, nostrils flared from the early morning exercise. Emily laughed again, basking in the pure enjoyment of the morning. She slid off her mount, her booted feet landing easily on the ground. Brushing off her breeches, she gave silent thanks that Ian was miles away. He never tired of chastising her for dressing like a man.

"There you go," she said, dropping Allegra's reins. "Enjoy your breakfast." The horse snorted twice, then sank her nose in the sweet clover.

It had been one week since her arrival at Glenview Manor, and already it felt like home. She loved her new residence, from the great expanses of old ivy crawling along the aging brick walls to the twenty rows of red rose bushes centered in the front lawn. The area stretched out, clipped and manicured in green splendor. Emily wondered if the gardener lay hidden in the boxwoods, shears open and ready, waiting for the next glossy leaf to sprout so he could trim it posthaste.

Rows of privet blended into each other, making it impossible to tell where one stopped and the other began. They wound around in a square pattern, forming a green maze that led to a center where a large white fountain sat. A stone angel perched atop the fountain, its wings suspended in the air, a steady stream of water spouting from its pursed lips.

But the land to the rear of the house was what captured
Emily's eye the most. There were several small and not so
small garden areas, randomly placed in the back lawn. One
was for herbs, one for wildflowers and one for vegetables. The
scent of lavender and honeysuckle filled the air to the west,
while a patch of vibrant pink and purple coneflowers called
one's vision to the east.

The manor itself drew her in with its simple yet elegant
furnishings. The rooms echoed pale green and creams with
hints of gold. No dark, brooding colors here. Emily especially
loved her bedroom, with its ivory walls and thick cream counterpane bordered with thin pale green piping. The draperies were
a rich cream damask, held back with golden tassels. White
vases carved with golden dragons adorned the dressing table
and nightstand. They reminded Emily of a vase Ian had given
her. It had been a remembrance of his past excursions to the
Orient. She wondered if *someone else* had been with him during
that trip, perhaps even touched that same vase and brought
back a few of his own.

Emily pushed the thought from her mind. She would not
dwell on *him*. She drew in a deep breath, letting the fresh air
fill her lungs and cleanse her mind. Allegra lifted her head and
whinnied, her ears pricked up and alert.

"What is it, girl?" Emily asked, following her horse's gaze
toward the hilltop that marked the perimeter of the Sandleton
property.

A lone figure sat astride a massive white horse, so still that
horse and rider appeared as one. Emily's heart skipped a beat.
Noah. She shielded her eyes from the sun, trying to get a better
view. Was it him? Had he returned? What would she say? The
rider lifted a hand in greeting and galloped toward her.

The sun shifted and Emily saw his golden hair. Her heart
sunk to her feet. It wasn't Noah. Her husband had not come
back for her.

The man brought his mount to a halt several feet from her.

"Good day, my lady," he said, his voice soft and low. He sat atop his huge horse, staring down at her.

"Good day, sir," Emily replied, calculating the distance back to the house. The intensity of his gaze unnerved her. Could she jump on Allegra and outrun him? Never.

The stranger smiled and laughed, the sound rolling over her like the summer breeze that blew his golden hair about his shoulders. "There's no need to fear me." His expression softened, revealing a dimple on the right side of his cheek. He was a handsome man of medium height and slight build. Almost too handsome, Emily thought, with his high cheekbones, lean jaw and sky blue eyes. She guessed his age to be somewhere in the midthirties.

"You startled me sir, nothing more," Emily replied, determined that this stranger should not think her a ninny. She was a grown woman now, married as well, and she needed to learn how to handle herself in these situations. After all, there would be no husband to rescue her.

"Forgive me," he said, smiling again, revealing an even row of very white teeth. He patted his horse and dismounted in one quick, fluid action, amazing Emily with his grace and form. Taking a step forward, he took a slight bow and extended his hand. Emily noted he was wearing tan gloves. "Allow me to introduce myself. I am Andrew Kleeton. I own the property to the west of Glenview Manor."

Emily smiled and placed her hand in his. "I am pleased to meet you. I am Lady Emily Sandleton, mistress of Glenview Manor."

"Ahh," Andrew Kleeton said. "Finally, we meet a member of the Sandleton family." He paused a moment. "And where pray might Mr. Sandleton be?"

The question was simple, yet the words struck her like a blow to the midsection. She wanted to tell him the truth. She had no idea where Mr. Sandleton was at the moment, nor did she know where he would be next week or next month. Or next year for that matter. And she had no idea what he was doing or with whom. Forcing back the anger and despair that threatened to escape in the form of blasphemous words, she pasted a smile back on her face and withdrew her hand. "Mr. Sandleton was called away on business." The words almost choked her. Business indeed!

Andrew Kleeton lifted a golden brow. "He left his new bride to attend business? When do you expect him to return?"

They were innocent words, spoken as a mere formality, she was certain, with perhaps a hint of curiosity, but they magnified Noah's absence tenfold. "He'll return when his business is complete." Emily tried to keep the sharpness from her voice, but she heard it in every word like a screeching wild bird.

"Ah," he said. "He should take care not to leave his beautiful young bride alone for too long." A strange light shone in his clear blue eyes, and Emily felt at that very moment Andrew Kleeton knew she was lying and knew also that she had no idea where her husband was or when he would return.

She cleared her throat and looked away. "Yes, well, when I do see him, I will pass along your regards." She smoothed back her hair and picked up Allegra's reins. "It has been a pleasure to meet you, Mr. Kleeton."

"The pleasure has truly been all mine, Lady Sandleton." Casting his reins over the pommel of his black saddle, Andrew Kleeton stepped forward, stopping mere inches from Emily. She could smell the woodsy scent of his cologne. "A woman who rides bareback is rare indeed," he murmured.

Emily blushed. "I'm certain there are not many who would share your opinion."

"Then they are fools. Forcing people to fit into society's mold is a travesty that begets nothing but boring, self-righteous men and simpering, sniveling women."

Emily stifled a giggle. "I do happen to know quite a few men and women who fit that description."

A slow smile broke out on Andrew Kleeton's handsome face. He leaned forward and whispered, "So do I." The blue in his eyes deepened to match the morning sky.

Emily smiled back, enjoying the quiet camaraderie of the moment.

"Allow me to serve as your footman," he said, bending down and lacing his hands. She placed a booted foot into the makeshift stirrup and swung her other leg over her horse, thankful that she'd worn breeches this morning.

Andrew Kleeton stepped back and dusted his gloved hands on his doeskin breeches. "Has anyone informed you, Lady Sandleton," he said, crossing his arms over his chest, "that your current manner of dress would appall the ton?"

"You don't think they would appreciate these," she said, pointing to her black breeches, "as the height of fashion? Why ever not, Mr. Kleeton?" Emily placed both hands on her hips in mock indignation.

Taking a step closer, Andrew Kleeton tilted his head and studied her attire. Then he shrugged and said, "I have no idea. Some people can be so narrow-minded."

Emily threw back her head and laughed. "My thoughts exactly."

The ride back to the stables took no more than fifteen minutes. As she dismounted and rubbed down Allegra, Emily's thoughts returned to her new acquaintance. Andrew Kleeton was charming and handsome. In some ways, he reminded her of Christopher, with his quick wit and easy smile. She hoped the rest of her neighbors possessed equally pleasant dispositions. Time would tell.

"Don't you trust me to walk your horse down for you?" a gruff voice called out, disturbing Emily's thoughts.

She turned to find the groomsman, Henry Barnes, standing several feet behind her and Allegra, his wizened old face scrunched up and disapproving.

"Of course I do, Mr. Barnes. I'm just used to taking care of Allegra myself."

The old man moved closer, crossing his arms over his thin

chest. His beady black eyes moved from her to Allegra and back again. "I promised the master I'd take good care of you and see to yer horse's needs, and I aim to do just that."

"Master?" Emily asked, confused.

Henry Barnes nodded. "Yup. The master hisself came to see me 'bout you and yer horse. Asked me to give you both special attention, seein' as yer such a horse lover and all." He uncrossed his arms and scratched his gray head.

The breath caught in Emily's throat. "Mr. Barnes, are you talking about my husband?"

The old man looked at her like she'd gone mad. "Beggin' yer pardon, Lady Sandleton, but there ain't no other master here. Hasn't been one since 'is uncle died ten years back."

"Glenview Manor is a family estate?" She had assumed her new home was just that. A new home. Certainly not one inhabited by Noah's ancestors.

"Sure is. Been in the family for ages."

"And was his uncle an Englishman?" Emily asked, growing more confused by the moment. Noah was an American.

" 'Course he was. They all was a bunch of bluebloods, earls and dukes and the like. 'Til the master's father up and moved 'em all to America." Barnes's thin lips turned into a frown as he shook his head. "If that didn't cause quite a stir. Yessirree. Quite a stir." He reached a scrawny hand up to rub the gray and white stubble on his chin.

"Noah is English?" The words came out as nothing more than a squeak.

Henry Barnes's gray head bobbed up and down. "Not only is 'e English," he whispered, "but when 'is old man dies, 'e'll be a duke as well. Don't claim it though and none of us is 'sposed to talk about it. 'E wants us to call 'im Noah, but it just don't seem right."

Noah was English? English nobility, no less! Henry Barnes's words swam in her head, swirling around, faster and faster, until they made her dizzy.

"I thought he was an American," she said, as much to herself as to the old man standing beside her.

" 'E's both, in a way. 'Is father is as mean as sin. I remember 'im. Always jealous of his older brother, the duke. One day, there was this big falling out and the master's father scurried 'em all to America." He snapped his bony fingers. "Just like that. Overnight. The master weren't more 'n eight years old. It tore the duke apart to see 'em gone. He never married, never had no kids and they was all like 'is own, 'specially the master. 'E looked just like the duke."

"But he came back?" Emily asked. Her husband was a stranger. She really knew little about him other than his name. And one day that would have a title before it.

"When 'e was about fifteen, he jest appeared one day. Still don't know how he got 'ere, exactly. Never did say. Only thing he told 'is uncle was that 'e weren't never goin' back to America while 'is father was alive. 'E went to school 'ere. You know, all them fancy ones, and then 'e joined the Royal Navy for a while."

"But he didn't stay with them." She did know that he and Ian had met at sea and traveled the world together.

Henry Barnes screwed up his face a minute, tapping his finger on his temple. "Nah, he didn't stay too long. Couple years, maybe. But 'e always kept in touch with 'is uncle and when the old man died, this all became 'is." Barnes set his beady gaze on Emily. " 'E coulda' thrown us all out on our ears back then. But 'e didn't. No sirree. 'E kep' us all on, ev'ry last one of us, paid us full wages and not a soul livin' in the big house."

Noah? The same man who had walked out of their marriage without a backward glance had provided jobs and homes for an entire household that housed no master? For ten years? It was incredible. Almost unbelievable.

"I don't mean to sound uncaring, Mr. Barnes, but why? Why would anybody do such a thing?" Especially a man like Noah Sandleton?

"Ah, there's the question," the old man said, smiling. It was a knowing smile, a smile that intimated she didn't know much about the man. His master. Her husband. And Henry Barnes was right. She didn't know much about him. Not much at all, Emily decided. And she knew less as the minutes ticked by.

" 'E said we was like family to 'im when 'e lost 'is own in Virginia. That's where 'e lived in America." Emily nodded. That much she did know. " 'E jest wanted to repay us for takin' care o' 'im and 'is uncle." He paused. "Like family. That boy's like family to me. To all of us."

"Did he visit often?" She had always pictured Noah aboard a ship or in some exotic land with a beautiful woman, not on his family's estate, conversing with an aging, wiry groomsman.

Henry Barnes shrugged his bony shoulders. "Not as often as we woulda liked. 'E came at night and left at night. Never wanted nobody to know 'e was 'ere. Kinda like he was tryin' to be secretive. Always brought us lots a presents though. I got a silver statue of a horse and a Chinese vase with a wild stallion carved on it."

Why would Noah want to keep his whereabouts a secret? That made no sense at all. Emily would have to ponder Mr. Barnes's words in the privacy of her bedroom that evening. Heaven knew there would be little else happening in that room.

"Lady Sandleton, you wished to have a word with me?" Edward Billington, Glenview Manor's butler, approached the rose-colored sofa Emily sat on and stopped a few feet away. He towered over her, his tall, lanky frame standing at attention as he awaited his mistress's bidding.

"Why yes, Mr. Billington, there is something I wish to discuss with you." She looked up at him and doubted her neck would stand much more straining to converse with him. "First, you must do me the favor of having a seat." When she noticed his hesitancy, she insisted. "Please. If nothing else, you will ease the crook in my neck. You are quite a tall man," she said, smiling up at him.

Edward Billington did not return the smile as he lowered himself onto the sofa. He sat with his hands folded in his lap, watching her. Emily poured him a cup of tea without asking if he'd like any. She knew he would have refused had she given him the opportunity to do so. Tea always calmed her and she hoped it would do the same for Mr. Billington. She needed him to relax so she could question him about her conversation with Mr. Barnes. She wouldn't offer the occasional shot of brandy Christopher used to put in hers, though. She'd save that for herself, after the meeting.

"You seem to know quite a bit about Glenview Manor," she said, handing him his cup of tea. He accepted the proffered brew, but Emily could have sworn his gray eyes turned cold just a moment, as though he wanted to refuse. Of course, they both knew it would be extremely rude to do so and Edward Billington was anything but rude.

He nodded, but offered nothing more.

"I've been here a week and know little more than I did when I first arrived. I thought perhaps you could tell me a little about the history of Glenview Manor, the inhabitants, that sort of thing." Why I had to find out from the groomsman that my husband is British? And a nobleman, no less!

The butler cleared his throat. "I assumed Mr. Sandleton had discussed these matters with you," he said, studying the steam rising from the tea. Why wouldn't he look at her? He had shifted positions at least five times in the two minutes since he'd taken a seat. Emily noted he sat ram-rod straight, several inches from the back of the sofa. She wondered what was making him so uncomfortable.

"Unfortunately, no. Mr. Sandleton left before I could become familiar with his estate or his employees. I was hoping you would be able to provide me with that information." There, she'd thrown the gauntlet. He could not refuse.

Edward Billington cleared his throat. "What exactly would you like to know?"

No, he couldn't be rude, Emily thought, but he could be very difficult.

"Tell me about yourself. How long have you been employed here?"

"I am a relatively new member to Glenview Manor," he said.

That told her nothing. "How new?" she prodded.

He pursed his lips as though he didn't want to let the words out. "Two weeks."

"Two weeks?" she echoed. He seemed to know too much to have been there for such a short time. And the other members of the staff held him in very high regard. Anytime she questioned one of them about their master or his comings and goings, they deferred the questions to Billington. All except Henry Barnes. He had told her more about her husband in ten minutes than the whole lot of them had in a week's time. So what power did Edward Billington hold over the staff of Glenview Manor? Was he privileged in some way? Had Noah bestowed some special authority on him during his absence?

She looked at Edward Billington as he sat on the edge of the sofa, motionless yet waiting. Like a big cat about to pounce, or perhaps retreat. His cold gray eyes gave away nothing as he stared at her. He was hiding something. She sensed it. This man was more than a middle-aged butler with thinning hair. Much more.

"Excuse me for being bold, Mr. Billington, but I find it quite odd that you have been employed by Mr. Sandleton for a mere two weeks and yet the entire staff defers to you. Why," she said as she gave him a small smile, "if I didn't know better, I'd say you wielded more power than I do where the staff is concerned."

He cleared his throat and set his teacup down on the mahogany table in front of him. "I said I have been at Glenview

INTRODUCING BALLAD,
A BRAND NEW LINE OF HISTORICAL ROMANCES.

As a lover of historical romance, you'll adore Ballad Romances. Written by today's most popular romance authors, every book in the Ballad line is not only an individual story, but part of a two to six book series as well. You can look forward to four new titles a month – each taking place at a different time and place in history.

But don't take our word for how wonderful these stories are! Accept our introductory shipment of 4 Ballad Romance novels – a $22.00 value – ABSOLUTELY FREE – and see for yourself!

Once you've experienced your first four Ballad Romances, we're sure you'll want to continue receiving these wonderful historical romance novels each month – without ever having to leave your home – using our convenient and inexpensive home subscription service. Here's what you get for joining:

- 4 BRAND NEW Ballad Romances delivered to your door each month

- 25% off the cover price (a total of $5.50) with your home subscription

- a FREE monthly newsletter, *Zebra/Pinnacle Romance News,* filled with author interviews, book previews, special offers, and more!

- No risks or obligations…you're free to cancel whenever you wish… no questions asked.

To start your membership, simply complete and return the card provided. You'll receive your Introductory Shipment of 4 FREE Ballad Romances. Then, each month, as long as your account is in good standing, you will receive the 4 newest Ballad Romances. Each shipment will be yours to examine for 10 days. If you decide to keep the books, you'll pay the preferred home subscriber's price of $16.50 – a savings of 25% off the cover price! (Plus $1.50 shipping and handling.) If you want us to stop sending books, just say the word… it's that simple.

If the certificate is missing below, write to:

Ballad Romances, c/o Zebra Home Subscription Service, Inc.,
P.O. Box 5214, Clifton, New Jersey 07015-5214

OR call TOLL FREE 1-888-345-BOOK (2665)

Visit our website at www.kensingtonbooks.com

FREE BOOK CERTIFICATE

Yes! Please send me 4 Ballad Romances ABSOLUTELY FREE! After my introductory shipment, I will receive 4 new Ballad Romances each month to preview FREE for 10 days (as long as my account is in good standing). If I decide to keep the books, I will pay the money-saving preferred publisher's price of $16.50 plus $1.50 shipping and handling. That's 25% off the cover price. I may return the shipment within 10 days and owe nothing, and I may cancel my subscription at any time. The 4 FREE books will be mine to keep in any case.

DN050A

Name _____

Address _____

City _____ State _____ Zip _____

Telephone ( ) _____

Signature _____

(If under 18, parent or guardian must sign.)

For your convenience you may charge your shipments automatically to a Visa or MasterCard so you'll never have to worry about late payments and missing shipments. If you return any shipment we'll credit your account.

☐ Yes, charge my credit card for my "Ballad Romance" shipments until I tell you otherwise.
☐ Visa ☐ MasterCard

Account Number _____

Expiration Date _____

Signature _____

Orders subject to acceptance by Zebra Home Subscription Service. Terms and Prices subject to change. Offer valid only in the U.S.

Get 4 Ballad
Historical Romance Novels
FREE!

A $22 value — FREE! No obligation to buy anything — ever.

BALLAD ROMANCES
Zebra Home Subscription Service, Inc.
P.O. Box 5214
Clifton NJ 07015-5214

PLACE
STAMP
HERE

Manor for two weeks. I have been in Mr. Sandleton's employ for much longer than that.''

"Oh? How long and in what capacity?''

"Years. I've had various duties, depending on the need at the time.''

Emily could feel the heat rising to her face. The man was deliberately avoiding her questions. Why? "Mr. Billington, it is becoming quite clear to me that you do not wish to answer my questions.'' Her fingers clenched around the delicate china cup she held as she waited for his answer.

A full minute passed before Edward Billington opened his mouth to speak. "It is not that I refuse to answer your questions, Lady Sandleton, but I am employed by Mr. Sandleton and cannot divulge information without his permission.''

"Oh. And how exactly do you obtain permission, Mr. Billington, when my husband isn't here? No, don't bother to answer that, because I know you won't anyway.'' She set the teacup on the table before she crushed it between her hands. "Henry Barnes said my husband was here recently. Is that true?''

"Mr. Barnes speaks out of turn.''

"At least he speaks.''

"Fools speak all the time and rarely say anything.''

"Where is my husband?'' Emily threw the question at him like a volley from a cannon. She saw his momentary look of surprise. He recovered within seconds, the mask of indifference back in place so quickly that she almost imagined she'd seen the look. But she hadn't. It had been real. Edward Billington knew where Noah was.

"Lady Sandleton,'' he said. The words were stiff and very precise. "You are his wife, whereas I am only the butler. Certainly, if anyone knew Mr. Sandleton's whereabouts, it would be you.''

He was a smooth one. Emily had to grant him that. This man knew how to turn and twist a phrase to make her question her own words. Almost. Emily leaned back against the sofa and pasted a smile of serenity on her face. "One would most

certainly think so, Mr. Billington. Unfortunately, that is not the
case in this instance, as we are both well aware. I think you
know that my husband doesn't plan to return to Glenview
Manor. And I also think you know where he is and how to
contact him. But, since, as you say, you cannot speak on this
matter without his permission, we will pretend that he is
'unavailable' for an indefinite period of time.'' Emily leaned
forward, attempting to close the distance between them. Edward
Billington inched back toward the edge of the couch. ''There-
fore,'' she continued, her words strong and steady, ''until further notice, I will be in charge of running Glenview Manor.
All questions and decisions will be handled by me.''

"Certainly you do not wish to be bothered with such a
tedious chore, Lady Sandleton. Mr. Sandleton left very specific
instructions as to how the house should be run so as not to
interfere with whatever pursuits you may entertain.''

Emily noticed the slight twitch in his jaw. He wasn't happy
with her announcement but he was making a very good show
of remaining indifferent.

"Why, it's no bother at all. I look forward to working with
the staff and learning all about Glenview Manor. And, since
my husband left *specific* instructions as to how his home should
be run in his absence, I will be most anxious to review the list
as soon as possible.''

Edward Billington remained silent, his bony fingers crossed
over his knees. Emily noted his knuckles were white. A dull
flush crept up his neck, staining his face and ears. He was either
very angry or embarrassed at getting caught in a lie of his own
making. And Emily was fairly certain the *specific* instructions
he referred to were a fabrication.

"Well, I believe that will be all for the moment, Mr. Billington,'' she said, rising.

"Yes, Lady Sandleton,'' he replied, unfolding his lanky form
into a standing position. He nodded once and turned toward
the door.

"Ah, Mr. Billington?''

"Yes, Lady Sandleton?" He had reached the door in less than ten strides and had his hand on the knob, ready to bolt. His gaze remained on the oak door in front of him.

"I'll expect that list no later than tomorrow morning." There. Let him stew over that.

"Yes, Lady Sandleton." The door opened and he was gone before she could take another breath. Or give another command.

Emily smiled to herself, shaking her head. Edward Billington could try one's nerves with his cold stares and one-word responses. She knew no more about Noah's whereabouts than she did before her meeting. Walking to the sideboard, Emily grabbed a crystal decanter and headed for the sofa. She could use a nice, hot cup of tea, with just a hint of something stronger to relax her. Then again, she thought as she poured a healthy measure of amber liquid into her cup, perhaps she'd skip the tea this time.

Chapter 10

Noah called himself a hundred kinds of fool for the note he'd sent Emily telling her he missed her. It had been almost two weeks and he'd gotten no response. Not a word from her. What had he expected, anyway? Even if she had received the letter, which was highly unlikely with a brother like Ian, she might well have torn it to shreds without reading it. Or she might have read it first and then torn it to shreds. Emily probably considered him among the lowest vermin on the face of the earth after the way he'd married her, bedded her and deserted her. He'd had no business trying to contact her.

So, why in the hell had he? He tried to tell himself he hadn't broken his promise to Ian by sending the note. It was just his way of trying to ease the pain he'd caused her. And a feeble attempt to make himself seem not such a horrible cad. He must have failed miserably, though, because every hour that dragged on without a response from Emily told him she wasn't pining for him anymore. That was one thing he'd learned about his wife. The woman could carry a grudge, especially if she had a reason. Well, she had more than one. She had several in fact.

It had been a stupid thing to do, he told himself. Even if she had received the letter and responded in a positive manner, what could he have offered her? He'd given his word to Ian, and unless he wanted to challenge him to a duel, Noah had to keep his word and stay out of Emily's life. His emotions were getting the best of him. He was moody and in a bad temper most days. He'd tried to take his mind off of Emily by concentrating on his spice and silk business, setting up meetings and arranging shipments with various merchants. Filling in time, passing the hours. That's what he'd been doing. But it was time to get back to the water. He couldn't wait any longer for a message that wasn't coming. A message he had no business waiting for.

Tomorrow, he told himself. Tomorrow he would leave England and head for the Indies. There was no reason to postpone the inevitable any longer. Billington would serve as his eyes and ears, sending him detailed reports on his wife. But Billington wouldn't be able to describe the way her gray eyes sparkled when she laughed, or the golden highlights that danced through her hair when the sun shone on it a certain way. His account would not mention the faint scent of lilac that drifted about her or the soft murmur of her voice in the night.

It would only contain facts. Details. Appointments. Noah would have to settle for this. As long as she was safe, he would save the rest for his dreams and lose himself in the sweetness of remembering her each night as sleep took him. As long as she was safe, he would stay away. But if anyone or anything threatened that safety, nothing would keep him from his wife. Not a brother, not a best friend, not a vow, not a duel. He would die to keep her safe.

"Mr. Billington, I'm going riding. I expect to return in time for my afternoon tea." Emily stood in the middle of the oak hallway, adjusting the gold trim on the sleeve of her forest green riding habit.

"If I might say, Lady Sandleton, this is certainly a departure from your usual riding attire."

"Yes, it is indeed." She knew he was referring to the customary white shirt and breeches she wore every day for her early morning ride with Allegra.

"Is there any . . . ah . . . particular reason that you're dressed in such a fashion?"

How nosy of him, Emily thought. Well, at least he did have the good grace to be hesitant about it. Which meant he knew it was none of his business but he wanted to know anyway. Why? she wondered. So he could check it off on his list of *specific instructions?* Was checking up on his wife Noah's unwritten request? Emily shook her head. That whole ordeal had been a laugh. When Billington presented her with the list the following morning, there had been six handwritten directives, beginning and ending with "do not overburden Lady Sandleton with mundane details." The handwriting was bold, sloppy and totally unfamiliar.

Emily had accepted the proffered list without a word. She'd stared at the single page for several moments. How could she dispute anything when she couldn't identify the handwriting as her husband's? After all, the only writing she'd ever witnessed was his signature in the marriage register. She had not considered that little obstacle the day before when she'd been so adamant about obtaining the list. Of course, Noah could have written the list. But Edward Billington could have penned it also. Or perhaps it had been the cook, or the scullery maid. The fact was, it could have been written by anyone. There had been no choice but to let the matter drop with a curt nod and a murmured thank you.

"Lady Emily?" Mr. Billington inquired, taking a few steps forward to close the distance between them. "Might someone be joining you today?" He asked the question as though he had a right to a response, and expected one. Emily wondered for the third time in as many days what his relationship to her husband might be that he should assume such an arrogant attitude.

"Why yes, as a matter of fact, I am riding with a friend today." *You'll have to pry the rest of the information from me, you nosy man.* She turned from him and headed for the door. Emily had taken no more than three steps before she heard his very precise voice behind her.

"I was not aware that you had made any acquaintances since your arrival at Glenview Manor."

He's dying to know what I am up to. Hiding a smile, Emily pulled the heavy oak door open and looked at him over her shoulder. "Well, I have, Mr. Billington." She stepped outside still holding the door open. "And he's quite a handsome acquaintance at that." With those parting words, she pushed the door shut and hurried down the steps, breaking into a run as soon as her booted foot reached the ground. The stables were several hundred feet away from the main house, and Emily's riding habit made running any distance quite difficult. Oh, how she wished she'd worn breeches! She could hear the steady, forceful steps of Edward Billington closing in on her, but her skirt was too constricting, the fabric too heavy for her to break away from him.

"Lady Sandleton! Why are you running from me? Please stop!"

"I can't, Mr. Billington," she called back to him. "I'm already late."

She heard him huffing behind her. "If you'll just hold up a moment."

Emily stopped in her tracks, planting her feet in the grass. He was starting to annoy her with his persistence. What right did he have to question her? After all, he was only the butler. Wasn't he?

Edward Billington rounded on her, his face flushed, his breathing heavy. "You are"—he drew in a deep breath—"riding with a gentleman?"

"If that is any of your concern, Mr. Billington, which I seriously doubt, then yes, I am riding with a gentleman."

"Who?"

She pressed her lips together for a moment before a blasphemous word escaped. And there were several that ran through her brain.

"It really is none of your business," she told him, crossing her arms over her chest in agitation.

"But it is Mr. Sandleton's," he answered, copying her stance with his long arms folded in front of him.

Rage engulfed her, sinking into every pore of her body. "How dare you?" Her body started to tremble. "If Mr. Sandleton were concerned, he would be here, wouldn't he?" Emily's voice was bold and challenging.

Edward Billington's gaze shifted to a point beyond her. He remained silent.

"Exactly," Emily threw back, trying to ignore the hurt that his silence caused. Even the butler knew Noah didn't care about her.

She turned to leave, feeling dejected and so alone.

"He would want to know."

Those simple words ignited a fire in her blood, angering her all over again. Spinning on her heel, she faced Edward Billington, fists clenched, mouth tight. "If he wants to know, then he'll have to ask me himself."

"How long have you lived at Penworth, Mr. Kleeton?" Emily asked.

"I purchased the property two years ago, but have only been living there for the last six months." He smiled at her, revealing two deep-set dimples on either side of his mouth. "And please, call me Andrew. Mr. Kleeton reminds me of my father."

Emily smiled back at him. "All right. Andrew," she said, testing his name on her lips. "Then you must call me Emily."

"Fair enough."

They sat in an open meadow on the north side of Glenview Manor. Finches and starlings danced around them, with an occasional skylark darting into the path. The melodies they created were gentle, soothing notes carried along with the early afternoon breeze. Emily closed her eyes, trying to block out her confrontation with Mr. Billington. She let nature's music wrap its arms around her, easing her worries, dissolving her anger.

"There's nothing quite so beautiful as nature in all of its naked glory." Andrew's soft words reached her. She smiled, but her eyes remained closed, basking in the warm rays of sunshine on her upturned face.

"I've always preferred the country to city life," she confessed.

"So, you did not go to London during the season?"

"I went kicking and screaming," she said.

Andrew laughed. "Well, I was there and I didn't notice anyone kicking or screaming. Wait a moment. I take that back. There were a few confirmed bachelors who got snagged by determined future mothers-in-law. Right into the marriage market, with their heads still spinning."

Emily laughed, opening her eyes to see his grin. He looked like a Greek god, his long blond hair bathed in sunlight, his skin a deep honeyed tone reflected by the rays. His handsome face was unmarred. There were no scars, bumps or bruises. No crooks in his nose. A vision of Noah's battered face the last time she'd seen him popped before her eyes. She blinked it away. Her smile faded.

"Emily?" She heard the concern in his voice.

Forcing a gaiety she no longer felt, Emily said, "Tell me, Andrew, how did you avoid being 'snagged' by some young girl's mother? Did you hide in a closet?"

"Emily!" he pretended outrage. "Of course not! Do you think me a coward? Not I," he vowed, grinning. "When I saw some willful mother approaching me with her simpering daughter, I merely pulled the nearest old woman into my arms and began dancing with her. It drove the mothers mad. And made my dance partners giggle like young schoolgirls. Quite a civilized way to avoid being captured, I might add.''

Emily laughed, forgetting about the shadow that had doomed her high spirits a few moments before. "You are incorrigible, Andrew Kleeton."

"Thank you, m'lady." He bowed his head in mock sincerity. "I wish I had met you last season. Then I might have swept you off your feet before Sandleton got to it."

His words were light and teasing, but there was no humor in the blue gaze that settled over her. It was dark, intense, and deadly serious. Emily shifted, uncomfortable with the way he was looking at her. She tried to lighten the mood. "Ah, Andrew, you say that now that I am a married woman, but I'll wager had I looked at you twice, you would have dragged *two* old ladies onto the floor."

"Perhaps," he said. "Then again," he sighed, all seriousness gone, "perhaps not."

She shook her head and laughed. Emily liked the man. He reminded her of Christopher. Andrew was intelligent and witty, and he possessed an amazing sense of humor. Like Christopher.

"I suppose we should be getting back," Andrew said, standing up and brushing bits of tall grass from his clothes. He held out his hand to Emily and she accepted the gesture, placing her hand in his. Her eyes drifted to the soft leather that covered his right hand. And his left.

"A war injury," Andrew said, following her gaze.

"I'm sorry," Emily said, looking away.

"Don't be. It happened a long time ago. I got tired of women fainting at the sight of all the scars, so I bought gloves. Boxes and boxes of them. All different colors, styles, textures."

"How clever," Emily said, slipping her hand from his and walking toward Allegra. The sun was high above them now, indicating they'd been out at least a few hours. It was time to head back to Glenview Manor. And the worrisome, inquisitive Mr. Billington.

The horses were chomping the tall grass, filling their bellies as they trimmed a path for her. Emily patted Allegra's neck, crooning soft words to her. Then, reaching for the reins, she mounted and turned toward Andrew. He was standing very still, his hand shielding the hot sun from his eyes, staring off into the distance. Emily followed his gaze, wondering what held his attention.

Off in the far distance, perhaps several hundred yards away, sat a lone figure on a horse. He seemed to be watching them.

"Andrew, do you know who that is?" Emily asked, a tiny prickle of apprehension running through her. Was someone spying on them? Who? And why?

"He's too far away to tell much," Andrew said.

"Why would anyone be—" the words hung in midsentence, unfinished. Billington! It had to be him. She couldn't wait to get back to the house to give him a piece of her mind. Spying, indeed! "I know who the culprit is, Andrew."

Not taking his eyes from the horse and rider, he replied. "You do? Who is it, Emily?"

"My overzealous, overprotective butler, Mr. Billington." She tapped her riding crop in her hand, beating a rapid staccato. "And I will take care of the situation as soon as I return to Glenview Manor."

Emily left Andrew at the corner of their properties, apologizing again for her butler's rude behavior. Andrew seemed quite bothered by the whole incident, almost outraged, vowing to intervene if Emily deemed it necessary. He felt someone had to look out for her welfare in her husband's absence. She didn't have the heart to tell him that was exactly what Billington thought he was doing by spying on her. Or that her husband might well have been the one to encourage such behavior. No, she was not about to discuss Noah with Andrew.

When she reached the stables, she dismounted and went in search of Henry Barnes. He was in one of the stalls, tending to a huge black stallion. She guessed it was Noah's. He had a wild, untamed look about him, as though he tolerated civilization, but barely. Like his master, Emily thought. Probably just wanted to be free. Like his master.

"Mr. Barnes," Emily began, trying to control the anger burning in her gut, "did Mr. Billington leave about two hours ago with one of the horses?"

The old man scratched his scraggly gray head. "No, ma'am."

He had to have taken one of the horses. Emily tried again. "He didn't come to you and request you saddle up a mount for him?"

That got a laugh from Henry Barnes. "No, ma'am. That old bag o' bones can't ride no horse. Hah!" He chuckled to himself.

"Well, then, did _anyone_ come to you and request one of the horses?" she asked.

"That'd be Jack," he said, nodding his head.

"Jack?"

"Jack, the stable boy," he said, as though that should mean something to her.

"Jack, the stable boy," she repeated, nodding her head in total confusion.

"Sure," he said, rubbing the gray stubble on his chin. "I sent 'im out after you."

"You did?"

"Sure. When I sees you all dressed up like one o' them fair ladies from town, I got to wonderin' wot was wot. An' since I promised the master ta make sure you was safe, I sent young Jack out."

"Noah—I mean Mr. Sandleton asked you to watch out for me?" This was incredible. Did the man have the whole staff on alert? If he cared so much, why didn't he just come home?

"Sure did. 'E knew I was good ta my word, or me name's not 'enry Barnes."

"But Mr. Barnes, you had no right to have Jack follow me." Did none of these people understand their positions?

"Had to. Yer the master's wife. Have ta keep you safe fer 'im."

"I see," Emily said. But she didn't. She thought the whole lot of them were crazy, including their master. Correction. Especially their master. What were they keeping her safe from? The only harm that had come to her since marrying Noah was a broken heart and he had been the cause of it.

"Heard ya went out with a man." He shook his head. "Should'na done that. The master ain't gonna like it."

"Who did you hear that from?" She had a sneaking suspicion she already knew.

"Ol' Billington. Crusty lot, ain't 'e?"

Among other things, Emily thought.

Henry Barnes laughed again. A full-bellied laugh that turned into a dry wheeze. "Ya shoulda seen ol' Billington run out 'ere, hollerin' up a storm ta git a body ta follow you. I done told 'im I already had Jack saddlin' up."

"Mr. Barnes, why were the two of you so concerned? I went riding with a neighbor. Period. Andrew Kleeton is a nice man. It was all perfectly innocent."

The old man cocked his head to the side, rubbing his chin again. "In all my years I learn'd one thing. Nothin' is ev'r perfectly innocent." He nodded his head, his black eyes narrowing on her. "Jest you remember that."

Emily wanted nothing more than to take a nap. It had been a trying afternoon and she felt bone tired. She'd decided to skip afternoon tea today. A soft, warm bed was much more appealing. Halfway up the winding staircase, she heard Edward Billington's voice.

"Did you have a nice ride today, Lady Sandleton?"

She whirled around to find him standing two steps behind her. Where had he come from? Emily hadn't heard him behind her. She must be so tired it was affecting her senses.

"Why yes, I did have a most enjoyable time today, Mr.

Billington.'' Putting special emphasis on her next words, she said, ''With the exception of the spy you and Mr. Barnes sent after me.''

Edward Billington's lips twitched. It was the closest thing to a smile Emily had ever seen on him. ''Do not consider him a spy, Lady Emily. He was more of an . . . observer.''

''An observer? And what exactly was he supposed to observe?'' Emily gripped the oak railing, pressing her fingers against the hard wood, willing her nerves to settle down.

''He was supposed to make certain that you were in no threat of danger,'' he replied.

Emily threw her hands up in the air. ''Danger!'' she cried. ''What sort of danger could possible overtake me in the middle of the country, Mr. Billington? There is nothing, I repeat, *nothing* here to cause me danger! The only thing jeopardizing my safety is the way you are treating me. It's enough to make me crazy!''

Edward Billington looked at her as though she'd already gone mad. It was then that Emily remembered where they were: on the staircase, in plain view and certainly in shouting distance for the rest of the household to observe their little confrontation. She peeked over the railing and saw several pairs of eyes staring back at her. They must have feared they would be the next targets of their mistress's wrath, for they scattered like dust, disappearing down the hall within seconds.

''Now, Mr. Billington,'' she said, turning back to the butler with as much dignity as she could muster, considering she had just created a scene in front of the entire household. ''I would like this foolishness to cease at once. I am not a child, and I do not expect to be treated as one.'' She took a deep breath. ''If, as you say, you are only following my husband's instructions, then I apologize for directing my anger towards you, but unless Mr. Sandleton relays his wishes to me directly and the reasons for them, this behavior must end immediately.'' *And since we both know he isn't coming back, this is a very polite way of telling you that I will take charge of my own life, thank you very much.* "Do we understand one another?"

"I understand what you are saying, Lady Sandleton."

Ah yes, he understands but he hasn't *agreed* to my terms. Clever. Very clever, indeed.

"And you will agree?" she persisted. I'll get him to say yes if I have to pull the words out of those thin lips.

Edward Billington stood ramrod straight and shook his balding head. "Unfortunately, no, I cannot abide by your wishes, Lady Sandleton. I have Mr. Sandleton's orders."

"To treat me as though I'm in prison?" Her voice shook in anger and frustration. "I am not permitted to ride my horse with a neighbor unless a spy is sent along for me? Will you be sending someone in to watch me sleep as well to be certain I don't try to escape in the night?"

"The neighbor—"

"Is a very nice, harmless man," Emily finished for him. "His name is Andrew Kleeton. He has resided at Penworth for the last six months, though he purchased the place over two years ago. His manners are impeccable. He behaved the perfect gentleman." She held out her hand and began ticking his attributes off on her fingers. "Mr. Kleeton has blond hair, blue eyes, medium build. Let's see," she said, tapping her finger to her chin. "Ah, yes. He is an excellent horseman and I believe, a confirmed bachelor, though he did travel to London for the season. He's also a superb dresser who wears gloves because of his scars."

"Scars?" The word was little more than a whisper.

"Yes, scars. It seems he suffered some terrible kind of accident that left his hands bad off. His solution was to purchase gloves in every style and color. Clever of him, wasn't it?"

"Very clever."

"Fortunately for him, the accident didn't seem to impair the use of his hands." She reached into the side pocket of her skirt and pulled out a card. "He sent me his card." She thrust it at him. "The penmanship is perfect, don't you agree?"

The butler didn't answer. He stood staring at the crisp white paper, his eyes narrowed to mere slits.

"Mr. Billington? What is it?" Emily peered at the card, lying open in his hand. Then she laughed. "I told you he was clever. Who would have thought to put that in there," she said, pointing to a silver-embossed design at the bottom of the card. "What is that little creature anyway? A snake?"

"Or a serpent. Either way, just as deadly."

Noah banged on the door again. He knew that two in the morning was well past the sociable hour to be calling, but this was urgent business. And Ian had damn well better be home. He was raising his fist to pound on the door again when it swung open. A startled young man dressed in a dark blue robe holding a lantern stood before him, terror written on his face. The butler. Noah remembered him and the way he used to gawk and stammer after Emily. He sympathized with the poor boy. Emily could tie him in knots and he was a grown man.

"M-M-May I help you, Mr. Sandleton?" he asked, not moving from the door.

"You could help me by letting me in," Noah said.

"C-C-Certainly, Mr. Sandleton." The boy was nervous, that much was obvious. Was he afraid of him? What had Ian told everyone about him? That he was a no-good rakehell who deserted his wife and beat on little children?

Noah pushed past the butler and stepped inside, removing his greatcoat. He was tired. Bone weary. That's what traveling nonstop for three days straight did to a man. No, he thought. That's what being married to Emily did to a man. He'd been mad with worry since the second he opened Billington's missive marked URGENT. Twenty minutes later, Noah was on his way back to England. Fortunately, they were in port along the coast and the *Falcon* had not been difficult to locate. And Billington had been with Noah long enough to know exactly where to look.

"I could use a drink," Noah said.

"C-C-Certainly, sir," the boy stumbled over his words. "W-Would you like coffee? Tea?"

"I was thinking more along the lines of whiskey."

The butler turned a deep rose. "O-O-Of course. F-F-Follow me, sir." He turned on his heel and headed down the long hall. The only sounds of night were the shuffling of the butler's slippers and Noah's booted feet following behind.

Once inside the study, the young man lit another lamp and then watched as Noah poured himself a whiskey.

"Come here, boy," Noah said. He tilted his head and threw back the whiskey in one gulp. He poured another.

The butler inched forward.

"For God's sake, I'm not going to hurt you. What's your name?" Why was everybody always afraid of him? Was he that intimidating?

"P-P-Pierce, sir. John Pierce."

"Well then, Pierce, come over here." He poured a second. "Here," he said, holding out the glass of whiskey. "Drink this."

"B-B-Begging your pardon, Mr. Sandleton, but I don't drink." Now his face looked purple. How could one face change colors so many times?

"Well, Pierce, tonight is an exception. Because as soon as you finish that drink, I'm going to ask you to go and wake Lord Kenilworth. Now come on, boy," he coaxed, nudging the glass into his hands. "Drink up."

Pierce eyed the amber liquid once more, as though it might be a brew from the devil himself, before he raised it to his lips, closed his eyes and swallowed. He coughed, sputtered, choked and gasped for a full minute. When he finished, Noah smiled, saluting him with his own glass. He downed it in one healthy swallow with a deliberate smoothness that only came with years of practice.

"Well done, Pierce. Well done. Now, it's time to go get him."

Pierce disappeared, stumbling a little in his hurry to obey. Or did he stumble in his hurry to be rid of Noah? Perhaps he really did instill fear in men, even when it was not his intention to do so. Why then hadn't it worked on his own wife? She'd certainly never feared him.

Emily. God, how he missed her. Billington's report had concentrated on this Kleeton fellow and his note. There had been very little mention of Emily herself, other than to say she seemed quite upset by his absence. Good. He hoped she missed him half as much as he missed her. If he had his way, it wouldn't be long before he'd see her again.

"What the hell are you doing here?" Ian's deep voice filled the room.

Noah turned around and nodded. "Nice to see you again too, brother-in-law."

"Damn you, Noah, why are you here?"

"Unfortunately, it's not a social call," he said, rubbing the back of his neck. God, but he felt every one of his thirty-one years. "Close the door, Ian."

Ian flung the door shut and stalked over to him, closing the distance between them in six long strides. "Talk. Now. You've got ten minutes." He folded his arms over his chest and stared at Noah.

Ian would never listen to him in his current mood. It was darker than black. Noah had to ease the tension between them. "Do you really wear all those clothes to bed?" he asked, gesturing to the blue silk pajamas and burgundy robe.

"Nine minutes."

Maybe that sort of humor couldn't be appreciated at this hour of the morning. He'd try another tactic. "If you're thinking of hitting me again, could you please avoid the nose area? You broke it last time and it still smarts."

"Eight."

Forget trying to change his mood. He always was something of a spoil-sport. Stubborn spoil-sport. "It's about Emily."

"Six."

"What happened to seven?"

"You just lost two minutes when you mentioned her name."

Noah took a deep breath and looked down at his whiskey glass. Empty. His gaze clashed with Ian's. "It's about Emily *Sandleton. My wife.*" He paused between each word, letting the silence heighten their meaning.

"One."

Noah ignored him. "She's been seeing one of her new neighbors." He hated the sound of that. It bothered him to think she might be interested in someone else when he couldn't get her out of his mind, day or night.

"Sounds like you've got a problem." Ian's tone was smug and not in the least sympathetic.

"His name is Andrew Kleeton. He's been at Penworth about six months. Obviously, I've never met him. Or heard about him until now, which concerns me."

"So he prefers beautiful women over men," Ian said in his usual dry manner.

Noah shook his head. "If it were only that simple. He sent Emily his card the other day inviting her to go riding with him and do you know what was on the card?" Without waiting for Ian to respond, Noah plowed forward. "It was an embossed drawing of a serpent."

"And?" He seemed nonplussed by Noah's revelation.

"A *serpent,* Ian."

"Are you trying to tell me you think it's Crowlton?"

Noah shrugged. "I don't know. But I damn well intend to find out."

"Wait a minute," Ian said, raising a large hand. "This all sounds very speculative and quite premature. The man's apparent fondness for reptiles does not make him a killer."

"My man, Billington, also told me Kleeton wears gloves all the time. Seems he was in a bad accident some time ago that left his hands scarred."

That got Ian's attention. "A fire?"

"Possibly," Noah agreed. "I think Emily may be in danger. If he is the Serpent, he may try to use her to get to me."

Ian let out a long breath. "I think I need a drink." He walked over to the side table and poured himself a whiskey.

"I want to go to her, Ian," Noah said.

"Impossible." He lifted the glass and drained it in one swallow. Then he poured himself another.

"She needs protection. Someone to be there all the time. Watch over her. Make certain she's safe. And keep an eye on Kleeton."

"I can do that from here. I'll bring her back to Marbrook," Ian said matter-of-factly.

"Do you really think she'll go with you? She's just settled into a new home and is not going to want you hauling her back here for no good reason. You can't tell her the truth without putting her in more jeopardy." He joined Ian at the side table and poured himself another whiskey. After taking a healthy swallow, he said, "So, what would you tell her, Ian?"

"I'll think of something. She might not like it, but she'll listen to me."

"Even if she does agree, you can't put the rest of your family at risk. Every one of you would be targets, including Augusta and the baby."

Ian was silent for several minutes and Noah could almost see his mind working, turning over possibilities, weighing obstacles, trying to determine the best course of action. Ian always had been a great tactician. That's one of the reasons he'd been such a great spy. When he spoke, his voice was quiet and firm. "I'll hire a bodyguard to stay with her at Glenview Manor."

"Who, Ian?" Noah asked, feeling the first waves of desperation wash over him, dragging him into the undertow, leaving him powerless. "Who but you and I would know how to handle a man like the Serpent?" Noah's left hand formed a fist as he tried to maintain control. His voice shook when he continued. "No one, and you know it." He was going to Emily, with or without Ian's permission. Before the end of the meeting, Ian would understand that. It would just be a hell of a lot easier having him on his side.

"We could contact the Crown and tell them of our suspicions," Ian said.

"And what would we tell them? I found a man living next to me who uses embossed serpents on his calling cards and wears gloves all the time? They'd think we were mad. Probably tell us we'd been on one too many missions." He rifled a hand through his hair. "It's not enough for them, Ian. They wouldn't bother with it and you know it."

"You're probably right."

"I'm going to her, Ian." There. He'd said those same words over and over in his head since the moment he'd read Billington's missive.

Ian's blue eyes narrowed. "What did you say?"

Noah met his level gaze and repeated, "I'm going to her." Ian crooked his head to one side, studying him. "Why?"

Noah stared at him. "Jesus, Ian, do you have to ask me that? I haven't slept in three days for worrying about her. Thinking I might get there too late. I *need* to see her and make certain she's safe. I'll go crazy if I'm not there. I have to protect her." He started pacing the room.

"Why couldn't you have displayed such honor a few weeks ago? *Before* you seduced her? Then she wouldn't even be in this predicament." His words stung like salt in a wound. An open, bleeding, raw wound. Noah had been tormenting himself with those same thoughts for the past three days.

He stopped his pacing and turned to face Ian. His voice was hoarse when he answered. "I love her, Ian. More than life itself." The bold, honest words left him feeling open and exposed.

"Does she know?"

Noah shook his head.

"If I do agree that you should go, how do you plan to keep

her safe? It's obvious that you can't present yourself as you are. If Kleeton didn't shoot you, Emily would.''

''I've got it all planned out. I wasn't known as the Chameleon for nothing,'' he said, referring to the code name he used during his espionage days. Noah's specialty had been transformation, walking into a building as a young man and hobbling out an old one. He could turn into anything given the right makeup and props.

''You'll go in disguise.'' Ian said, a hint of a smile on his face.

''The name's Cyrus Mandrey,'' Noah replied, lowering his voice to a raspy imitation of his character. ''I'm going to have bushy brown hair and a beard and mustache,'' he continued in that same voice. ''With glasses this thick.'' His fingers extended an inch. ''And nobody, but nobody's going to touch Lady Sandleton.''

''Even her husband?'' Ian asked, raising a dark brow.

Noah dropped the guise. ''About that promise, Ian. Would you consider releasing me from it?'' He braced himself, preparing for the worst, praying for the best.

Ian rubbed his chin. ''I never thought you'd fall in love and certainly not with my little sister. I don't think it's my decision any longer, Noah. Now, it's up to Emily.''

''I just want to know that when this is all over, I can try to win my wife back without worrying about you showing up with a pistol.''

''Agreed.''

''Or a strong left hook.''

Ian laughed, a full deep sound that echoed in the quiet room. ''Now, let's have a drink and settle the details. If that bastard is still alive, I want him exposed as soon as possible.''

Chapter 11

"Ian!" Emily shrieked, bounding across the room to throw herself into her brother's arms. "It's so good to see you!" She hugged him tight. "I've missed you."

He smiled, putting his big arms around her. "And I've missed you, Emily." Ian looked down at her. "It's pretty boring without you. There's no one running around the house screaming and yelling, getting into mischief." He hugged her tighter. "Well, I take that back. Lucas is moving around a little and he can let out a pretty good holler when he's hungry."

Emily laughed. "How is my little nephew?" she asked, her voice softening as she thought of him.

"He's wonderful and getting bigger every day." He released her but kept hold of her hands. "Let me have a look at you." His smile deepened as he studied her through blue eyes the color of an evening sky. Emily still thought him the most handsome man she'd ever met. Handsome and exasperating, she thought, remembering the argument that erupted between them the last time she'd seen him. He'd wanted her to stay at Marbrook and she'd wanted to venture off to Glenview Manor.

"I have something for you," he said, reaching into his vest pocket and pulling out a letter. "It's from Chris."

"Christopher!" She took the letter and hugged it to her chest.

"Go ahead, open it. I'll pour myself some tea while you read it."

Emily raced to the sofa and sat down, studying her name on the outside of the letter. Emily St. Simon. Christopher would have no way of knowing what had happened during the past several weeks. She wasn't certain she wanted to tell him. Not when everything had turned out so badly.

She read the letter twice, all six pages of it. He described the beauty of the land, from the rolling hills to the blossoms on the dogwood and cherry trees. The soil was the color of terra-cotta and just as hard, which made running a plantation a great challenge. There were hundreds of acres of tobacco plants, all thriving in the warm, sunny Virginia climate. It was nothing like England and Christopher loved everything about it. Emily wondered if he'd met any interesting women yet, or perhaps a woman who might hold a special interest for him. She thought it was time to bring it up in her next letter. After all, he was twenty-eight and the only remaining unmarried St. Simon. But she might not tell him that. How could she possibly explain that she had married the man who helped him get to Virginia, but he had abandoned her on the night of their wedding?

She would sound like a complete fool if she told him that. Maybe she could just tell him that Noah and she had gone their separate ways, but he was providing a very comfortable lifestyle for her with the exception of a nosy butler and an overprotective staff. Christopher would see right through that ruse. He knew she would never settle for an arrangement of any kind. No, not her. She had to dive headfirst into anything she tackled. Even love. There was no halfway about it. She was a fool.

Perhaps she should just stick to niceties and talk about the weather, Allegra and maybe a few old excursions with Belle.

And she probably should make mention of coming to America again, since every letter she'd ever penned had begged him to convince Ian to permit her to join him. If she said nothing about it, he would become suspicious. The truth was, she no longer had the burning need to get there and she knew why: Noah.

Emily folded the letter and stuck it in the pocket of her lilac day dress. *Oh, Christopher, I fell in love, just like you said I would one day. But you didn't tell me he might not love me back. You never told me that.*

"Are you happy here, Emily?"

Ian's words sliced through her thoughts. "As happy as a woman can be under these circumstances," she answered, her voice soft and wistful like a summer breeze dancing through the night.

Ian's thick brows drew together in a frown, but he remained silent, waiting for her to continue.

She leaned forward and poured herself a cup of tea. Next came two lumps of sugar and a drop of cream. As she stirred the hot brew, Emily watched the swirling designs the spoon made as the cream blended into the tea. Blended and disappeared, leaving only a trace behind. Just like her husband, who'd worked his way into her heart, marking her forever, and then disappeared.

"Living as a married woman without a husband is not a situation I ever considered," she said, sipping her tea.

"You could be a married woman living with a husband you detest," Ian offered.

Emily smiled at her brother over the rim of her cup. Dear Ian. Situations of the heart always made him uncomfortable. "Yes, well, there is that to be thankful for."

"Speaking of that situation, there is something I wish to discuss with you," Ian said.

Her hand jerked and a small spot of tea sloshed onto her lilac gown. "What situation?" Noah? Ian was going to discuss *Noah* with her?

"I'm concerned Noah might try to return to Glenview Manor."

"Ridiculous." Noah would never return. He'd made his choice and it hadn't been her.

"I have reason to believe that he might try," Ian said. "For a time, anyway."

"He wouldn't dare," Emily said through clenched teeth.

"Noah sent me a letter telling me he would like to see you again," Ian said, his eyes trained on her.

"He did?" She swallowed hard. He wanted to see her again? "Well, does he plan to come alone or would he be bringing Desireé and Monique too?"

Ian almost choked. "What do you know about Desireé and Monique?"

"They're his mistresses." She waved a hand in the air as though it were of no consequence to her. Inside she was seething, angry with Noah for being such a worthless scoundrel, and with herself for the tears she'd wasted over him.

"They'll be available, I'm sure," Ian said.

When he tires of his wife, Emily thought. Damn the man. Did he think he could just walk back into her life without so much as an apology or an explanation and she would accept him with open arms? Well, he could think again.

"Of course, I told him it was out of the question. I said you had no desire to see him. But Noah never has been a gentleman. He'll do what he wants. Or try to, anyway. That's why I've taken certain precautions to ensure your safety," Ian said, standing and walking toward the door. "I'll be back in a moment." He opened the door and murmured something to Billington, who must have been standing right outside. Spying on her, no doubt. Emily knew firsthand how easy it was to "overhear" a conversation through a door.

Emily heard a soft, raspy voice a moment before she saw a tall, burly man enter. Her gaze riveted to his hair. There was so much of it. Everywhere. It covered his head like a brown, bushy nest, falling to just below his shoulders. His eyebrows formed a straight, thick line and his mustache flowed into a full beard that extended a good two inches below where she thought his chin might be. He wore thick spectacles that distorted the shape of his eyes and she was much too far away to discern their color. Emily guessed there was no more than a few inches of skin on his face that wasn't covered with hair or spectacles.

"Emily, I'd like you to meet Cyrus Mandrey," Ian said. "Your protector."

The bushy-haired man nodded and said, "It's a pleasure to meet you, Lady Sandleton."

"My . . . protector?" she echoed, darting a puzzled look at Ian.

"Mr. Mandrey is going to make *certain* Noah doesn't bother you," Ian said.

"But that's absurd. And totally unnecessary." Emily shook her head in disbelief. A hired protector? Ridiculous.

"Emily," Ian said in that tone that told her he was tired of their bantering. "The only way I will allow you to remain at Glenview Manor is if Mr. Mandrey stays with you."

"But Ian—"

He cut her off before she could say more. "Or else I will take you back to Marbrook in the morning."

Emily took a deep breath, trying to find a way to reason with her brother. She had no need of a protector. Especially not one that looked more like an animal than a human being.

"I don't mean to be difficult," she began, keeping her voice level so he wouldn't detect her growing irritation. "But I don't need a protector. Noah may be a lot of things, but he would never hurt me."

"I'm not concerned about physical violence. I'm talking about the emotional wreckage he'd leave behind," Ian said, his voice rising with every word, "with his *inevitable* departure. And he would leave, Emily. It's in his blood. Maybe not right away. It might take several weeks or months. Perhaps even a year. But one day, when you've just come to believe he'll be with you forever, he'll be gone. You'll wake one morning to find a note on your pillow. No apologies, no excuses. And you'll live each day after that wondering when or if you will ever see him again. Do you really want to live that kind of life?''

Emily closed her eyes and shook her head. She couldn't speak for the lump in her throat. It felt like one of Mrs. Florence's biscuits was lodged there, making it difficult to breathe and impossible to speak. Ian was right, of course. Seeing Noah again would only spell disaster. Tears pooled in her eyes as she met Ian's gaze.

He stepped forward and took her cold hands in his. When he spoke his voice was gentle and soothing. ''I don't want you to go through what you did last time,'' he said. ''It was much too painful. For all of us.'' Emily knew he was referring to the days after Noah's departure when she'd remained abed in a deep, depressive sleep, refusing to eat or drink.

Cyrus Mandrey cleared his throat. ''If I may be so bold as to speak, Lady Sandleton. Perhaps your husband regrets his actions and wishes to make honest retribution. Perhaps he wishes nothing more than to see his wife again and grow into old age with her.''

Emily stared at the bushy half-animal, half-man standing before her. How dare he speak to her about Noah's possible intentions? He knew nothing about Noah other than what Ian had told him. ''If you believe that, even as a *remote* possibility,'' she said, her words as cold as a winter storm, ''then you are implying that my husband has a heart and a conscience. I know firsthand that he possesses neither.'' Dismissing him with her eyes, Emily turned to Ian. ''I accept your proposal. At least for a while, until we are certain there are no attempts to return. Please discuss the details with Mr. Mandrey, giving him any background information he might deem necessary. And make it perfectly clear that I do not wish to hear any further speculation from him as to why my husband may be trying to contact me.''

Ian nodded. "It's for the best, Emily."

She didn't respond. "Now if you'll excuse me, I feel a headache coming on."

"Oh course." Ian gave her a brief hug. Emily ignored Cyrus Mandrey altogether as she brushed past him on her way to the door, but she felt his eyes follow her, watching her every move.

When the door closed behind her, Noah dropped the guise of Cyrus Mandrey and his words rushed out in low, fierce tones. "Did you have to paint such a black picture of me? She hates me! Did you see the look in her eyes when you mentioned my name?"

Ian laughed, not trying to hide his amusement. "I told you that you'd have to win her back."

"But you didn't tell me you were going to make it so difficult," Noah said, scowling.

"I had to make her realize the danger of letting Noah back into her life," Ian said, all traces of humor gone. "It was the only way I could get her to accept the presence of Cyrus Mandrey. And we need him to protect Emily and investigate Kleeton."

"I can't wait to meet Andrew Kleeton," Noah said, slipping back into Cyrus Mandrey's raspy voice.

"I'm certain you will soon enough, my man. Soon enough."

Noah sat at a small table in one of the guest bedrooms. He would have preferred sleeping in the master suite. Right next door to his wife. Or, better yet, with his wife in his bed. But that would have to wait. The success of this mission depended largely on Noah's ability to convince Emily that he was nothing more than a bodyguard with absolutely no resemblance to her husband.

He had tried to change his physical appearance as much as possible. The bushy hair on his head, the full mustache and beard, the thick glasses, and the extra padding in his shirt were attempts to achieve that goal. A slow, shuffling gait replaced his usual purposeful stride. And when he spoke, the smooth warm, sensual tone that turned many a woman's knees to jelly became Cyrus Mandrey's gravelly voice, not unlike the sound of sand rubbing on paper.

"I want you to tell me everything you know about Andrew Kleeton," he said, leaning forward to whisper the words. He remembered his wife's uncontrollable penchant for eavesdropping. For all he knew, she could be on the other side of the door right then.

"Most of what I know I included in the missive I sent you." Edward Billington sat in a companion chair of cream and pale green brocade, his lanky form bent forward toward Noah. "Apparently, Penworth belonged to the Duke and Duchess of Twidale until their deaths two years ago. Kleeton purchased the property at that time, but did not take up residence until six months ago. As for the man himself," Billington continued, placing one long, bony finger on his chin, "he is of medium build, longish blond hair, light blue eyes, dimples on either side of his mouth, perfect unblemished face. One might consider him quite handsome if one were interested in that sort of thing."

Noah rubbed his nose. His crooked, twice-broken nose. "Does Lady Emily seem 'interested in that sort of thing'?" Noah knew he shouldn't have asked the question. He really didn't think he wanted to know the answer, and yet he *had* to know.

Billington looked at him, his long face showing no surprise over the strange question. "No, I wouldn't say she seemed interested."

Noah breathed a small sigh of relief. When this whole ordeal was over he was going to have a difficult enough time winning Emily over without any outside complications.

"Though it's hard to tell." Billington's words struck him in the gut like a lead ball.

"Oh?"

"Well, sir, I have only observed them together on one occasion, and that was yesterday when Mr. Kleeton came to take

Lady Emily riding. It's difficult to formulate an opinion based on such limited information.''

He should have known better than to ask Billington a question involving emotions.

"Forget I asked,'' Noah said, annoyed with himself for asking the question in the first place. "Let's move on. What about his hands?''

"Gloved. To somewhere above the wrist, but I couldn't determine how far.''

"Well, we'll have to find a way to get them off, won't we?'' Noah asked, crossing his arms behind his head and stretching his booted feet in front of him.

Billington's lower lip twitched. "My thoughts exactly, sir.''

"Good. Are there any other matters we need to discuss?''

"Well, there is one small situation that I would like to bring up.'' Billington's mouth puckered up as though he'd just bitten into a lemon.

Noah nodded, curious as to what subject had put such a distasteful look on his face.

Billington cleared his throat and said in a very low, precise voice, "It's about your wife, sir.''

"My wife?''

His lips puckered again. He hesitated a moment and then the words flew out like a cannon ball. "She is quite willful, sir. *Quite* willful.''

A shadow of a smile played about Noah's mouth. "Ah, I see. She's given you a mighty chase, hasn't she, Billington?'' He could just imagine Emily and Billington together. They were about as compatible as oil and water.

Billington pulled out a handkerchief and mopped his balding head. "She's always questioning me, sir. Not in the quiet, demure manner of a woman befitting her station, but boldly and brazenly, like a''—he hesitated a second—"man might do.''

"Are you calling my wife masculine, Billington?'' Noah asked, raising a bushy eyebrow. Too bad Billington couldn't

see his lips twitching beneath all the hair. Then he would know
Noah was only joking with him.

"Oh no, sir. Not at all." He sat up very straight in his chair.
"It's just that, at times, she can be quite . . . undisciplined."
A small bead of sweat trickled down his right temple.

"A hoyden?" Noah supplied, cocking his head to one side.

"No! No sir," he shook his head several times to press
the point. Be damned. The man had actually raised his voice.
Billington had shown emotion. That was a first.

Amazing, Noah thought. Edward Billington, the shrewd, no-
nonsense, proper man who never lost his composure, had come
undone because of his wife. Noah started to chuckle low in his
throat. Emily could drive a man to Bedlam; he could attest to
that. Somehow, she'd found a way beneath Billington's cool,
carefully honed exterior, chipping away one argumentative
word at a time, to release the emotions in the man. Negative,
unfortunately, but emotions nonetheless.

Noah guessed it was time to stop tormenting the poor man.
Emily had most likely tortured him enough with her obstinate,
questioning ways. "How would you like it, Billington, if Cyrus
Mandrey took over Lady Emily's comings and goings? You
wouldn't have to be responsible for her. No more questioning,
no more following her around, no more being *responsible* for
her?"

Billington let out a long sigh and seemed to slump backward
just a little in his chair. "I would be most appreciative of that,
sir," he said, mopping his forehead again. "Most appreciative
indeed."

Cyrus Mandrey took another sip of claret. Emily hadn't
spoken more than five words since they'd sat down to supper
fifteen minutes before. And he'd had to practically drag them
out of her. But he hadn't missed the furtive glances she threw
his way when she thought he wasn't looking. She seemed to

be studying him, watching his every movement down to the way he buttered his roll and chewed his pork.

Enough was enough. Setting down his fork and knife, he sat back in his chair and folded his hands over his stomach.

Emily looked at him, a forkful of mashed potatoes poised in midair. "Is the food not to your liking?" she asked, plopping the potatoes into her mouth.

"The food is fine."

She raised a golden eyebrow and swallowed. "You're not much of an eater," she commented, her eyes glancing over his half-full plate.

"On the contrary. I love food."

She nodded and took a small bite of pork, chewing thoughtfully. "If the food is fine and you love to eat, then why aren't you eating?"

"It's the company," he said.

Cyrus watched as a crimson flush inched up her neck, spreading to her cheeks. He loved to see Emily blush and wondered if the color had spread downward, toward those lush, ripe breasts. He felt himself harden.

"I beg your pardon?" she said, her voice a mere squeak.

Shrugging, he said, "You've been staring at me since we sat down."

"I have not been staring at you." Emily glared at him.

"Yes you have. And I know it's not because you're entranced with my good looks," he laughed, gesturing to himself. "Obviously, you're puzzled about something. What is it?"

The flush deepened. Emily stared at her plate.

"Lady Emily, we will be spending countless hours together. It is best if we're honest with each other from the beginning." He was surprised a bolt of lightning didn't shoot out of the sky and strike him. Honesty, indeed. If she knew the truth right now, she'd fly across the table and scratch his eyes out. Of that he was certain.

"I-I-I was just wondering," she began, her eyes remaining

on the plate in front of her. "Why did my brother select you, Mr. Mandrey?"

"I was the most qualified candidate."

Her head shot up. She opened her mouth to speak, then clamped it shut.

"You were about to say something," Cyrus prodded.

She shook her bent head so the only thing he could see was a golden crown of ringlets bobbing back and forth. "Come now, Lady Emily, confess."

"It was nothing, Mr. Mandrey, nothing at all." He admired the shimmering brilliance of her hair as the light danced over it. She'd worn it pulled back in a loose twist at the nape of her neck, a few tendrils escaping their confinement to trail about her shoulders. He liked it. Compelling. Seductive. Like the woman.

Cyrus shook his head, forcing himself to concentrate on the task at hand. "Honesty, Lady Emily."

The golden tendrils floated back and forth as she shook her head. "I can't be honest at the risk of being cruel," she said.

Ah. So that was it. She doubted his ability to protect her, but didn't want to hurt his feelings. A hint of a smile appeared beneath his beard. "You are concerned that I might not be an adequate protector," he ventured.

She didn't answer.

"You think I might not be able to run very fast if need be due to the, ah, somewhat impaired movement in my legs." Well, at least he'd played the part well.

Her head sunk lower.

"And I might not see the suspect or could possibly apprehend the wrong one due to these very thick spectacles I wear." He reached up to finger the thick glass.

"Or perhaps this has nothing at all to do with my ability." He took a sip of claret before speaking. "Perhaps you are so repelled by my homeliness that you can do nothing but stare at me in pity and disgust."

That got a reaction. Her head shot up, fire in her eyes as she declared, "That is not true! I do not think you're ugly."

"Nor do I. I merely said homely." Cyrus smiled. "There is a difference, you know."

She looked at him as though he'd gone mad. Then a giggle escaped her, followed by another. "A man with a sense of humor. How unique," she said, giggling again.

Cyrus raised his glass to salute her and took another drink. "Now, why don't you tell me what's bothering you?"

A faint pink tinge washed over her cheeks. "I guess I do have some doubts as to your ability as a protector," she said, looking at him. Her gray eyes seemed so contrite, so full of sympathy and concern, he almost wanted to tear away the disguise and show her who he really was. Almost.

"Please, do not apologize for your thoughts, Lady Emily. They are perfectly normal, considering the circumstances. Would an army feel comforted to learn their weapons were butter knives? How would an expert horseman feel if he was expected to show his skill on a wooden rocking horse?"

"Why do you make fun of yourself so, Mr. Mandrey?"

"I have learned to look beyond what appears to be, to find what is. Appearances are of no consequence to me. They rarely tell the true story. I was hired for my skill as a strategist and my cunning as a tactician. If I deploy these using the proper methods, brawn and speed will not be necessary."

"I see. And you feel you will be able to avoid an actual confrontation?"

"I do."

Emily picked up her fork and began toying with her food. "I feel compelled to warn you that my husband may be equally skilled in such maneuvers."

Cyrus stared at her. Why would she say a thing like that? "Has he ever displayed certain capabilities that would lead you to believe this?"

"No, not exactly. But there's something about the way he

moves. It's almost catlike, as though he could sneak up on a person when they least expected it.''

She'd noticed that? Noah would have to start walking with a heavier foot when this was all over. Trudge, that's what he would do.

"And he has a very keen intelligence. I've seen him giving his full attention to one person and then turn and answer another before they've asked the question.'' She swirled her mashed potatoes in a circle. "I can't explain it. I just feel it.''

Perhaps Emily should be the one in the espionage business. She could ferret out everyone with a hidden agenda, starting with Andrew Kleeton.

"Thank you for your concern, but I have been well-trained,'' he said.

She smiled and nodded, slicing off a piece of roast pork.

Time to do a little prying. "What are your plans for tomorrow?'' he asked.

"My plans?'' she repeated.

"Plans for the day. Your agenda. What will you be doing all day?'' Dear God, he hoped it wasn't going to be shopping or attending a tea, though the choices in the area for either diversion were limited.

"Nothing much. I plan to go riding with Mr. Kleeton in the morning, then I'll return for lunch and work in the garden until tea. I hadn't thought much past that. Why do you wish to know?''

He ignored the question. "Who is Mr. Kleeton?'' He'd get her version of the suspect.

She smiled. A rather large, happy smile, as though the thought of him made her warm inside. Cyrus clenched his fist under the table. "He's a neighbor. We go riding together every morning.''

Every morning! Billington had neglected to mention the frequency of Emily's contact with Andrew Kleeton. "Every morning,'' Cyrus repeated when he had control of his temper.

"Yes,'' she nodded, scooping a spoonful of peas into her mouth and chewing. "He's an avid horseman and enjoys the ride." She smiled again. "He's also been quite insistent about escorting me about the area so I won't have to ride alone."

I'll just bet he has, Cyrus thought. Like the fox escorting the hens to the hen house. He couldn't wait to meet the man. Tomorrow couldn't come soon enough.

"How thoughtful of him," he said in a dry, raspy voice.

"Yes, it really is quite thoughtful, isn't it? He's such a gentleman."

Cyrus didn't comment. "I look forward to meeting Mr. Kleeton tomorrow," he said.

"You do? Why?"

She really hadn't figured it out yet. Sighing, Cyrus looked at her through his spectacles. They were nothing more than cut glass. He could see everything in minute detail. The distortion came from the side of the onlooker, and the illusion contorted his eyes, making them appear much smaller than they actually were.

"I'll just be doing my job, Lady Emily. Where you go, I go. Everywhere. With a few minor exceptions, that is. If you have difficulty figuring out what those might be"—he gave her a little half-smile that he doubted she could see beneath his beard—"I'll be happy to spell them out for you."

She sat there huffing and puffing and getting indignant over his words and the way he'd said them. "Mr. Kleeton is hardly a suspect. Nor am I. I don't see why you have to follow us as though we're prisoners." She started tapping her knife on her plate.

If you only knew that your Mr. Kleeton is the number one suspect, who could well be a murderer and a traitor, you'd run so fast your head would spin. Cyrus shrugged. "You'll have to ask your brother. Those were his instructions."

"I will," she said. "I most definitely will." She lifted her head and thrust her chin out. Cyrus wanted to laugh. Nobody was more mercurial than Emily. One minute she was weeping and the next she was ready to poke somebody's eyes out. Probably his.

Best to just let her stew about it for a while. Like it or not, he was accompanying her on her ride with Kleeton tomorrow. He pushed back his chair and stood up. Emily remained seated, staring at her plate. "What time will you be riding in the morning?"

She looked up and blurted out, "Early." She paused and gave him a sly little smile. "Very early." Emily was up to something, he could almost see the wheels turning in her beautiful head. "I'm an early riser."

"How early?"

"I'll be leaving at six."

Cyrus studied her. He had not pictured her to be an early morning person. He'd bet his last coin she was trying to goad him. "Fine, I'll see you then." He nodded his head and prepared to leave. He knew he should just walk out the door, but something pulled at him to stay. He couldn't resist the temptation to best her right now. Turnabout was always fair play, especially where Emily was concerned. "One more thing," he said, resting his hands on the back of his chair. "Please extend my compliments to the cook."

"I will." She was back to speaking in one-syllable words again.

"Might I request a meal of my choosing sometime in the near future?" he asked.

"Of course."

Cyrus's gaze met hers. "I'd like to start off with cream of asparagus soup." He heard her gasp. "For the main dish, I'd like roast duck"—she went white—"and red potatoes." Her eyes grew wide as though she'd seen a ghost. From the past, he thought, stifling a chuckle. Cyrus nodded again and said, "You can pick the dessert." With that, he shuffled out of the room, leaving Emily staring after him.

Chapter 12

At five forty-five the next morning, Cyrus Mandrey knocked on Lady Emily's door.

It creaked open a few inches and a very tired, half-asleep Emily peered out at him from beneath heavy lids. Her hair was unbound, falling like a golden cloak over her shoulders. It was obvious she had just crawled out of bed.

"Are you ready?" Cyrus asked, tapping his riding crop.

"Ready?" Her voice was low and throaty, heavy with sleep. The sound washed over him, stirring his desire for her. A few more inches and he could be inside her room. A few more feet and he could be in her bed. A few more lifetimes and he might stand a chance. *Patience,* he told himself. Patience was the key to all treasures, including his beautiful wife.

"I believe you told me you were riding with Mr. Kleeton at six o'clock this morning," Cyrus said, placing his hand on the door. If he could just inch it open a little more, he might be able to see what she was wearing. There was no harm in looking. It was probably one of those virginal white gowns like she'd worn on the ship. Though with Emily's curves it had looked anything but innocent on her.

He pushed the door forward just a hint.

She didn't seem to notice as her eyes drifted shut. He could see a few more inches. More than enough as he caught a glimpse of her splendid breasts and full hips, swathed in a light, filmy material. The gown clung to her curves, swirling about her, lending an ethereal quality to the whole creation. Had this been part of her trousseau, he wondered. For her husband?

Cyrus leaned forward, the faint scent of lilac drifting to him, filling his senses. Just one more inch.

Emily chose that moment to fall against the door, hit her head on the wood and come awake with a shriek.

"Emily, are you all right?" Cyrus stepped forward and touched her arm.

She was staring at him with a strange look on her face. Her hands fell to her sides. She no longer seemed aware that she'd shrieked in pain, or that she'd hit her head, or now stood before a veritable stranger half clothed.

"Your voice," she whispered.

"My voice?" he repeated, dropping it a full two octaves to reach Cyrus Mandrey's level.

"You called me Emily," she said, unable to take her eyes from him.

"I apologize," Cyrus said. "In my concern for your safety, I forgot my manners." *And I forgot my senses because I was too busy ogling your body.*

"But your voice," she said again. "It sounded just like . . ." Emily closed her eyes a moment. When she opened them again, Cyrus saw the faint shimmering of unshed tears. "It was nothing," she said, pressing her fingers to the sides of her eyes. "If you can give me ten minutes, I'll meet you at the stables."

"Certainly. Are you sure you're all right?"

"I'm fine," she managed. "Just fine."

Cyrus backed out of the room. "I'll see you in ten minutes," he said, pulling the door shut. As he started walking down the hall, he thought he heard a sniff and a sob coming from Emily's room. He stopped to listen, but the sound was gone. Swearing under his breath, he headed for the stables.

The morning air was fresh and brisk, reminding him that summer would soon blend into fall. Tiny droplets of dew painted the lawn in glossy attendance like an artist creating his masterpiece. Chirping crickets faded in and out as the last of the night sounds dissolved into day. Cyrus smiled as the stable came into view. He looked forward to seeing Henry Barnes and Flash.

"Mr. Barnes," he called out, entering the stable.

"In 'ere," he hollered from one of the stalls. Cyrus figured it would be Flash's. Old Henry had a penchant for the stallion, said their spirits were alike, wild and free.

"Hello, Mr. Barnes," Cyrus said, stepping up to Flash's stall. The horse whinnied at the sound of another voice, jerking his head up.

"Who are you?" His black beady eyes scrunched up to get a better look at the stranger before him. Henry didn't like strangers, said they couldn't be trusted. He believed in two things. Family and the Sandletons.

"Name's Cyrus Mandrey, Mr. Barnes."

"Wot are you doin' 'ere?" He'd gone back to brushing Flash.

"I've been hired to protect Lady Emily," he said.

That got his attention. His old withered hand stilled on Flash's back. "Be damned. I knew it! I told the little miss, the mast'r would'na like it if she went all ov'r the countryside with anoth'r man." He grinned and the lines on his forehead and cheeks deepened. "Hah!"

Cyrus cleared his throat and hid a smile. "Actually, Mr. Barnes, I have been hired to protect Lady Emily *from* her husband."

"What?" he yelled. Flash whinnied again and threw his head up, tossing it from side to side. "There boy, it's a'right," Henry said, stroking the stallion's black coat. "It's a'right."

The horse calmed under his gentle touch and soothing voice. "That don't make no sense, mister. No sense a'tall."

Cyrus shrugged.

"Why a'body can see the master would nev'r do no 'arm to 'is wife. 'E loves 'er."

The conviction in Henry's words took Cyrus aback. "Why do you say that?"

"Plain and simple as the nose on yer face," Henry said, nodding his head. "When 'e talked to me 'bout 'er comin' 'ere, 'e was all concerned 'bout her. Wanted the best fer 'er. But it's the way 'e talked 'bout 'er. 'Is voice got all soft and cozy like. I could tell. Plain and simple."

Had it been that obvious that he was totally besotted with his wife? Apparently so. To everyone but the one person who should have seen it. His wife. But then he'd made every attempt to hide it from her. When this was all over, he'd make certain Emily never had a reason to doubt him or his love again.

"If'n you ask me, ya oughta be protectin' her from that pretty boy, Kleeton."

"What do you know about Andrew Kleeton?" Cyrus asked, his words edged with steel.

"Enough to know I don' like 'im." Henry pointed a bony finger at Cyrus. "Keep yer eye on 'im. 'E's the one to watch."

Before Cyrus could ask any more questions, the sound of Emily's voice reached them. "Mr. Mandrey?"

"Over here," Cyrus called out, glancing at his pocket watch. They were already fifteen minutes late. Emily had said they were to meet at the north end of the property at six o'clock. It would take a solid ten minutes to get there if they left now, and they still had to saddle the horses. They would be at least thirty minutes late. Would Kleeton wait? Cyrus had a feeling he would. If Kleeton were the Serpent, he'd use any opportunity to see Emily to further his quest for her husband. If he weren't, Cyrus believed he would still wait for her in an attempt to coax her into being his own personal conquest. Both thoughts sickened and enraged him.

"I'm ready. I must have overslept."

Cyrus turned to greet her. The words he'd planned to say got stuck in his throat. Emily stood before him, dressed in a royal blue riding habit trimmed in gold. She wore her hair in one long braid that reminded Cyrus of nautical rope. He still wasn't used to seeing her in regal attire. Most of his memories had her garbed as a boy in breeches and an oversized jacket. Or as a servant in thick muslin and sackcloth. Or as a temptress on the *Falcon* in a gown sans underclothes. Or, and this was his fondest memory, as a full-blooded woman, warm and naked beneath him.

"A little early fer you ta'day, ain't it, Lady Emily?" Henry Barnes said, grinning.

A rose tinge spotted her cheeks. "Is it?" she said, not looking at Cyrus.

Henry Barnes laughed and shook his head. " 'Les my clock is off, I don' see you fer anoth'r three hours."

Emily picked at something on her jacket. No doubt an imaginary speck of lint, Cyrus thought.

"Don't mind him," she whispered. "He tends to get confused."

Cyrus nodded and stifled a laugh. Emily had a penchant for getting caught in traps of her own making. "Now for a mount. Would there be any objection if I took this one?" he asked, pointing to Flash.

"No," Emily said, so quickly he wondered if she'd heard the question.

"No?" Why would Flash matter to her?

"He's quite spirited," she said, clenching her kidskin gloves.

"I'm a superb horseman," he countered. *And Flash is my horse.*

"You might get hurt." She twisted the gloves between her hands.

"I'm a superb horseman," he repeated. What was the matter with her?

Emily threw a desperate look at Henry Barnes, who stood

off to one side, a huge grin on his face. She was waiting for him to say something to bail her out of her predicament. He lifted his shoulders and shrugged.

"He's only ever had one rider." There she went with those gloves again.

"He'll get used to me," Cyrus said, more curious by the moment.

"One rider." She emphasized the words.

"And?"

"My husband," she said, her voice a mere whisper. "Noah is the only person who has ever ridden Flash. He's his horse. No one else rides him."

For a second, Cyrus was so dumbfounded he couldn't speak. For whatever reason, Emily had protected something that was his, and she'd been quite adamant about it. He wanted to shout with joy. It wasn't exactly a profession of love from her, but it was a start.

"Fine. You should have said so in the first place." He turned to Henry Barnes, who was still grinning. "I'll take the chestnut in the corner."

Ten minutes later, they were saddled and ready to head out. Henry Barnes caught up to Cyrus and motioned him aside with a bony hand. "Jest thought I'd tell ye, case you didna' notice, I think she's in love with 'im too." With that, he stepped back, crossed his wiry arms over his chest and laughed.

Cyrus saluted Henry as he left the stables. He had little time to ponder Henry's comment because Emily was several paces ahead of him. *Is she in that much of a hurry to meet Kleeton?* The thought didn't set well. It took little effort to catch up with her. She was an expert horsewoman, but this land was his turf. He knew every crack and crevice, dip and valley on the estate. And his mount, Speed Demon, was nearly as fast and spirited as Flash.

As they neared the north point of the property, Cyrus saw a lone figure atop a huge white stallion. Blood rushed to his head. He could feel the anticipation pumping through his veins.

In a matter of seconds, he would face the man who might be the treacherous traitor and ruthless killer he'd exposed seven years ago. And if it was, the man would be Peter Crowlton. The Serpent. And Crowlton would want revenge.

Cyrus gripped his reins tighter and followed Emily's lead, breaking into a full gallop, shortening the distance to the rider and the answers to the questions pounding in his brain. Within minutes, they pulled their mounts up, stopping several feet from the man Cyrus knew must be Andrew Kleeton. Billington had always been accurate with his descriptions, and he had not failed in this instance. Andrew Kleeton was quite handsome in an almost pretty manner. His features were fine-boned and delicate, his hair blond, his eyes blue, his nose thin and straight. Nothing like Noah Sandleton. And unlike Noah, who could intimidate with a mere look, this man seemed incapable of frowning, much less cold-blooded killing.

But looks could be most deceiving.

"Why hello, Lady Emily. As always, it is a pleasure to see you again." Andrew Kleeton's voice was soft and velvety. Like a caress.

"Thank you, Andrew. I'm looking forward to our ride today." *Andrew?* She was on a first-name basis with a potential killer? "I . . ." She hesitated, "I would like to introduce you to Mr. Cyrus Mandrey. Mr. Mandrey, this is Mr. Andrew Kleeton."

Both men nodded.

"Mr. Mandrey will be staying at Glenview Manor for a while," Emily said.

Longer than a while, Kleeton. Much longer. If I have my way, I'll be staying. Period.

"How nice," Andrew murmured, his blue gaze scanning Cyrus's shaggy head and thick glasses. "Are you a relative? A cousin perhaps?" The small smile that played about Kleeton's well-curved lips told Cyrus he thought him a buffoon, no matter who he was.

"Not . . . exactly," Emily said, shifting in her saddle and casting a sideways glance at Cyrus.

She doesn't want to tell Kleeton why I'm really here, Cyrus thought.

An uncomfortable silence settled over the trio, as the two men waited for Emily to speak again. She fumbled with her reins, almost dropping them. Allegra sensed her mistress's discomfort and lifted her head up, snorting and pawing the ground. The stallions eyed one another, nickering and blowing. Cyrus reached out to place a hand on Speed Demon's mane and the horse stilled.

"Forgive me," Kleeton said, his words directed at Emily. "It was not my intention to embarrass you, yet it seems I have done exactly that. I was merely being polite, nothing more."

Emily's cheeks turned bright pink. "You have nothing to apologize for, Andrew," Emily said. "It is just that the circumstances surrounding Mr. Mandrey's presence are a little"—she paused—"embarrassing."

"Then we needn't discuss it," Andrew said simply.

"I want to." Emily pushed back a stray lock of hair. Cyrus watched the byplay with growing irritation. Kleeton had her eating right out of his hand. He knew what to say and how to say it to get exactly what he wanted and make it look as though he had no part in it.

"It really isn't necessary," Kleeton said.

Emily smiled a sweet, innocent smile just for Kleeton. Smiles like that should be reserved for her husband, Cyrus thought, his dislike for the man increasing tenfold. Andrew Kleeton was smooth. Too smooth.

"Mr. Mandrey has been hired as my protector." She laughed. "The whole thing is quite ridiculous really. He's supposed to guard me from my husband."

That remark got a reaction from Kleeton. It was subtle, nothing more than a slight flinch of his left hand. But Cyrus saw it. He also saw the gray leather covering that hand.

"Guard you from your husband?" Kleeton asked. "I'm afraid I don't understand."

"Nor do I. I tried to tell Ian that it wasn't necessary, but he refused to listen. He gave me two choices, one of which was Mr. Mandrey. Had I chosen the other, I would have been back in his home last evening."

"Then I shall be indebted to Mr. Mandrey for keeping you here," Kleeton said, giving a slight nod in Cyrus's direction.

"I've only been at Glenview Manor a short time, but it feels like home already." Her gray eyes sparkled as they scanned the countryside, taking in the fields and rolling hills peppered with elm and ash trees. A small pond sat several hundred feet away, surrounded by clumps of orange and yellow daylilies. "It's breathtaking," Emily sighed, entranced by a handful of starlings, darting in and out of the pond.

"Yes, it is," Kleeton agreed, but his eyes were on Emily, not on the pond. He thought *she* was exquisite. Cyrus balled his hands into fists, wishing he could sink one of them into Kleeton's perfect nose. Then it wouldn't be so perfect anymore. The man had nerve, trying to seduce his wife right in front of him. Of course, he didn't know that Noah Sandleton was within ten feet of him, disguised under a brown wig and beard.

"Let's race," Emily said, a glimmer of excitement in her voice. "Andrew, Mr. Mandrey is an accomplished horseman too."

"Bravo," Kleeton said, but his words sounded flat.

"Hah!" Emily yelled, digging her booted heels into Allegra's sides. The mare bolted off down the hill at lightning speed. Kleeton's horse fell in behind with Cyrus in a close third. Horse and rider leaned low and flat over their mounts, bending to the wind. Kleeton overtook Emily when they came out of the second hill. Cyrus passed her a few minutes later. He set his sights on the back of Kleeton's tan jacket and dug his heels into Speed Demon's side, calling out praise as they soared through the field. Kleeton must have sensed his lead was in jeopardy, because he pulled out his riding crop and whacked his mount seven times on the hindquarters. Despite the bitter bite of the crop, the white stallion slowed, as though he'd been ridden all-out too early in the game and had nothing left.

Cyrus took advantage of the animal's distress, sailing past him, head low, knees in tight. He raced on for several hundred feet before glancing back to see how his competition fared. Kleeton had slowed his horse to a trot but Emily was still barreling forward in a valiant effort to finish the race. Pulling up on Speed Demon, Cyrus settled him into a light canter as he waited for Emily.

"My goodness," she called out in a breathless voice, falling into pace with him. "You certainly are a superb horseman."

"Speed Demon is a superb horse," Cyrus said. "That makes all the difference in the world." He glanced behind to see Kleeton gaining on them. Another thirty seconds and he would be bearing down upon them. Cyrus groaned.

"I say you and Speed Demon are the perfect match. You practically flew over the field!" Emily said, her face alive with excitement.

"Perhaps you're right, Lady Emily," Cyrus agreed. "But isn't that life? Finding the right match?"

"What do you mean?" She cast him a sideways glance, her golden brows pulled down in puzzlement.

"When a person finds his perfect match, he can do anything. A lame man with a lightning-fast horse can fly." He stopped his horse and turned to face her. She must have known he was referring to himself, because she became very still. "And an unworthy man with an honest woman can turn into the most trustworthy husband in the world."

He watched her face as his words sunk in. She looked stricken, her gray eyes wide, her face pale. "Not always, Mr. Mandrey," she said, her words flat and empty. "Not always."

Cyrus opened his mouth to speak, but Andrew Kleeton was upon them. "That was quite a show, Mandrey. Quite a show," he said, his blue eyes assessing Cyrus with renewed interest.

Cyrus shrugged. "As I told Lady Emily, Speed Demon is an excellent horse."

Kleeton nodded. "Avenger and I are not in the habit of losing." He patted the big white stallion with a gloved hand. Cyrus's attention focused on the gray leather molded to Kleeton's hand. Beneath the leather hid the truth. A truth that could either expose Kleeton as a criminal or pardon him as an innocent.

One way or the other, Cyrus would find out.

"And that, I believe, is checkmate." Cyrus moved his bishop to trap Emily's king.

"You win," Emily conceded on a sigh. "Again."

Cyrus smiled at her. It was difficult to see the smile beneath all that hair, but she could hear it in his voice as it softened and lost some of its hoarseness. She rather liked it that way, though he didn't do it often enough. In the three weeks since his arrival at Glenview Manor, she had grown accustomed to spending hours at a time with him. They rode horses every morning at eight o'clock, a compromise between Cyrus's choice, which was six o'clock, and hers, which was ten. Andrew Kleeton did not accompany them on their early morning jaunts, but was included in the afternoon ones. Evenings were quiet, simple affairs with dinner and card games or chess afterward.

It was amazing to Emily that she felt so comfortable with this man who just a few short weeks before had been a complete stranger. Perhaps it was his unpretentious manner or his silent strength that enabled her to relax with him. And he seemed to be able to sense her moods and anticipate her reaction, sometimes before she herself did.

"Would you care for coffee?" She remembered he preferred coffee to tea.

"No, thank you. I'm stuffed. Everything was delicious as usual. I've never had such excellent lamb. And the cherry tarts were exquisite."

Emily laughed. "I thought you liked the tarts. How many did you have? Four? Or five?"

"Six," Cyrus said, his laughter soft and low. "And did you see how pleased the cook was when I complimented her? She was ready to bring out ten more."

"She'll probably expect me to eat as many when you're gone. I'll be as big as a house if you don't stop with your compliments," Emily said.

Their gazes locked, but Cyrus said nothing. Emily wished she could see his eyes beneath the wire spectacles he wore. She believed that the eyes were the conveyors of true emotion, and she felt at a distinct disadvantage with a man who could hide behind two pieces of thick glass.

"Perhaps you won't be dining alone after I leave." His words were quiet, devoid of emotion.

"Well, I do suppose Ian and Augusta will come to visit me from time to time." Emily tilted her head in thought. "And I do have a very good friend who would love Glenview Manor. I could invite her for a long weekend stay if her father and brothers will consent. Of course, Andrew would be invited."

Cyrus's bushy brows creased into a straight line. "I wasn't thinking of Kleeton."

The sharpness in his tone surprised her. "You don't like Andrew, do you?"

"No, I don't."

That comment surprised her. He was usually neutral and tried to understand both sides of a situation, with their accompanying consequences, without choosing sides. But the subject of Andrew Kleeton was different. Both men had been dropping subtle insults at each other for the previous two days. Andrew considered Cyrus Mandrey a servant who took far too many liberties in his limited position as temporary protector to Emily. He saw no reason why the man had to follow them about when they went riding. After all, Andrew was an excellent marksman and just as handy with a sword, or his fists for that matter. He

could protect Emily from this invisible threat of a husband that
loomed over Glenview Manor.

As for Cyrus, she didn't know what it was that made him
dislike Andrew so. But she intended to find out.

"Would you be so kind as to tell me exactly what you find
so offensive about Andrew?"

He took a sip of his sherry. "I dislike any man bent on
seducing another man's wife. Especially if it's one I'm supposed to be protecting."

"How can you say that? Andrew is *not* trying to seduce me!"

"What do you call it?" he asked, folding his arms over his
broad chest.

"I call it being a friend."

"Then he's trying to become an awfully familiar friend."

"That's absurd," she answered, shaking her head.

"Is it?" He stood up, bracing his hands on either side of
the mahogany table, and leaned over, shortening the distance
between them. "Are the two of you not on a first-name basis?"

"You know we are. That is of no consequence," she
answered, a little intimidated by his closeness. His face, at least
the part not covered by hair, was much younger than she would
have guessed. Emily had thought him well into his forties, but
realized he was probably on the low end of thirty.

"It is of consequence," he bit out, revealing a set of even,
white teeth.

He's got nice teeth too, Emily thought, watching his mouth
move. She didn't hear the words because she was concentrating
on his mouth and the hint of two well-shaped lips. Sensual
lips. On Cyrus Mandrey?

"Emily?"

"What?" she asked, wondering what other secrets lay hidden
beneath all that hair.

"You haven't heard a word I've said." His words were thick
with frustration.

"Hah!" She jumped up from her chair, placing her hands
on her hips. "You just called me Emily. Not *Lady* Emily. If I

call you Cyrus, does that mean you and I are involved in a clandestine relationship?''

Cyrus shook his head. ''Of course not.''

''Good.'' She smiled. ''Then you may call me Emily and I will call you Cyrus.''

''Don't change the subject, *Emily.*'' He leaned farther over the table, moving closer to her. ''Does Andrew not find every possible opportunity to touch your person?''

''No!'' she said. He was so close she could smell his spicy cologne.

''Does he not act as your personal footman, assisting you as you mount and dismount Allegra?'' She heard the anger in his voice, buried beneath the hoarseness.

''Yes, but—''

He cut her off. ''Does he not clasp your arm as he walks you about, trying to locate the *perfect* spot in the field for you to sit?'' Cyrus didn't give her a chance to respond. ''And when he finds that perfect spot, does he not place his hand at the small of your back, guiding you to your seat, lingering just a little longer each time?'' His voice rose with each accusation until it became nothing more than a dark, menacing growl.

''It's not like that,'' she whispered, a tiny thread of fear wrapping around her with each angry word he spoke. She looked away, trying to distance herself from him. This was a side of Cyrus Mandrey she hadn't seen before. A violent, dangerous side.

''Look at me, Emily,'' he commanded.

She bent her head down, studying his large hands splayed across the table. Strong, tanned, capable hands. With calluses. She hadn't noticed them before. Cyrus Mandrey did not seem like a man who engaged in manual labor, but his hands belied that fact.

''Look at me,'' he repeated in a voice that brooked no argument.

Emily squared her shoulders, raising her head to meet his gaze. She stared at his dark eyes through the lenses of his spectacles. The glass was so thick it was hard to make out the actual color of his eyes. Dark brown? Black?

"He caresses you with his voice," Cyrus continued, "in soft, low tones, so you have to lean close to hear him."

"Andrew speaks in the pleasant, cultured tone of a true gentleman. Unlike others I know, who shall remain nameless." Emily knew she sounded cold and haughty, but Cyrus deserved it. He had no business making cruel insinuations about a man he barely knew.

"Kleeton is no gentleman," Cyrus said. "And you know nothing about him other than what he's chosen to reveal to you." He crossed his arms over his broad chest. "For all you know, your Mr. Kleeton could be a thief. Or a murderer."

"That's absurd," she said. He had no right to make such accusations. Andrew Kleeton had been nothing but kind and considerate since the morning she'd met him. Like a brother. Like Christopher.

"What I find so absurd is how you can be so trusting of a complete stranger and so critical of your own husband?" he flung back.

Emily felt the anger, hot and consuming, bubble and boil over, coursing through her veins, filling her soul with fire that flowed like flames through her next words. "My husband doesn't deserve my trust." Her hands balled into fists so tight she could feel her nails digging into the flesh of her palm.

"How can you be so certain?" he asked. "Perhaps there are circumstances which sent him away." There was something in his voice that reminded her of the cold, desolate winds of winter, whipping over the land, leaving it stripped and barren.

Emily ignored the voice, ignored the feeling that Cyrus himself was the wind whipping over the land, alone in pain and despair. She could think of nothing but closing the wound he seemed so determined to scratch open. If she permitted even the tiniest possibility that Noah had not *wanted* to leave her, then the great wall of anger that protected her from loving him might come crashing down, piling onto the ground like so much rubble. And it would crush her and all the defenses she'd spent weeks developing. She'd be left alone, naked and exposed. And vulnerable once again to the man who could make her body burn, stripping her pride away, with a single heated look.

As if suddenly realizing he had gone far beyond the bounds of propriety, Cyrus straightened away from the table, cleared his throat and spoke. "My temper got the best of me. I spoke out of turn. Please accept my apologies."

He looked so perfect, so proper standing there, his words cool and devoid of emotion. Emily rather thought she liked the heated version of Cyrus Mandrey much better than the lukewarm one he presented to the world.

"He's a *friend,* Cyrus," she said, wanting to make him understand and hoping to divert his attention from further talk of Noah. "I care about him like a brother, nothing more."

She thought those words would soothe him, but he was around the table, bearing down on her before she could say another word. "Andrew Kleeton is not your brother," he said, his voice darker than the night outside. "And you are a married woman."

His words, full of cold accusation and unspoken assumption, matched the tone of his voice, sending Emily to the brink of losing her composure. She was teetering, close to falling over the precipice into the oblivion of rage and recourse. "I am well aware of my marital status," she hissed.

Cyrus took a step closer. His trousers touched the hem of her yellow gown. Emily inched backward.

"Then perhaps Mr. Kleeton needs to be reminded of it." He leaned toward her. "So he will stop trying to get into your bed."

Emily's hand flew up to slap him, but Cyrus caught her by the wrist. His grip was hard and punishing. They stared at one another, neither speaking, as silence filled the room, deepening the chasm between them like unbanked floodwaters surging forward, harsh and unforgiving.

Cyrus was the first to speak. "I won't apologize for speaking the truth. The man wants you in his bed. Period."

He released her then, letting her hand drop to her side. Without another look, he turned on his heel and left. Emily stared after him, her anger forgotten for the moment. She replayed the last several seconds over in her mind, the part where he had turned to leave. Emily could have sworn Cyrus walked out the door with calm, purposeful strides and not a single shuffle.

Chapter 13

The house vibrated with tension. Everyone felt it, from the footman to the chambermaid. There were no raised voices. No slamming doors. No stomping feet. Not a single disagreeable word. Only silence. A silence so dark and deep it crushed out any thoughts of smiles and laughter, smothered the very idea of lightheartedness or humor. It began to eat away at the inhabitants of Glenview Manor like an insidious disease, gnawing at their souls, stealing their peace of mind. They were jumpy, all of them, avoiding Cyrus and Emily as much as possible. Cyrus didn't blame them. He didn't much like his company these days either.

He knew he should put an end to it all and try to settle things with Emily so the household could get back to normal. But after three days, he was still furious with her. Last night as he lay in bed, staring into the darkness, he admitted the anger he felt had little to do with Emily's trying to slap him. No, the red-hot fire in his gut was because of her unwillingness to believe anything bad about Andrew Kleeton. Or anything good about her husband.

He paced back and forth on the Aubusson rug in the library, stopping occasionally to glance out the double-paned window. Emily was kneeling on the grass, her gloved hands covered with rich, brown dirt as she separated a clump of herbs. She looked at peace. Serene. Content. Cyrus cursed. How could she look so damned happy when he was so damned miserable?

And how could she honestly not know that Kleeton wanted to bed her? Couldn't she tell by the overblown praise he gave her? Did Emily really believe it when Kleeton told her she had hair the color of the sun, as though a hundred fairies had danced through it with their wands dipped in gold? Or that she was so beautiful, so exquisite, she reminded him of a Greek goddess? Cyrus shook his head. What rubbish! He'd almost fallen off his horse when he'd heard Kleeton murmur those words. It had taken every ounce of willpower not to spring from Speed Demon and pummel the man.

Emily was an intelligent woman. Certainly she could tell when a man was feigning sincerity for ulterior motives. As in wanting to feel the silk of that luxurious golden hair running over every inch of his naked body, or finding out just how beautiful and exquisite her body was minus clothing.

Cyrus swore again. If Noah had made any of those ridiculous comments to her in the guise of a compliment, she would have flung a chamberpot at him. Or jabbed him with an iron poker. But not Andrew. He was too perfect, too polished. Beyond reproach. And Emily refused to consider a dark side of him. Or a light side of Noah.

It had been almost four days since their argument. They were both becoming quite adept at avoiding each other whenever possible. Cyrus had received a note from Emily via Billington the first morning telling him she was feeling a little under the weather and would not be taking her early morning ride for the next several days. It was just as well because Cyrus didn't trust himself to be alone with her for fear he'd wring her neck or try to shake a bit of sense into her.

Meals were another somber affair. Cyrus tended to bury

himself in a book during breakfast, and other than a slight nod of his head when she entered, he ignored the beautiful woman at the other end of the table. He called forth all his tactical skills to elude Emily during the other meals by dining before or after the scheduled time, which changed daily. Apparently, Emily had no more desire to see him than he did her. As for Kleeton and the afternoon rides, Emily gave those up as well, at least for the moment.

For all his apparent elusiveness, Cyrus knew where Emily was and what she was doing at all times. If she roamed about in the gardens, working among the herbs or wildflowers, which she seemed to do quite a bit, he would watch her from the library window. If she decided to take a stroll among the roses, or walk the privet maze, Billington followed her. If Emily ventured to the stables, which she did every day, Cyrus trailed several paces behind. Henry Barnes was a ready ally who was more than willing to report his mistress's comings and goings once he learned Cyrus didn't like Andrew Kleeton any more than he did.

Evenings stretched out long and lonely. There were no more after-dinner chess games or comfortable conversations. No more soft melodies drifting through the air as Emily's fingers roamed over the ivory piano keys. Only the echoes of silence rang through the manor, louder and more deafening than a crowded ballroom at the height of the season.

"Sir?" Billington's voice brought Cyrus out of his dark musings. He turned away from the window. Billington advanced toward him with measured steps, his lanky body moving with its usual air of quiet superiority.

"What is it, Billington?" His eyes shot to the white card in the older man's hand.

"This, sir," the butler replied, holding out a plain white envelope with Emily's name on it, "is from Mr. Kleeton."

Cyrus snatched the envelope away and tore it open. He scanned the contents, his bushy brows pulling in a straight line. "It looks as though I am about to get a peek into Kleeton's

lair." He looked up, the hint of a smile playing about his lips.
"Emily has been invited to tea tomorrow afternoon. Isn't that
nice, Billington?"

Edward Billington looked at his employer and nodded, his
upper lip twitching into a semblance of a half-smile. "Very
good, sir. Very good indeed."

The carriage rolled along the dirt road, winding its way past
rows of elm and ash, their leaves fluttering in the soft breeze,
glittering like tiny jewels. Small clouds of dust kicked up around
the wheels, partially obscuring the mosaic pattern the sun's
rays cast on the ground as they filtered through the green foliage.

Cyrus stared out the window. He and Emily had been in the
carriage less than ten minutes, but it seemed like hours. The
scent of her lilac perfume drifted to him, filling his senses,
calling to him. He stared harder. Her soft, even breathing floated
through the carriage, wrapping around his body like a whisper,
tugging at his heart. And his groin. He closed his eyes, blinking
hard. A vision of Emily, naked and writhing beneath him, swept
through his mind. Soft. Supple. Sensuous. His eyes shot open.
Damn, but it was hot in that blasted carriage. Cyrus reached
for his cravat, loosening the knot. Riding in the carriage had
been a big mistake. He knew he should have saddled Speed
Demon instead. It would have been a lot safer for him to travel
alongside the carriage, several feet from the sight, sound and
smell of Emily.

Casting a sideways glance at her, he noted she continued to
stare out the window, oblivious to his current state of distress
or the fact that she was the cause of it. Her hair was perfect,
every golden lock in place under the pale green bonnet trimmed
in gold. Hands adorned in cream kidskin remained folded in
her lap, resting on the neat folds of her pale green gown. Emily
appeared calm, cool and unperturbed, unlike Cyrus, who was
as wild as a tempest and as hot as the devil himself. Emily
could do that to him. And it galled him.

He couldn't think straight when she was so close. That was the whole reason they were in their current predicament. He'd lost his temper and said things he shouldn't have, all because when he looked at her, smelled her lilac scent, heard her soft voice, he lost his objectivity. Damnation! Never had he been on an assignment where he'd done that. He had always prided himself on his ability to remain detached, aloof. In character.

Until now. Emily made him feel things he'd never felt before and it was proving very difficult to keep his cover as Cyrus Mandrey. Because Noah Sandleton felt anything but detachment from his wife. And because of this, he interfered with his own character. Noah kept creeping in like a thief, stealing an extra moment whenever possible, lingering on a word, fabricating excuses to spend time with her. Cyrus Mandrey would not have done that. He was here to do his job in a professional manner, without emotion or personal attachment. But Noah wouldn't let him, taking every opportunity to snatch a slice of time for himself until Cyrus Mandrey and Noah Sandleton intertwined, creating a dangerous, deadly situation.

Cyrus Mandrey wouldn't have lost his temper, or forgotten to shuffle along, or spoken in Noah's voice. He would have completed his mission with as little emotion as possible, and then disappeared. That's what had always made Noah such a good operative. He could lose himself in whatever role he was playing. So much so that it was difficult to find a trace of Noah Sandleton in any of his characters. Until now. Noah was seeping into the persona of Cyrus Mandrey, little by little, day by day.

It was time to get a grip on the situation and force Noah out of the picture, or at least control him, before he made another mistake. If Kleeton were the Serpent, he'd be a trained observer, skilled at detecting the slightest anomaly. And that could prove fatal.

Cyrus pulled his gaze back to the woman seated across from him. Her eyes had fluttered closed, her head tilted back to expose the slender column of her neck. His gaze lingered on her chest, mesmerized by the slow, even movements of her breasts. He leaned back against the velvet squabs and sighed. There was no way he could play the role of Cyrus Mandrey without Noah's thoughts and feelings taking over. No way at all.

Penworth was an old estate, older than Glenview Manor, with vine-covered brick walls and overgrown privet and arborvitae cowering along the pathways and main entrance. Clumps of overgrown grass and weeds crowded out the few spindly roses that fought through the thick greenery, struggling for a hint of light.

Cyrus walked ahead of Emily, reminding her of a soldier blazing the path.

Cyrus.

She felt a tug of guilt. It had been days since they'd exchanged a civil word. Longer than that since they'd laughed or shared honest conversation. And Emily missed those times. All of them. Cyrus had only been trying to protect her because he felt Andrew was a threat. Emily knew that. But it hadn't been necessary. Andrew was a gentleman. He wasn't trying to get into her bed, for heaven's sake. Emily felt the heat rise to her face. Only one man had ever tried to do that. And he'd succeeded with very little effort.

Noah. He was the cause of the rift between herself and Cyrus. Emily clenched her fists, feeling the soft kidskin against her palms. Everything always came back to Noah. Her anger. Her frustration. Her broken heart. She blinked hard to push that last thought away. If Cyrus hadn't tried to make excuses for Noah's actions, implying that he might well have good reasons for leaving, Emily wouldn't have lost her temper and this whole argument would never have taken place. He always seemed to rally for Noah, giving him the benefit of the doubt, making an excuse for his absence. Emily knew why he was doing it. She'd figured it out weeks ago.

Cyrus was trying to protect her feelings by fabricating forgivable reasons for Noah's leaving. But there was no use trying to sweeten a bitter pill. Emily knew Noah Sandleton for the ruthless, uncaring rakehell he was, even if Cyrus did not.

"We're here to see Mr. Kleeton." Cyrus's low, gravelly voice pulled Emily back from her thoughts. She looked up and gasped. A short, squat man with a black patch over his right eye was staring straight at her. His good eye, if it could be considered that, was a rheumy faded gray. His sallow complexion matched the few strands of hair remaining on his head. He was dressed in black, from the ill-fitting jacket that stretched over his round middle to the black boots on his small feet.

He made no move to let them in, nor did he speak. His thin lips curved downward into a frown.

Cyrus cleared his throat and tried again. "Would you be so kind as to announce us to Mr. Kleeton? He's expecting us."

The man backed up from the door an inch at a time. Cyrus took that opportunity to shoulder his way through, taking Emily by the hand and pulling her with him. She heard the click of the heavy wooden door behind them. Turning, she saw the butler's pudgy hands pushing the heavy brass lock through the bolt. A shiver ran down her spine as she imagined being trapped inside this house.

Thank God Cyrus was with her. She promised herself that she would apologize for their silly little spat as soon as they were back inside the carriage headed home. And to think she almost tried to sneak away to Penworth without him. Emily clung to his arm as they walked down the hall. It was mid-afternoon, nearing the end of summer, yet Penworth felt like midnight in the dead of winter. Dark. Dismal. The butler stopped in front of a large black double door and knocked.

"Come in," Andrew Kleeton's voice called from the other side.

The butler opened one of the doors, stepping back to permit Cyrus and Emily entrance. A stale, sour odor reached Emily as she walked past the strange creature of a man. She felt his hard, one-eyed gaze on her and moved closer to Cyrus.

Andrew Kleeton rose from the black, overstuffed chair he was sitting in and approached them. He was the one bright spot in an otherwise gloomy, formidable room. The casual elegance of his coffee-colored superfine jacket, cream breeches and snowy white cravat were at odds with his surroundings. He didn't belong here. It was too dark, too depressing. Andrew wasn't like that. He reminded her of sunshine and light, with his blond good looks and gleaming smile.

"Emily, how good to see you," he said, bestowing one of those smiles on her and taking her hand.

If she kept her gaze fixed on his summer-blue eyes, Emily could almost forget where they were. She could just about blot out the strange little man with one eye standing behind her, except for the sour smell that filled her nostrils. But it was hard to ignore all the darkness that threatened to envelop her, pull her in, bury her alive. Emily's gaze darted to the black brocade draperies that covered the windows, barring even a sliver of light from entering. She stared at the sofa and chairs, all done in matching patterns of black. And more black.

What in the world was Andrew doing in a morbid place like this? It reminded her of death. She shivered.

Andrew nodded in Cyrus's direction. "Mandrey."

"Hello, Kleeton." Neither man made any attempt to extend a hand.

"If there is no objection," Andrew said, "I had rather thought to share a quiet cup of tea with Emily."

"That's why we're here, isn't it?" Cyrus asked, his words laced with sarcasm.

"I meant alone."

"Why?" Emily heard the steel edge to the words.

Andrew's eyes narrowed just a hint, and then he smiled again. "I have some issues I wish to discuss with Emily. In private." His upper lip curled a moment before it flattened.

Cyrus crossed his arms over his burly chest. "My job is to protect Emily. Where she goes, I go."

"Are you still worried about Noah Sandleton? You needn't

be.'' Andrew Kleeton strode to a brocade-covered window and pulled back the fabric. ''Even your Mr. Sandleton couldn't get through these.'' Black iron bars, set close together, ran the entire length of the window, blocking anyone from entering. Or exiting, Emily thought as cold fingers of uneasiness crept along her spine. Penworth reminded her more of a prison with each passing moment.

''Emily?'' Cyrus asked, ignoring Andrew.

''Yes, I'll be fine, Cyrus,'' she said with more conviction than she felt. Her gaze traveled about the room, from the huge sword displayed over the mantel to the flickering lamps casting eerie shadows on the walls. What was Andrew doing here? It was the tenth time she'd asked that question in the ten minutes since she'd crossed the threshold of Penworth. He didn't belong here, not in such morbid surroundings. Perhaps this was the décor of the previous residents, the duke and duchess of something or other. Emily couldn't recall their names, but would bet these hideous furnishings bore their stamp.

But what about the monster of a man behind her? Emily could still hear his thick, heavy breathing, still smell the sour cabbage odor emanating from his person. Was he a castoff from the duke and duchess as well?

''In that case, I'll be waiting right outside the door,'' Cyrus said. He turned to leave.

Andrew Kleeton addressed the butler. ''Thank you, Charles, that will be all. Would you please send Mrs. Rothmore in with our tea?'' He smiled at Emily again. ''Oh, and have her see to Mr. Mandrey's needs.''

The sound of labored breathing diminished, as did the smell of something akin to a rubbish bin, signaling the butler's departure. As the door closed, Emily let out a long breath.

''Andrew,'' she asked, removing her bonnet, ''where on earth did you find that . . .'' Emily hesitated, ''. . . man?'' Dreadful, horrid, frightful, shocking, monstrous were more appropriate descriptions, but she didn't want Andrew to know how much he bothered her.

"Charles? He's harmless, Emily," Andrew said, taking a seat beside her on the black sofa. He leaned back, crossing a booted foot over his knee. "Charles is the product of our country's illustrious prison system. When I found him, he was nothing more than a bloody, beaten piece of human flesh, his eye gouged out and his tongue ripped from his mouth. He'd been thrown in a shallow grave, left to bleed to death."

Emily gasped as his words sunk in. Prison. Beaten piece of human flesh. Left to bleed to death. Questions thundered in her brain, rolling over one another, fighting for the answers like the hooves of a hundred horses charging into battle. What was Andrew doing near a prison? Why was this man Charles beaten and left for dead? What crime had he committed? Why did Andrew's fine lips twist into a cruel smile, his eyes glazed, as though he relished the tale and wanted to say more? Perhaps expand on the hideous mutilation of the butler and describe each gory detail?

Emily shuddered and wrapped her arms about herself. Andrew's gaze snapped to hers, his eyes warm and smiling, making her think she must have imagined the cold steel of a moment ago, must have dreamed the demonic curl of his lips. This was Andrew, she reminded herself. Kind, generous, polite Andrew. And she was overtired, that was all.

Andrew reached over and patted Emily's hand. She felt the soft leather of his tan glove. "Aren't you going to ask me what I was doing near Newgate?" he asked, his voice the texture of brushed velvet. "Aren't you even a little curious?"

Emily looked at him and nodded, feeling foolish for acting so skittish about the tale of a man and his misfortune. She should concentrate instead on Andrew's valiant rescue effort and the fact that Charles was still alive, disfigured or not.

"I am something of an amateur writer, though it's a well-kept secret." Andrew laughed and shook his head. "I have always written and kept journals of my travels, writing about everything, no matter how insignificant. Human suffering intrigues me. Exploring Newgate seemed logical. I wanted to understand the mechanisms of a prison, from the dank, musty interior of the cells to the warped, sinister minds of the guards and the broken, hopeless spirits of the imprisoned.''

''To fight the cause of the oppressed?'' Emily asked, thinking him nothing short of a hero.

''To test the limits to which a human will go before he loses reason, blurs all sense of right and wrong and is willing to compromise himself and his ideals,'' Andrew answered.

Emily frowned. She had not expected that answer and didn't know what to make of it. ''But why is he compromising himself?''

Andrew leaned toward her, his summer-blue gaze locking with hers. ''Greed and power, Emily. It all boils down to that. Greed and power.''

''Greed and power?'' she echoed. ''As in everyone has a price at which he or she will give over and perform in a particular manner?'' Her voice rose an octave. ''Or for the assurance of a certain amount of control, one can also be persuaded to surrender one's values?'' Emily felt a wave of anger course through her, heating her cheeks. ''I most strongly disagree with you, Andrew. If one has true conviction, no amount of money or power will lure him from that conviction.''

Andrew laughed, a full and hearty sound that filled the air, lightening the somber mood. ''Oh, Emily,'' he said, grinning, ''of course you believe in conviction and principle. That's what makes you who you are.'' His words were soft and gentle as the wind whispering through the trees. ''That's why you are so very special. And you are, Emily. So very special.''

Emily smiled, mistaking the heat in his voice for genuine brotherly affection. ''As are you, Andrew. Thank you for being such a good friend.''

His lips tilted upward, a faint suggestion of a smile playing about his mouth. ''Friends.'' The word rolled about his tongue.

''Good friends,'' Emily said, smiling again.

''Ah, yes,'' he repeated. ''Good friends.''

A knock on the door signaled their refreshments had arrived.

"Come in, Mrs. Rothmore." The door opened, but it was Cyrus, not Mrs. Rothmore, who bore the silver platter of tea and assorted cakes, cookies and scones. He advanced and, without a word, placed the tray on the mahogany table.

"Your new duties suit you, Mandrey," Andrew said, nodding toward the silver tea service.

Cyrus ignored his words and turned toward Emily. "Is everything all right?"

"Of course, Cyrus," Emily said, puzzled by his excessive concern. "Everything is fine."

"I'll be outside," he said. Turning on his heel, he quit the room.

"He's the reason I wanted to speak with you in private," Andrew said, nodding his blond head toward the door.

"Cyrus?" Emily asked, holding her cup while Andrew poured the steaming brew for her.

"Yes. Mandrey. I think you should get rid of him. The sooner the better."

"I can't do that!" Emily exclaimed, wondering at the animosity that flowed through his words.

"How do you think he can protect you when he can't take his eyes off of you long enough to notice the threat of danger?"

Emily stared at him, unwilling to hear the words, much less understand them.

"The man's in love with you, Emily. Surely you can see that."

"That's absurd, Andrew. Cyrus is concerned for my welfare, nothing more. Certainly nothing on a personal level." Emily sipped at her tea, finding it odd that Cyrus had said exactly the same thing about Andrew. She didn't believe either one. More likely, they were using her as a prize to be won in their war against one another, a war fought for nothing more than the sake of beating the other.

Emily would have no part in their games.

"Emily, I tell you, I've been watching the man. He's in love with you," Andrew persisted.

"Funny, Andrew, but Cyrus said the same thing about you." Emily met his blue gaze, her face somber and unsmiling. "The two of you have been at odds since the moment you met. I suggest you deal with one another on a private level and stop putting me in the middle."

Her words cast a shadow of gloom over the conversation, matching the dimness of the room. "Very well," Andrew said. "Perhaps that is exactly what we need to do. Settle matters in private."

"Good," Emily said, breathing a sigh of relief. At least one of these men was being reasonable. Cyrus had been about as easy to move as the stone fountain on the front lawn of Glenview Manor. But Andrew's next words made her realize he was just as stubborn as Cyrus, though in a more diplomatic, genteel manner.

"And when Mandrey is gone, I will take over full protection of you against your errant husband, when and if he ever shows."

"Andrew—"

"Don't worry, Emily," Andrew said, waving a gloved hand in dismissal, "I can handle *ten* Noah Sandletons." He had the slow, steady smile of a tiger watching his evening meal romp about in the tall grasses. Deadly. Dangerous. A sick feeling of dread rolled over her, wrapping her in its heavy embrace. Emily didn't doubt his words.

The carriage pulled away from Penworth, Andrew's words clinging to Emily like a hot summer night, still and close, almost suffocating. *I can handle ten Noah Sandletons.* There had been sincerity and conviction in those words. And determination. For the first time in all of her encounters with Andrew, Emily had detected a steely tenacity, hard and cold, that had heretofore lain buried under an air of gentlemanly civility. But she had seen it today and it surprised and confused her.

What would happen if Andrew and Noah ever met one another? Though Noah could intimidate through sheer size and dark looks alone, Emily sensed Andrew would not fall prey to such tactics. Rather, he would remain undeterred, employing craftiness and cunning to achieve his goal. Whatever goal that might be.

The only bright spot in the whole situation was her relative certainty that Noah would not show himself. Seeing her again had most likely been a passing fancy, fleeting and gone, like their marriage. Emily closed her eyes and took a deep breath. She needed to relax. Her head lolled back against the velvet squabs. Everything would be fine.

Noah was nothing but a memory, and an unpleasant one at that, who tended to resurface when her defenses were down.

"What the devil is going on?"

The harsh, sharp tone of Cyrus's words startled Emily out of her dark thoughts.

"Nothing. Really. I'm fine," Emily rushed on before realizing that Cyrus wasn't listening to her. He hadn't even been looking at her, much less addressing her. They had rounded the bend toward home. Glenview Manor sat several hundred yards ahead of them, in stately, vine-covered elegance.

But the front lawn leading up to the manor was anything but stately or elegant, and this is where Cyrus's attention lay. Two men, one tall and skinny, the other built like a mountain, romped about the front lawn like children on a Sunday afternoon. Emily watched in amazement as they ran to the huge fountain, drenching themselves with water spouting from the stone angel's pursed lips. She spotted a third trying to climb the privet hedge.

From the distance, their manner of dress appeared similar: breeches, loose fitting shirts, jackboots. Most wore caps. Only one man stood out from the rest and Emily would have recognized his tall, lanky build anywhere. Edward Billington volleyed back and forth between the men like a black bouncing ball, his long arms gesturing to the house in short, choppy movements. He appeared to be trying to get everyone inside, probably to calm things down, regain control, avoid a spectacle, as was the typical Billington style. Little did he realize that he was almost more entertaining to watch than the men cavorting on the lawn. Edward Billington in a state of agitation. Emily smiled.

"Damn them," Cyrus whispered under his breath.

Emily looked at him and sensed the tension in his body from the quiet stillness that emanated from him. He did not look pleased. Not at all.

She peered out the window, trying to get a better glimpse as the carriage rolled around to the middle of the drive. The men stopped their play as all eyes centered on the elegant black carriage bearing the Sandleton crest. It was then that Emily saw their faces, young, old, stubbled, clean-shaven, familiar ones that brought a smile and a tear to her heart. Before Cyrus could stop her, she leapt from her seat and flung the door open, bounding down into the waiting arms of the *Falcon*'s crew.

Chapter 14

"I tell you, Miss Emily, er, I mean *Lady* Emily, the cap'n was dyin' without you." Big Tom's full lower lip pulled into a pout as he shook his shaved head. "Jest dyin'."

"Yep, it's true enough," Amos piped in, popping a piece of roast duck in his mouth and chewing it with great thought. His sun-weathered face resembled well-worn leather, creases and all. "The cap'n was miserable before he left. And ornery." He shook his gray head and laughed. "He was a sight to be around, let me tell you."

"He's in love." All eyes turned to the red-haired youth who'd uttered the words. Jeremy's face turned five shades deeper than his hair. "It's just my opinion, is all," he muttered, bowing his head to stare at his plate.

Cyrus tapped his fingers on his glass of claret. When this was all over, he'd thrash every one of his men, starting with Big Tom, and he'd save an extra one for Jeremy. Or two, perhaps. They were making Noah look like a milksop, a weak-kneed, spineless fool, and there wasn't a damn thing he could do about it. From the moment Emily had bounded out of the carriage, Cyrus knew trouble was ahead. And he had been right. For the past several hours he had heard nothing but what a sorry excuse for a man Noah had become since parting from his beloved wife. It was downright sickening.

"He'll come fer you now," Amos said around a mouthful of candied yams. "Sure enough, he will." The other men, their mouths filled with samplings of roast duck, boiled potato and candied yams, grunted in agreement.

Emily shot a quick glance in Cyrus's direction. Was she worried for Noah's safety? Did *she* think he'd try to come to her? One look at her plate told him something was bothering her. She'd flattened her potatoes, topped them with smashed yams and dumped shredded roast pork over the whole mess. And she hadn't taken more than two bites, though he couldn't blame her on that count. It was not the most appealing presentation he'd ever seen.

Clearing her throat, she swallowed hard and looked around the table. Her gray eyes glistened with tears like stars on a cloudless night. Cyrus didn't miss the slight tremor in her hand as she smoothed back a stray lock of hair. "Thank you, each of you. You've all been so kind, trying to protect me, make me feel better by telling such high tales about your captain." Her smile was bright, too bright, as though it masked a pain buried deep in her soul where joy once dwelt before betrayal and despair blotted out its memory, leaving behind an empty, all-consuming grief. "But," she continued with just the slightest quiver in her voice, "we all know there isn't a weak bone in Noah's body. He's proud and fierce and . . ." she hesitated, stumbling over the next word as though her tongue refused to say it, ". . . de-determined. And you all know he's determined not to be saddled with a wife."

The men all started talking at once, their loud, raucous voices filling the dining room, drowning out Emily's protestations. A shrill whistle burst through the clamor, piercing the air like an arrow, quieting the group in an instant.

All eyes turned to the man who'd issued the edict. John

Judson reached out and patted Emily's hand. His blue eyes roamed over the misbegotten group that was more family than his own blood relations. He stroked his white beard with his free hand, a gesture the crew knew he employed when he was deep in thought. The room remained silent, waiting.

The oak chair squeaked under John's weight as he turned to face Emily, his paunch spilling over the ornately carved arm. His rough, reddened hand remained on her smooth, slender one, offering comfort and strength. It amazed Cyrus how this woman could make a man, any man, regardless of rank or station, want to help her, slay her dragons if need be. Just as John was doing now.

"I've known Noah a long time, Lady Emily," John began, holding her gaze with his honest blue eyes. "As I told you before, he's a good, honest man. When he left us several weeks back, he told me he wasn't returning until he had you with him. Those were his exact words." His voice was soft and low, like the lapping of the tide on sun-weathered rocks. "And I believe him."

Cyrus watched as a shimmering tear escaped and trickled down her cheek. "But where is he, John? He's had plenty of time to get here." The sadness in her voice ripped at Cyrus's gut. She reached up to swipe at another tear. Brave Emily. He wanted to stand up and rip off his wig, throw his glasses and beard on the ground and end this cruel game right now. His fingers shook. He clenched his hand to still himself.

John's broad shoulders lifted. "Perhaps he's here. Somewhere." His blue eyes glanced over Cyrus, then settled back on Emily. "Have faith in him, Lady Emily."

" 'E's the cause of it all," Big Tom said, pointing a sausage-sized finger at Cyrus. "We heard he was hired ta keep the cap'n away from Lady Emily. If'n it wasn't fer 'im, they'd be together already."

Emily shook her head. "Well, that's not exactly—"

"That's right," Amos cut her off as though she hadn't spoken. Scratching his gray head, he muttered, "Wot business is it o' his if the two of them git together or not?'' He leaned forward.

"I agree." Jeremy's voice squeaked with feeling. "He had no business interfering with them. They would have worked it out. They—they—" he stuttered, "love each other." His ears flamed, but he kept his level green gaze on Cyrus, challenging him to answer.

"Gentlemen, there's something you should know," Emily began.

"The kid's right," Big Tom said, hitting the table with a beefy fist.

"Right 'e is!" Amos seconded, his scrawny fist following suit.

Within seconds, the table resounded with shouts as the men pounded their fists on the hard oak, shooting venomous gazes at the man they now held responsible for their captain and his lady's separation.

Cyrus watched in amazement, moved that these men would remain so loyal to their captain. Or perhaps it was his lady whose allegiance they now served. Either way, they were hell-bent and dead set against Cyrus. It was time to settle things down before they came after him, pounding on him with the same vigor with which they were attacking the table. He could not afford another broken or bruised body part.

Slamming his fist down, he roared, "Enough!"

The room fell quiet, all eyes watching in startled silence.

Cyrus stood, his hands resting on the white linen tablecloth. He eyed each man, holding his gaze until the other man looked away. Big Tom sunk his head down. Amos looked off to the right and scratched his ear. Jeremy turned several different shades of red and planted his eyes on the ceiling. None of the other men were bold enough to hold his gaze.

Except John Judson.

John sat back in his chair, hands crossed over a stomach that reminded Cyrus of rising bread, soft and rounded, expanding to twice its normal size. His blue eyes, usually warm and full of spirit, were staring with dead intent at Cyrus. It was as though he could see behind the bushy wig and beard, behind the thick glasses and raspy voice, to the man who lay beneath the layers of extra padding. To the man who was their captain. His friend. And Emily's husband.

Clearing his throat, Cyrus looked away and addressed the men before him. "You men may hate me and hold me responsible for the separation of your captain and his wife." This statement brought a round of low grumbles, washing over and past him like a wave, settling back into the dark depths of silence. "And I say," he paused to give his next words added meaning. "If your captain truly loves Lady Emily, *no one* will keep him from her." His hands balled into fists. "Not me or Lord Kenilworth. Or the devil himself. If he truly loves her, Sandleton will find a way to be with her. Period."

The men hadn't expected this backward rally for their captain. It was clear in the way they looked at one another, muttering low under their breath, scratching their heads, shifting their gazes between Cyrus and John Judson. They were confused, off balance, disturbed. Each man was prepared to hate Cyrus. He could see that in the way they narrowed their eyes at him, hear it in their harsh accusations, feel it in the tension vibrating throughout the room. They all wanted to hate him, to pounce on him for wreaking havoc on the lives of two people they cared about. But now they couldn't, not after the words he'd just spoken. And that rubbed them raw. Noah knew his men; they'd probably want to get in a punch or two just to work off some of their frustration. He didn't miss the glaze in Big Tom's beady eyes. It usually meant he was ready to launch an attack on some unsuspecting victim. Cyrus rubbed the bridge of his nose, feeling the bump with careful fingers.

John settled the matter like a captain gathering his men around him to prepare for battle. He had the direction, the determination, the faith to lead his men and the wisdom to impart this knowledge to them. When John spoke, they listened. Only one man commanded more respect from these men.

Unfortunately, Noah Sandleton was hiding behind a wig and beard at the moment. Worse yet, the man he was posing as was the object of these men's ire.

"Listen here, men." John's quiet voice stilled the clamor in the room. "Mandrey's got a point. He's only doing his job. Nothing more, nothing less. You have to respect him for that." John grinned. "And when Noah shows up," he said as his blue eyes twinkled, "and we all know he will, he'll only be doing his job when he trounces this unlucky gent."

" 'E'll beat 'im to the bones," Big Tom said, nodding his head back and forth.

"Noah will string 'im up by his boots," Amos chimed in, cackling like a wild man.

"He takes care of his own," Jeremy said, his young voice trembling with emotion.

Cheers traveled around the room. John raised his hand to silence them. "You do have one thing working in your favor, Mandrey," he said, stroking his long beard in casual speculation. All eyes settled on Cyrus.

"Pray, Mr. Judson, what might that be?" These men had him all but buried. If one believed the roar of the crowd, the only advantage Cyrus might have against Noah would be a head start away from Glenview Manor. Immediately.

Leaning forward, John's lips turned up in a slow, easy smile as his blue gaze traveled over Cyrus's face. "I was just thinking that a few nicks and bruises would never show under all that hair." He tilted his white head to the left. "And those glasses would hide a broken nose real well. Yes sir, Mr. Mandrey. You might just consider yourself a lucky man. A lucky man indeed."

"I'm sorry, John, but I just don't see Noah returning to Glenview Manor," Emily said as she poured coffee into his cup. They were sharing after-dinner coffee in one of Emily's favorite rooms. She called it the Cream Salon because everything from the thick Persian rug to the damask draperies, brocade sofa and overstuffed chairs shone in various shades of cream. Cream vases lined the fireplace mantel, each displayed in various sizes and shapes with Oriental designs etched on them. A huge silk print of a dragon done in white, gold and cream hung over the mantel. Square cream pillows with gold tassels accented the sofa and chairs. In the corner of the room rested a stack of four very large pillows of the same cream color and gold tassel design as those found on the furniture.

These particular pillows had intrigued Emily, and when she was certain no one was about, had kicked off her slippers and crawled onto them. And toppled off. Apparently, stacking them four high and sitting on them was incorrect. She was much more successful when she placed each one on the floor and chose one. Sometimes she scattered them about and stretched her body on all four. It felt like she was lying on a big, fluffy cloud. She'd done that a few times and fallen fast asleep. Mr. Billington had caught her once and, much to her amazement, made no comment other than to ask if she were comfortable, to which she had pushed the tangled mass of hair from her eyes and replied yes, very much so. He'd bowed and left then, and she almost thought she'd seen a shadow of a smile on his thin lips. But she told herself her brain was addled from sleep. Billington never smiled.

This room brought her peace, imposing a calm, quiet serenity that she often sought. She needed that feeling tonight. Especially as she sat with John, waiting for him to bring up the one subject that could tear down her wall of tranquillity in the blink of an eye: Noah.

Emily set the heavy pot down, making a production of preparing her own steaming brew. Two lumps of sugar and a spot of cream. Stir together and blend to a dark tan. Place spoon on side of saucer. Anything to avoid discussing Noah.

"He'll be here, sure as my name is John Judson." There it was, the first words out of John's mouth. His words were spoken with such conviction, such certainty, that Emily didn't have a heart to tell him she was just as confident he would not return.

Why would he when he had Desireé and Monique to warm his bed? Why should he when he'd been forced into a marriage he didn't want with a woman he didn't love? Emily felt her stomach clench. Of course no well-bred woman would ever discuss such delicate matters. Especially with a member of the opposite sex.

Emily plunged forward. "John, you've known Noah for ages. Please don't try to spare my tender sensibilities." She sipped her coffee, meeting his blue gaze over the rim of her cup. "I know about his women. I saw the clothes, or whatever you might call those wisps of material, in his armoire. He's probably off on one of his adventures, lazing about in some port." Her voice trembled. "Too drunk on wine and lust to know or care where he is." She'd thought those words more times than she could remember, but saying them aloud to another person was like shredding the last flimsy bits of hope into a hundred pieces of nothingness.

John shook his bushy white head. "You're wrong, Lady Emily. Dead wrong."

Emily blinked. She did not want to hear his soothing words. Everyone was trying to spare her feelings, protect her from the truth. Cyrus, John, Amos, Big Tom. Even young Jeremy. She could feel the tears threatening. Why couldn't she think of Noah without crying? Where was her calm? It wasn't working. She could feel it slipping away. Why couldn't she say his name without hearing the quiver in her voice, feeling the tug at her heart, as though at any moment she would fall apart. When would it stop? When would it all be over? Emily feared the answer and so she pushed it away, buried it deep inside her mind. *Breathe,* she told herself. Just breathe and think of nothing else. Relax. But it was no use. The bitter truth always dug its way out, clawing forth, taunting her with words she refused to believe. It would never be over, the voice promised. Never. Not in one day or one year or one hundred years. Never.

"No," she said, blocking out the words swirling through her brain, teasing her with harsh reminders, twisting her thoughts.

"No," she repeated, pushing them back, forcing them into the black abyss of denial.

"Yes, Lady Emily. You're wrong about Noah." John's voice was a gentle, soothing balm to her tense nerves, even if his words were not. "There've been no other women since the wedding. I'd wager there hasn't been one since the day he laid eyes on you."

Emily wanted to laugh, a dark, hysterical laugh at those words that couldn't be further from the truth. Instead, she raised an eyebrow, forcing herself to remain quiet.

John held up a big fleshy hand. "Now just wait a minute, Lady Emily. I'm getting the feeling that you think you're the only one who's unhappy with this marriage situation." He shook his head. "Not so. Noah was miserable the last time I saw him."

A sinking feeling settled in the pit of Emily's stomach. "Of course he was miserable, John. I knew that." It was bad enough surmising his unhappiness and knowing she was the cause of it, but having someone confirm those thoughts was even worse.

"Sure enough he was miserable, but not for the reason you think. I went to visit Noah a few days before the wedding. Do you know how I found him? Do you know what he was doing?"

It would not have been ladylike to tell John she had a fair idea of how he'd spent his last days of bachelorhood. She wasn't supposed to know about *those* kinds of places. Emily kept her true thoughts to herself and simply shrugged.

"Well, I'll tell you, little lady. I found him drunker than a dog and more miserable than a bird without wings."

Because I clipped them.

"And all because he had to marry you and leave." His blue gaze searched her face. "He didn't want to leave you, Lady Emily. He wanted to be a proper husband, a real husband."

The words shook Emily. The cup she held fell from her hands, splattering hot coffee onto her blue gown. Even the warmth of the steaming liquid soaking through petticoats to her skin could not rid the chill that ran through her body.

John jumped up from his chair. "I upset you. I'm sorry. Let me help." He handed her his linen napkin, his big frame standing right beside her as though to ward off any further accidents.

"He . . . he *wanted* to marry me?" she asked, her voice one note above silence. Hearing the words aloud sounded foreign, even to her and she'd dreamed them a thousand times. Noah had wanted to marry her? He'd never said anything, never indicated by even the smallest degree that he would be amenable to such an arrangement. But then she hadn't seen him until ten minutes before the wedding either. And afterward, Emily blushed with remembering, there hadn't been more than a few minutes of talking before passion carried them away on a tumultuous ride.

"I'm so confused, John." She massaged her temples with the tips of her fingers. "You said he wanted to marry me, but he had to leave. Why, John? Why did he have to leave?"

John sat down next to her, sagging the cushions with his weight. "I can't say, Lady Emily. I wish I could. All I can tell you is that he had a good reason. You'll have to hear the rest from him."

It was on the tip of her tongue to ask him what kind of "good reason" could permit a man to desert his wife, but she decided against it. John was too loyal. He'd never tell her something he thought should come from her husband. Emily sighed, resigning herself to the question she'd asked every night for the past several weeks. "And how will I do that, John, when I have no idea where he is?"

John smiled, "You will. If I know Noah, he won't wait much longer. I'm surprised he hasn't come to you already."

"Well, it's not that easy, John," Emily said. "Cyrus Mandrey is here for the express purpose of keeping Noah away from me."

The old sailor threw back his head and let out a deep-bellied laugh. "Dear girl, do you really think one man is going to keep Noah from what's his?" John laughed again, clasping his big hands together. "Ah, well, time will tell. Yes, it will."

Emily was about to say more when a harsh rap on the door interfered.

"It's us, Lady Emily. Come to say g'night." Emily smiled at the rough, gravelly voice on the other side. Big Tom must be sending Mr. Billington into fits of apoplexy. She could hear the butler's precise voice trying to persuade the group to wait, beseeching them to employ a little patience. The door burst open and in piled Big Tom, Amos, Jeremy and Mr. Billington.

"We wanted to say g'night, but this bugger tried to stop us," Amos said, pointing a bony finger at Edward Billington. "Told us to use some 'reserve.' Wot's that?"

Big Tom screwed up his face and scratched his head with two beefy fingers. "I dunno. Jeremy, wot's a reserve? Is it like me mum's preserve? The strawberry kind?"

Jeremy crossed his long, skinny arms over his nonexistent chest. "Hmm. I think it's something we do. Like . . . like . . ." his voice drifted as he tried to come up with a plausible answer.

"For your information, gentlemen," Mr. Billington said, his voice filling the room. "To practice reserve means to exercise self-restraint, control of one's actions."

"Huh?" The three sailors looked at one another. "Exercise what?"

"I think what Mr. Billington is trying to say is that he wanted you to wait until you were invited to enter," Emily said, her voice soft and gentle. "He was only doing his job."

"All 'e knows how to do is walk around like 'e's got a stick in 'is behind and a bunch o' lemons in his mouth," Amos said, casting the butler a disgusted look. Big Tom and Jeremy howled.

Mr. Billington straightened, long arms at his side, shoulders back, feet square and centered. And his mouth *was* puckered in a look of sour distaste. As though he *had* a bunch of lemons in there. Emily stifled a giggle. Amos was dead center with his description.

"Amos, he was only thinking of me. Isn't that what all of you have been trying to do since the moment I saw you again?" She stood up and walked toward them, stopping between the three sailors and the butler. "You've tried to protect me, worry over me, guide me. That's all Mr. Billington is doing and I have to admit, sometimes I make his job very difficult." Her mouth turned up at the corners, giving the men a mischievous grin.

Emily threw Mr. Billington a sideways glance, hoping he would play along with her explanation. He stared at her, the sour expression gone, replaced with open-mouthed confusion. It was probably as close to gaping as Mr. Billington had ever come. Emily gave him a small smile and turned back to her three friends. She knew Mr. Billington thought her less than one step above this lot standing before him, thought of her as nothing more than an assignment given by his employer, and a distasteful one at that. But she was offering him a way to save face with these men. All he needed to do was accept it by remaining quiet. And that, Emily knew, would prove very difficult for the ever correct, self-righteous Mr. Billington to do.

"Maybe we was a little hard on 'im," Big Tom said, cracking the knuckles on his right hand. His beady eyes ran over the butler. " 'E jest got some strange ways, is all."

"We ain't used to 'em. We ain't used to havin' a body look down 'is nose at us ever' time we fergit our manners." Amos puffed out his bony chest. "Noah never done that. And we met all kinds of royalty. All kinds," he repeated, taking a step closer to Billington.

Emily held her breath as Mr. Billington met Amos's hard stare. He offered no rebuttal, no drippingly sarcastic commentary, though Emily knew his repertoire contained much of it. She thanked the heavens he chose this moment to hold his tongue.

"Big Tom and Amos said it all fer me. Nothin's left to be said." Jeremy grinned and punched Big Tom in the shoulder.

The burly man grabbed the young boy and hoisted him in the air as though he were one of the many cream cushions accenting the room. Amos let out a hoot and shouted, "Get 'im Jeremy. Get 'im where it counts."

Jeremy thrust his fingers under Big Tom's armpits, tickling him until the giant let out a screech and dropped him on the hard floor.

Anxious to avoid another altercation between these three men and the butler of Glenview Manor, Emily took a step forward and said in a low voice, "That will be all, Mr. Billington. Thank you."

He looked at her, his gaze hard and steady. And unfathomable. Had a whisper of kindness just passed across his face? Had she imagined those ever-narrowed gray eyes relaxing just a little, the tight lips smoothing out, the frown gentling? She couldn't say, and before she could consider it further, he gave her a curt nod and exited the room.

"All right, *men,*" John's commanding voice addressed the laughing, tickling trio who resembled naughty children more than seasoned sailors. "It's time we bid Lady Emily good night. We need to be on the road by dawn. The *Falcon*'s got a schedule to keep."

The jostling, teasing gestures from the men died down and they approached their captain's bride. "Yer the most beautiful, kindest woman I ever met, Lady Emily," Big Tom blurted out, casting his eyes downward. "You got a heart o' gold an' the cap'n's gonna be back soon. 'E knows how to spot riches. And yer a jewel." Emily saw the heat color his face and knew he had just paid her a rare compliment. She reached out, grabbed both of his beefy hands in hers and leaned over to plant a soft kiss on his cheek. The faint smell of cabbage reached her nostrils. She was surprised Mr. Billington hadn't lectured them on the basics of hygiene. It appeared he himself had exercised some "reserve" where they were concerned.

"Good-bye, Big Tom. Thank you." He smiled at her then, a wide, toothless grin that lit up his homely face. The long scar on his forehead flattened.

Amos was next. "Thank you, Lady Emily, fer lettin' us in

yer home.'' His eyes met hers and she saw in them the light of wisdom that came from years of experience, situations and circumstances. Life had been Amos's tutor, mere words found in books had not. ''You treated us like the cap'n does. Like friends.'' He nodded his gray head, the lines in his leathery face standing out, spreading like a fan with his grin. Amos reminded Emily of an oak Christopher had cut down years ago, its middle marked with a series of rings denoting its age. They had counted fifty-seven rings. She wondered if the lines on this old sailor's face would outnumber ones on the oak.

Emily leaned over and kissed his sun-beaten cheek. ''Goodbye, Amos,'' she whispered.

Jeremy was next. His face with its smattering of freckles was the same vivid hue as the scarlet roses on the front lawn. He twisted his hands a few times, his green eyes darting around the room, bouncing from the right to the left, up and down, before settling on Emily's chin.

''Thank you for coming, Jeremy,'' Emily said. Maybe if she started the conversation he would feel more at ease. He blushed an even deeper shade of red. Magenta? Like the gladiolas in the back of the manor. Just as vibrant. Just as noticeable.

She tried again. ''You all came to ensure my safety. Your captain would be very proud of such a noble act.'' As the words spilled out, Emily questioned the truth of her own words. Would Noah really be pleased that his men journeyed to see her? Intruded upon his personal affairs? Bandied his name and emotions about, giving the impression that he was a besotted husband who wanted nothing more than to reunite with his wife? Somehow, she doubted he'd take kindly to that description. A faint smile played about her lips. Too bad he'd never know his loyal men had unwittingly made a fool of him for her sake.

''He'll come to you. I know he will.'' Jeremy's words rang with the innocent fervor of one who had never known the bitter taste of love's betrayal.

Emily blinked hard. Twice. It wouldn't do to have Jeremy see her fall apart and cry an ocean of tears. Better to do that in private, where no one but herself would bear witness to the pain she felt inside. She gave him a quick hug and whispered, "Thank you, Jeremy."

She watched the youth turn away, his face settling back to its pale pink hue. There wasn't more than a few years' difference in their ages, but it may as well have been decades. Jeremy still resided in a cocoon of naiveté, where love prevailed and good triumphed over evil. Emily had been stripped of those beliefs the day Noah left their marriage bed.

A single tear escaped, trickling unchecked down her cheek. A light touch on Emily's arm reminded her that she was not alone. She turned around to find John looking at her, his warm blue eyes studying her with quiet intent. He reached out and covered her cold hands in his big, rough ones.

"Oh, John," Emily whispered, "what am I going to do?" She was so confused. Did she want Noah to return or didn't she? The words that spilled from her mouth said she never wanted to see him again, believed he'd never come back, but the secret corners of her heart told a different story. They still held onto some of Jeremy's innocent fairy-tale beliefs about happily ever after.

"Jeremy's right, you know." John smiled at her, his soft voice wrapping around her like a warm blanket. "Noah will come to you." His blue eyes bore into hers. "And then it will be up to you to decide if you'll listen to your heart or your pride."

Sleep wouldn't come. The hours ticked by, creeping toward morning as Noah watched the dark edges of night give way to the gray shades of dawn. He lay on the bed, arms propped behind his head, staring out the window. Soon it would be time to shroud himself in a mass of bushy hair, don a pair of thick spectacles and pad his chest. It would be time to play the part of Cyrus Mandrey.

Noah sighed. Each day it was becoming more difficult to

pretend he was a trustworthy, nondescript do-gooder by the name of Cyrus Mandrey. And it was becoming equally difficult to feign anything but polite interest in Emily when all he wanted to do was take her in his arms and bury himself inside her sweet silkiness. Emily's presence swirled around him, making him a prisoner to his own senses. He heard her soft voice everywhere he turned. In his dreams, he saw her golden beauty unfolding like an exotic flower, felt the satiny touch of her skin beneath his fingers, inhaled the fragrant lilac scent on her body, sipped the honeyed nectar from her full lips.

He grew hard at the thought. But that was nothing new to him. For the past several weeks it hadn't taken more than a smile, a look, a word from Emily, no matter how innocent, to make his manhood throb with need. She wielded a power over him, like a sorceress casting a spell, making him want her as no woman ever had. Noah swore under his breath. Soon, he would go to his wife and no one would stand in his way. Not Kleeton, or Ian, or even Cyrus Mandrey. Very soon, there would be nothing between him and Emily but the feel of her satin skin against his.

It was time to speed up his plan. Things were moving too slowly. Noah's thoughts turned to Andrew Kleeton. Was he just a quiet country gentleman, harboring no darker side of himself other than a macabre taste in decorating? Or was he a cold-blooded, ruthless killer, waiting to strike again? It was time to find out, Noah decided as he sat on the edge of the bed and reached for his breeches.

Was his name Andrew Kleeton or Peter Crowlton? Noah splashed water on his face and reached for a towel. Gentleman or traitor? He opened a drawer and pulled out his wig and beard. Neighbor or nemesis? His booted feet strode to the closet where he pulled out a fresh shirt and jacket. Innocent or guilty? Grabbing his spectacles, Noah fitted them to his face and looked at his reflection in the oval mirror.

A stranger stared back at him. He had created Cyrus Mandrey. Had Peter Crowlton created Andrew Kleeton? Noah thought of the calfskin gloves that Kleeton never removed. Quite possibly, he thought as he closed his bedroom door with a soft click. Quite possibly indeed. As he headed down the spiral staircase in the direction of the dining room, he plotted his next move.

The smell of bacon and fresh-brewed coffee reached him before his booted foot hit the bottom step. He could hear the soft din of plates and utensils. There was very little conversation. Cyrus smiled to himself and entered the room. The *Falcon*'s crewmen were taking advantage of Cook's culinary expertise, heaping their plates with crispy bacon, sausage patties, fried potatoes and three different variations of eggs. Bowls of fresh strawberries brightened the table along with an assortment of nut breads, tarts and pastries.

"I can see this beats young Jeremy's cooking any day," Cyrus commented, taking his seat at the head of the table. He reached for the silver pot and noticed all eyes were on him.

"Is something wrong?" No one said a word. He ran a hand through his full beard. "Is something stuck somewhere?" Cyrus patted his hair and mustache.

Amos coughed into the silence. Big Tom cleared his throat. John's blue eyes narrowed. Jeremy was the first to speak. His face matched the strawberry jam on his knife. "Pardon me, Mr. Mandrey," he asked, his green eyes wide with confusion, "but how did you know I was the cook?"

Cyrus stared at the boy. Damnation! How indeed! He'd known because Jeremy had been practicing his sad culinary skills on the whole crew since he'd been hired on board the *Falcon* seven months before. He'd known because underneath the hair and spectacles of Cyrus Mandrey resided their captain, a man who'd tasted every one of Jeremy's meals, from his lumpy porridge to his hardtack biscuits.

Cyrus cleared his throat and held Jeremy's gaze. He couldn't look away or show any sign of confusion. All eyes were on him. Watching. Waiting. "That's an easy one, Jeremy. I served a short time on a ship and the rule was the youngest member got kitchen duty." His laugh was light and disarming. He hoped. "At the time, that was me. If the rule still applies," he said as he scanned the crusty lot of sailors before settling his gaze back on Jeremy, "you've got this room beat by at least ten or more years."

Jeremy grinned and nodded his red head. "Right you are. Big Tom is eight and thirty. Amos is . . . is. . . . How old *are you,* Amos?"

The old sailor laughed and spat out, "Old enough to know better!" The crowd let out a whooping holler that put a twinkle in Amos's eyes.

"C'mon, Amos," Jeremy persisted. "Tell us how many years you been stomping on this ground?"

Amos leaned back in his chair, scratched his stubbled chin and looked at the ceiling. "Let's see." He counted on his fingers. "I was fifteen when I sailed on the *Tempest,* spent ten years with them, six on the *Runaway,* twelve on the *Lady,* and seven on the *Falcon.*" He paused, moved two fingers up and down, shook his head, raised three fingers, then two more. "Damnation!" Amos threw his hands in the air. "How the hell old am I, anyway?"

Big Tom grinned, the gaps between his teeth wide and uneven. "Old. Older 'n all of us put together."

"I am?" Amos leaned back in his chair and scratched his gray head.

"You're fifty," John said, nodding at him. "And full of more energy than the lot of this sorry group. Now eat up. We have a long trip ahead of us."

The rest of the meal passed in relative silence except for the occasional clink of glass or scrape of silverware to plate. When the men were finished, they bade Cyrus a hasty good-bye and went to gather their bags. John and Cyrus were the only two remaining in the room.

"More coffee?" Cyrus offered, extending the pot.

John held up his hand and shook his white head. "I'm stuffed. My compliments to the cook."

"I'll see that she gets them."

The room fell into silence, laced with a fine tension that hinted of things unspoken.

"So you've sailed before," John said, his blue gaze intent. Cyrus nodded. "A few times."

"I've been sailing for more years than I can remember. Used to be captain of my own ship, until I met up with Noah." He leaned back in his chair and folded his hands over his rounded belly.

"Then you are managing quite well in his absence?"

John shrugged. "Well enough. Might as well get used to it. Once he and Lady Emily patch things up, he won't be back."

"Would that bother you?" Seven years was a long time.

"I'd miss him. Noah's like a son to me. Never had any children of my own." He pinched the bridge of his nose.

"And he must think of you as a father." *You were more of a father to him than his real father.*

"That would be a real honor." John held Cyrus's gaze, his blue eyes misty.

"It would be an honor for him too." Cyrus swallowed hard.

John said nothing for a full thirty seconds. "He's in love with her, you know."

"I know." The words were low, rough with feeling.

"He'll come for her."

Cyrus nodded.

"She loves him too."

"Does she?" Cyrus felt a deep pain in his chest.

"She does. But she's been hurt. She's afraid. He better have a damn good reason for leaving her like that."

"I think he does," Cyrus said.

John sighed. "Then they'll have to get past their stubborn pride, past the hurt and anger, to find the love."

"Can they do it?" He asked the question as much to himself as to John.

"If their love is strong enough, if they fight hard enough, then they can."

Cyrus said nothing. There were no words left to say.

John pushed back his chair and stood up. "I'd best be on my way before the men start trouncing the flowers again."

Cyrus stood up also. He approached John and held out his hand. "Good-bye, John."

The older man clasped Cyrus's hand with both of his. The blue eyes that studied him brimmed with unshed tears. "Good-bye, Captain," he whispered.

Cyrus's eyes widened in shock and confusion. John smiled and squeezed his hands. "You're like a son to me, boy. I'd know you anywhere."

There was no time to respond as Big Tom's voice bellowed through the door. "All set, John."

Releasing his hand, John stood back and raised his right hand in a salute. "Good luck, my boy. Good luck." Then with one last smile, he was gone, leaving Cyrus alone with his thoughts.

Chapter 15

Cyrus tapped on Emily's door once more, a little louder this time. He thought of calling Julia, her maid, to check on her, but decided against it. If Emily were feeling under the weather, he wanted to see her himself. Make certain it wasn't anything serious. She had to be ill. Perhaps a case of the ague. What else would keep her in bed until eleven in the morning?

"Emily." He tried to keep his voice raspy but not too loud. It proved to be a difficult task. If he could just borrow Noah's deep drawl, it would have Emily throwing the door open posthaste. Or hiding under the counterpane. John's words pounded in his head, beating through his thoughts like Ian's fist had beaten his body. *She loves you.* Was it true? Did she still love him despite his desertion? Could she still love him?

Cyrus heard a groan from behind Emily's door, followed by running footsteps and horrible retching sounds. Emily was ill! He threw open the door and burst into her chambers. She was huddled in a corner, kneeling over a chamber pot, her golden mane falling in a tangled mass down her back.

"Emily." Cyrus hated to see her this way. He knelt down

beside her, stroking her hair back from her pale face. "Let me help you." He heard the anguish in his voice.

She shook her head and threw up again. Her forehead was warm and sweaty. A cool cloth might feel good. "I'll get you a cloth," he said, scrambling to his feet. By the time he had the damn thing ready, she'd been sick two more times. Cyrus knelt down and pressed it to her forehead.

Emily hunched over the chamber pot, her breathing quick and shallow. The cotton of her batiste nightgown clung to her in a white sticky mess. Cyrus rotated the cloth between her forehead and the back of her neck. Wisps of damp tendrils escaped the limp mass that Cyrus held in his hand.

Long moments passed with nothing in the room but the sound of their breathing. When it seemed as though the worst had passed, Cyrus ventured a word. "Emily?"

Nothing.

"Emily?" he persisted. "What happened?"

She didn't even try to lift her head. Oh my God, he thought, she's dying right before my eyes. "Emily!" His words were harsh, urgent.

"What!" she yelled, flinging back her head and eyeing him with wild gray eyes.

He looked at her in shock. She seemed to be quite alive now. Not on the verge of death as he'd feared a moment ago. Actually, she appeared almost angry.

"Are you all right?" She didn't look all right. Not at all. She was watching him as though she wanted to pounce on him and scratch his eyes out. And then do some other bodily harm to him. "Emily?" He kept his voice soft and even, as though talking to a child.

Her brows creased into a straight line, but she said nothing.

"Do you think you ate something that disagreed with you?" His words were gentle, patient.

"No." She looked away.

"Perhaps some sort of stomach upset?" He wiped her mouth with the wet cloth.

"No." Her eyes squeezed shut.

He was running out of possibilities. "You seem so sick. What could have made you so ill?"

No answer.

"I'm going to call a doctor."

"I don't need a doctor." Her voice was firm and unbending.

Cyrus shook his head. "You've been ill twice in the last five minutes. You're all hot and sweaty. You say you didn't eat anything that turned your stomach." He shrugged. "Someone has to tell us what's wrong."

"I know what's wrong." Her words were faint, as though she couldn't muster the energy to speak them.

"Then dear God, woman, tell me. What's wrong with you?"

Emily closed her eyes and slumped forward. "I'm pregnant."

Cyrus stumbled back as though he'd been kicked. Pregnant? He tried to clear his head, make some sense of what she'd just said, but the thought of Emily pregnant scattered his logic like wind scattering the leaves.

"Pregnant?" he croaked. Pregnant! With his child! He was going to be a father.

"Pregnant," she whispered, burying her face in her hands. She did not seem at all pleased with the prospect of carrying his child. The thought weighed in his gut like a lead ball.

"You're not ... pleased ... about the baby," he said. He had no experience in this area, none at all. Should he tell her that her husband would be thrilled with the news of a child? Or should he not mention her husband at all? Or perhaps he should just offer her another cool cloth and not say a word.

A huge sob escaped her. Emily looked up at him, her gray eyes rimmed in red, tears streaming down her cheeks. "My baby has no father."

Cyrus rifled a hand through his thick hair. "Of course he has a father." To hell with watching his words. "And when he finds out, he'll be delighted. You'll see."

She shook her head, fresh tears spilling from her sad eyes. "No. He doesn't want me. He'd never want a baby."

The words twisted his gut like a knife, sharp and deep. *Does she really believe that? Does she think her husband some kind of monster?* Cold, hard bands of anger grabbed him, pulling him to the limits of his patience.

"Do you want the baby?" The question was direct, devoid of emotion.

Emily swiped at a stray tear. "Of course I do."

He forced himself to say the next words. "And do you love him?" Cyrus held his breath.

"That has nothing to do with it," she hissed.

"It has everything to do with it," he growled. "Answer me, Emily. Do you love him?" His gaze bore into her, willing her to speak the words.

Emily pushed the hair from her face and sat back on her heels, staring at him for a full minute before her head dipped a fraction of an inch. It wasn't a full nod, just a little movement downward and then up again. But for a man as desperate as he was for another chance, it was enough.

"You love him." The words spilled out before he could stop them.

"Cyrus! I really do not want to discuss this any further."

He had pushed her too far, forced her to admit something that she probably kept locked away in the dark recesses of her heart, safe from everyone, even herself. He shouldn't have pressed her in her weakened state, but desperate men take desperate measures and he was well past desperate.

His heart lightened at the words she'd spoken. He longed to take her in his arms and pledge his eternal love. They needed to strengthen their fragile bond as husband and wife, before time and circumstance got in the way. He would shed his disguise along with his pride and go to her tonight. And then he would show her just how much he loved her and their unborn child.

Cyrus's gaze settled on Emily. She was leaning against the wall, eyes closed, long lashes caressing her pale skin. He thought her the most beautiful woman he'd ever seen, even in her weakened condition. With great care, he scooped her limp body into his arms and carried her to the bed where he laid her down as though she were more fragile than the finest piece of china. Folding the covers about her shoulders, he let his fingers trace a pattern along the slender column of her neck, ending at the delicate hollow of her cheek. Soon, very soon, she would be his again.

He pressed Speed Demon on, eager to set his plans in motion. Penworth loomed before him in the distance, cold and unwelcome. Not a splash of color anywhere. There were no flowers in the beds, no blooming trees or vibrant shrubs on the lawn. Everything was the darkest green or the dullest brown. Drab. Oppressive.

Speed Demon trotted along the circular drive, ears perked, head high. A huge, darkly clad figure appeared from the side of the house. He stopped several feet from Cyrus.

"I'm here to see Mr. Kleeton," Cyrus said, studying the big man. Big was not the proper term for this individual. Neither was tall. Both were drastic understatements. The man staring at him as though he'd just as soon crush him with his bare hands rather than look at him was twice the size of Big Tom. And several times meaner if the snarl on his face was any indication.

"Is Mr. Kleeton in?"

The giant crossed his burly arms over his chest and planted his feet. He said nothing.

Perhaps he had his tongue ripped out too, Cyrus mused. Another prison escapee? He'd lay his money on it. He wondered what other creatures of misfortune inhabited the walls of Penworth. Before he could consider the matter further, the front door opened and Andrew Kleeton stepped out, dressed in black from head to toe.

"Ah, Mandrey," he said, smiling, "what a pleasant surprise." Neither the smile nor the words contained a hint of warmth.

"Did I interrupt something?" Cyrus cocked a brow. "Looks like you're headed for a funeral."

Ignoring the question, Kleeton posed one of his own. "Why is it when someone dresses in black people think of death? Or evil? I find the color quite soothing to my senses, calming actually."

"Is that why the inside of your house looks the way it does?" Cyrus decided not to tell him what he really thought of the gloomy, morbid interior, though the thought ran through his head. Penworth reminded him of a dungeon he'd seen in Morocco once, cold and dark, a place where death lurked in every corner, waiting for the opportune moment to snatch its next unsuspecting victim.

"Penworth suits me," Kleeton replied without answering Cyrus's question.

It wasn't necessary. Penworth's owner was just as dark and foreboding as his home. But he wouldn't say as much to Kleeton. At least not yet. He needed this bizarre man with his black-gloved hands to think he trusted him enough to help him trap Noah Sandleton. That was the only way the plan would work.

"There's something I need to discuss with you," Cyrus said, anxious to set his plan in motion. His gaze darted from Kleeton to the monster on the lawn.

"But of course. Gerald, please take care of Mr. Mandrey's horse."

The big man approached Cyrus and waited for him to dismount. He said nothing as he took the reins and turned away. Cyrus noted a large chunk of his left ear was missing.

Forcing his gaze away, he walked toward Andrew Kleeton. "Was his tongue ripped out too?" he asked, pointing toward Gerald.

Kleeton laughed as they entered the house and headed down the hall. "Hardly. Gerald, for all his size, is quite shy. He rarely speaks."

"Is he another prison escapee?" He'd bet his last coin on it.

They entered the study and Kleeton headed to the sideboard, his back to Cyrus.

"Not actually an escapee. His time was up. He had nowhere to go. I happened to be doing research at Newgate and took pity on him." Kleeton poured two whiskeys and turned around, his blue gaze settling on Cyrus. "He's very loyal, Mandrey. He'd kill anyone who tried to harm me."

Cyrus raised a bushy brow. "I'd say that's a little more than loyal. More like mad."

Andrew Kleeton smiled, his white teeth gleaming in obvious contrast with his dark attire. And the black furnishings in the room. "Some still believe in 'an eye for an eye,' " he said, handing over a whiskey.

"Do you?"

He shrugged. "In certain cases." Cyrus noted the slight flare of Andrew's nostrils, the twitch on the right side of his jaw, the slow inhalation of breath. He could tell Kleeton wasn't as nonchalant about the whole matter as he'd like him to believe.

"What kinds of cases?" he pushed on.

Kleeton drained his whiskey in one swallow and headed back for another. Cyrus sipped his, curious about this man in black who shone like the radiance of the sun one moment and hid like the blackness of night the next.

"There's no formula, no exact rule by which one decides when retribution must be taken into one's own hands. It's a knowing, a certainty that justice must be served in a certain manner, dealt with in one swift blow, without the protection of the law. And nothing will satisfy until the punishment is delivered. Because in these instances, the law is powerless, hiding behind its laws and dictates, trying to preserve the rights of individuals who do not deserve to have those rights protected."

Cyrus eyed him over the rim of his glass. "You sound as though you speak from experience." *If you're Crowlton you've got more blood on you than a leech during a bloodletting.*

Kleeton's blue eyes narrowed. "Do you really want to know,

Mandrey, or are you making polite conversation? Because if we start to drag out our old battle scars, things could get ugly and we'd both have to take off our masks.''

"Touché." Cyrus raised his glass in a mock salute and drained his glass. The man was no fool. He might present himself as nothing more than a polished, reserved country gentleman, but underneath the well-groomed façade, Cyrus sensed the restless edginess, the raw determination of a man with a mission. One who would achieve his goal no matter the cost. Cyrus recognized it because the same feral tenacity pulsed in his veins. Both men sensed the other was hiding something and both were just as determined to discover what it was.

"You said you had something to discuss?" Kleeton changed the subject with the finesse of one long accustomed to evading personal questions. Not that Cyrus would have pressed the issue. He heard the challenge in Kleeton's voice and knew he was warning him not to dig around in his past unless he wanted a few of his own skeletons unearthed. Which Cyrus did not.

"I think Sandleton has returned."

Kleeton raised a golden brow. "Oh?"

"I saw footprints beneath two windows."

"It could've been the gardener."

"Could've been," Cyrus agreed. Now was the time to plant the seed. "But the figure running from the house at five this morning was not."

That got Kleeton's attention. His blue eyes darkened. "Did you follow him?"

Cyrus shook his head. "He disappeared before I got my second boot on. But he couldn't have known I'd seen him." It was time to dangle the proverbial carrot. "He'll be back."

"How can you be so certain?" Kleeton balled his left hand into a fist.

"Simple. He thinks our guard is down. All of these weeks have passed without a sign of him. Nothing. Sandleton expects us to get careless. He's going to strike soon and take Emily away." Cyrus toyed with his empty glass, waiting for Kleeton's response.

"Then we'll have to get him before he gets her." Simple words, spoken as a vow, understood as a commitment, taken as a promise.

Cyrus almost smiled. It appeared Kleeton needed little prodding to join the cause against Noah Sandleton. Very little at all. If indeed he were the Serpent, then he'd waited years for this confrontation, living and breathing hatred and revenge as a form of daily sustenance.

"Good. I'll count you in." *Better to work with the enemy than against him.*

"What do you want me to do?" Kleeton asked.

Take off your gloves so we can end this whole charade. "I need someone to monitor the perimeter of the properties. He might enter from your end, since Penworth is closer than any of the other properties." Cyrus rubbed the back of his neck. "I have to keep my eyes on Emily. Keep her close to the house. No more horseback riding, at least for the next couple of days."

Kleeton's lips quirked upwards into a smile. "She won't like that."

Cyrus shrugged. "I'm sure she won't. But she'll have no choice." His gaze darted to Kleeton. "You were in the military?"

"For a short time." The smile pressed into a flat line.

"Do you know anything about surveillance?"

"A little."

"Good."

"I'll start tonight."

Cyrus nodded. "If you catch him, bring him to Glenview Manor. Immediately. Don't harm him. Lord Kenilworth will deal with Sandleton."

"I can't guarantee his safety, Mandrey," Kleeton said, his words cold and harsh, like this past morning's frost. "Accidents happen all the time. Surely you know that in your line of business." The gleam in his eyes unsettled Cyrus, making him more determined to end this whole scheme as soon as possible. A gnawing in his gut told him Kleeton was dangerous, like a powder keg waiting to explode at the hint of a spark. Cyrus could see it in his cold blue eyes, sense it in his words. If Kleeton captured Noah Sandleton, he wouldn't deliver him to Glenview Manor as ordered. At least not alive.

"He's not a criminal, Kleeton."

"That's a matter of opinion." Cyrus hadn't missed the bitterness in those words. How could Kleeton harbor such intense feelings of dislike for a man he didn't know? Unless he'd spent years building on that hatred?

"You have no quarrel with Sandleton. You don't even know the man, so why should you desire to mete out his punishment?" Cyrus threw out the challenge, daring Kleeton to answer.

"He's committed a crime against Lady Emily. That's reason enough to want the man punished." Cyrus didn't believe the words. There was too much emotion in them to fit Andrew Kleeton. He was a man of cold, calculating responses, who didn't often permit emotion to interfere with the interpretations of his logical, precise mind. Which meant he was hiding something.

Ignoring Kleeton's words, he said, "I think it best if we not discuss our plan in front of Lady Emily. No need to cause her undue concern."

"Agreed," Kleeton said. "I'll begin my duties this evening."

Cyrus's lips twitched. "I see you're already dressed for the part." He gestured to the other man's black shirt and breeches. And his black gloves. The words were no sooner out of his mouth than he began to wonder at his own words. Who and what was Andrew Kleeton? Stalker? Predator? Enemy? Traitor? Murderer? Cyrus found it easy to believe that the man standing before him like a dark angel, with a strange gleam in his eyes, could be any or all of these.

* * *

The stone felt cold against his fingers as he edged his way along the narrow passage. The lantern dangling from his hand provided a flickering pathway, permitting no more than a few paces of illumination before him. Just enough so he wouldn't stumble. It had been years since he'd explored this passage, with nothing on his mind then but adventure and curiosity. Tonight, as he traveled the dimly lit path, he felt as if his entire future were at stake.

What if she turned him away? What if the hurt and anger she'd suffered were etched into her heart? Too deeply to forget? Too deeply to forgive? He ran a shaky hand through his tousled hair. It felt so good to be rid of that damned bushy mop. He imagined her fingers twining in his hair, sweeping that ever-errant stray lock from his forehead, playing with the tumble that fell about his nape. Such thoughts were pure torture because they elicited images that were vivid, erotic, carnal in nature and had nothing to do with the forgiveness he sought. His mind couldn't be clouded with visions of lovemaking, at least not yet. Perhaps if he were very lucky, that would come later.

But the floodgate of sensuality burst open and Noah felt himself harden at the very thought of making love to his wife. It had been such a long time. He tried to push away the vision of her sweet, supple body as it responded to his touch, writhing beneath him, above him, beside him. His manhood throbbed, aching for release. She was inside him, coursing through every fiber of his being, pulsing, wanting, teasing, and he couldn't extinguish her heat. Nor did he want to.

Noah reached the small door that led to the master bedroom. He fitted the key in the lock and rested a hand on the handle, waiting for his breathing to steady. Emily was only one room away. So close. All he had to do was step over this threshold and walk the ten steps or so to her door. His heart pounded in his chest with such force he was surprised she couldn't hear it in her chambers.

How many times in the past several weeks had he wished she would see him as her husband and not a bushy-haired protector by the name of Cyrus Mandrey? It was obvious she'd grown quite attached to Mandrey. But he couldn't say she felt the same way about her husband. Getting her to admit she loved him was worse than he'd imagined. He had the feeling she would have rather emptied her stomach again and would have if she'd been given the choice. But he'd persisted and forced her to answer him. Not that a little half nod of her head was any great proclamation of love. But it was a start.

And then there was the baby. His baby, he corrected, feeling a tightness in his chest. Strengthened by the thought of his unborn child, Noah opened the door and stepped into his chambers. His gaze fell on the small strip of light beneath the adjoining door.

Emily was awake. Noah took a few steps closer. He could almost smell the scent of lilac in her hair, on her skin. Another few steps and he pressed his ear to the door. The whole house was abed. Nothing stirred. Noah gave a light rap and waited. Nothing.

Inching the door open, he peered inside. Emily was asleep, propped up with two pillows, an open book resting in her left hand. Her golden curls cascaded about her shoulders, a plump lock falling onto the swell of her breast. The white nightgown she wore was prim and proper, though the laces at her neck had come undone and showed a glimpse of golden skin. Her breathing was slow and even. Peaceful. Perhaps he should leave her with her dreams and return tomorrow night. His thoughts and desires jumbled together, making it difficult to sort out the best course of action. Logic told him to leave. Emotion forced him to stay.

Noah stepped closer, drawn to Emily like a moth to a flame. He had to get closer to her, had to touch her, breathe in her scent. Setting the lantern on the bedside stand, he leaned over and lifted a locket of her hair, caressing its silky texture, letting it spill through his fingers like spun gold. God, but she was such a beautiful woman. He'd give up everything he owned to be with her again, see the passion in her eyes, feel the tremble of her fingers as she touched him, hear the sharp intake of breath as he stroked her woman's heat, smell her lilac scent enveloping him as he buried himself deep inside of her.

He laid gentle fingers against her cheek, drinking in the soft, silky essence of her skin. The pads of his callused fingertips trailed a path from her cheek to her mouth, stopping to trace an outline over each full lip. Noah wanted to kiss her, taste the honeyed nectar that she had once so freely offered.

Her lips moved and he jerked his hand back as though he'd been burned. *Emily was waking up.* He held his breath. His gaze darted to her eyes. They remained closed, covered by a thick fringe of lash. Noah let out a silent breath of relief. Tiny beads of perspiration popped out along his forehead. He stood glued to the floor, straining his eyes to detect the slightest change in breathing pattern or eye movement. Part of him wanted her to awaken, to find him standing over her. The other part was petrified that she would do just that.

Reaching out a shaky hand, Noah placed his palm on her belly. Where their child rested. His child. A fierce wave of possessiveness washed over him, for both mother and child. But there was another feeling creeping along his spine, clutching at him and wrapping its long tentacles around his heart. It was an emotion that was foreign to him, for he'd experienced it not more than once or twice and that being long ago. He knew it for what it was, though, as it made his heart beat faster, jerked his breath out of his throat, pounded his gut and clamored in his brain.

It was fear. Fear in its most primitive form. Fear that the woman he loved would turn away from him, deny him a second chance, look on him with hatred instead of love. And the baby. Would she deny him that too? Noah backed away, one step at a time, though he was so caught up in the maelstrom of emotion that he didn't remember making a conscious effort to move. Another step backward and his booted foot hit the door with a dull thud. He couldn't face her tonight. Not tonight. He was too afraid. And Noah Sandleton was never afraid of anything.

He would have to deal with that demon, come to terms with it, before he went to Emily. Noah slipped through the open door, closing it behind him, and headed for the secret passage. Not until he was ready to enter the black opening did he remember that he'd forgotten his lantern. Cursing under his breath, he stepped into the darkness and pulled the door shut. It was going to be a long night, he thought, as his fingers felt for the cold, hard surface of the wall. A long night indeed.

Emily awakened early the next morning feeling quite refreshed. She raised her arms above her head, stretching like a cat in the sun, and yawned. Her stomach didn't rumble or lurch in warning. Of course, she'd eaten nothing more than clear beef broth and a few wafers. But it was a start.

Emily recalled the terrible time Augusta had when she was pregnant. She'd almost had to carry the chamber pot around with her for the first several weeks of her pregnancy. Everything upset her, from a drop of chicken broth on her tongue to a whiff of roast pork. Ian had been by her side, worrying over her, ministering to her, loving her.

Emily felt a pain in her stomach that had nothing to do with being pregnant. There would be no one to care for her, to be with her as she swelled with child. She thought of Cyrus and her heart warmed. Dear, sweet, dependable Cyrus. He was the one who'd wiped her brow and carried her back to bed when she was too exhausted to move. He was the one who had taken care of her. But he wasn't her husband. He wasn't Noah.

She'd dreamed of him the past night, just like she had every night, except this time it seemed so much more real. He had been standing over her bed, watching her with those deep-set brown eyes, his full lips unsmiling. There was tenderness in his expression as he lifted a tanned hand and trailed his fingers over her face and neck, memorizing them. She had wanted to do the same, touch the slight crook in his nose, trace the small scar over his right eye, brush her fingers along his lips, but her hands wouldn't move. No matter how hard she tried, they would not move.

Calming herself with a deep breath, Emily detected a faint hint of spice. Her eyes snapped open. She inhaled again. The spicy scent filled her nostrils. Only one person wore that type of cologne. Noah. Emily shook her head, trying to rid herself of morning cobwebs. Last night had been only a dream. Just like all the others. The whispered words, the gentle touches. Only dreams.

Emily threw back the covers, anxious to get dressed and out of her chambers before her imagination got the best of her. Next, she'd be thinking she had spotted him beside her bed. One thing was certain, Noah could wreak havoc on her emotions, even in sleep. As her bare feet touched the floor, her gaze landed on the bedside stand. She froze. A black and silver lantern, one that she had never seen before, rested on the edge of the sturdy oak table.

Was it him? Was he back? Had he been in her room? Had her dreams been real? Had his touch been real? The questions bounced around in Emily's head. What to do? Perhaps there was a logical explanation for the lantern. What would that be? she wondered. Who would be so bold as to wander into her room in the middle of the night? No one but her husband, her heart answered. Emily felt a flutter in her stomach and reasoned it away as nerves.

Should she tell Cyrus? No! She couldn't tell him; he was after Noah. Someone might get hurt and for all of Cyrus's supposed training as a tactical expert or whatever it was he'd said, he would probably be the injured party. He lacked the ruthless tenacity she'd seen in Noah. On the other hand, Noah's guard might be down and he might fall prey to Cyrus's patient persistence. She wouldn't risk hurting either one of these men, which meant Emily would have to deal with the potential "situation" herself.

Moving over to the bedside stand, she gripped the lantern, imagining Noah's warm hands on the handle only hours ago. If it had been him invading her chambers last night, she wanted no outside intrusion when he came again. And as she clutched the lantern close to her, she knew he had come to her last night. She also knew he would be back. This time she would be ready. Walking over to the closet, she opened the door and pushed aside several gowns, placing the lantern on the floor behind a lavender and peach muslin gown.

His secret was safe. For now.

Chapter 16

Cyrus avoided Emily the entire day. There were too many issues to address and seeing her tantalizing beauty would only take his mind off pressing matters. Such as the realization that he was a coward. Never in his entire life had he behaved like one. He couldn't even fathom the possibility. Until last night. The fear of losing Emily had done it, driven him away as though he were being chased by demons. He'd spent the rest of the night nursing his self-disgust along with a bottle of whiskey.

He was in a foul mood today. Blacker than the soot on a chimney sweep's cheeks. Lack of sleep and enough whiskey could do that to a man. So could a woman. Cyrus swore under his breath, the events of last evening pounding in his head. Tonight would be different. He would not act the coward again. When the house fell quiet, he would go to Emily and ask her forgiveness. As her husband. Her lover. Her friend. But not as a coward.

And she would accept it. Period. He hoped. Then he would lay his head on her soft, full breasts and let sleep take him.

The thought of those firm, ripe mounds of creamy flesh stirred his manhood. Perhaps he wouldn't sleep right away. Provided Emily was amenable to the idea. He cursed again. Why shouldn't she be? After all, they were husband and wife. She'd admitted she loved him. They'd been apart a very long time. She was carrying his baby, for God's sake. Why wouldn't she be agreeable? *Why,* he ripped a piece of paper in half, *wouldn't,* he slashed at another with his letter opener, *she be agreeable?*

A knock on the door saved a third piece of ivory stationery from mutilation.

"Yes?"

"It's Billington, sir. You wished to see me?"

"Come in." Cyrus guessed it was time to apprise Billington of his plan, seeing as it was already in motion. He sighed, raking a hand through his hair. His fingers stuck in the tangled mess. God, he'd be blasted happy when this was all over. It wasn't bad enough that the sight of Emily made his objectivity sail out the window, he had to deal with a matted mop on his head every day! Damn, but it itched.

Billington entered and approached his employer.

"Have a seat, Billington." He lowered his voice. "As I told you before, Lady Emily has a very bad habit of eavesdropping. I don't want to have to holler at you from across the room."

The butler's lips twitched. It was almost a smile. "So you have said, sir. But I do think we are safe for the moment. Lady Emily is napping in the study."

"She is? Why?" Odd that she didn't walk the short distance to the privacy and comfort of her own quarters.

Billington's mouth curved upwards. Cyrus saw a show of teeth. It was a definite smile.

"Billington, is something wrong?" In all the years he'd known the man, never once had he seen him smile.

"No, sir," he replied, fighting to pull his lips into their customary straight line. "I believe Lady Emily is sleeping in the study because of the pillows."

"Pillows?" He was making no sense. Billington always made sense. It had to do with that damnable smile.

Clearing his throat, Billington flattened his lips and said in his most serious voice, "She's sleeping on them, sir."

"Sleeping on the pillows?" Cyrus repeated. Emily's chambers were equipped with two of the softest, down-filled pillows at Glenview Manor. He'd made certain of it. *Why* is she sleeping on the pillows, Billington?"

The older man lifted a bony shoulder. "It would appear Lady Emily is enamored with them. They're the rather large ones you brought back from one of your excursions to the Orient. For the past two days, she's been bringing books in there after lunch and reading." He leaned over and whispered, "She's fallen asleep both times. I made certain she was covered with a blanket so she wouldn't be chilled."

"That was very thoughtful of you, Billington. Thank you." Cyrus stared at him. Emily had gotten to the old man, melted some of that icy exterior. He never thought he'd see the day. Poor Billington. He didn't stand a chance now. Next he'd be throwing down his jacket in mud puddles so she wouldn't have to get her feet wet. Cyrus shook his head.

"You wished to see me, sir?"

"Ah, yes, there is something I need to discuss with you. I embarked on a little plan yesterday that involves our neighbor, Mr. Kleeton."

Billington raised a thin dark brow but said nothing.

"I told him I spotted Noah Sandleton this morning, running away from the estate."

"And did he believe you?" Billington asked.

Cyrus nodded. "Of course. He had no reason not to. The man may not care for me, but he wants Noah Sandleton and it has nothing to do with his misplaced loyalty for Lady Emily."

"Are your suspicions about Mr. Kleeton proving correct?"

What he meant to ask was whether Cyrus felt Andrew Kleeton was the elusive figure from his past. The Serpent. "I don't know." Cyrus rubbed the back of his neck. "I just don't know.

There's something about the man that reeks of deceit. It's in his eyes, behind all that blue. It's as if he's always watching, calculating, assessing those around him, one word, one action at a time. I can even detect it in his smile. If you look past the flash of white, you'll see nothing but cold, stark emptiness, like falling into a deep, unfathomable pit.''

"What of his hands?'' Billington asked.

Cyrus shook his head. "Nothing. Not one blasted thing. He keeps them well covered in every color and texture imaginable.'' He clenched his fists, his next words sharp and fierce. "You can't know how tempted I've been to pin him down and rip them off. But since I can't do that, I've decided to include him in a little search for Noah Sandleton.''

"How so?''

A small smile crept onto Cyrus's lips. "Kleeton will patrol his property and the surrounding estates in search of Noah.''

"And never find him,'' Billington added, nodding his head in approval.

Cyrus cocked a bushy brow. "He'll find him all right, but not yet. Not until I've had an opportunity to observe him, learn some of his secrets, test his skill. When I've done that, Noah will let himself 'be found' and if Kleeton is the Serpent, he'll waste no time striking.''

A deep line furrowed Billington's shiny forehead.

"What is it, Billington?'' He'd known the man too long to not know when something was bothering him.

The older man sniffed twice, cleared his throat and ventured, "It sounds dangerous.''

"What did you say, Billington?'' He couldn't have heard him right.

"I said, sir,'' Billington began, squaring his shoulders and sitting even straighter than before, "that the plan sounds dangerous.''

"Dangerous?'' Cyrus wanted to laugh. "Dangerous?'' He did laugh. "Billington, you and I have worked together for years. This little event is *nothing* compared to what we've been through." He laughed again. *"Nothing.* Surely you realize that."

Billington's gray eyes met Cyrus's. "Lady Emily wasn't involved then."

"Lady Emily? What's she got to do with any of this?" The old man was going soft on him. He liked him better hard and crusty. Covered with layers and layers of crust.

"If Kleeton is the Serpent, he'll go after what Noah Sandleton cares about most." His careful, precise voice faltered. "And that would be Lady Emily."

Silence filled the room, thick and heavy, dragging Cyrus down under the threat of Billington's last words. Like sacks of sand, the words hung on his shoulders, echoed in his brain, coursed through his blood. His fists clenched and unclenched. He grabbed the letter opener to still his hands.

"If he touches her, I'll kill him with my bare hands." Cyrus's words choked out the silence, his promise of retribution pounding through his veins. No one would hurt Emily. He would see to that.

Noah slipped through the opening of Emily's door, his eyes never leaving her face. She looked like an angel in sleep, her golden hair flowing about her, soft and shimmering. He felt his heart pounding in his chest as he moved closer to the side of the bed. There was no turning back tonight. He would confront her, ask her forgiveness, pledge his love, and pray to God she took mercy on him. The scent of lilacs drifted to him, urging him closer. Noah leaned over, closing his eyes, reveling in the sweet fragrance that beckoned him. Closer, closer, until he felt the silken tendrils of her hair. God, but he wanted to feel her hair across his naked body, teasing, tempting.

His lips planted light, gentle kisses in her hair. Desire coursed through every pore of his body. It had been so long since he'd touched her, so long since he'd kissed her. His manhood throbbed as he thought of her full, ripe lips. He opened his

eyes and stared at her mouth, so inviting, like sun-kissed berries
waiting to be plucked. His head lowered, hovering mere inches
from her mouth. Her breath fanned against his face, heating
his blood. His eyes drifted shut. He was about to taste a slice
of heaven.

Instead, he felt a blow from hell, right square at the back of
his neck. *What the hell?* He jumped backward, rubbing the
tender spot on his neck. "Damn you, Emily," he muttered,
glaring at her.

"Stay right where you are," she said, backing up to the
farthermost corner of the bed.

"Up to your old tricks again, Emily? What was it this time?
Another pitcher?" Whatever she'd used, her aim was perfect.
His neck hurt like the devil.

She shook her head and he watched the golden curls whirl
about her breasts. He wondered if she knew he could make out
her entire shape beneath that pristine nightgown she wore. From
her position on the bed, with the lamp shining in just the right
direction, her charms left little to the imagination. Of course,
he had already been privileged enough to see those charms
minus clothing.

"So what did you attack me with, Emily?" Noah watched
her chest heave and saw the dark hint of a nipple through the
white material. No, there was no way she knew.

She swallowed twice. "One of those vases with the dragon
on it," she whispered.

He raised a brow. "One of *my* vases? From China?" He
saw her lower lip tremble.

"It's fine. No harm done," she said, pulling a white and
gold vase from beneath the covers.

"That's a matter of opinion," he said, massaging the muscles
in his neck.

"Leave, Noah. I have nothing to say to you." Her quiet
words echoed off the walls as though she'd shouted them.

"Like hell," he said, trying to keep his anger in check. He'd come here to see his wife and ask her forgiveness, not engage in battle.

"Don't you dare come one step closer," Emily said, jumping from the bed and grabbing an old fire iron from the fireplace. She crawled back onto the bed and stood up, gripping the bottom of the iron with both hands, readying her swing.

If he weren't so damned annoyed and sore, the sight of Emily wielding a fire iron would have made him laugh.

"Now just leave, before you force me to use this thing," she said, swatting the iron through the air.

"For what, dear wife?" He cocked a brow. "Jousting?"

"For keeping you away," she said, her voice two octaves lower than normal.

"Ah," he replied. "I am indeed filled with fear."

"Not one step farther," she whispered, crouching low, reminding him of a hunter preparing for attack.

Noah looked her square in her big, gray eyes and moved his booted foot forward. One step.

"I'm warning you," she hissed in hushed tones. "I'll use this thing."

Dropping his hands to his sides, he advanced two steps. "You would maul me with that thing?" His gaze darted to the fire iron in her hands. "Scar me and beat at my head and body?" Her grip loosened, the iron slipped a fraction. "You would wish that for me, dear wife? You would be my attacker?" He took another step.

"No. No," Emily whispered, shaking her head. "I . . ." her lips trembled, ". . . don't want you . . . to be hurt."

Noah forgot about the dull ache in his neck. He almost smiled. He and Emily were talking, making progress, even if she didn't realize it.

"Nor do I want you to be hurt. Especially by me," he finished, his gaze locking with hers. He had to keep his head about him, play it smart, especially now, with Emily on the brink of catapulting into his waiting arms.

She swiped at her left eye, still keeping a grip on the iron with her right, but it was looser, less forceful than before. "It's too late for that, Noah. Much too late," she whispered, the sadness in her voice tearing at his gut. So much for catapulting into his waiting arms.

Noah squeezed his eyes shut and pinched the bridge of his nose. *Think. Keep her talking. Don't let her close you off or it will be too late.* He said the next thing that popped into his head. "Why do you keep whispering?"

Her gaze shot to the door. "Cyrus might hear."

"Cyrus?" What in blazes did Cyrus have to do with anything?

Emily wet her lips, hesitated a moment and then plunged forward. "He's the man who's been hired to protect me." Her small chin shot up an inch. "Against you."

"Against me?" How should he handle that remark? Humor and sarcasm. "Is he the hairy ape that's been following you around like a long-lost puppy?"

"He is not a hairy ape. For your information, Cyrus Mandrey is my friend and protector, which is certainly more than you ever were."

Noah winced. "You don't need that fire iron when you've got a mouth like that for a weapon, Emily."

He could tell by the spark in her eyes that she was far from finished. She'd assumed her feet-apart, chin-up, hands-on-hips stance that told him she had much to say and he would be the lucky recipient of her diatribe.

"Cyrus is a noble, honest man of integrity, whose opinion I value. I trust him and his judgment." Her voice raised just a hint with her next words. "*He* would never lie to me."

Noah raked a hand through his hair. Cyrus. Who would have thought he'd be competing with himself? "Then why don't you call your *hero* to come to your rescue? Surely he will save you from your cruel, wicked husband?"

Her eyes narrowed to gray slits. He watched her delicate nostrils flare, her mouth flatten, her hands grip the end of the iron. Catapulting, he thought. He'd be catapulting all right, straight into hell if he couldn't cool her temper.

"Uncaring," she hissed.

"Uncaring what?"

"Ruthless," she spat out.

"Emily?" He took another step forward.

"Deceitful," she growled, raising the iron.

"Emily?" He held up a hand.

"My cruel, wicked, uncaring, ruthless, deceitful, arrogant husband," she said, taking a swing in the air. The iron whacked the bed, the force of the impact unbalancing her. Noah took that moment to dive toward her, throwing his arms about her waist and tossing her onto the bed. He wrested the fire iron from her with his right hand, pinned her arms behind her head with his left and clamped a thigh over her lower body.

"Let me go, you beast." She was glaring at him, her chest heaving, her breath coming in broken, choppy gulps.

Noah was breathing hard too. He'd forgotten how exhausting his wife could be, both in and out of bed. Though he had pictured quite a different scene in bed.

Emily bucked underneath him, her knees just missing his groin.

"Keep it up, Emily, and I'll take that behavior as an invitation," he drawled, a hint of a smile playing about his lips.

She froze. Color seeped into her cheeks, spreading down her neck.

"Now that we're both more comfortable," he said as he reached out with his right hand and brushed a stray lock of hair from her cheek, "why don't you tell me why you didn't yell for Mr. Mandrey to come to your rescue?"

She looked away. "Cyrus is very skilled in tactical maneuvers."

He waited. And waited. Silence stretched in the room like shadows on the wall. Noah grew impatient. "And," he prompted.

"You wouldn't stand a chance," she whispered.

"Would it matter?" His gaze bored into her, commanding her to meet his gaze.

Emily turned her head to look at him. She opened her mouth to speak but no words came out.

"Answer me, Emily. Would it matter?" He held his breath, waiting for her response.

Her gaze flitted to his shoulder, his chest, his arm. Anywhere but his face. "On the other hand, you are quite a bit larger than Cyrus and you might just end up hurting him."

"And you wouldn't want Cyrus hurt." He felt a rush of anger spreading through his body, one pulse at a time. How ironic that she would rush to protect one man and condemn another. He wondered what she would say if he told her the truth about Cyrus Mandrey.

"Of course not." Three simple words, spoken with such conviction. Who would have thought they could wound so deeply?

"And me? You wouldn't mind if I got a jab or two, would you?" His words sounded harsh, bitter. "Maybe another broken nose?" She kept her head turned away, not meeting his gaze. Damn it, she was supposed to love him. She'd admitted it the other day. Had her feelings changed already? Had she only spoken the words so Cyrus would leave her alone? *Had she lied?*

"Look at me, Emily." She buried her head farther into the pale green of the counterpane. Noah closed his fingers around her chin and forced her to face him. "Look at me, Emily." His words were gentle, like a warm caress on a summer's eve.

Her gaze met his and he felt a huge lump wedge in his throat. Two shimmering tears trailed down her cheeks. Unbidden, he was certain. Unwanted, most definitely. Were the tears for him or Cyrus Mandrey? He had to know.

"You would care if something happened to me?" he asked, his voice low and soft.

Emily nodded. Just a little movement of her head, but Noah saw it. "But I wouldn't want to," she said, as though afraid to let him see her true feelings. It hurt to hear the words, to see the look of pain on her face, but he couldn't blame her for her hesitancy. He'd left her without a word. No good-bye. No explanation. Nothing.

"Of course, you wouldn't want to," he murmured. "I understand." Noah let out a ragged breath. "God, but I've missed you, Emily."

He felt her stiffen beneath him. "It's not that simple, Noah." Her words felt like a bucket of cold water on his emotions.

"There's much to be discussed. Much I need to explain. But right now," he ran a finger from her satiny cheek to the fine line of her jaw, "I want to know if you missed me half as much as I missed you."

Luminous, gray eyes widened, but only for a second, before a cloud of indifference blanketed them, masking the truth. She shook her head, trying to deny the pure, honest response of need and longing that had shimmered in her eyes the moment before her guard came up. But it was too late. Noah had seen it, recognized it for what it was and determined he would hear her say the words. For herself, so she could stop pretending. And for him, so he could start believing in their love.

"Did you miss me just a little?" He held his breath.

She shook her head. A single tear escaped her left eye.

Noah ignored the dull ache in his chest. "Not even one little bit?" he coaxed, his gaze burning into hers, trying to strip away the fear that shielded the truth. He'd seen it a few moments ago, knew it was there, but she had to admit it, accept it, or they would have no chance for a future together.

He held his breath as she opened her mouth to speak, and he watched her lips move, but no sound came out. Sound wasn't necessary. He'd read her lips and seen the answer. Noah hung his head in defeat. She'd said no. Not just no to his silly little question, for he knew she'd missed him. The answer was in her eyes before she put up her guard. But her attempt to deny the truth told him she was saying no to a much larger question. His wife was saying no to trusting him, believing in him, loving

him. There would be no second chances. All that and she hadn't
uttered a sound.

"No." That one whispered word reached him, clung to him
in his despair, like a lifeline around a drowning man. Had
Emily spoken or was it his imagination? Noah lifted his head,
searching her face, looking for answers. She met his gaze, her
eyes brimming with tears. "I . . . missed"—she drew in a
shaky breath—"you . . . very . . . very . . . much." Her voice
was hesitant, full of sadness and resignation. It must have cost
her dearly to utter those words.

Noah leaned over and brushed his lips across hers, a soft,
gentle balm meant to heal and comfort.

"And I missed you so very, very much," he murmured, a
breath away from her lips. His head dipped again and he placed
a chaste kiss along the slender line of her jaw. "So very, very
much." His lips trailed a path to her ear.

Emily moaned low in her throat. He buried his face in her
hair. God, but she felt wonderful.

"Why did you leave, Noah?"

Her words didn't really surprise him. He knew she would
expect answers, want to know why he'd left and where he'd
gone. Noah wanted to be honest with her. He knew he needed
to be if they were to make a go of their marriage. Problem
was, if he told his wife the truth, he would betray his best
friend. As for where he'd been these past several weeks, he
couldn't tell her that either without risking her safety. He'd
have to settle for a half-truth until this whole thing was over.

And pray Emily would accept it and maybe trust him just a
little.

Noah lifted his head and met her steady, gray gaze. She
wanted answers, expected them as a matter of course, needed
them if they were to begin again.

"I can't say. Not yet."

He felt her stiffen beneath him, saw her mouth thin into a
straight line. She was pulling away from him, closing him off.
Noah couldn't let her do that. Not again.

"Emily, listen to me. I *can't* tell you, yet. But I will. Soon."
He heard the desperation in his voice. "All I ask now is that
you show patience, just a little while longer." She turned her
head away, closing her eyes.

"*I had no choice.* If you believe nothing else, believe that.
I never would have left you. I have dreamed of nothing but
holding you in my arms every night. I have felt the pain of my
leaving a thousand times and it has been worse than any hell
I ever could have imagined." He touched her hair, her cheek,
her lips. "Please. Please, Emily. Give me your trust just once
more. I promise you'll not be sorry."

"You ask too much, Noah," she whispered.

"Five days. Give me five days with no questions and on the
night of the fifth, I will reveal all." He held his breath, waiting
for her response.

"Three days. You have three days to tell me the truth."

Three days wasn't much time. He'd have to force Kleeton's
hand. Soon. But if Emily was willing to consider the bizarre
arrangement, who was he to quibble over a few days? Right
now, he could think of nothing but the sound of her sweet
voice and the feel of her soft body beneath him. His manhood
throbbed with hopeful anticipation. He'd been hard from the
minute he entered her room.

The tone of her next words reminded him that he might be
in her bed but they were still a long way from sharing any
intimacy. "And will I see you every night until then?" she
asked, her voice cool and distant. "Or will you just pop in
whenever it suits you?" Her eyes were on him, challenging,
accusing.

"That will be up to you, dear wife," he said.

"How did you get in here without Cyrus seeing you?" Her
golden brows turned downward.

Noah smiled. He'd wondered when she'd get around to asking him that question. "That's a secret I can share. The library
has a secret passageway leading into the master chambers. If
you walk around the bookcases to the left, you will find a small

door that will take you right into my room. My uncle had it
built several years ago, though no one but myself, and now
you are aware of its existence.''

"Whatever for?''

"Who knows? Most likely to amuse himself.'' Noah grinned.
"We Sandletons love a good intrigue.''

She shook her head. "You're probably all crazy, the whole
lot of you.''

He gazed down at her full, pink lips. "You're probably
right,'' he murmured, lowering his head to taste her mouth.
Emily moaned low in her throat as she parted her lips. Noah
teased her bottom lip, tracing it with his tongue, savoring the
sweetness before delving into the honeyed depths of her welcoming mouth. Their tongues touched, gently at first, reveling
in the wonder of rediscovery. Soon it wasn't enough. Noah
groaned, thrusting his tongue deep into her mouth, over and
over, feeling as though he'd burst when Emily began to suck
on it.

Without breaking the kiss, Noah settled himself between her
legs and loosened his grip on her arm. He wanted to feel her
hands on his body, all over, touching, pleasuring, exploring.
His fingers stroked her neck, trailing downward to the ties of
her nightgown. Flesh. That's what he needed to feel as he
loosened the ties and pushed the thin material aside, his fingers
skimming her silky skin, working up the undersides of her
breast, tracing her nipple, making Emily moan. Noah's hand
cupped her breast, his fingers stroking her hard nipple in small
circles until Emily whimpered beneath his touch.

She grabbed at his shoulders, her fingers traveling down his
arms, stroking hard and fast, then moving to settle on his
hips, where she pressed him further down into the cleft of her
womanhood. Noah lay hard and heavy between her legs, cursing
the thin material that separated them. If not for that one little
wisp of white, he'd be buried deep inside his wife right now.
Just the thought made him pulse with need. God, how he wanted

her. And needed her in a way that was much more elemental than pure physical desire.

He loved his wife.

His hand worked its way along her thigh, brushing caresses down her leg as he pulled her gown up to touch naked skin. He stroked the soft, creamy flesh on the inside of her thigh, traced a path from her knee to her ankle and up again. Emily trembled in his arms, making soft little mewling sounds into his mouth. Her hips moved up and down in a slow, sensual rhythm, like a dancer feeling the music in her soul.

Tearing his mouth from hers, Noah muttered, "I can't take much more, Emily. You're driving me mad."

She laughed, a low, throaty sound, heating his blood all the more. Noah lowered his head and took her pink nipple in his mouth, devouring the ripe bud with his lips, his tongue, his teeth.

"Love me, Noah," she whispered. "Love me. Now."

The growl that escaped his throat sounded more like that of an animal than a human. He pulled away from her, yanking open the buttons of his shirt with unsteady fingers. He felt like an animal driven to mate, with a need he couldn't control. Nor did he want to. Nothing existed for him but Emily lying before him with her nightgown bunched around her hips, her long legs open and inviting. Noah tossed the shirt to the floor, kicked off his boots and reached for the buttons on his breeches. Emily stopped him, placing her hand over his.

"Let me help you." His mouth went dry as he watched her tongue dart out to wet her lips. Her smile was slow, sultry. Noah swallowed. Hard. His manhood throbbed, pulsing just inches beneath her fingers, begging for attention. He let his hand fall away, mesmerized by her smile, the touch of her hand stroking his belly.

The buttons popped open, one agonizing moment at a time. It was heaven. It was hell. Noah sucked in his breath, his eyes glued to the nimble fingers working the buttons. When the last one popped, his manhood sprang free, jutting out like a soldier standing at attention. He watched her hand close around him, felt the slow, even strokes of her fingers gliding along his shaft. Blood rushed to his brain, filling his head, pushing out all thoughts save the need to be inside her. Now.

Unable to stop himself, Noah jerked in her hand, pumping once, twice, a victim of his desire. Her hands felt so damn good on him. Too good. If she didn't stop right now, it would all be over before it got started. He reached out and grabbed her hand.

Emily met his gaze, her big gray eyes full of confusion. "You . . . you didn't like that? I'm sorry," she whispered, her face turning crimson.

His ragged breathing filled the room. He liked it all right. Every single bit of it. Her eyes were on him, deep, soulful eyes that tugged at his heart. And his groin. The mixture of innocent and siren drove him wild. His gaze slipped to her full, round breasts exposed for his blatant perusal. The creamy mounds of flesh topped with pink rosebuds invited his eyes, his hands, his tongue. Oh yes, he liked everything about Emily.

"Noah?"

His head snapped up from her breasts. What had she asked him? Oh yes, she wanted to know if he liked her touch. How could he answer a question like that in words that would not offend her? Telling her the truth might scare her. After all, she was still a relative innocent where lovemaking was concerned. She'd only been with him a few times and there was still so very much to learn. Like how to substitute her mouth for her hands. Or lay on her belly with her legs spread wide while he entered her from behind. A groan of need and anticipation escaped him. He was more than cocked and ready.

"Emily, believe me, you're driving me wild." Noah let out a harsh laugh. "Too wild as a matter of fact." He wanted to tell her that a few more strokes from those nubile fingers would have sent his seed spewing all over her like a blast from a cannon. Instead, he opted for a more delicate explanation. Blunt honesty. "Sweetheart, you want me inside of you. Right?"

She nodded.

"Well, three more strokes and it would've been too late for that." She should be able to figure that out.

"Oh. I see," she said, pulling her gaze from his.

Noah laughed low in his throat. "No, dear wife, I doubt you do." He yanked off his breeches and knelt between her legs, his hands enjoying the silken feel of her against his callused fingertips. "I want to see you naked. Take off your gown."

Emily shifted her weight, pulling the nightgown over her head until she lay before him in naked splendor. "God, but you're beautiful," he murmured, lowering his head to mesh his mouth with hers. The kiss deepened, tongue mating with tongue, burning out of control as they ran their hands along each other's flesh, each touch more desperate than the last.

Reaching his fingers between their bodies, Noah found her swollen nubbin and caressed it with a feather-light touch. Emily gasped into his mouth, her hips jerking off the bed in excitement and surprise. He worked his fingers over the sensitive flesh, stroking his way to her woman's heat. She was hot and ready, wet with desire. Noah probed a finger into her heat, feeling the tightness close around him.

Emily's hips moved in a slow rhythm, rising to meet the stroke of his finger. He caught her moans in his mouth, his tongue delving deep, showing her what he would soon be doing with another part of his body. She wanted more. He could tell by the fast, uneven movements of her hips. Even the flick of his thumb on her clitoris didn't ease her obvious need. Only one thing would do that.

"Now, Noah," Emily murmured against his lips. "Make love to me now."

Noah pulled back, rising to his knees. His gaze burned into her with promise, love and desire. Emily Sandleton was his wife. There would be no more separations. He cupped her buttocks and leaned over her welcoming body. She was his. Forever. He watched her eyes turn smoky with passion as he entered her in one long, slow stroke, burying himself to the very core of her womanhood. Her legs closed around his thighs, hugging him to her, trying to draw him closer still. He felt her nails on his back, trailing down his hips, his buttocks. He pumped into her, saw her smile and pulled back. She lifted her hips to coax him back. Noah pumped again, feeling her tight heat grip him.

With painstaking slowness, he eased out of her, almost all the way, until she moaned. Three times, four, he repeated the sensual torment. When he reached six, his control burst, passion pouring over him like a tidal wave, pulsing through his body, filling him with a wild need to bury himself to the hilt in her hot, sweet body. Noah plunged into her. Deeper and deeper he went, losing a piece of himself with each thrust. Emily matched him thrust for thrust, nails clawing, legs high and snug over his back, mouth fused with his in a savage kiss.

It was heaven and hell melded into one. The desire to go on like this forever, to reach for the stars, the moon, the sky warred with the need to find fulfillment as soon as possible, to float back to earth on a cloud, in peace and harmony.

Emily cried out first, her body rigid, her woman's heat sending tiny spasms coursing along Noah's manhood. She clung to him as he drove into her one final time. He threw back his head and shouted her name, spilling his seed deep into her womb. Noah drew one last breath and collapsed, his sweat-slicked body covering his wife's like a shield of armor. She was his. Forever.

"I love you, Emily," he whispered. There. He'd said it. Noah closed his eyes and inhaled the scent of lilac mixed with the aftermath of their lovemaking. He smiled. Very soon they would be able to put their stormy past behind them and start anew. Just the three of them. His heart clenched at the thought of his child. A real family, built on love.

A real family built on love . . . built on love. The words waltzed around in Noah's head as he drifted off. Real family . . . built on love. Love. Love. Something wasn't right. The words didn't feel right. Love. Love. Understanding rolled over Noah like Flash's hoof in his chest.

Emily hasn't said the words. Not once. There was no "I love you." No, "By the way, we're going to have a baby." Nothing. He only knew about them because she'd admitted those things to Cyrus, her friend and protector. Too bad she hadn't seen fit to make such an announcement to him, her husband and father of the baby. The thought rankled, stirring a coil of anger and jealousy deep in his gut.

What the hell did she think she was doing by telling Cyrus Mandrey and not him? He wouldn't tolerate it. Noah opened his eyes to find Emily staring straight ahead. So much for the slim hope that she'd fallen asleep and not heard his profession of love. Emily had heard it all right. And ignored it.

This was ridiculous. She loved him. He knew it. He'd heard it himself. Well, in a manner of speaking he'd heard it. It was of little consequence that Emily had spoken the words to Cyrus. The fact of the matter was that she *had* spoken the words. And she would speak them again. To him.

"Emily?" Perhaps she just needed a little coaxing.

"Yes?" Her gaze remained fixed straight ahead.

"Did you hear me a moment ago?" He tried to hide the hint of annoyance from his voice. "When I said I loved you?"

She nodded.

"And?" Just say the words. His right hand clenched into a fist.

"Thank you."

"Thank you? *Thank you?*" Noah grabbed her chin and forced her to look at him. "I just told you that I loved you and all you have to say is thank you?"

Her eyes darted to his chin. "I don't know what else to say."

He could feel his heart pounding in his chest and wondered if rage or despair was the cause. Damn her, she was not going to tell him. "Well, I can tell you one thing," he said, his eyes narrowing to slits, "any other woman would be dying to hear those words from me."

That got her. Her gray eyes darkened like a storm cloud about to burst. She hadn't liked that last comment. Her words spilled out in a downpour of emotion. "Then perhaps you should take your *words* and speak them to someone else."

"Fine. Maybe I will." He was well past angry now. Furious was even too tame a term for what he felt. Noah threw back the covers and got out of bed. Rage. That's what filled him. Pure, white-hot rage. Where were his damn breeches? Lying on the floor with his shirt and boots and his tattered, bruised pride. So much for good intentions.

Noah pulled on his breeches, the feel of Emily's gaze boring into his back. He had to get out of here. Now. Before he said anything else he would regret. Shoving his arms into his shirt, he turned around and began buttoning it.

One quick glance at Emily told him his wife was just as eager to see him leave. She held the counterpane with both hands, clutching the material under her chin. Noah gave a harsh laugh, his eyes scanning the full length of the bed.

"A little late for modesty, isn't it?"

"Get out of here," she hissed. *"Now."*

Noah finished the last button on his shirt and walked toward her, stopping inches from the bed. He leaned over and smiled. "You like that word, don't you, Emily?"

She pulled the covers closer. "I don't know what you're talking about."

His smile deepened. "Just a few minutes ago you were begging me to make love to you. *Now.*"

"Temporary insanity," she spat out.

"I don't think so." He reached out to fondle a plump curl. Emily tried to jerk away, but in an instant Noah trapped her between his arms. They stared at each other, locked in a battle of wills. "You may not say the words," he said with a voice that was soft and clear, "but there's no denying what happened in this bed, and we both know it." He let go of her arms and straightened. "And it will happen again. We both know that too, Emily."

"Don't you dare come back," she said, her voice rising an octave.

Noah laughed. "Or what?"

Her eyes narrowed. "Or I'll have to stop you." He heard the feeble threat in her words and it angered him more.

"That's right, Emily. You have a *protector*. Cyrus Mandrey, isn't it?" He cocked his head to the side. "Fair enough. By all means, you may inform Mr. Mandrey that I will be returning tomorrow evening, but I would like to make one small suggestion." Noah's voice lowered, taking on the tone of a true conspirator. "Why not wait until after you've had your woman's release? Maybe it will make you less cranky. What do you say?"

Emily scrambled off the bed and reached for the Chinese vase just as Noah opened the door to the master chambers. He cast one last look back and saw her arm cocked, preparing to launch her weapon. "I'll see you tomorrow night," he said, unable to resist one last jab before he pulled the door shut. Seconds later, a sharp thud hit the door, followed by a loud crash.

Noah shook his head and wondered why, of all the women he'd known, he had to fall in love with one as impossible as this one.

Chapter 17

Emily finished tying a pale green bow in her hair and turned toward the mirror. Her eyes narrowed as she studied herself. Everything looked the same. Same eyes, nose, mouth, hair. She squeezed her eyes shut. Who was she trying to fool? Everything was different now.

Her stomach lurched and she pressed a hand to still herself. Was she about to be sick? It had been two days since her last bout with the chamber pot, and she prayed she could make it two more. Besides, the jumping in her stomach had been going on all night.

Well, most of the night, she corrected herself. Ever since Noah left.

Her head pounded with the thought of her husband. She rubbed her temples. All she needed was a headache to go along with her riotous stomach. Not only had the man wreaked havoc on her emotions, battering down her defenses with little care or concern, now he was affecting her body as well. Damn Noah Sandleton.

How could she have been so foolish as to let him touch her

again? She should have known better. She did know better. But it hadn't mattered. Not when he was standing before her in all of his fierce, masculine glory, like a determined warrior come to claim her, his eyes glittering with desire, his mouth uttering soft, sensual promises of unexplored pleasures. No, she couldn't deny him, not any more than she could deny herself a breath of fresh air. And that was the real reason her stomach kept somersaulting all over the place. It had nothing to do with morning sickness and everything to do with lovesickness.

Emily swung away from the mirror, disgusted with her own weakness. Her gaze fell on the bed. Images of Noah's naked body moving over hers sent a flash of heat coursing through her, centering on the most private part of her body. She was a prisoner to her own sexual desires, trapped in a gilded cage, captive to the holder of the key.

Noah.

Last night, he'd uttered the words she had waited so long to hear, only to find that she didn't trust him enough to believe them. Too many lies had passed between them, too much hurt, too much betrayal. He wanted to hear her speak the same words, but she couldn't, not when she had no idea where he'd been or if he'd be staying. Emily knew he'd come back tonight, but what about the next? And the next? What would happen when she became swollen with child and no longer appealing? Would he still come to her, if for nothing else than to hold her in his arms at night?

And what of the day? Would he spend time with her, talking and laughing, even playing cards like she and Cyrus had done on many a long night? Would Glenview Manor hold enough excitement to keep him here? Would she? The questions ripped Noah's love words into tiny shreds, tossing them out as unbelievable and inconsequential. There was too much at stake. Emily couldn't tell him. Not until she was certain he wasn't leaving again. Not until he proved his love. Then she would tell him her truth, the one she kept carefully guarded, even from herself: She loved her husband with every fiber of her being. Today, tomorrow and always.

When the time came, if circumstances permitted and God smiled down upon her, then she would pledge her love to her husband, but not a moment before. And then she would tell him about the baby. It was all quite simple to reason out without a certain pair of dark brown eyes boring into her. Very simple indeed.

Emily's stomach growled. It didn't lurch or jump, or even somersault. It simply growled, a natural response to a desire for food. Thank God. At least something felt normal. Smoothing her pale green gown, she headed for the door, wondering what delicacies the cook had conjured up. Blueberry tarts sounded appealing this morning. Or perhaps a cranberry muffin slathered in thick, creamy butter. Her mouth watered. Then again, there was always poached eggs and toast. But she had a taste for a slice of cured ham too. And a big bowl of fresh strawberries. It all sounded wonderful. How would she ever decide? Her stomach growled again. On second thought, maybe she'd just have them all.

She was so preoccupied with thoughts of breakfast that Emily almost didn't see Mr. Billington coming out of the study.

"Oh, good morning, Mr. Billington," she said, turning toward him.

"Good morning, Lady Sandleton," he said with a hint of softness in his usual, precise voice.

Emily bestowed a dazzling smile on the butler. Ever since she'd stuck up for him in front of Noah's men, he seemed to have softened toward her, the crusty edges smoothing out, sometimes even disappearing. She rather liked this side of the man and took every opportunity to encourage more of the same behavior.

"Is Cyrus in there?" she asked, inclining her head toward the study.

Billington shifted his weight to stand in front of the doors. "Cyrus?"

Emily smiled. Mr. Billington had a very good way of answering a question with a question, especially when he didn't want to answer it. But she was onto his little tactics and could play the game almost as well as he could. "Yes. Cyrus," she said, crossing her arms over her chest. "You recall him, Mr. Billington. Tall, broad, bushy brown hair, beard, glasses. Does he sound familiar?"

Mr. Billington's lips twitched. "Quite."

"And?" she prodded.

"And?" he countered.

"Is he in the study?" Before Mr. Billington had a chance to answer, Emily heard Cyrus's low, raspy voice through the door. One sleek brow shot up. There was no denying her protector's distinct voice.

"Ah, yes, Lady Sandleton, Mr. Mandrey does happen to be in the study at the moment."

She gave Mr. Billington one of her "I already knew that" smiles and waited for him to step aside.

He didn't move.

Emily sighed. The man might be softening up a bit, but he still had a long way to go. "Excuse me, Mr. Billington, may I pass?"

The butler took a deep breath. "Mr. Mandrey is in a meeting at the moment and asked not to be disturbed."

"A meeting? Cyrus?" Who would he be meeting? As far as she knew, Cyrus didn't know anyone in these parts, with the exception of Andrew and he couldn't stand the man. So who could it be? A cold chill ran up her spine. He'd found out about Noah and contacted Ian. Ian was in there! Her heart skipped a beat. She didn't like the odd look on Mr. Billington's face. Like he was trying to hide something. Or protect someone. Noah? Was Noah in there? Had Cyrus found him?

"I need to see Cyrus. Immediately." If Noah was in there, she had to help him. He would be just foolish and arrogant enough to underestimate Cyrus because of his disarming appearance.

"But Mr. Mandrey—"

"I *need* to see Cyrus, Mr. Billington. Now." The quiet persistence in her voice must have warned him that it would be useless to argue any further. Without a word, Mr. Billington stepped aside.

Emily bound through the door, words flying out of her mouth in an incoherent jumble. "I can explain, Cyrus. I can explain everything."

Two pairs of eyes stared back at her, one with spectacles, the other a summer sky blue.

"Andrew?" Her mind reeled. What was Andrew doing here?

"Hello, Emily," he said, giving her one of his winning smiles as he rose from his overstuffed chair to greet her.

"Emily? Is something wrong?" She heard the concern in Cyrus's voice.

Shaking her head, she squeezed her eyes shut a moment. Her hands trembled. She'd almost mentioned Noah's name. Almost given him away. No matter how angry she was with him, she had to protect him. For her own sake as well as his. If Noah left now he'd never be able to prove his love and she'd never trust him, never pledge her love to him. His simple "I love you" would haunt her forever.

"What did you want to explain, Emily?" Cyrus asked, his voice gentle.

"Nothing," she blurted out. "Nothing at all." Her gaze swerved to Andrew. "Why are you here, Andrew?" Her curiosity equaled her desire to steer the subject away from her odd behavior.

Andrew's smile was full of compassion and understanding. "Mandrey wanted my permission to scout my properties. He spotted your husband the other night."

"Kleeton." She heard the warning in Cyrus's voice, like steel wrapped in velvet.

Andrew waved a gloved hand in the air, dismissing Cyrus. "Why not tell her, Mandrey? She needs to be aware so she can protect herself."

"That's my job," Cyrus shot back.

Andrew cocked a golden brow. "You can't be with her every minute. And you won't let me stay with her, either."

Emily's gaze shot from Andrew to Cyrus. "Cyrus? Is what Andrew says true?" She held her breath.

Cyrus stepped away from the desk and walked toward her, stopping when they stood face to face. His expression was solemn, his voice quiet. "Yes. I found footprints beneath the windows the other night and saw someone running from the house." He sighed. "I am assuming the man was Noah."

"No," Emily said. "It can't be him. He wouldn't come back." Her hands balled into tight fists. She looked away, afraid Cyrus would see the lie on her face. The situation was worse than she thought.

"We think he'll come to you, Emily. He's probably already tried." Andrew's words sliced through her.

"Have you told Ian?" she managed to ask. Her chest hurt, like a big fist had landed flat in the center, stealing her breath.

"There's no need to alert him yet, until the job is done," Cyrus said. The small reprieve faded, overshadowed by the promise of impending doom.

She bit the inside of her cheek to keep from showing undue emotion. It would not do to appear distressed. Cyrus watched her, his gaze intent, his mouth silent. He was only doing his duty. She understood that. As she was doing hers.

It was past time to get out of that room, out of that situation. The four walls were closing in, stifling her breath, choking her hopes with every word that passed between them. Emily needed to clear her head and formulate a plan to help her husband. And she needed to do it now.

Hazarding a glance at both men, she willed her voice to remain steady as she said, "Well, then, gentlemen, it seems you have everything under control." She pasted a smile on her face. "I will leave you to your strategies." She nodded her head and turned to leave. Her hand was on the knob when Cyrus's soft voice reached her.

"Emily, you will let us know at once if Noah tries to contact you?" It was a statement disguised in the politeness of a question.

"Of course," she said and quit the room.

Emily sat up in bed, two pillows propped behind her, and tried to read. She'd been on the same page for the past twenty minutes. Her eyes flew to the clock. Eleven. She slammed the book shut. It was useless to try and concentrate. Nothing could hold her attention. Nothing except the conversation she'd had that morning with Cyrus and Andrew. *Cyrus had seen Noah.* Could he tell she was lying about having seen him? She'd tried to sound so convincing, but it was difficult to lie to Cyrus. He was such an honest, noble man that it made her feel guilty even though she knew she had no choice. Noah needed her help, though he most likely would have a different opinion on the subject. He was too bullheaded, too stubborn to see trouble when it stared him in the face. And she was not about to let him get carted away before he proved his love for her.

Emily smoothed the French lace on the bodice of her silk nightgown. The nightgown she was to have worn on her wedding night. It was beautiful, adorned with miniature satin rosettes and tiny seed pearls. The plunging neckline left little to the imagination, exposing ample amounts of creamy flesh for an admirer's perusal. She told herself the only reason she was wearing it tonight was that it happened to be the first thing she grabbed. And her cotton nightgown had a small tear in it from last night. Emily felt her cheeks heat as she recalled the way she'd flung the gown aside, eager to please Noah with her nakedness.

She jerked the bodice together with her right hand. This was ridiculous. What was wrong with her? Who did she think she was trying to fool, half dressed in a flimsy swatch of material with a closed book in her hand and both eyes fixed on the door? She might have told Noah to stay away, said the words, even frowned and shook her fist at him, but Emily knew in her heart she wanted him to come tonight, needed him to come. And one look at her half-naked body and Noah would know it too.

Throwing back the covers, Emily scrambled out of bed and yanked open her wardrobe. She must hurry. Rifling through layers of white cotton, she found a simple nightgown, tied at the neckline and devoid of lace. Functional. That's what it was. If Noah did decide to show up, she would not have him thinking she had taken extra pains with her appearance.

The soft click behind her told her she was too late. Emily froze, her back to the door, the gown bunched in her hands.

"Well, well," Noah's deep voice poured over her like fine brandy, "if it isn't my little wife." She heard his footsteps moving toward her. "What a delicious surprise," he murmured. Emily felt his breath on the side of her neck, warm with a hint of tobacco. A chill ran down her arms. Her fingers twisted the fabric she held.

I will not show him I care.

Noah touched her hair, a brief, light caress, traveling from neck to back. His fingers trailed over the juncture of her hips, stroking her through the lace, heating her bare skin. Emily tensed, forcing herself to ignore the pulse of desire coursing through every fiber of her body, pretending she didn't feel the liquid heat pooling low in her belly.

"You wore this for me?" Noah asked, running his hands up the sides of her waist to the undersides of her arms, brushing past the swell of her breasts.

"No!" Emily closed her eyes against the onslaught of sensation rippling through her breasts. His fingers outlined the plump flesh, circling each mound with calloused fingertips, touching everywhere but the tips. She needn't look to know the peaks were hard and quite visible through the thin fabric. Perfect for his mouth, aching for his tongue. A small moan escaped her lips.

"You want me as much as I want you, Emily," he said, his

voice ragged and heavy with desire. His breath fanned the hair
by her left ear. "Stop fighting it." His fingertips brushed her
nipples.

Emily tried to concentrate, tried to keep her wits about her,
but Noah stripped away her convictions, one flick at a time as
his thumbs worked her swollen nipples.

"We shouldn't be doing this," she whispered, leaning back
into the solid comfort of his chest.

Noah's big hand moved down her body to cup her mons.
He pressed her back into his thighs, her buttocks rubbing against
the hard shaft of his arousal. "We most definitely should be
doing this," he murmured, lifting her nightgown to bury a
finger in her woman's heat.

Emily rocked against him, trying to get closer to his touch.
Her hands reached back to stroke his erection. Noah jerked
against her. "I can't . . . ahhh," she moaned as his thumb
circled her swollen nubbin, "let you . . . ," she groaned, moving
against his finger, "hurt me . . . again."

"No," he said, ripping his breeches open, "not again. Never
again," he whispered on a ragged sigh. His manhood sprung
free, brushing against Emily's hand. She circled his shaft, ran
her fingers the length of him, smiled when he growled low in
his throat. Noah pumped into her hand, a slow, methodic rhythm
that begged her to join in. Emily moved her hips, back and
forth, swaying to meet him and the driving need raging in her
blood.

"Noah," she breathed at the feel of his shaft pulsing against
her buttocks.

"Open your legs for me, Emily," he pleaded, running his
hand along her inner thigh. Emily spread her legs, her hips
arcing in a circle. She pushed forward, straining to meet the
gentle hum of his fingers on her nubbin. Ecstasy. Pure, simple,
sensual ecstasy. She leaned backward and felt the slick, swollen
tip of his manhood, begging entry.

There was no denying him. Emily wanted Noah, needed him.
Now. "Yes, Noah," she whimpered, "oh, yes."

He grabbed her hips and surged into her with such force that she almost lost her balance. She felt him inside, warm and pulsing. Needing, just like her. Emily reached out to brace herself against the wardrobe, arching her hips and planting her feet to meet the storm that was about to erupt.

"That's it, Emily," Noah said, reaching around to stroke her nubbin as he moved in and out of her with slow, even strokes. "Get ready." He kissed her neck. "Once you explode all over my fingers, I'm going to ram into you like a wild bull." His tongue circled the soft flesh on her shoulder. "Understand?" He stilled, waiting for her response.

Emily jerked back against him, needing to feel him full and hard inside her. "Yes . . . yes." His fingers skimmed and caressed her clitoris, his manhood pumping in and out of her with measured restraint. "Yes," she groaned as a whirlwind of sensation grabbed her, thrusting her into a vortex of sensual oblivion, spinning, spinning out of control. "Yes!" she screamed, as she felt herself come apart, pulsing against the shaft that thrust into her, creating new waves of ecstasy with each careful stroke.

"Hold on, Emily," Noah ground out, "we're going for a ride." He grabbed her hips, driving into her, filling her to the hilt. Noah hadn't lied. He surged into her like a mating bull, thrusting and jerking, all signs of the controlled lover gone. With one final plunge, he groaned and spilled his seed inside her.

Emily didn't know who moved first. Had Noah carried her to the bed and tucked her in with the tenderness of a loving husband, or had she dreamed it? And had he made love to her a second time with such exquisite care that she had sobbed? Fantasy meshed too closely with reality for her to tell the difference. But how could she be expected to when she had dreamed the dream so many times that it had become real? And was he lying beside her now, flesh and blood and warm male? There was only one way to separate fantasy from reality.

She opened her eyes and stared into a broad, hairy chest.

Noah. It hadn't been a dream. He had done all of those *things* to her, every one of them. And she had done her share of *things* to him, too. Heat crept up her neck to her cheeks. How would she ever face him when she had told him not to even try to enter her chambers or she'd boot him out? Well, not only hadn't she given him the boot, she'd welcomed him, with eagerness and open arms. Emily winced. And open legs. He'd think her a wanton, no better than one of his mistresses, flaunting herself around in that lacy nightgown. That had started everything. If she had only worn a serviceable gown, none of that would have happened.

"Emily?" Noah's deep voice ran over her like warm honey.

"Yes?" She stared ahead, right into his hairy, intimidating chest. Images of her fingers roaming over that chest, running her bare breasts along it, feeling the tingle of crisp hair on her nipples flashed through her mind. Emily jerked her head down. That was a bigger mistake. The sheet rode low on Noah's slim hips, exposing another, much more dangerous part of his anatomy. She squeezed her eyes shut, refusing to think about what she'd done with that body part.

"Emily?" There was a hint of amusement in his voice.

She kept her head low, eyes shut tight.

He chuckled. "Would you look at me, please?"

She shook her head.

"You have to look at me sometime."

"Not necessarily," she mumbled into the sheet.

He sighed and she guessed he was trying to be patient. "I'm your husband. You've seen me naked before, Emily." He touched her shoulder. She flinched but he didn't remove his hand. "And I've seen you naked, too."

"It was the nightgown," she blurted out.

"The nightgown?" he repeated.

Her head bobbed up and down. "If I hadn't worn it, none of this would have happened."

"None of what?" he asked, his voice rising.

"This," she said, waving a hand in the air, but still refusing to look at him. "Me. You. Naked. Together. Doing *things*."

"And *that's* what you're upset about?" He took a deep breath and let it out on a long sigh.

"I told you not to come back and you did anyway."

"You knew I would," he said, annoyance clear in his voice. "And if I hadn't, you would have been even more upset."

Emily said nothing.

"Isn't that right, Emily?" he prodded.

"That's beside the point." It was, wasn't it? "I told you not to come and you did and if I hadn't been wearing that wanton nightgown none of this would have happened."

Noah was silent for a full minute. When he spoke, his words touched her like a caress, heating her body. "You could have been wearing a sackcloth and I would have done the same things to you, Emily." She felt his gaze boring into her. "I like doing *things* to you, Emily. I like it a lot. As a matter of fact, there are a few *things* I would like to do to you right now." His fingers inched down her back, tracing circles on her skin.

"I acted like a wanton." She buried her face in her hands. "Probably no better than Desireé or Monique."

His laughter came out in gulps, as though he'd tried to restrain himself and couldn't. "Desireé and Monique? Really, Emily." He laughed again.

"I know," she said, shaking her head in misery. "I acted no better than one of them."

The laughter stopped. Noah's strong fingers found her chin and forced her head up. "Listen to me, Emily," he said, his brown eyes blazing as he scanned her face. "You are my wife. We shared passion in this room and it was wonderful. If you deny everything else about us, for God's sake, don't deny that." Hard brackets formed around his mouth. "Maybe you wanted to kick me out tonight. Maybe you still don't trust me. Maybe the passion carried you away. But whatever happened had nothing to do with the damned nightgown or wanton behavior.

It had to do with passion. And need. Don't apologize and don't be ashamed of it.''

She watched him, saw the twitch in his jaw and knew she had hurt him. "I said nothing about love because I can see you're not ready to discuss it.'' Noah sat up, rifling a hand through his dark brown hair. "You think I only want to use your body to meet my baser needs.''

The bitterness in his words stung, but she pretended they didn't bother her. "I told you, Noah, I won't let you hurt me again.''

"Yes,'' he replied with a knowing look, "I do recall you mentioning that today, though it took you a rather long time to get the words out.''

Emily's eyes narrowed. Of all the cruel, vile, indelicate things to say. She pulled the sheet up, covering her breasts. "You told me this whole charade would be over in three days, Noah. That's tomorrow.''

His hands balled into fists. "I can count.''

"Good.'' Emily's chin shot up. She bit the inside of her cheek to keep from crying. Who was this man who stared back at her with such coldness? Could it be the same one who had made love to her less than an hour before with such consuming passion? He seemed a stranger now with his dark, brooding stare. How was it possible to feel such closeness one minute and such distance the next?

"Let's get some sleep,'' Noah said, reaching over to put out the lamp. "We'll talk about this in the morning.''

Emily's hand snaked out to grab a muscled, dark forearm. "Wait!'' she whispered, surprised at the panic in her voice. "You can't sleep here.''

Noah shrugged her arm off and cocked a thick brow. "I can't?'' His words were soft, too soft.

"No. No, you can't,'' she stammered, feeling self-conscious and awkward. And very naked. Emily tugged on the sheet to cover her bare leg, but Noah's thigh weighed it down. Reaching over, she yanked the counterpane up, unaware that her breasts were exposed and dangling like inviting melons, waiting to be touched and tasted.

"Good night, Emily," Noah said, as though he hadn't heard a word of what she'd just said. He leaned over and snuffed out the lamp, casting the room in darkness, save the sliver of moon that slipped through the gap in the draperies.

"But you can't—"

"I know," he sighed. "I can't stay with you tonight," he said, settling himself back and pulling Emily into the crook of his warm embrace.

He wasn't going to leave. This just wouldn't do. What if Cyrus came knocking on her door in the morning? What if she were sick? Noah would be too smart not to guess she was with child. She could tell him it was an upset stomach from last evening's meal. Of course, that would be another lie. What was one more lie in the long trail that paved their relationship? Her stomach twisted into a knot. Lies. Would she and Noah ever stop telling each other lies? Was he lying to her now when he professed his love? She didn't know and it filled her heart with such overwhelming sadness that she ached. Emily felt the moisture in her eyes and blinked the tears away. There would be no tears. Not with Noah so close she could feel his breath on her hair.

"Good night, Emily." His words floated to her, soft and sensuous in the night.

He wasn't going to leave. *And* he was drifting off to sleep. The knowledge pricked every nerve in her body. Well then, fine, let him stay, but she'd see he got no sleep. "Cyrus saw you the other day," she said. That would rouse him.

"Hmmm."

One mumbled half-word was not the response she anticipated. "He's determined to catch you."

"Hmmm."

"And he asked me if I saw you." *There. Stew about that for a minute or two.*

"Did you tell him you saw every inch of me?" The laughter in his voice was too much.

"You!" Emily tried to struggle from his hold but Noah held her down like a nasty pest. "Don't you care that Cyrus is after you? Could catch you? That I could have turned you in?" Emily maneuvered a few inches, trying to work her way to her side. Noah's arm went with her, landing on her hip. Her bare hip. She squirmed but he only pressed her deeper into his side. Emily froze when she felt the coarse hair on his legs brushing the inside of her thighs.

"You wouldn't turn me in." The certainty in his voice annoyed Emily. She didn't know what bothered her more, the fact that he was right or that he knew he was right. "As for Mandrey, I'll take my chances."

"You do that," she hissed, angry at his arrogance. "But you have one more day to end this charade and if you don't, I *will* turn you in."

"And see me hang by my ankles," Noah added, as though Emily's threat didn't bother him one bit.

"Toes," she ground out.

"Toes?"

"I'll see you hang by your toes. Much, much more painful," she assured him.

Noah chuckled and pulled her closer. "Dear wife, how will I ever get used to such unadulterated adoration?"

Chapter 18

Emily rolled onto her stomach, arms outstretched, uncurling one finger at a time as she shed the last layers of slumber. Her body felt warm, languid, like a rose gifted with the full bounty of sunshine. She sighed, Perhaps she'd drift back to her dreams a little while longer. Noah would be there. He always was, touching her with strong, tanned hands, watching her with dark, unreadable eyes, tasting her with full, firm lips. Emily smiled. Yes, she would dream just a little longer.

A rap on the door jolted her from her thoughts. "Emily, wake up. It's eleven o'clock. Are you planning to sleep all day?" Cyrus's voice rasped through the door.

"I'm . . . awake," Emily said on a yawn.

"It's a gorgeous day. I thought we'd take a walk if you're feeling up to it."

Emily buried her head under the pillow. She'd rather get back to her dream but Cyrus was much too persistent to leave her alone. Besides, dreams were just that. Dreams. She preferred to keep hers tucked away in the recesses of her brain for midnight perusing or early morning wanderings. Throwing back

the covers, Emily flung her legs over the side of the bed and
called out, "Fifteen minutes, Cyrus. I'll see you then."

She heard him turn away, whistling as he went down the hall.

Twenty minutes later, Emily grabbed two buttermilk biscuits
from the sideboard, tucked them in a napkin and headed out
the door. Cyrus was waiting for her on a bench near the maze.

"Good morning," she said, smiling at him.

"And good afternoon to you," he returned, smiling back.

"I guess I was more tired than I realized." And who wouldn't
be with a virile, demanding husband like Noah Sandleton?

"It's to be expected of a woman in your condition."

He was referring to the baby, of course. A pang of sadness
struck Emily as she realized Cyrus knew about her unborn
child but Noah did not. She pushed her feelings away. It wasn't
time to tell him yet. Emily had to see if he'd keep his word
and then she would tell him. Sometime, within the next twelve
hours, she would know if she'd been betrayed. Again.

Why couldn't Noah be more like Cyrus? Dependable, honest,
trustworthy, sincere? They probably weren't even part of his
vocabulary. "I'll miss you when you're gone, Cyrus."

"I'll miss you too, Emily," Cyrus said as they rounded a
corner of the rose garden and headed into the maze.

"What will you do when you leave here?" She hated to
think of him alone.

He smiled. "There's a certain woman I intend to contact.
And if she'll forgive my stupid, selfish, uncaring ways and give
me another chance, I'll be the happiest man in the world."

"You?" Emily squeaked. "Are in love?" He nodded and
she was sure he was blushing beneath his bush of hair. "That's
wonderful!" She let out a peal of laughter, grabbing his hands
and giving him a quick hug. "I am so happy for you, Cyrus!
I had no idea!"

He looked a little sheepish. "Nor did I, to tell you the truth.
But watching you made me do a lot of thinking. I left her
without much explanation, and a lot of things unsaid. I don't
plan on making the same mistake twice."

"I can't even picture you being selfish or uncaring. Or anything but an honorable, noble man." *Unlike some men I know.*

"Love makes people do crazy things, Emily. Remember that. I wouldn't be surprised if your husband felt the same way."

The smile faded from Emily's face. "Well, time will tell, Cyrus. Time will tell." *Sooner than you think.*

He wasn't coming. It was eleven fifty-two and she sat alone, fully dressed on a high-backed chair in the corner of her room, staring at the cream swirled wallpaper in front of her. All of the promises, hopes and dreams ticking away. Why had he even come back? she wondered. Why couldn't he have left her alone? Why did he have to make her care so much that losing him a second time would be almost unbearable? Why couldn't he love her enough?

Emily rested her head against the wall, wishing she could still her weary mind from the constant torment of loss and betrayal. She closed her eyes, trying to ignore the ache in her back. After two hours in a wooden chair without a cushion, she longed for the softness of her bed. Eight more minutes. She would wait right here with every stitch of clothing on. Far from the bed. She wanted to keep her wits about her so she could deal with his soft voice and searching eyes. Seductive charm. That's what he had and more than his fair share of it too.

Something brushed her forehead, soft and gentle as a summer's breeze. Emily murmured in half sleep, her head falling to the side. Another feather-light touch grazed her neck. She lifted her hand in silent protest and found her fingers molding something hard and scratchy. Her eyes flew open. Noah leaned over her, inches away, his stubbled chin stroked by her fingers. Emily snatched her hand away, burying it in the fold of her blue gown.

"Why aren't you in bed?" he asked, his brown eyes as soft as warm honey. Emily's stomach jumped at the tenderness in his voice. He was doing it to her again. With no more than a few soft-spoken words, Noah tied her up in knots, blurring her judgment like raindrops on a windowpane.

"I was waiting for you." She kept her voice even, void of emotion. Her gaze flitted across his face and she noted the weary lines of fatigue etched around his mouth and eyes. He looked older, tired, less self-assured. Something was wrong. She could sense it.

"You should be resting." His gaze darted to her stomach, settled there a few seconds and then moved to her face. Almost as if he knew there was indeed a very real reason for her to be resting at such an hour. Almost as if he knew about the baby.

Emily blinked that thought away. No sense in looking for complications, not yet, anyway. The sad, uneasy look in his eyes sent a shiver of foreboding up her spine.

"You're not going to tell me what this is all about, are you?" Emily folded her hands in her lap, squeezing them so hard her knuckles turned white.

"I need a little more time."

Six words, that's all it took to shatter her dreams, crush her hopes for a life with the man standing before her. Six small words. One sentence. Her future with Noah Sandleton inked out before it started.

"Then there's really not much else to say." Emily looked away. She felt dead inside, snuffed out. Only the pain from the nail marks in her palms reminded her she was still alive.

Noah raked a hand through his mussed-up hair. "I know what I told you, Emily. And I thought I would have everything under control by now. But I *need* a little more time."

Emily shrugged, a ghost of a smile playing about her lips. "Take all the time you *need*, Noah. Take a week, a month, a year, if that's what you *need*. But don't expect me to wait for you or welcome you back as my husband."

He cursed under his breath. "Can't you be reasonable? Can't you trust me just a little longer?"

"We haven't trusted each other since we met in the Fox's Tail."

"Then isn't it time to start?" He knelt down on one knee, covering her cold hands with his strong, warm ones, his brown eyes melting into hers. "For God's sake, Emily, don't do this," he pleaded.

"Don't do what, Noah?" she asked, her voice empty and lifeless. "Don't ask questions?" The right side of his jaw twitched. "Don't expect answers?" His nostrils flared. "Don't be difficult?" His eyes narrowed to brown slits. "Don't intrude on your plans?" His hands tightened on hers.

"Stop it," he ground out.

"Stop what, Noah?" She disengaged her hands from his grasp with quiet firmness. "Stop asking for the truth?"

"Yes, damn it! I mean no. No! Stop behaving like a child and be reasonable." Noah massaged the back of his neck. "Give me a little more time."

Emily folded her arms across her chest. "Sorry. Time's run out. Where have you been all this time, Noah?" Her eyes searched his face. "Why did you leave me on our wedding night?"

Noah glared at her. "I told you, I am not at liberty to say at the moment."

"And I told you, I am not interested in excuses."

Noah stood up and paced the room, plowing all ten fingers through his hair. "Damn you, Emily," he muttered.

"*Damn you*, Noah," she shot back, a spurt of feeling pumping into her cold veins.

He gave her a dark look and a scowl before he rounded on her, stopping less than a foot away. Emily studied her hands, willing him to go away. But she knew from experience that nothing was that easy. Not with Noah Sandleton.

"You're too upset to be rational right now, Emily. You're saying things you can't mean." Noah rubbed his jaw, studying her with quiet intent. He reminded Emily of a commander strategizing before battle. Only this skirmish would hold no victory for him, only the bitter emptiness of defeat.

"If you say so, Noah." The man was persistent to the point of being downright exhausting.

"I know so," he said, enunciating each word with careful eloquence. And then the dagger came, twisting, grinding into her heart. "I love you, Emily."

Those were the words Emily couldn't bear to hear. She didn't believe them, couldn't believe them and perhaps that was why the pain seeped to her very soul. A surge of anger, hot and piercing, gripped her, making her want to lash out, make him feel her pain, hurt him as he had hurt her.

"Words, Noah. Only words," she murmured, feeling their weight squeezing her chest. What was love without trust?

"Believe what you will. One day you'll know the truth." Emily kept her head bent, refusing to look at him. She must keep her armor in place, not let him find the slightest chink in it. "I'll be back tomorrow night and then we'll talk." He turned on his heel to leave.

Emily's head shot up. Their gazes clashed, gray steel with amber fire. "No. I won't trust you again, Noah. Leave tonight and you'll be spared. Stay and I won't be responsible for the consequences."

"You would see me captured, treated like a common criminal?" He advanced a step, crossing his broad arms over his chest, daring her to answer.

Emily remained silent.

Noah threw a hand in the air. "Do what you will. I will see you tomorrow night." With those last words, he turned and stalked out of the room, leaving Emily staring after him.

When she was certain he was gone, she rose from her chair and moved to the bed. She was cold. So cold. And empty inside. Emily lay on the bed and turned her face into the counterpane. Only then did she allow the tears to come.

Emily tried to hide the puffiness in her eyes the next morning but knew Cyrus noticed their swollen state. But he was too much the gentleman to ask pointed questions. Unlike one particular person she knew. Brown eyes and a slow smile danced through her mind. That man was no gentleman, she reminded herself, shaking him from her thoughts. He was a scourge, a scoundrel, a rakehell. Her husband. She sighed. And the cause of so many tears.

"Kleeton should be arriving any moment," Cyrus said, cutting into her thoughts.

"Good." She patted a stray lock of hair into place.

"Why is he coming?" Cyrus asked, taking a seat beside her on the sofa.

Emily hesitated. She hated lying to Cyrus but couldn't very well tell him the truth, so she settled on a half-truth. "It's nice to have a visitor on occasion. Andrew is aware of our 'situation' and it's not as awkward inviting him to tea as it would be a new neighbor." Emily gave Cyrus a wistful smile. "After all, Cyrus, how would I explain your presence?"

Cyrus shrugged his bulky shoulders. "Soon enough, it won't matter. I'll be gone and you can invite the whole town if you want."

"Yes, soon enough it won't matter," Emily echoed, her gaze settling on the row of books harboring the secret panel that opened to the secret passage. She had wanted to check the passage out herself days ago, but hesitated, worried that Noah might be hiding in its dark recesses. Now she was certain she would not be undertaking any grand explorations. The fear of seeing Noah again was too real, her emotions too raw.

Last night as she lay on her bed, spent and exhausted from tears, Emily felt the pang of hurt and betrayal and vowed she'd never again let Noah close enough to hurt her. And she'd meant it. But this morning, when she woke in the gray dawn, crumpled and mussed, in yesterday's gown, she remembered the heat in his eyes, heard the pleading in his voice as he begged her for a little more time. "I love you, Emily." Noah's words rolled over her, like waves beating against rocks, wearing her down, a little at a time.

This morning she didn't know what she wanted to do. Didn't know which she'd regret more, leaving Noah or not leaving him. And that's why she'd sent Andrew the invitation to tea.

Emily needed someone to listen to her dilemma. Cyrus was out of the question for obvious reasons. Augusta was too far away and even if she weren't, Emily wouldn't risk creating a rift between her and Ian. Belle was touring the Continent with her aunt. So there really wasn't anyone left save Andrew.

Andrew would know what to do. He'd been supportive throughout the whole ordeal, concerned only for her safety and best interest. Andrew would help her make the right decision. Now all she had to do was find a way to be alone with him, which meant fabricating an excuse to get Cyrus out of the room.

A single rap on the door signaled Andrew's arrival.

Cyrus rose and opened the door. Emily saw Andrew's blond head just outside the door. He and Cyrus exchanged a few words, but their voices were too low for Emily to make out what they were saying.

"Hello, Emily," Andrew said, advancing into the room with a dazzling smile on his handsome face. Emily returned the smile and placed her hand in his. Today he sported cream calfskin gloves, the same color as his jacket and breeches.

"Andrew, thank you for coming on such short notice," Emily said. She shot a glance toward Cyrus, who was watching the exchange with mild interest. The sooner she got this over with, the better. Her stomach twisted in knots of anticipation and indecision.

"It's always a pleasure to see you, Emily." His voice was soft and smooth, like his gloves.

"Cyrus, would you mind very much seeing to tea? And would you speak with Cook about the lemon pastries and raspberry tarts I asked her to prepare? I have a sudden craving for them." Emily smiled at Cyrus, hoping he wouldn't realize she was just trying to get rid of him.

His raised brow and tilted head told her he was onto her game, but Cyrus, being Cyrus, would comply with her request. He would never embarrass her in front of Andrew. Unlike another individual, who would relish the idea.

Cyrus gave her a slight nod and said, "I'll be back shortly."

As soon as the door clicked behind him, Emily turned to Andrew. "Andrew, you must help me," she whispered. "I'm in a terrible mess and I don't know what to do."

Andrew's summer-blue eyes shone with concern. He leaned toward her and adopted her same tone. "Whatever is troubling you, Emily?"

"It's Noah. He came to me the other night." She felt the heat in her cheeks. "He told me in three days' time I'd know why he left and why he couldn't return. It seems it had nothing to do with Cyrus being here. It was almost as if there was another, much more serious reason he couldn't come to me." She shook her head, rubbing her temples. "I'm so confused."

She didn't see the unnatural light in Andrew's eyes. "Of course you are," he whispered, soothing her shattered nerves. He took her hand in his. "Go on," he urged. Emily felt grateful to have a friend such as him. She had done the right thing by telling him.

"Last night, he told me he needed more time." Emily hesitated, swallowing the lump in her throat. "I refused him." Her eyes filled with tears. "I said some horrible things, Andrew. I just wanted to protect myself from being hurt again."

"And now you wonder if you did the right thing?" His quiet words voiced the uncertainty she'd felt since Noah had stalked out of her room.

Emily nodded, a stray tear escaping to trail down her cheek. She swiped at it with the back her hand.

"How did he get into your room, Emily?"

"Oh. Well," her gaze shot to the bookcase. "There's a secret panel that opens a passageway leading to his room." What did it matter if she told Andrew?

"Where is this secret panel?" Emily looked at Andrew, wondering at the sharpness in his voice, the keenness in his eyes.

"It's behind the third row of books in that case over there," she said, pointing to several volumes of red-leather-bound volumes.

Andrew let out a long breath, as though he'd been holding

it. She must have imagined his reaction. What did he care if Noah harbored a secret passageway in his home?

"Telling me was the right thing to do, Emily," Andrew said, leaning back against the couch and taking her hand with him. Emily didn't notice. Her heart and her mind were tangled with thoughts and feelings, all centering around Noah Sandleton.

"I just don't know what to do, Andrew. Part of me wants to hate him, but the other part won't let me. And I'm carrying his child," she murmured.

"Give it time, Emily," Andrew said with the wisdom of a sage. "Just another day or so," he said, reaching up to push back a stray lock of hair. "Everything will work out according to a plan much larger than yours or Noah's. You'll see," he said, his gentle words a balm to her restless soul.

She gave him a tear-streaked smile and whispered, "I never knew you to be a religious man, Andrew. Thank you. Thank you for your comforting words." Emily squeezed his hand. "I'll wait and let the divine plan follow its course."

Andrew smiled. "And so it shall be, Emily. So it shall be."

He had to make her see reason. He just had to, Noah told himself as he strode into the darkened library with nothing but a small lamp to illuminate his path. Damn, but the woman was bullheaded. He'd thought he'd be able to force Kleeton's hand in three days, thought the man would have slipped up in his overzealous endeavor to trap Noah Sandleton. Noah hadn't missed the gleam in Kleeton's eyes when he mentioned Noah's name. He'd bet his entire wealth that the man posing as a country gentleman was a notorious traitor and cold-blooded killer.

But hunches weren't enough. Not with stakes this high. Peter Crowlton had slithered away once before, hidden behind God knew how many rocks, escaping capture for years. Well, he wouldn't escape again. Not if Noah could help it. Tomorrow, he'd force Kleeton's hand. He'd confront him, not as Cyrus

Mandrey but as Noah Sandleton. And he would see what secrets lay behind Andrew Kleeton's gloves.

Noah pressed the panel to engage the hidden door. As he pushed it open and stepped inside, his thoughts turned toward his wife. Why in the hell had she called a meeting with Kleeton? And he knew damned well it was a meeting, not a social call as she would have had Cyrus believe. What was she up to now?

He turned around to close the door. A sharp object lodged against his throat, freezing him in his tracks.

"Well, well," a familiar voice said. "If it isn't the ghost himself."

"Crowlton," Noah rasped against the blade. "Traitorous bastard."

The blade dug into his flesh. "Watch it, Sandleton. I've waited a long time to see you bleed. Seven and a half years to be exact." His breathing was harsh and labored against Noah's ear. "I want to savor every minute of this. I want to feel the fear in your heart as I raise my knife in final revenge, see the helplessness in your eyes as I slit your throat, hear the short, choppy rasps of breath as life spurts out of you. I want to remember *everything* for years to come."

"You can't remember anything if you're a dead man," Noah ground out.

Crowlton laughed. "Always the hero, aren't you? Well, you'll be no hero today. You'll pay dearly for what you did to me." He paused. "With your life."

Noah heard the bitterness in his voice, felt the fury as the Serpent's hand trembled against the blade, digging deeper, drawing blood.

"You did this to yourself. You wanted it all, no matter the stakes. It didn't matter who got hurt or *killed,* so long as you were in charge." If he were going to die, he'd make damn certain he had his say first.

The blow to the back of his neck was swift and sharp, placed with enough precision to drop Noah to his knees. The lantern fell to the ground, but remained upright. Before he could recover, Noah suffered the toe of Crowlton's booted foot in his side. He slumped forward, groaning.

Crowlton snorted. "I did what I had to do. I had the power, don't you understand, Sandleton?" His words were fervent, demanding recognition. "I was in control, within two missions of absolute power." He towered over Noah, the tip of the blade glinting in his left hand. "Until you ruined everything."

"You . . . were," Noah rasped, sucking in air, "a traitor . . . to your . . . country and . . . fellow agents."

Another kick landed in his side. "I was a *businessman,* nothing more. My allegiance was to whoever gave me the most coin. Now, turn around, Sandleton. I want the satisfaction of seeing the life drain from your face when I slit your throat."

Noah tried to lift his head as a wave of nausea rolled over him. He felt dizzy and lightheaded at the same time. He had to fight, had to gather his strength and his wits or he would soon be nothing but a lifeless pool of bloody flesh. Ignoring the pain in his side and the ache in his head, he rolled himself over and slouched against the stone wall. It felt cool and soothing on his head and neck.

"I want you to see what you did to me," Crowlton said, yanking off his black gloves in two swift movements. "Look, Sandleton. Look at what your fire did," he hissed, thrusting his hands forward in the dim light. Noah's gaze narrowed on the gnarled extremities in front of him. They were covered with layer upon layer of thin white skin, stretched and crossed over one another, forming a grotesque pattern of human flesh.

Noah looked away. Crowlton snatched his hands back. "You are the cause of this, Noah Sandleton," he raged. "You! And would you like to guess how I came to be so disfigured?" He leaned forward, his blue eyes glinting. When Noah didn't respond, he burst forth, "I tried to grab the files you torched. All those names, with dates, assignments, everything. All up in flames. With a single match you stripped me of my power and turned me from the best espionage agent in the country to a wanted criminal."

"They were onto you, Crowlton," Noah said, meeting his cold stare. He had to try to distract him, keep him talking. Perhaps then he'd let his guard down and Noah could strike. Should he go straight for the knife or tackle him at the waist?

"Don't even try it." The words hit him like one of Crowlton's boots in the gut. It knocked the wind out of his half-formed plan. Crowlton was a master of many things: espionage, strategy, tactics, weaponry.

But he was human. Or as close to human as a traitor could be. What was his weak spot?

"I would have taken care of you sooner, but there were too many people after me," Crowlton said, tossing the knife from one hand to the other. "Too many tracks to cover. And then you were gone, disappearing for years. But I decided to wait it out, certain that one day you would return. Too bad I had to kill the old duke and duchess next door, but I needed their home and they refused to sell. Of course, their wastrel of a son had no choice, not after I bought up all of his markers and threatened to call them in. Poor dumb bastard. Most humans are such a pitiful lot, don't you think?"

Noah rested an arm on his knee, staring straight ahead, wondering at Crowlton's incredible arrogance. He didn't think he could ever be beat. Not by anyone, least of all a man without a weapon. That was his weakness.

"And then," Crowlton went on, "stroke of luck would have it that your beautiful wife arrived at Glenview Manor." He smiled. "Alone. Without her husband. That was a true gift and I will be forever indebted to you."

"Leave Emily out of this," Noah said, clenching his fists at his side. If he had a knife, he'd drive it right through the bastard's heart before he could utter another word.

"Oh, but I can't. She's become such an important part of this whole, ah, shall we say, situation?"

Rage, red hot, threatened to boil over and explode throughout Noah's body. He wanted to charge him, but he thought about it and held back. He must be rational.

"I don't know what you're talking about," he spat out, his eyes zeroing in on Crowlton's knife.

"Of course you don't." Crowlton gave a short, harsh laugh. "You weren't here, were you?" He tilted his blond head to one side and rubbed his smooth chin. "Well, not the whole time anyway." Reaching into his pocket, he pulled out a brown ball and tossed it to Noah. Before it touched his fingers Noah knew it was Cyrus Mandrey's beard.

Crowlton threw back his head and laughed. "Clever, Sandleton. Very clever. They didn't call you the Chameleon for nothing." His smile faded. "But you're no match for the Serpent."

"I'm unarmed." What could he do to even the odds?

"That you are. Too bad for you, isn't it? Well, as I was saying, your wife will be my prize. I think I deserve something after ferreting you out, don't you?"

"Don't touch her." It took every ounce of strength not to lunge at the bastard.

"Don't touch her." The words rolled over Crowlton's tongue like soft velvet. "Is that a request or a demand? Either way, it seems you have little control over the situation."

Noah looked away, trying to fight the strong urge to wipe the smile off Crowlton's face. Permanently. His gaze fell on the lantern, the sole source of illumination in this otherwise black passage. The flame flickered and danced within the confines of the glass. One sharp blow to the lantern would snuff out the flame, blanketing them in darkness, evening the odds.

"I can't wait to touch your wife's soft, creamy skin. Sink myself into her warm, wet heat." He paused, his voice little more than a whisper. "Again."

Again. The word pierced Noah's heart with more pain than any knife could ever cause. Again? Emily? Emily and Crowlton? No, anything but that. He refused to believe it. Emily loved him. Didn't she?

"Did she tell you she's with child?" From the guarded look on Noah's face, it was obvious she hadn't. "I see." He flipped the knife in the air, caught it by the blade and flipped it again. "Emily's going to have a baby, Sandleton. My baby."

"Liar!" Noah roared, kicking the lantern with his right foot and lunging for Crowlton. Blackness covered them as he wrapped his arms around the other man, wrestling him to the floor. Noah was much larger, but the Serpent was wiry and hard to hold down. A slice of pain ripped Noah's side as he felt the sharp blade sink in, drawing blood. He reached for Crowlton's forearm, missed, and suffered the slash of a blade on his forearm.

"Damn liar!" Noah hissed, slamming his fist in the area of Crowlton's face. The sickening sound of crushing bone filled the air, followed by a low groan. Noah punched him again. Harder. His left hand reached up, swiping the air, searching for Crowlton's arm. He found it, yanked it down over the Serpent's head and banged his hand hard on the wood floor several times. "Damn liar," he rasped. The knife fell from the Serpent's hand, and Noah felt for it, grabbed it and lodged it against his nemesis' throat.

"You lied." Noah trailed the knife along Crowlton's neck, pressing harder into his skin with each passing second. "Admit it." He waited for the confession. The only sound he heard was Crowlton's labored breathing and mumbled groans. "Admit it!" Noah said, determined to force the words from his enemy's lips.

A slow gurgle filled the air. It was half-laugh, half-gasp. "Who do you think told me about this place? I win, Sandleton, I win," Crowlton whispered. "My baby, not yours. Mine."

Noah sank the blade into Crowlton's neck, twisted it until he felt pools of blood oozing on his fingers. Then he twisted it again, trying to wipe out the words. Harder. Deeper. But it was too late and Noah knew it. The Serpent lay before him, dead, his throat slashed beyond recognition. It should have been a welcoming victory, but the win was cold and empty.

Peter Crowlton was right. He'd won.

Noah dropped the knife and wiped his bloody hands on his

breeches. He tried to stand, but the pain in his side kept him doubled over. He felt for the wall and edged along, one step at a time, his right arm bracing his weight. Blood seeped through his fingers from the deep gash on his side. Noah winced. Crowlton knew how to place his blows. Every one of them, he reminded himself, thinking of his last words.

"My baby, not yours. Mine." Had Crowlton told the truth? Had he seduced Emily as his ultimate revenge? Or had Emily gone to him of her own will, lain with him and let him father her child? Is that why she hadn't told him about the baby? The questions teemed in his head, making him sick with thinking of them.

Noah took another shuffling step and thought of his wife's conversation with Cyrus the morning she'd been sick. She'd admitted it was Noah's child, hadn't she? But what else could she have said under the circumstances? *I am carrying Andrew Kleeton's baby in my belly?* And there was plenty of opportunity for a distraught young bride and an experienced seducer to share a liaison before Cyrus showed up. *And* Emily had told Kleeton about the secret passageway.

Emily had betrayed him. The realization tore at his gut. Did she know Kleeton's true identity? Was she in on his scheme? Perhaps waiting at this very moment for her lover to join her in her bedchamber and inform her of her husband's demise? Noah felt the bile rise to his throat. God, but he wished he could just expel this whole distasteful mess from his stomach and be done with it. But the pain of betrayal was much more severe, much more insidious, invading every part of his body from head to heart. And it would remain with him forever.

Noah reached the door leading to his room. He rested a sticky hand on the knob, hesitated a moment and then pushed it open, thinking of Emily and her betrayal.

Chapter 19

She must have heard the door open, because no sooner had he hobbled over the threshold than she came running toward him, shock and surprise on her face. "Noah! What happened?" Emily was a good little actress, he'd give her that. She actually seemed concerned about him. But he knew better. She was probably wondering about her lover.

He settled into a large cream tufted chair, mindless of the blood he tracked behind and about himself. Leaning back, Noah pinched the bridge of his nose and rubbed his eyes.

Emily sank down on the floor beside him, grabbing his free hand. Tears streamed down her face. God, but she was beautiful. Beautiful and deceitful, he reminded himself. "Kleeton's dead," he said, relishing the words. *Your lover, the father of your baby, is dead.* That's what he wanted to say, but it would all come out soon enough.

"What happened, Noah?" She held his hand with such force, looked at him with such concern in those smoky gray eyes, that he could almost believe she cared. Almost. Crowlton's words stayed with him, never far from the surface, tormenting him, driving him mad.

"Kleeton jumped me in the passageway. He tried to slit my throat, but I beat him to it." That's all she needed to know.

A look similar to horror shadowed over her face. "But why? I don't understand."

Noah shrugged. "Perhaps he wanted you to himself." He pulled his hand away and rubbed his neck. "I need Billington."

"Of course," she mumbled, scrambling to her feet. "I'll get him right away." Noah heard her slippered feet hurrying toward the door. He tried to take in a deep breath, but his side hurt too much. Damn, but he felt weak. His head fell back against the plush cream fabric of the chair and he closed his eyes, waiting for Billington.

Within minutes, Edward Billington rushed to Noah's side. "Sir, you requested my assistance?" Noah opened one eye and would have laughed if the pain weren't so bad. Ever the gentleman, even in a burgundy stocking cap and matching silk robe, Billington stood before him, tall and erect, awaiting orders. He didn't look the least bit perturbed, but why should he? Billington had patched him up on more than one occasion.

Before Noah could answer, Emily half ran into the room, water sloshing over the sides of the basin she carried. "Mr. Billington, I need your help," she panted. "He's bleeding." Noah wondered at her almost panicked voice. She needn't put on such a show for him or Billington. They'd seen it all before, the best plots of deceit imaginable. Emily clanked the basin on the floor and produced a cloth from the pocket of her robe. She dipped it in water and rung it out. Her slender hands moved toward him, holding the cloth.

Noah snatched it from her. "That's Billington's job," he snapped. He did not want her touching him, not after she'd lain with his enemy. His eyes shot to her stomach. Not when she was carrying Crowlton's child.

"Noah? I-I just want to help," she murmured. There was

no need to look at her face to know there were tears in her
eyes, but she would get no comfort from him

"Haven't you already helped me enough? You almost got
me killed." He ignored her gasp and turned to Billington.
Holding out the cloth, he said, "Here. Do what you need to
do."

Billington took the cloth but hesitated, his gray eyes darting
to Emily. "Sir, perhaps Lady Emily could help."

"No. I said she's *helped* enough. If you can't do the job
then both of you leave me the hell alone and I'll do it myself,"
he snarled. Billington clamped his mouth shut and didn't say
another word. Within minutes, he had assessed the wound,
applied pressure and a dressing. The other cuts were superficial
and needed less attention. He was quick, efficient and familiar
with the task.

Emily sat in a chair a few feet away, her eyes never leaving
his face. Noah pretended to ignore her, but he felt her presence,
smelled her lilac scent, saw the cascade of golden curls trailing
from her shoulders. He told himself he hated her for her betrayal
and part of him did. But a deeper part couldn't hate her and
still wanted her, even now, in the hour of her greatest deceit,
and he despised himself for his weakness.

There was only one solution.

"Billington, in the morning I would like you to send a few
servants to help Lady Emily with her packing." Only one
solution, he reminded himself.

"What are you talking about, Noah?" Emily jumped out of
the chair, hands on hips. "Where are we going?"

Noah forced himself to meet her gaze one last time. She
stood before him, a mixture of anger and confusion etched on
her beautiful face.

"*We* are not going anywhere," he said, his voice cold and
emotionless. "You, on the other hand, are going back to your
brother's."

"What?" She took a step closer. Then another. He could
see the light spray of freckles on her nose. "Why? Noah, why

are you doing this? Last night you told me you loved me and today you can't even look at me.'' Her voice trembled. ''Why, Noah?''

He waved a hand in the air, annoyed with her questions. ''Spare me the theatrics, Emily. It will do you no good. You know better than anyone the reason for my decision.''

She inched closer, her small hands balled into fists at her sides. ''Do I? Do tell, what *is* the reason? Is it because I couldn't trust you enough to admit my love for you before? Because I wanted to be certain you wouldn't leave again? Is that what this is all about?'' Emily's voice rose to a fever pitch and Noah knew half the household perched on the other side of the door. He cared less.

''Let it be, Emily. You know the reason. Don't embarrass yourself any further, just leave. Tomorrow,'' he finished on a ragged sigh. Why did it cause him such pain to say the words?

Emily's eyes widened in disbelief. *''I will not leave, Noah Sandleton.* I love you and you told me you loved me. I am not running away.''

''Tomorrow, Emily,'' he repeated, his eyes burning into hers.

A single tear trickled down her cheek. ''I love you, Noah. I'm sorry I didn't trust you enough. Please forgive me,'' she whispered, bending over to place a light kiss on his forehead.

Noah jerked back before her soft lips touched his skin. The look of hurt and shock that crossed her face would remain carved in his brain for all time. But it was the only way. He had to make her leave. Now. His salvation depended on it.

Emily straightened and squared her shoulder, a proud, fierce warrior preparing for battle. Her gray gaze traveled over his face, from eyes to nose to hair to chin and back again, as though she were memorizing it. When she spoke, he had to lean forward to hear her words. ''I'm carrying your child, Noah.''

''No!'' he roared, half jumping out of his seat. The pain in his side forced him back down. ''Do not,'' he bit out, ''speak of your bastard child as mine!''

Her eyes rounded in disbelief at his words.

"That is not my child! It was your lover's and I'll be damned if I'll be cuckolded just because he's dead." He slammed his fist on the arm of the chair.

"Andrew?" she asked, as though trying to make sense of Noah's rambling tirade. "No! No, Noah. It wasn't like that at all. Andrew and I were just friends, nothing more. How could you think such a thing after we ... after we ..." She swiped a tear with the back of her hand and shot a pleading look at Billington, who had faded to the far end of the room. "Tell him, Mr. Billington, tell him the truth."

"I don't want a goddamn testimonial from Billington. I heard it from your lover's own mouth," he said, the words bitter on his tongue.

"It's not true, Noah. Why would Andrew say something like that?"

"Because it was the truth?" Noah replied, sarcasm dripping on each word. "I know you and I have never shared much in the way of the truth, but some people think honesty is a virtue, though I do doubt he was one of them."

Emily ignored the cruel words. "If you don't want to ask Billington, then let's find Cyrus and ask him. He'll tell you the truth."

Noah shot a sharp look at Billington, who coughed and sputtered into his hand. "Sorry. Can't do that," Noah said, clenching his jaw.

"Why not? Cyrus won't mind losing a little sleep. I'm surprised he hasn't woken up yet."

"I'm not," Noah said, a ghost of a smile playing about his lips.

Emily's eyes narrowed. "What did you do to him, Noah? Did you harm him? Where is he?" Her voice rose with each rapid-fire question.

Noah shrugged. "Gone."

"Gone?" she echoed, staring at him. "Gone?" Emily inclined her head, trying to get into his line of vision. Noah avoided her gaze, fixing his eyes on the Ming vase on top of his bureau. Her words beat at his defenses. "He can't just be gone."

Raising a weary hand, he signaled Billington. God, but he just wanted to be done with this whole mess. So many lies. Too many lies. No wonder he and Emily never stood a chance. "Billington? Would you care to enlighten Lady Emily?"

Emily's gaze flew to Billington. The butler cleared his throat. Once. Twice. Three times before daring to speak. "Ah, Lady Emily, it seems as though Mr. Mandrey is no longer with us." He shot a reproving glance at his employer.

Noah scowled back. "Because?"

Billington straightened his shoulders. "Because," he dragged the word out, then stopped. "Because," he coughed, "he's been called away on an emergency." He finished in a rush, the words tumbling over each other in a blur. So much for Billington's very precise manner.

"What kind of emergency?" Emily asked, taking a few steps toward Billington.

"Billington." Noah didn't try to hide the warning in his voice. Or the exasperation. He wanted to make a clean break from this whole business. And he didn't want Emily thinking her knight in shining armor, or in this case her protector in hairy disarray, would rescue her. She might as well learn right now that there was no such thing as charming princes or happily ever after. He'd been foolish enough to forget that for a short time and he would pay for his error. The pain of love, loss and betrayal had seared his heart, scarring him worse than the Serpent's hands.

Billington moved toward Emily. His expression softened. "It seems there's been a bit of confusion concerning Mr. Mandrey," he began in a gentle voice. "Actually, quite a lot of confusion." There was a long pause. His throat worked, but no sound came out.

What was wrong with the old crust? Had he gone soft on him after all these years? Of course, he was just one more sap ready to do Emily's bidding. Well, he would no longer be included in that number. "I'm Cyrus Mandrey," Noah ground out.

Emily whirled around in disbelief. "What? You?" A short, choked laugh escaped her. "Where is he, Noah? What have you done with him?"

"He's me," he said, giving her a small salute. "I'm him. Ask Billington."

She turned to the older man, a question on her face. Billington nodded, a quick, curt gesture as though someone held a string around his neck, forcing him to respond.

"But you can't be Cyrus," Emily said, advancing on Noah. "Cyrus is gentle and warm and caring." Noah stiffened but she didn't seem to notice. "He's honest and trustworthy. Filled with integrity." He heard the conviction and admiration in her voice and it irritated him.

"Of course I couldn't be him," he snapped. "How could I possibly know anything about those qualities?"

He watched the color stain her cheeks. "Nevertheless, I *was* Cyrus Mandrey. If you are so inclined, the wig and beard are in there," he said, pointing to the secret passageway, "but they might be a little bloody."

Emily closed her eyes, her hands reaching up to rub her temples. "Why, Noah?" The words weren't more than a whisper.

"The man you knew as Andrew Kleeton and I had a score to settle. I had to ensure your safety first, before I took care of him." That was as much as he was going to tell her about his past life.

"I see." Her voice wandered off. "This was just like a play. The characters weren't even real." Emily's gaze moved to the butler. "And Billington?"

"Is not really a butler," Noah said, eyeing her.

"Oh." She looked at him then and he saw the hurt and torment in her eyes. "This was all just an act, wasn't it? All of it?" she breathed.

He knew what she was asking him. She wanted to know if

his words of love were real, if the passion they had shared meant something or was just part of a well-thought-out script. His heart clenched, pounding against his ribs so hard it hurt.

You have to save yourself. He met her gaze and nodded. The words stuck in his throat, but he pushed them out. "It was all part of the plan."

She gasped and turned away, running for the shelter of her room. He heard the door close behind her, and he knew he'd been successful in shutting her out of his life. Forever. Resting his head against the cushions, Noah let out a sigh and gave himself up to the pain.

Emily scanned the chamber one last time. Empty. Nothing left to indicate she'd ever been in this room, ever shared intimacies here with her husband that made her blush. Everything looked the same, but nothing would ever be the same.

Noah had stripped away every vestige of pride along with any hope for a reunion. He'd done it with such cruel callousness that she found it hard to believe he'd ever looked at her with warm, caring eyes or spoken soft, gentle words of love and devotion. But it hadn't really been him, she reminded herself. That person was an actor playing a part, reciting lines from a script, not from his heart.

It would be best to be away from Glenview Manor as soon as possible. It looked as if Noah planned to continue his life here and he had made it quite obvious that she would have no part in it. Emily gathered her wool cloak and with one last glance left the room.

Her bags and trunk were packed and waiting. She'd declined a proper breakfast, preferring a cup of cocoa and toast in her bedroom. Emily's emotions were too raw to risk an encounter with Noah this morning, though he probably felt the same way. But not for the same reason.

He just wanted her out of his life in the most expeditious manner possible.

Emily's hand trailed down the oak railing, the polished wood smooth under her fingers. She would miss this place. It had felt like home. Reaching the bottom stair, she pulled on her cloak, took one last cursory glance behind her and stepped outside into the brisk fall sunshine.

Of course, she knew Mr. Billington and Henry Barnes would wish her farewell. And perhaps Cook and maybe even the shy young maid who changed her linens. But she did not expect to find a line of servants peering at her from the top step to the carriage door. It appeared as though the entire household had come to send her on her way. Tears sprung to Emily's eyes as she worked her way among the crowd, hugging and exchanging kind words with the well-wishers.

"Best of luck to ye," Mrs. Connelly, the scullery maid, whispered, her bony hands clasping Emily's.

"We's heartbroken by it all, jest heartbroken," Cook murmured, the flesh under her chin jiggling with each shake of her head.

Mrs. Reeves, the downstairs maid, couldn't speak for the tears streaming down her face. Emily gave her a quick hug.

"Thank you. Thank you all," she said, fighting back tears. "I will miss all of you."

She worked her way through the remaining servants, hugging and reminiscing.

"I ain't gonna git all teary-eyed, so don't go expectin' it," a gruff voice said in her ear.

"Mr. Barnes." Emily smiled.

Henry Barnes clasped her upper arms, shaking his gray, frizzled head. "He needs ya, the boy does. Too bad, 'e's too stubborn ta admit it."

Emily did not want to discuss Noah's shortcomings. He'd made his decision, and judging from the line of sad faces surrounding her, they'd all pay for it.

"Take care, Mr. Barnes. Thank you for taking such wonderful care of Allegra. I'll send for her as soon as I'm settled."

A shadow fell over the groomsman's weathered face. "Take

344 *Mary Campisi*

as long as ya need. No problem.'' Emily met his black-eyed gaze and saw sadness in its depths. She hugged him and stepped away, turning to the final well-wisher.

Mr. Billington.

He stood tall and erect, just as he had the first day she'd seen him. But that's where the resemblance ended. Where once his gray eyes were cold and emotionless, now they harbored warmth and compassion. The pinched, sour lemon look was gone, replaced with a softer, more relaxed visage. And sometimes, like right now, his lips actually curved into a semi-smile.

Mr. Billington guided her away from the ears of the crowd. He cleared his throat, a habit she now knew signaled nervousness. ''Maybe when he settles down, things will appear differently to him.''

Emily shook her head, a wistful smile haunting her lips. ''No, Mr. Billington. I don't think so.''

He shifted his weight from one long leg to the other. ''You were caught in the middle of a very dangerous situation. Mr. Sandleton could think of nothing but ending it.''

''There's no need to make excuses for him, Mr. Billington. You were there. You heard what he said.'' Emily sighed, tired of talking about Noah, tired of thinking about him. ''I don't know or have any great desire to know about Noah's conflict with Andrew or whatever his real name was. Whether Noah admits it or not, the baby is his. Period.'' She straightened her shoulders. ''And that will be his loss.''

''What will you do now?'' Mr. Billington asked, searching her face.

''I suppose I have no choice but to return to my brother's for the rest of my confinement.'' She shrugged. ''But after the baby is born, I'll seek a house for myself and the baby.''

Mr. Billington nodded, opened his mouth to speak and closed it again. Some things were better left unsaid.

Emily gave him a gentle smile and clasped his long, bony hands. ''I will always remember you, Mr. Billington. Thank you.'' Her smile deepened. ''For everything.'' Before he could see the devastation on her face, she hugged him and ran for the safety of the carriage.

Not until the wheels rolled down the cobbled drive, away from Glenview Manor, did she give herself over to the gut-wrenching grief in her soul. Then the tears came.

Noah brought the bottle to his lips, tipped his head back, and let the amber liquid trickle down his throat in a slow, steady burn. He'd discarded his glass hours ago, after the third drink, he thought. The past several hours blurred before him, nothing more than a haze of jumbled words and vague images teeming with numbed emotions. He wiped his mouth with the back of his hand and set the bottle down.

Why in the hell was he drinking anyway? He couldn't remember. Screwing up his eyes, he forced himself to concentrate. *Something had happened. What?* Noah looked down at his rumpled shirt. It was torn and splattered with red. Blood. There had been a fight. A violent one. He had killed a man. A glimpse of terror flashed through his mind. There was a face to go with the dead figure lying on the cold floor. Noah pinched the bridge of his nose. The image sharpened.

Peter Crowlton, the Serpent, lying face up, bathed in red, his lifeless blue eyes open, a twisted smile on his lips. Noah grabbed the bottle and took a healthy swig, ignoring the liquid trickling from the sides of his mouth.

Another vision swayed before him. Emily. He pushed her sweetness away with another swallow and a curse. He would not think of Emily.

A light rap on the door disturbed his soulful musings.

"Come in," he said, his voice hoarse from lack of sleep and too much liquor.

Edward Billington entered, his expression more stoic than usual.

"Is she gone?" Noah asked, torn between pride and hope.

A slight nod of Billington's balding head told him more than he wanted to know.

"Good," he muttered, lifting the bottle again. When it was halfway to his mouth, Noah noticed Billington's gray eyes fixed on him. "What are you looking at?" The raw meanness in his voice echoed throughout the room.

"Nothing, sir." Billington took a step forward. "I was just observing your choice of breakfast beverages."

Noah held the bottle back, squinting one eye, trying to bring the print into focus. "Damn if I know what it says, but I know what it is." He held the bottle up. "And besides," he continued, his words slow and purposeful, "I haven't slept yet, so this is not breakfast." He took another swig. "Mmm. Whiskey. Want a taste?"

"No, thank you, sir." Billington approached Noah and pulled a white envelope from his pocket. "This is for you, sir," he said, holding out the envelope.

Noah rubbed his stubbled chin. "Read it to me, Billington. I'm having a little difficulty focusing at the moment."

"Yes, sir," Billington replied, opening the envelope and pulling out a single sheet of paper.

Noah sat back against his leather chair and rested his hands over his belly. "Just give me the gist of it, man. Don't bore me with the whole thing."

Billington's eyes scanned the paper. "Very well, sir," he said, looking up to meet Noah's bleary gaze. "It seems as though the entire household has resigned."

"Resigned?" Noah echoed. "Resigned from what?"

"From your employ, sir," Billington said, clearing his throat.

"That's ridiculous."

Billington extended the paper. "They've signed their names, sir."

"They can't resign," Noah barked, slamming the desk with his fist. "They're as much a part of Glenview Manor as the house itself." His eyes narrowed. "Why do they want to leave?"

"It seems they took a great liking to Lady Emily and sympathize with her."

"Of course," Noah said, his voice quaking with anger. "Everyone wants to rush to do her bidding. Fine. Let them feel sorry for her. See if it feeds their bellies. We'll replace every last one of them." He slashed his hand through the air. "Get on it right away, Billington."

The older man cleared his throat and coughed. "I'm sorry, sir," he said in a quiet voice. "I won't be able to do that."

Noah looked at him, tilting his head to one side. "Why the hell not?"

"My name is on this list as well."

"You?" Noah sputtered. "You? Resigning?"

Billington squared his shoulders. "I'm afraid so, sir."

"Because of *Emily?*" He braced his elbows on the desk and rubbed his temples. *Billington couldn't leave.* "I thought you two didn't even like one another."

"We came to an understanding of sorts," Billington confessed. "I hold Lady Emily in the highest regard."

"I see," Noah said, but he didn't. He didn't see one damn thing.

Billington cleared his throat again. "Now that I am no longer in your employ, sir, I would like to make one comment."

Noah raised a dark brow and waited.

A dull flush crept up Billington's cheeks. "Lady Emily loves you, sir. She did not betray that love. Peter Crowlton knew she was your weakness and he pressed his advantage, telling you a terrible lie. If you believe him, then he lives on, not in an unborn child, but in you, festering and growing, until his hatred becomes your hatred. And it will destroy you."

"She told *him* about the baby, not me," Noah said, letting the pain spill over his words.

Billington shrugged. "She also told Cyrus, but you didn't accuse him of fathering the child."

"That's absurd."

"No more so than what you are suggesting." Billington took

a step closer. "But if you've a notion of putting matters right, you had best be on your way. Her carriage left over twenty minutes ago."

Noah sat slumped in the chair, his face buried in his hands. He didn't move, nor did he see Billington's lips twitch.

"She still loves you though, despite what's happened," Billington said. "Though she did mention America again." He paused, tapping a long finger to his pointed chin. "Is it possible, sir, that Lady Emily would forgo her brother's house and set sail for America? In her condition? A pregnant woman, traveling alone? Do you think she would?"

Billington's words swirled about the empty room, crashing to the ground in a careless heap. He turned just in time to see Noah's large form bounding out the door. Edward Billington smiled and, for the first time in his adult life, threw back his head and laughed.

Noah flew down the road on Flash, hoping to catch a glimpse of the Sandleton carriage at each turn. But as he rounded each bend, he saw nothing but a vast stretch of trees and road before him. Had he somehow missed her? Had she taken a different course? Panic, cold and feral, gripped him, squeezing his heart. Was he too late?

Billington's words echoed in every hoofbeat. *America. America. America. A pregnant woman traveling alone.* Noah pressed on, harder and faster. The carriage shouldn't be much farther ahead. Unless she'd decided on a different route? *One that did not lead to her brother's house.* Dread washed over him, frightening him with possibilities.

Just as he was about to turn around and head in the opposite direction, Noah spotted the carriage. Urging his mount forward, he came up alongside the black conveyance and signaled the driver to stop. He slid to the ground and grabbed the carriage door, flinging it open to find his wife, wide-eyed and open-mouthed, staring back at him.

"You're not going to America," he said. She may as well know he would fight to keep her and his unborn child with him.

"I'm not?" She stared at him as though he were a madman. He might well look like an escapee from Bedlam in his current rumpled, unshaven state.

"No." His words were firm, brooking no argument. "Unless you want to go after the baby is born." He paused, swallowing hard. "Then, if you'd like, we can visit my family and Christopher."

"We can?" she whispered, her full, pink mouth quivering.

Noah smiled. "We can. Whatever you want." He climbed into the carriage and took her hands in his. "I love you, Emily. I've always loved you," he said, his voice ragged with emotion.

"You—you do?" she stammered, her gray eyes misting with tears.

"I do," he murmured, stroking her cheek. "With my whole heart. I've been such a fool. I almost let my hatred destroy our love." He placed a hand on her stomach. "I want *our* baby, Emily. Very much." Noah leaned over and brushed his lips over hers. "Thank God for Billington," he whispered, trailing kisses along her jaw.

"Billington?" Her breathy voice made him hard. God, but she felt good. He wanted her. Now.

"Hmm." Noah nuzzled her ear, his tongue running along the delicate, pink rim. "He told me you loved me. Always would. And then he said something about you taking off for America." He wondered if she would be amenable to a private stroll. Just far enough off the road to lie down in the grass and pull her on top of him, heat to heat. His manhood throbbed with the thought.

"Noah!" Emily pulled away far enough to see his face. "I didn't say that!"

He held his breath. "You didn't. You *don't* love me?"

She reached up to brush back a lock of hair from his forehead. "No, silly," she said, smiling. "I *do* love you. And I always will. That part is true, though I don't recall telling Mr. Billington that. But I said nothing about America.''

A slow smile spread over Noah's face. ''I'll be damned. I didn't think the old crust had it in him to play matchmaker.''

''Mr. Billington?'' Emily's tone sounded doubtful.

''Remind me to increase his wages. Oh, I almost forgot.'' He grinned. ''He quit. I'll rehire him and then increase his wages.''

''Mr. Billington quit?''

Noah nodded, chuckling. ''It seems my entire staff resigned because of you. Billington too. They thought I mistreated you and wanted no part of the ogre who drove you away.''

''But they've been with you for years,'' Emily said, resting her hand on his thigh.

Noah clenched his jaw. His wife was still much too innocent. She had no idea what her small hand was doing to certain parts of his body at that moment. ''They all love you, Emily,'' he managed in a thin voice, aching to feel her fingers on his manhood.

Tears sprung to her eyes. ''Thank you, Noah. Thank you for your love.''

He took her in his arms and kissed her, pledging his heart, his love, his future to her. Always.

''From this day on, I want us to be completely honest with each other,'' Emily murmured against his lips.

''Completely?'' Noah sucked on her upper lip.

''Completely,'' she sighed, curling her fingers in his hair.

Noah smiled against her lips. ''All right, then. I've spent the last several minutes trying to think of a way to coax you into going for a walk in the fields.''

''Why didn't you just ask me?'' she whispered.

''Because walking isn't really what I want to do with you in those fields,'' he confessed, laughing low in his throat.

''Oh?'' she asked, her voice light and teasing. And very seductive. Perhaps she wasn't as innocent as he thought. ''What did you have in mind, Mr. Sandleton?''

"Well, since I've taken a vow of complete honesty, I suppose I'll have to tell you." Noah nuzzled her neck and whispered in her ear.

Emily sucked in her breath. "Why, that's shocking! Absolutely shocking, Mr. Sandleton." She pulled away to meet his heated gaze. He could see the desire in her eyes. Her head tilted to one side as she considered his words, a slow smile forming on her full lips. "Which field? Right or left?" she asked, pointing to either side of the road.

"Both," he replied, his hand slipping behind her head to urge her toward his mouth. Their lips met, fused, melted into one another, forging unspoken promises, pledging heartfelt desires, offering a glimpse of heaven.

Grasping freedom. At last.

ABOUT THE AUTHOR

I started writing my first romance novel when my children were babies. I would read fairy tales to them during the day and work on my own version of "happily ever after" when I tucked them into bed. Now, years later, I am thrilled to be publishing my first novel, *Innocent Betrayal.* I am equally thrilled to be the mother of five unique, energetic children, ages 9–16. Our house is always a little crazy, never quite clean, full of raucous laughter and good food. It's full of animals too (no, not the kids, but a black lab, a goldfish and two gerbils). When I find a few quiet moments, I read, garden, experiment with my own interpretation of art or walk my dog and plot my next scene. And sometimes, I even get to spend a little time with my very patient, very understanding husband, who keeps me on course and is without a doubt my biggest fan.

I would love to hear from you c/o Zebra Books.